TAINTED

TAINTED

A Dr. Zol Szabo Medical Mystery

ROSS PENNIE

ECW Press

Published by ECW Press,
2120 Queen Street East, Suite 200, Toronto, Ontario, Canada M4E 1E2
416.694.3348 / info@ecwpress.com

LIBRARY AND ARCHIVES CANADA CATALOGUING IN PUBLICATION

Pennie, Ross, 1952-
Tainted : a Dr. Zol Szabo medical mystery / Ross Pennie. -- Pbk. ed.

ISBN 978-1-77041-021-3
ISSUED ALSO IN ELECTRONIC FORMATS:
978-1-55490-860-8 (PDF); 978-1-55490-343-6 (EPUB)

1. Title.

PS8631.E565T33 2011   C813'.6   C2010-907843-8

Cover image: © Roberto Pastrovicchio / Arcangel Images
Cover and text design: Tania Craan
Typesetting: Mary Bowness
Author photo: Sherry Smith, Keepsake Photography
Printing: Transcontinental   1   2   3   4   5

Mixed Sources
Product group from well-managed
forests, controlled sources and
recycled wood or fiber
www.fsc.org Cert no. SW-COC-000952
© 1996 Forest Stewardship Council
FSC

The publication of Tainted has been generously supported by the Canada Council for
the Arts, which last year invested $20.1 million in writing and publishing throughout
Canada, by the Ontario Arts Council, by the Government of Ontario through Ontario
Book Publishing Tax Credit, by the OMDC Book Fund, an initiative of the Ontario
Media Development Corporation, and by the Government of Canada through the
Canada Book Fund.

 Canada Council   Conseil des Arts
for the Arts   du Canada   Canada   ONTARIO ARTS COUNCIL
                                             CONSEIL DES ARTS DE L'ONTARIO

PRINTED AND BOUND IN CANADA

ECW PRESS
ecwpress.com

This book is dedicated to Dr. Bob Nosal and his team of professional women and men at the Halton Region Health Department whose mission, every day, is to protect us from ourselves.

CHAPTER 1

They say when you're home alone and the phone rings, you're an extrovert if you jump up, grab the receiver, and delight in a familiar voice.

Zol Szabo let it ring.

He sipped his Scotch and nestled his lanky frame deeper into the buttery leather of his recliner. A north wind, sweeping across the western shore of Lake Ontario and howling up the Niagara Escarpment, rattled the living-room windows. Zol stroked the furry spine of Cory, the ginger cat who hunkered into his lap. They both gazed at the blue flames licking the simulated logs in the fireplace. Only a light November snow was forecast for tomorrow. Zol chuckled. Max would be disappointed. No snow day.

Zol cocked his ear and listened past the nagging of the phone for the sound of pleas from the bedroom upstairs. All seemed quiet up there. Max had finally settled, but it had taken two bowls of cereal, a glass of water, three adjustments to his night light, and a great big hippopotamus hug. As usual, Zol had stayed calm through each interruption, tingeing his voice with frustration only at the sixth or seventh petition from the seven-year-old's bedroom doorway.

The ice cube in Zol's glass, floating in two fingers of twelve-year-old Glenfarclas, clinked and snapped. Overripe apricots, cedar wood, and peat smoke kissed his nostrils. He closed his eyes and drew in a mouthful, letting the whisky dance across his tongue and down his throat.

He drank alone only during this bedtime ritual — and always just one shot, a single malt poured over a single ice cube in the single crystal tumbler left in the house. Francine had smashed five of them against the ceramic floor, the double-door fridge, and the wide-screen television before slamming the door on their brief marriage.

Who could be calling at this hour?

It might be that reporter from the Hamilton *Spectator* on the prowl for more details about a cluster of seven cases — with three deaths — of invasive streptococcal infection in a home for the elderly. The man's heated words from earlier in the week still rang in Zol's ears: "The residents are petrified. And their families are scared stiff. Surely it's the moral duty of you docs at the health unit to stop this epidemic before any more grandparents are consumed by flesh-eating disease."

It was not quite ten o'clock, too early to be Zol's boss, Peter Trinnock, MD, LMCC, CCFP, FRCPC, MCPHA, chief of the Hamilton-Lakeshore Public Health Unit. Trinnock's workday hours were so much taken up by rounds of golf in summer, putting matches in winter, and protracted lunches all year round that he seldom caught a glimpse of what was happening under his nose until late in the evening. He'd find himself caught off guard by the ten o'clock news on TV, then blast Zol via telephone for not keeping him in the loop.

Zol had practically burned his boss's retirement day into his calendar. He reckoned that if he didn't make any major errors or misjudgements he'd be promoted from *associate* to *chief* medical officer of health for the municipality of Hamilton-Lakeshore when Trinnock stepped down next May. In fact, Zol was counting the days until Trinnock's departure and the relocation of his office from the building's dingy rear to its prestigious front.

At the continued ringing from the kitchen, Cory flashed his tail and looked at Zol as if to say, "Damn, we only just got settled."

Zol gulped another mouthful of Scotch, put down his glass, and heaved Cory from his lap. Then he grabbed the phone by its throat.

Dr. Hamish Wakefield's voice always gave him away with the first syllable. Singer's nodes, he'd told Zol before the operation. A consequence of his years as a boy soprano. But the biopsy of his vocal cords revealed no explanation for the roughness in a voice that still rasped no stronger than a whisper. Behind his back, the doctors and nurses called him the Whispering Warrior — on account of that voice, his short haircut, and the utter concentration he brought to the specialty of infectious diseases.

"What's up, Hamish?" said Zol.

"I'm calling from the office." Hamish's words hissed breathlessly down the line. "Came across something I thought you guys should know about."

"At this hour? Geez, you need a diversion outside the halls of academia. A hobby or a love interest."

"No time for either. Listen. Have you ever met Julian Banbury, the neuropathologist here at the med centre?"

Zol's job kept him in touch with the regional coroner, but he'd never dealt with any of the other pathologists at Caledonian University's tertiary-care facility. "Don't think so."

"You'd remember him, believe me. He's got a big scar across his neck and such severe exophthalmia that you'd think —"

Zol passed the phone from one hand to the other. "It's okay, I'm with you."

"Anyway," Hamish continued, "he's our local brain-infection guru, and a couple of weeks ago he came back from holiday. More like a mini sabbatical. And now he's catching up on three or four months' worth of brain autopsies."

Zol pictured a lineup of buckets on the dissection-room floor, a pickled brain floating in each one. He touched his nose, almost feeling the sting of formaldehyde that permeated the pathology seminar room when he and Hamish were students together seven years ago at the University of Toronto.

"Well," Hamish continued, "Julian said that three of the brains show signs of CJD. One man, two women."

"The last case reported on my patch was about eighteen months ago. A retired Anglican minister," Zol commented. "Big write-up about him in the paper when he died."

The article had described the congregation rallying to provide palliative care in the minister's home — twenty-four hours a day for several months. But why the alarm bells tonight at ten o'clock? It took twenty years for the Creutzfeldt-Jakob agent to cause disease after entering the body. These cases must be reflecting events two decades old. Hamish really did need a distraction in his life to lure him away from the constant seduction of Mistress Medicine.

Zol gazed at the glass of Scotch out of his reach on a table in the living room. "Three cases within three months does sound like a cluster," he said. "But probably just a coincidence. I'll get my team to look into it later this week. Right now, I've got most of my nurses and health inspectors working on that outbreak of necrotizing fasciitis at Shalom Acres. That's one giant can of worms."

"But Zol . . ." A gulping sound echoed down the line as Hamish sucked on the water bottle that seldom left his side. He needn't have bothered. His voice remained as croaky as ever. "I've got to tell you — Julian Banbury is calling it *variant* CJD."

Zol felt the blood drain from his face as the facts began to percolate. Three locals dead from tainted beef . . . meaning humans infected with BSE prions, those contagious, mis-folded proteins that cause Bovine Spongiform Encephalopathy, a universally fatal, brain-rotting disease. Hamish had graduated top of their class at U of T, and thanks to him Zol had memorized the Krebs cycle long enough to pass his final examination in biochemistry, but . . .

"I hope to hell your pathologist is jumping to conclusions," Zol said. "Is he a bit of a grandstander?"

"Not at all," said Hamish. "These people are all under fifty, Zol. Too young for *regular* CJD. Banbury is adamant. The microscopic features in their brains — the amyloid protein plaques — are diagnostic of *variant* CJD." He coughed and gulped, then coughed again. "The same as they're getting in England after eating mad cows.

That's three local residents —"

"Infected with mad cow prions. I hear you."

"Now do you see why I called you this late?"

"Mother of God." Zol rubbed at his temple. "You know what this means, eh? I sure do. My dad was a tobacco farmer."

"I don't think BSE has anything to do with tobacco," Hamish replied in the flat, humourless tone that came out whenever he was anxious or concentrating.

"I know," Zol said. "It's just that I've lived through what happens when agricultural commodities get stung by the fickle prick of scandal."

Zol pulled a chair out from the kitchen table and dropped into it. Hamish had just handed him a Chernobyl-sized problem. It would make last year's countrywide panic over one Alberta steer with BSE look like five minutes of rain at a Sunday-school picnic.

Neither man said anything. Cory jumped into Zol's lap and purred while Zol absently stroked his back.

Hamish broke the silence. "What do we do now?"

Zol gave Cory a pat on the rump then pulled out the loonie he always kept in his pocket. The coin was not for spending but for fingering whenever life's tensions mounted. Much cleaner than his father's chewing tobacco, and it didn't cause cancer.

Zol tightened his grip on the phone. "I'm sure not going to call the *Spectator*," he said. "Or Elliott York at head office in Toronto. I can't go reporting the country's first cluster of human BSE until I've got a whole lot more details. Just a sec." He set the phone on the table, dropped Cory onto the floor, and fetched his Scotch, draining it in two mouthfuls. "We'll have to be careful," he continued. "I can almost feel York and his Toronto cronies breathing down my neck already. And after them, every agricultural and public-interest lobbyist in the country."

"And the media outlets. Like that stupid Lassa fever wild-goose chase, two years ago."

"You knew from the start the woman only had malaria."

"Problem was, my senior colleagues with the big mouths and

bigger egos wanted it to be Lassa. Better for their fame and fortune on the speakers' circuit."

Zol stared at the flames dancing in the fireplace and pondered the implications of this cluster — for the food industry, for his health unit, for his career. He weaved the dollar coin faster and faster through his fingers.

A staccato of clicks from Hamish's computer keyboard scurried down the phone line. "I can clear my calendar for tomorrow afternoon," Hamish said. "You can come to my office, if you like. Have a look at the charts of the three cases."

Zol rubbed at an ache beside his eye. It would take him most of the day to bone up on mad cows, prions, BSE, and human-variant CJD. There were newspaper clippings, medical journals, and the Internet to scour. He'd have to duck tomorrow's staff meeting, always a time guzzler at best. "We better maintain as low a profile as possible. Can you bring the files over to my house? Say, tomorrow evening? I'll feed you supper."

"I guess this can wait until then. Let me pick up a pizza. Or how about Thai or Chinese?"

Zol coughed, and then grunted.

"Oh, right," Hamish replied. "Take-out never darkens your doorway."

"Just bring your appetite. And a bottle of wine. I'll see you at seven."

At five thirty the next morning, an hour before his alarm was set to buzz, Zol jerked awake. He heard the thump of the paper hitting the front steps and dashed downstairs to retrieve it. A blast of arctic air whistled through his T-shirt and boxers as he dusted the snow from the newspaper's plastic sleeve. On the way back to his bedroom he stopped in the pantry and pulled two Cornish hens from the freezer for tonight's dinner. The birds always impressed guests, who considered them more exotic than they really were. At the Stratford School for Chefs, Zol's instructor had called them the runts you could quickly stuff and overprice whenever relations with your banker were looking dicey.

The five years he'd spent as an apprentice chef, though barely a decade in the past, seemed like another lifetime altogether. Had the frenetic life in steamy restaurant kitchens been any less satisfying than his life as a public-health physician? He'd sweated plenty in both environments.

Leaving the hens to thaw in a bowl of ice water, he retreated to the warmth of his bed and scoured the newspaper. A suicide bombing in Jerusalem. A political assassination in Sweden. A rumoured record-setting private donation to the medical school at Caledonian University — right here in Steeltown. But no mad cows in Ontario and no hint of citizens with variant CJD.

A couple of hours later, downstairs at the breakfast table, Zol spooned up a final mouthful of cereal. In their daily father-and-son race to the finish, Max's bowl was almost always the first to be plunked onto the kitchen table, empty and triumphant. Zol downed a final triplet of flakes ahead of the few neon oat rings straggling at the bottom of Max's bowl. "I win!" Zol said.

"But look," said Max, holding up an empty glass, "I finished my juice. You didn't drink your coffee yet."

Zol winked at his son. "Okay, Max. I won the cereal event but you won the beverage round."

Max beamed as he put down his juice glass, oblivious to his handicap. His left hand, stiff and claw-like, had been fettered since the moment of his birth. But to Max it was just the understudy who stole the show.

It was strange what a man could be grateful for, like being thankful that the stroke your son had suffered at birth affected only one hand — not his legs, not his speech, not his intellect. And certainly not his ability to play an entire catalogue of electronic games.

His breakfast bowl empty, Max crimped his latest pocket video gadget in his left palm and jabbed at its buttons with his right. A minute later, at the sound of clatter from the front door, he looked up from the screen, grinned broadly, and slid off his chair. Even after three years as their beloved housekeeper, Ermalinda knocked like a visitor and waited for Max to run to the door and throw it wide open.

Ermalinda wasted no time in exchanging her parka for an apron and lifting the dirty dishes from the table. She swooped them into the sink and plucked the phone from its cradle as it began to ring. Without a word, she passed the handset to Zol.

"Did you see today's paper?" said Hamish, coughing into the line. "See the story about that huge donation coming to our medical school? It's going to be announced today that the donor is Bernard Vanderven, the auto-parts magnate. I've seen the press release."

"Two hundred million. That's a hell of a lot of coin."

"His wife is one of the three CJD victims I was telling you about. Vanderven's been saying she died of a heart attack. He's going to earmark half his donation for cardiac research."

"She was a bit young for an MI, wasn't she? What did her autopsy show?"

"That's just it. It didn't show even a hint of heart disease."

"That's strange."

"Her coronaries and myocardium were perfect. After all, she was only forty-three." Hamish took several gulps, probably of a double café latte made with his expensive machine. "But . . ."

"But what?" Zol demanded. Something more than CJD was bothering Hamish. But didn't the guy even allow himself a few minutes to eat a peaceful breakfast?

"Her CJD wasn't advanced enough to kill her. Julian Banbury's report makes that very clear."

"Hmm. What was the official cause of death before Banbury got a chance to examine her brain?"

Hamish rustled some sheets of paper that sounded as if they were right next to his telephone. "The death certificate says cardiac arrest due to ventricular arrhythmia, cause unknown."

A bit of a stretch considering the woman's heart appeared pristine at autopsy. "But you told me that the original autopsy didn't find —"

"Yes, I know," said Hamish, his voice rising. "It didn't turn up a darn thing that could explain the woman's death. Not in her heart. Not anywhere. But the duty pathologist had to come up with an official diagnosis for the death certificate so the body could be released to the funeral home. I guess arrhythmia seemed to fit the bill at the time." Hamish gulped, then continued. "I *did* notice a couple of other things."

"What?"

"Toxicology showed Joanna Vanderven had a blood alcohol level that would put her way over the driving limit, and moderate levels of lorazepam, fluoxetine, and oxycodone."

Zol strolled into the dining room as far as the phone cord would permit and closed the door. The Vanderven woman had downed an explosive cocktail: a generous measure of alcohol, a few pills to counter anxiety and depression, and a potent narcotic. "Sounds like she was one unhappy woman. Did anyone suspect she'd overdosed intentionally?"

"Not as far as I can tell. The toxicology results only came in this week."

"Yeah," said Zol, "the provincial lab always runs a backlog, sometimes several months. Autopsy specimens aren't exactly their priority." The belated results probably held the key to Joanna Vanderven's death: the alcohol she ingested could have acted in combination with the three powerful drugs to tip her into respiratory arrest — a final sigh through blue lips, the heartbeat ceasing a few minutes later. The autopsy could have missed that scenario.

"Anyway," Hamish continued, "no embarrassing questions were asked. The coroner agreed with the duty pathologist's arrhythmia diagnosis and signed the death certificate. Case closed."

"Until a few months later, Julian Banbury discovers that her brain is riddled with variant CJD."

"Not exactly riddled," said Hamish. "Not enough to kill her, but you've got the picture."

A quizzical frown flashed across Hamish's brow.

"Max likes his apple juice in a wineglass," Zol explained, "particularly when we have company."

Hamish turned to the sink. He pumped a measure of liquid soap into his palm, lathered his hands, and rinsed them under the tap. He turned the faucet off with his elbow and dried his hands. Only then did he open the cupboard and lift out the glasses.

After they'd made quick work of the Cornish hens, Zol dispatched Max to the TV room with a large bowl of chocolate ice cream. And while Hamish went to retrieve his briefcase from the front hall, Zol poured two measures of Glenfarclas. The shiraz had loosened neither Hamish's collar nor his tongue over dinner. Maybe a Scotch would help.

Hamish returned and placed three dossiers on the table. "Well, here they are," he said. "Our cases." He was smiling for the first time since he'd arrived.

Zol handed him a glass of the Glenfarclas and lifted his own. "Cheers," he said. "And here's to a speedy investigation."

Hamish, still smiling, saluted with his glass. "Yes — to an efficient investigation." He squinted at the amber whisky, then set his glass on the table without taking a sip. The smile left his face as suddenly as it had appeared. "Let me ask you, Zol. Is it ghoulish to love doing this outbreak stuff?"

"There's nothing wrong with feeling a passion for our work."

"Well . . . there's not much else in *my* life."

Zol looked away, toward the TV room door, and felt a little guilty at being blessed. He had Max to put the punch in his job, transform the work of public-health medicine into a vital calling where every aspect mattered more with each passing year. Yet he shared with Hamish that lonely kinship, the yearning of the single man. He downed another mouthful of Scotch and pointed to the neat stacks of paper tethered with long staples. "Hey! I thought you weren't allowed to take charts out of the hospital."

Hamish's cheeks flared. "I'll be sure to return them tomorrow before anyone notices." He picked up a chart and ran his finger along the top of the front page. "Joanna Vanderven, age forty-three. We already talked about her — apparent cardiac death on June twenty-second. Positive toxicology for drugs and alcohol." He pointed to the next chart. "Danesh Patel, age forty-nine. Immigrant from India. Hit by a car while crossing Upper James in front of Platinum Honda — he was a salesman there. Killed instantly. That was June twenty-eighth."

"I think I remember that from the news," Zol said. "Wasn't it a hit and run? Did they ever find the guy?"

"I don't know. No details of the accident made it into the chart. All we've got is the death certificate and the report of the preliminary autopsy, performed before Julian Banbury came back from his sabbatical." Hamish opened the chart and read from the pathologist's post-mortem summary: "Multiple contusions, lacerated liver, ruptured abdominal aorta, intracerebral hemorrhage."

Zol pictured Patel's brain in his mind's eye: the large hemorrhage like a blood-red egg, produced by the blow from the fast-moving car; such bleeding, obvious even to the naked eye, had been documented long before Banbury examined paper-thin slices of the brain under his microscope.

Hamish took a mouthful of Scotch and was struck by a string of explosive coughs. He dropped the chart and spluttered into his fist. "Sorry — I'm not — used to — this stuff."

"Here," said Zol, lifting a jug. "I'll add a little water. Easier on the throat."

Hamish wiped his eyes and lips with a tissue, then pointed to the name on the third chart. "Hugh McEwen, age thirty-six. A dentist. We did our degrees in biochem together at U of T. Nice guy, but we lost touch." Hamish paused and dipped his head. "Committed suicide. In his office. Saturday, September fifteenth. Pronounced dead at the scene by the coroner." Hamish swallowed hard, then lifted the chart and riffled its pages. "There's not much here. A brief hospital admission two years ago for an appendectomy, a trip to Emerg with a sprained knee last year, and the preliminary autopsy report — again, minus the latest brain findings."

"Not much to go on, eh?" Zol said. "The three of them died fairly close together — June twenty-second, June twenty-eighth, and September fifteenth."

"But did they get infected at the same time?" asked Hamish. "And when did they start showing the first signs of their disease?"

"It all hangs on how long ago they ate the tainted beef. And where. Our best hope is that they've all got ties to Britain and dined on mad cows in England."

"Good point — the English connection. That would be the perfect solution."

"But only if it were true," Zol said. "And we'd have to prove it beyond a reasonable doubt."

Hamish lifted his well-diluted Scotch, pursed his lips, and sipped carefully. "You make it sound like a court case."

"It's the court of public opinion," Zol said. "As soon as the news of these cases gets out, the press will be watching every move we make." With his emotions lubricated by the wine and the Scotch, anger rose into his throat. "And they'll fall all over themselves trying to run ten steps ahead of us." He thumped his fist on the table. "The stupider we look, the bigger the headlines."

Zol's heartbeat quickened as he pictured Health Canada, the Ontario government, the Canadian Food Inspection Agency, and the Canadian Cattlemen's Association all thrown into a maelstrom of panic. Pandemonium far worse than a few soon-forgotten headlines. The Americans, the Europeans, the Japanese shutting their borders to almost everything edible produced in Canada. And years of negotiations to reopen them. He wiped his palms on his trousers and took up his pen. "Let's make a list of questions we need to answer."

"For a start," said Hamish, "did all three actually eat beef?"

"And did they live in the United Kingdom during the mad cow epidemic?"

"That's the key point."

"And our best hope for a quick solution that's politically painless," said Zol.

"The victims might have travelled to other countries," Hamish suggested. "Patel was from India. Does that ring any bells?"

"Not that I know of. Lots of malaria and tuberculosis, and more HIV than they'll admit."

"You're right, this isn't tropical."

"Focusing locally," Zol continued, "we need to know where they bought their groceries."

"And did they ever go to butcher shops?" said Hamish.

"Probably not," Zol replied. "Most people don't these days."

Hamish leaned on the table and scanned the growing list. "We'll want to know which restaurants they ate at." He rubbed at an apparent stiffness at the back of his neck. "And we can't forget the iatrogenic causes of CJD."

"Good point," said Zol. The alcohol, though great for loosening the mind and promoting creative connections, had begun to take the edge off his memory. "Let's see. . . ." He paused, his hand hovering above his notepad. "There've been concerns about transmission as a result of neurosurgery performed with contaminated instruments. And reports of cases acquired through corneal transplantation. And from injections of growth hormone extracted from pituitary glands. But recipients of corneas and growth hormone harvested from infected donors developed regular CJD, not the variant type, didn't they? What a tragedy — regain your sight or grow a few extra inches, then die prematurely because your brain is riddled with infectious prions."

As Zol continued writing, Hamish tipped back another mouthful of Scotch and dabbed his lips with his serviette. "We'll need to ask about any recent deaths among family members."

Zol looked up from his list and held Hamish's gaze. "What are you suggesting?"

"Maybe there've been more of these cases than anyone realizes."

"What do you mean?" Zol said, his mind jolted to sharpness.

"Families eat together — they get exposed to BSE prions together. None of these three had obvious CJD when they died."

"And if Vanderven, Patel, and McEwen hadn't had autopsies, we'd never have found out about their variant CJD, which means . . ."

"There might have been others infected among their families," said Hamish, raising his index finger. "*And* their friends and neighbours."

Zol poured himself another Scotch and let a mouthful warm the back of his throat. The workload of hunting down more cases, the ramifications of finding them, were almost too much to contemplate. "You realize," he said to Hamish, "we can't openly investigate these deaths by asking questions about variant CJD."

"And why not?"

"As soon as there's a hint of Julian Banbury's revelation, the press will get wind of our investigation and they'll throw the entire country into a panic. I can see it now — economic chaos." But what excuse could they give the grieving families for asking so many penetrating questions about their lives and their habits? "How about this?" he suggested. "We'll tell them that their loved ones showed features of an encephalitis. We'll explain that the health unit is conducting a routine set of interviews, just like we do for other infections like food poisoning, diarrhea, and meningitis."

"It might buy us a little time," Hamish said, his tone hesitant. After a moment his face brightened slightly. "I suppose we wouldn't actually be lying. CJD *is* one of the transmissible spongiform encephalopathies. It can rightly be called a form of encephalitis."

"We can even hope that people might jump to the conclusion that we're investigating West Nile."

In the summer and early fall the newspapers had been full of alarming stories about mosquitoes and West Nile virus encephalitis. The exaggerated headlines had been a headache at the health unit, but perhaps they could be used as a smokescreen.

Hamish pressed his hands together, as if in prayer. "But what if we're asked point-blank what sort of encephalitis the victims had, and was it really West Nile virus?" His face looked grave as he shook his head. "We can't lie."

"At first, we might have to," Zol said.

The colour drained from Hamish's cheeks. "But we're professionals. We can't lie." He scowled and pointed his finger at Zol's chest. "And you're — you're a public figure. You can't breach that trust."

"Look, Hamish," Zol replied, his tone flat and firm, "for a little while, we might have to play with the truth. For a greater good."

"But . . ."

"We'll say we're not sure what we're dealing with, that we're still gathering our facts."

"But we're . . ."

"It's true. We *are* still gathering our facts. Surely you can live with that?"

"Hell's bells, Zol. I'm a diagnostician, not a detective. Supposed to be a disciple of Hippocrates, not Sherlock Holmes."

"Come on — right now, I need you to be a bit of both. You have to admit there's a tremendous amount at stake. And you did say you loved this outbreak stuff."

"Well, yes."

"And you're the guy with the best brain for this job."

Hamish flushed. "Stop buttering me up." He picked up his Scotch, sighed, and returned it to the table. "Look — I'll do my best. If anyone jumps to the wrong conclusions, thinks we're investigating West Nile or something else, I won't correct them. But you'll have to do the lying and the politicking. I don't have the stomach for the backroom intrigue you put up with at your health unit."

"Okay then," Zol said with relief. "We won't actually lie. We'll just keep the facts to ourselves until we're set to divulge them." He gripped Hamish's arm. "And when we're asking all our picky questions, we'll use the 'better safe than sorry' line. At our office, we're good at that."

Zol found himself wondering, and not for the first time, how much time and money had been wasted over the years by that four-word catchphrase. How many unexpected consequences had it triggered? Antibiotics rendered useless after decades of frivolous prescriptions for minor colds. Classrooms demolished after the discovery of harmless mould inside their walls. Teddy bears banished from bedrooms after someone said they could make kids wheezy. But now they had hold of a real problem. And it felt great to grapple with it.

"What about Julian Banbury?" Zol said. "Can we get him to keep a lid on his findings until we've completed our investigation?"

"He might keep this quiet for a week, not much longer."

"Can you . . ."

"Yes, I'll talk to him."

The phone started ringing. Zol looked at his watch: ten thirty. He knew who it must be. Call Display confirmed it: P. Trinnock.

"Hell," said Zol. "I'm not talking to him tonight."

CHAPTER 3

At seven thirty the next morning, Zol backed the minivan out of the driveway and headed along Scenic Drive toward the health unit, on the Escarpment at the western end of Concession Street. He'd walked to work a couple of times the previous summer, but forty minutes twice a day was time away from Max he wasn't prepared to spare, no matter how good it might be for his heart. Maybe he should get a bike in the spring. It would be a beautiful ride along Scenic Drive, through the grounds of the psychiatric hospital, then along the dizzying edge of the Niagara Escarpment, a corridor of limestone terraces and old-growth forest that snaked all the way from Niagara Falls to Georgian Bay. The United Nations had deemed the eight hundred kilometres of cliff face a World Biosphere Reserve; as a public-health official he felt vaguely guilty about soiling it with noxious fumes twice a day from the tailpipe of his minivan.

In the distance to his left, beyond the city's gritty port, Lake Ontario's western bow shimmered in the low-flying sun. The dazzle of the watery horizon always lifted his spirits no matter how daunting the current office crisis. Even the motley smokestacks, bristling and flaring from Hamilton's lakeside steelworks, offered no more than a dubious threat to life up here on the Escarpment. Hamilton natives referred to this lofty part of the city as the Mountain, but in the seven years since Zol had moved here, he'd never been able to see anything remotely hilly about this dead-flat plateau.

He parked, then climbed the stairs to his fourth-floor office, taking the steps two at a time but pulling heavily on the banister. His breakfast coffee had yet to dissolve the stubborn grains of sleepiness that lingered in his head. Last night at lights out, a fringe festival of images had disturbed his sleep — drooling cows, disintegrating brains, jeering reporters. He awakened twice with a start, breathless, his heart pounding, his T-shirt soaked in sweat. As he strode past the dark reception desk and headed for his office, he felt the excitement of the impending investigation, then shuddered at the hornets' nest he might soon be splitting open.

He logged on to his computer and answered the three emails that demanded immediate responses. Then he emailed Anne, the secretary he shared with his boss, and asked her to cancel all his meetings for today. He clicked Send, then scanned the potholed parking lot outside his window. No postcard view over the Escarpment for the *associate* MOH. Just cardboard cartons and paper coffee cups spilling from the dented garbage bins huddled at the edge of the tarmac. A red Honda was parked in the lot not far from his minivan. He dialled Natasha's extension and got a busy signal. Good. She was at her desk.

Natasha Sharma completed her master's in epidemiology eighteen months ago, after earning a degree in biology. She'd finished top of her class and impressed everyone as the best applicant for the vacant communicable-disease epidemiologist position. She'd proved her mettle within her first six months by unearthing the culprit behind an outbreak of 120 cases of bloody diarrhea: E. coli in the undercooked sausages at a Croatian wedding. She discovered that the bride's mother had ordered the toxin-laden canapés be served prematurely to keep the six hundred guests occupied while the bride underwent a meltdown between church and banquet hall. Something about a spirited flower girl and a handful of rhinestones torn from the bridal gown. Natasha said the altercation made perfect sense, but Zol reckoned it was pointless for any man to try to understand that part of the puzzle.

He tried Natasha's number again. Still busy. He strode down the hall to her office and stood in her open doorway.

Natasha tugged on the short, fly-away curls at the nape of her neck. A scowl and a fist had replaced her trademark poise and charm. She enunciated every syllable as though forcing it through the telephone and rolled her eyes in response to her mother's daily ritual.

"I already told you, Mamaji," said Natasha with a rapid shake of her head, "if you invite him, I am not coming." Catching sight of Zol, she squared her shoulders and picked up a ballpoint. "Gotta go. Dr. Szabo just came in. I'll call you after work," she said, and hung up.

Zol stepped into the room and closed the door behind him.

Natasha stood up and swept the folds of her dress. "Sorry, Dr. Zol," she said, glancing toward the phone as though her mother were still attached to it.

Zol smiled and waved away Natasha's embarrassment. He knew her Punjabi mother phoned every morning with some urgent family matter and managed to steer the conversation toward the discovery of another suitor for Natasha to look over — *just this once*.

Gripping the file folder of notes he'd made last night with Hamish, he lowered himself into the chair in front of Natasha's desk. "Something big has landed in our lap," he said, "and I need you to drop everything." He hoped he didn't sound too sombre.

Natasha's dark eyes glowed with alarm. "But at Shalom Acres," she said, "they've still got tons of questions about their invasive strep outbreak. I was going to —"

"Don't worry about Shalom Acres. We'll find someone else to go over there." He rubbed his palms together. "First off," he said, "what I've got to say is strictly confidential. The implications for the unit, for the entire country, could be enormous."

Natasha put down her pen. "I understand. I won't discuss —"

"I know you won't." They both eyed the ballpoint on her desk as though it were a secret recording device.

"Do you know Dr. Hamish Wakefield, the ID specialist?" Zol asked.

"He's the shy man, mid-thirties, blond, gravelly voice, and perfectly ironed shirts, right?"

Zol brushed a cluster of Cory's cat hairs from the sleeve of his blazer. "I never noticed his shirts, but yeah, gravelly voice. My age, or a couple of years younger."

Natasha smiled. "I've seen him present at Grand Rounds over at the medical centre. He seems really smart."

"He dropped a bombshell on us yesterday." Zol recapped the details of the three cases of variant CJD while Natasha, her chair pulled tight to her desk, jotted on a crisp, yellow pad. She shook her head at the story of Joanna Vanderven, the philanthropist's wife; she gasped at the details of Dr. McEwen's suicide in his dental chair; she nodded as though already familiar with the incident when Zol recounted the hit-and-run death of Danesh Patel, the car salesman.

Zol took a deep breath and raised his eyebrows. Natasha's sandalwood scent cast a soothing wave through his nostrils. They would solve this together, he told himself. All three victims must have lived in foreign parts far enough in the past to acquire their variant CJD by eating tainted meat outside Canada.

Natasha's lips tightened, and she narrowed her eyes. "I'm afraid there's a problem with the foreign beef angle," she said, tapping her notepad with her pen. "The Patels are strict vegetarians. I know the family. Mrs. Patel is a fanatic. Reads the labels on everything."

"You've got to be kidding. Was the husband just as strict?"

She nodded. "He always seemed the type who'd keep peace in the family at any cost. Just like my dad."

Stale coffee churned in Zol's stomach. "Damn. So much for our blame-it-on-English-beef solution."

"I'm sorry," she said with an embarrassed smile. Then she added quickly, "One thing, though. The Patels *did* live in England for a while. Before they came to Canada. I'm not sure when, but I can find out."

"Okay! So we might still have our English connection." He lifted the file folder and waved it in the air like a flag. "I'll be grateful for every bit of insight you can offer."

"We can plot the epidemiological curve," Natasha said with bright notes of optimism in her voice. "Let's see . . . the deaths occurred June twenty-second, June twenty-eighth, and September fifteenth, so the curve looks like this." She sketched a graph on her notepad, then looked enquiringly at Zol, as if the visual depiction of the deaths and the dates might have cracked some sort of code. When he didn't say anything, she shrugged and frowned. "Doesn't tell us much, does it?"

He stood and gazed through the window. Pedestrians crowded the sidewalk, their coats fastened and necks wrapped against the November wind. For a moment, he longed for their humdrum office jobs — predictable hours, nothing more at stake than shipments of hamburger buns, toilet seats, and paper clips. "You know," he said, turning away from the window and shaking himself out of his daydream, "a traditional epi curve might not be much use. CJD's incubation period is ten or fifteen years. That's too long to let us link these cases together in time or place."

"Unless," said Natasha, her voice rising, "this cluster is the first indication of some brand-new kind of variant CJD."

He felt a tightness in his throat. Was this some new form of rapid-onset CJD? A Canadian variant? Hamish had said they should be prepared for other cases to turn up, already dead or still alive. But how many more?

"That's a bold thought, Natasha. But not one I'm ready to swallow at this point," he said, trying to sound more confident than he felt. He pulled a tissue from his pocket and wiped his palms. "Our best hope is to discover that their lives intersected at a common factor — a decade ago and a continent away. As far away from Hamilton as possible."

Natasha drew her fingers through the curls at the back of her neck. "Where do you want me to start?"

"By interviewing Mrs. Patel. In her home. See what you can dig up." He smiled. "That Croatian wedding case showed you're an expert at digging toxins out of nibbles."

Two hours later, after scanning his bookshelves for articles about CJD in the back issues of the *New England Journal of Medicine* and the *Morbidity and Mortality Weekly Report,* Zol sat at his computer searching public-health databases on the Internet. Bit by bit, a blend of lime and cedar insinuated itself into the office, like an unexpected guest. Hamish had splashed on that unmistakable scent last evening before arriving for dinner. And now he was standing in the office doorway, wearing the expectant face of someone hoping to be noticed. He'd unbuttoned his winter coat and was clutching his briefcase to his chest, quietly shifting his weight from one foot to the other. It was obvious he'd discovered some important facts about the case: his eyes were smiling, and his lips formed a satisfied smirk, like Cory the cat depositing a freshly killed mouse at Zol's feet.

"You've got some good news," Zol said, rising from his chair. At six-foot-two, he was a head taller than Hamish. "I can see it written all over your face."

Hamish smiled, thrust his gloves into his pockets, and unwound his scarf. "I think you're going to be pleased."

"Terrific!" Zol said, smacking the air with his fist. "Banbury reviewed his slides? No CJD after all?"

"No, that's not it."

"Damn."

Hamish placed his scarf and coat on the rack in the corner of the room. He turned and shrugged. "Sorry." He pulled up a chair and sat down, then lifted a tooled leather notebook from his briefcase. He reached in again and brought out a bottle of imported spring water. He unscrewed the cap and took a swig. Before setting the bottle on Zol's desk, he hesitated. "Do you have a coaster?"

Zol threw up his hands. "Forget the coaster! Tell me the good news."

"First, you have to congratulate me for finding the dentist's widow and chatting her up for a tonne of details, all before ten thirty in the morning."

"Yeah, you're right. You did great. Now start talking."

Hamish opened his notebook. He'd inscribed a title page: Mad Cows — And Englishmen. "I phoned Brenda McEwen first thing this morning," he began. "She remembered me from U of T. The three of us were undergrads together. Hugh, Brenda, and me." He took a swig from his bottle. "She invited me right over. I was there by nine." He put down the bottle and fingered his notebook, clearly in no hurry to turn beyond the title page.

Hamish would try even the patience of Job. "And?" Zol said, spinning a get-on-with-it gesture with his hands.

"She reminded me that she and Hugh . . ." Hamish smiled and raised his eyebrows, as if on the brink of serving up the *pièce de résistance*. "Well, it turns out that she and Hugh lived in England for a couple of years. And — get this — he had a passion for British sausages." He paused and pursed his lips, putting on his professorial expression. "They call them bangers, you know."

"I know that," Zol said sharply. Why did university docs always figure they had a monopoly on knowledge and brains? "I also know that bangers are usually pork, and there's often veal or beef in the mix."

Hamish turned and coughed a string of staccatos, as if covering his embarrassment at Zol's unexpected roughness.

Zol shifted in his chair and tugged at the collar of his shirt. Hamish's cologne hung in the overheated air. Zol was about to remove his jacket but thought better of it; any movement on his part might distract Hamish into stalling further. "When did Hugh live in England?"

Hamish tightened his lips. "I'm getting to that." He tipped his bottle and swallowed another mouthful. "After we finished our biochem degrees in ninety-one, he went to Oxford. Spent two years there as a Rhodes Scholar. Brenda went with him."

"That's twelve years ago," Zol said.

Hamish beamed. "Yes. And it's perfect. Exactly within the incubation period of variant CJD."

Zol nodded. The timing of Hugh McEwen's years at Oxford *was* spot on. And his passion for British sausages seemed like a clincher. Zol had been dismayed at the hole Natasha had punched in the English beef connection, but could she be wrong about Danesh Patel? Could the man have been a closet carnivore? Zol gestured at his computer. "When you arrived I was digesting the latest reports from England. So far, they've had seventy-two human cases of variant CJD."

"I know," Hamish said. "I reviewed that ProMed posting this morning. Not too helpful. They're releasing so few clinical details we can't tell how closely our three cases match theirs."

"Tell me about the bangers," Zol said flatly. Once again, Hamish had leapt ahead of him.

"Hugh loved them. Ate them for breakfast every single day during their years in England. Brenda said she got sick of frying them up."

"Any other culinary infatuations?"

Hamish scanned his notes. "Just a few. Seville orange marmalade, Scottish shortbread, smelly cheese, and Swiss chocolate. He was addicted to the stuff."

"Addicted to what?"

"A certain kind of Swiss dark chocolate. With creamy centres. His favourites were . . ." He peered at his notes and began to count the flavours on his slender fingers: "Raspberry, kiwi, passion fruit, and hazelnut. Half a pound a day."

"That is a heck of a lot."

"Funny, eh? A dentist addicted to chocolate. I wonder if his patients knew about it?"

"It's not that easy to find Swiss chocolates with fondant centres in Hamilton. I only know of one place that sells them."

Hamish uncrossed his legs and straightened the crease in his trousers. "Four Corners Fine Foods. Just down the street from here." Triumph shone in his eyes. "Hugh made a pilgrimage there every Saturday. Had a standing order of four pounds a week."

"Good God!" Zol said. "Anyone who eats that much chocolate is bound to rot more than their teeth."

"And die happy." Hamish smiled, then frowned and covered his mouth. "But Hugh McEwen was no happy dentist. For the past few years he'd been having difficulty swallowing. Could only eat meat that was thoroughly ground up. His wife blended most of his meals, including his favourite Viennese sausages and English-style bangers."

Zol pictured one of his festive rack-of-lamb dinners tossed into a blender. A terrible assault on fine ingredients. "That sounds like an esophageal stricture," he said. "Or that condition where the far end of the esophagus doesn't open properly when you swallow."

"You mean achalasia," Hamish said, narrowing his eyes and raising a forefinger as if instructing a student. "Brenda's description fits it exactly."

Zol raised his hands and spread his fingers. Sometimes Hamish's pedantic manner was just plain annoying. Zol took a deep breath, tucked his hands beneath his thighs, and reminded himself that Hamish was a rare friend — obsessive and finicky, but unfailingly loyal and too socially insecure to be an egotist.

Hamish picked at the flecks of lint on his necktie, then ironed it smooth with his palm. After a moment he said, "Hugh saw a gastroenterologist who performed a manipulation every few months. His wife didn't know much about it, except that the treatments did improve his swallowing for a few weeks each time."

"What about his suicide?" Zol asked. "How long had he been depressed?"

"Only recently. But it wasn't exactly depression. More like a change in personality. Since early June he'd been distractible, getting angry over trivialities. Brenda found him weeping in the bathroom a few times."

"Any confusion or memory loss?"

"He cancelled his workday a number of times. Always at the last minute. Walked out without warning — threw his staff into a tizzy."

"Had he been given a psychiatric diagnosis?"

"Refused to see a doctor."

"And then," Zol said "within three or four months, he kills himself."

Hamish bit his lower lip. "Sunday, September fifteenth. In his dental chair. Morphine, midazolam, and nitrous oxide." He gulped several mouthfuls from his bottle. "Very sad. I remember him as a really nice guy. Always in a good mood."

Zol picked up his pad and jotted several lines. After a few moments, when Hamish had regained his composure, he asked, "Anyone else in the family sick, depressed, forgetful?"

"Brenda's grieving but she seems okay — between bouts of tears. They have just the one child, a nine-year-old girl. She missed school for a couple of weeks after her father's death, but her mother said she's pretty well back into her routine."

"What did Brenda think when you asked so many questions about Hugh's eating habits? Did she twig to the CJD angle?"

"She was relieved to hear that the pathologist found something in his brain that might explain —"

Zol threw his hands into the air. "Hamish!" he said. "You didn't tell her about the amyloid plaques and the mad cow —"

Hamish flinched and drew back in his chair. "Of course not." Red blotches sprouted on his neck. "I approached it like we agreed. I told her that the preliminary tests showed he had some sort of brain disease, probably an encephalitis." He tossed his notebook onto the desk. "If you're not going to trust me, I might as well —"

Zol caught sight of his huge, threatening hands and tucked them under his thighs again. He stared into the dark screen of his computer.

Hamish walked to the window.

Several moments passed. Neither man spoke.

In the dingy side yard of the Chinese restaurant across the street, plastic bags and cardboard boxes fluttered beside the overflowing garbage bins. A battered wheelbarrow lay on its side, its tire missing.

Zol broke the silence. "I'm sorry, Hamish." He rubbed his temple with his fingertips. "It's just that the implications of these cases have me spooked."

Hamish turned from the window and forced a smile. "I know. We might be out of our depth."

"You did dig up a lot of details in one short visit," said Zol.

"Do you want to hear the rest?"

"Shoot."

Hamish lifted his notebook from the desk and flipped it open. "Okay," he said, "Brenda buys their meat only at Kelly's SuperMart, never at butcher shops. Beef, lamb, pork, and chicken. No exotic meat or game. And Hugh loved a certain kind of smelly cheese. But I mentioned that already. He always bought it himself."

Zol shrugged at the cheese; the British authorities swore that variant CJD couldn't be transmitted in dairy products. On what seemed like a whim, a chef's curiosity perhaps, he asked, "What sort of cheese?"

"Brenda said it smelled disgusting. She and her daughter never touched it."

"What was it called? Limburger?"

Hamish checked his notes. "Head cheese."

Zol clapped his hands and laughed from deep within his belly, his tension evaporating. "Oh, Hamish. You're a riot."

Hamish's cheeks flushed. Furrows creased his brow. "What?"

"Head cheese isn't *cheese*."

"What do you mean?"

Zol tapped his own cheek. "It comes from the head."

"What?"

"Pig's head. It's pickled pork. A sort of sausage made from tongues and cheeks and snouts." He stuck out his tongue and touched his nose with his forefinger.

Hamish shivered and looked away. "Yuck! No wonder Brenda wouldn't touch it." He straightened his tie, then patted the pockets of his shirt and suit coat. "Can't find my pen. Can I borrow yours for a sec?"

Zol handed him his fountain pen.

Hamish drew a line through *head cheese* and printed *pork sausage* above it. "This pen writes pretty nicely," he said, clearly anxious to change the subject. He wasn't used to being caught out on the job. "I've seen this before. Weren't you using it last night? It must be an antique."

"Eighteen ninety-five. The first leak-proof model that could be carried in a pocket. It's a Parker. Belonged to William Osler."

Hamish fondled the black ebonite shaft, ran his fingers along the sterling silver clip. "William Osler? *The* William Osler? The internist who founded Johns Hopkins medical school?"

"And wrote the first medical textbook. Of course, you know he grew up right here. From my back yard, I can look over the Escarpment and imagine I see the street where his father's church used to be. It sounds silly, but when I'm holding Osler's pen I feel inspired to go that extra mile," Zol said, surprising himself with this stirring of emotion. "But back to bangers and blended meals. Hugh McEwen was into ground meat in a big way. For more than a decade."

"It sounds like we're on the right track, eh? With Hugh and his English bangers? Patel and Joanna Vanderven were immigrants; if they've got connections to England we might get this solved before your boss gets back from his retreat."

Zol threw him a puzzled frown. "How did you —"

Hamish laughed. "Know about the retreat?" He was enjoying the moment, feeling good about stealing the upper hand. "Your secretary told me."

"Yeah. Trinnock's up in cottage country for the next few days. He and all the other health-unit bosses are meeting in Muskoka. And thank goodness, too. It'll give us a little breathing room. I just couldn't face him when I saw his name light up last night on my Call Display."

Zol glanced at his watch. With any luck, Natasha would have found Mrs. Patel by now. His pulse quickened as he pictured Natasha, her graceful fingers poised over her notepad, her sharp mind discovering the unlikely thread that would link the vegetar-

"This is as loud as I get."

"Oh, yeah. Sorry," he said, then ex
who'd arrived at the Emergency Dep:
tion in his right arm. He'd been bitt
entire upper limb was infected —
painful. The man had a fever but wasr

"By the look of the wounds, the
mad about the idea of being turned in
with a chuckle. "But seriously, I need
start him on. Do mink carry any kind

"Extremely painful, eh?" said Ham
"Won't let me near his arm."

"Sounds pretty bad. Give him a tet:
ten minutes. What's his name?"

"Aah, you got me there. Too many
remember them." There was the soun
checked his notes. "Here it is: Kroon
him in zone two."

Hamish rang off. He started to call
the guy was on holiday. The trainees
closed the phone, placed it on the pass
few facts he'd been given.

He'd never treated a mink bite. He
farms there were in this part of Ontari
oric in the news, mink farmers did
offering guided tours of their operatio
against rabies? Did mink's teeth carry
cat- and dog-bite infections? And wl
mink encephalopathy? He remembere
a mink ranch somewhere in the Am
was it? Or Wisconsin? But that was a
not in people. It had nothing to do w
animal handlers. One thing did bother
was extremely painful. Hamish shudd
light ahead, and pressed the accelerato

ian car salesman with the Rhodes Scholar dentist.

The phone rang, its red flashing light indicating that Anne was calling from her desk at the reception area in front of Trinnock's office. She might have been classed as a secretary, but she was the administrative heart of the health unit. She never interrupted if she knew Zol had a visitor. A knot of apprehension gripped his stomach, banishing his sense of euphoria.

"Sorry to disturb you, Dr. Szabo." Anne sounded rattled. "I know you're busy with Dr. Wakefield. But there's a man on the line. He said — he said I'd be sorry if — if I didn't put him through immediately."

"Did he give his name?"

"No. He sounds like an older man, with an accent. European, I think."

"Did he say what he wants?"

"I tried to take a message, but he won't speak to anyone but you."

"I guess you'd better put him on." Zol cupped the mouthpiece with his palm and turned to Hamish. "This sounds like a touchy relative from Shalom Acres. Everyone's been pretty upset over there lately. I'd better speak to him."

Hamish scanned his notes as if hunting for unfinished business. "No problem. I'll catch up with you later."

"I have a feeling," said Zol, "we're going to be dumped from our frying pans into a whole lot of fires before this roast gets carved."

A hint of barnyard odour hung like a stain in the air as Hamish entered zone two, the Emergency Department's eight-bed examination room. And when he opened the privacy curtains and entered Ned Krooner's cubicle, the stench of manure hit him like a punch in the chest. A wild-looking man lay propped on the bed, and two tall men stood on either side of him. For an instant, Hamish braced himself against the expected taunts of the burly trio. Hamish had been the short kid on the block who sang in the church choir three times every Sunday, and hazing had been a fact of his life. These days, it rarely happened, not with patients anyway. His status as the specialist protected him. But old feelings never died. Instead, they gained power with age.

The man on the bed held his right arm against his bare chest. He cradled the limb — bruised, bloated, and covered in punctures — as though it were a wounded animal. A week's growth of whiskers grizzled his face. His bloodshot eyes crinkled with pain and fatigue. His cheeks were flushed with fever, and his dark hair was matted to his sweaty forehead. Clods of mud from his work boots soiled the bedsheet.

The man on the right stood trim and neatly groomed, his jaw square and clean-shaven. His blue jeans bore a crisp crease, his loafers a recent polish. He looked the youngest of the three. He smiled without humour and shot out his hand, shaking Hamish's with firm confidence. "Lanny Krooner," he said. He pointed to the even taller man standing on the far side of the bed. "My brother Morty."

Morty, his long hair wild, his clothing smeared with mud and who knew what else, had the stooped posture of a shy man too tall for his self-esteem. He stared in the direction of Hamish's knees and grunted.

"And of course this here's my brother Ned," Lanny said. He narrowed his eyes and stared straight into Hamish's. "You're gonna make sure he doesn't lose his arm, eh, Doc?"

Hamish couldn't be certain of anything about this new patient. He'd barely caught sight of the injured limb, let alone given it his

CHAPTER 4

On
Me
far southeast of the city, Hamish
his thoughts while three men lath
from his Saab. When he'd in
Caledonian two years ago, he'd b
that Mud Street was no muddier

The car wash was the perfect
tions. Impenetrable to pagers an
from an intrusive world. Zol's ou
Brenda McEwen had been a sla
uncalled for. Hamish picked at hi
knew more than he was letting
English beef connection. Hamish
windshield. The white noise of th
did nothing to quell his trepidatio
left the car wash and turned cauti

His cellphone trilled immediat

"Hamish Wakefield speaking."

"Hi, Hamish, it's Jeff Suszek
Caledonian. "Got a case for you.

professional observation and careful thought. So far, the only thing he'd assessed was the reek of the man's clothing. "I don't know yet. Give me a chance, eh?" Hamish said. "I just walked in, for heaven's sake." He regretted his tone immediately. Worrying that his voice and eyes had betrayed his annoyance, he countered with a forced smile, hoping it conveyed enough empathy to keep these muscular men from turning on him.

He donned the pair of gloves he'd pulled from a box mounted on the wall and took a step toward Ned.

"Don't touch it," Ned shouted, his voice full of fear. "It — it really hurts."

"I'll be careful," said Hamish, leaning in to pry Ned's fingers away from his chest so he could examine the palm of his hand.

Lanny pounced, forcing his arm between doctor and patient. "He told you — don't touch it."

Hamish recoiled and stood perfectly still. He felt like a sapper disarming a time bomb.

"I'm serious," Ned said. "Please . . ." He sniffed, tears spilling onto his cheeks. "Don't touch it. Nowheres."

Hamish had seen this before with flesh-eating disease. The pain, beyond excruciating, reduced tough men to tearful waifs and their families to Rottweilers. He made a show of withdrawing his hands. "Okay. Sorry. Okay, I won't touch."

Lanny fired a warning glare and withdrew his arm.

Hamish eased forward again, his hands by his sides. "I'll just look."

Ned's right upper limb had swollen to twice its normal size. Every crimson slash and puncture pouted with pus. The bloated fingers were the size of sausages.

"Quite a mess, eh?" said Hamish, hoping to break the ice by stating the obvious.

The three men nodded. Ned pleaded with his eyes.

"Now, Ned," Hamish said, speaking slowly and with as much reassurance in his voice as he could muster. "I want you to roll your hand forward like this." He inverted his own palm, like a panhandler on a street corner. "I need to see your palm."

Ned grimaced. "Can't. Hurts too much."

"You can do it. Just take it slowly."

Bit by bit, holding his tongue between his teeth, Ned rolled his palm away from his chest and exposed the fleshy underbelly of his forearm.

Hamish leaned in. There it was: a telling strip of purple-grey flesh, partially hidden on the inner surface of the forearm. It was time to get the detailed history, the nuts and bolts that would assemble this ugly picture into a complete diagnosis. "When was the attack?"

Lanny did the answering. "Tuesday."

Good God. They had let this arm fester for more than a week. "You mean a week ago?"

Lanny glowered. "Yeah, and don't you gimme a hard time about it. Heard enough from that nurse." He jabbed his thumb in the direction of the nurses' station on the other side of the curtain.

Hamish put up his hands. He tried to clear his throat with a couple of coughs. "All right, no problem," he said, his voice croaky. He tried to see into the injured man's face, but Ned kept his head down. "Tell me, Ned," he asked, "have you been bitten like this before?"

"Never," Lanny replied. "Not in twenty years o' mink farming." Lanny scanned the cubicle as if to confirm they were still alone. "The mink that done this was acting strange. Restless, eh? Funny look in its eyes for a couple o' days."

A wave of apprehension filled Hamish's chest. "Did it have rabies?"

"Impossible. All them mink are vaccinated. Besides, I keep 'em in sheds, eh? Locked in cages."

Despite Lanny's assertion, rabies was lethal and potentially contagious. It would have to be ruled out for certain. "We should send the animal to the federal lab in Ottawa. They can test the brain for rabies virus. Just to be sure."

"It's already dead," Lanny said. He folded his arms. "We burned it." His eyes dared Hamish to make a federal case of it.

"Okay," said Hamish. "No problem." The real issue wasn't rabies, anyway. It was the terrible state of this arm. "How long has Ned been in this much pain?"

Lanny shifted on his feet and wiped his mouth with his palm. "We thought it was just scratched and bruised, eh? Until the fever started. A couple o' days ago."

Hamish asked a few more questions about Ned's general health. He was forty-one, had never had a serious illness, didn't take any medications, and smoked cigarettes and the occasional joint of marijuana.

Hamish pulled off his gloves and planted his feet in preparation for conveying his diagnosis. The cubicle pressed hot and close, the stench of sweat and manure almost overpowering. He tugged at his collar. "It's going to sound like a big deal," he said, concentrating on the choice of each word, "but I've got to tell you. This is flesh-eating disease."

Ned jerked his head. "Shit." His eyes were ablaze with fear and pain. "Shi–it."

A shudder shocked Morty's stooping hulk. He produced a disgusting noise from the back of his throat and swallowed hard.

"I knew it," Lanny said, the pulse at his temple beating furiously. "I just knew it." He set his jaw and clenched his fists. "But there's no goddamn way you're takin' his arm."

"It's — it's not that bad," Hamish said, struggling to remain in the driver's seat, to project a confidence he didn't feel.

Lanny's cheeks flushed to crimson. "What do you mean? You said it was flesh-eating. That means, you know . . ." He cupped his hand beside his lips and mouthed, "amputation."

Hamish shook his head. "I've seen quite a few cases like this, and we've done pretty well with them." He pointed to the back of Ned's hand and along his arm where the tissues were inflamed but not too far gone. "There's still some healthy enough flesh in that arm, but we can't waste any time. Ned's going to need surgery this afternoon."

Ned raised his good fist like a club. "I don't care what you do. Just get rid of the goddamn pain."

"We've got a terrific plastic surgeon here. Dr. Blayne. He'll open the wounds, clean them up, and trim away the worst of the damaged tissue. You'll feel better almost immediately."

Hamish paused. Should he make a promise he wasn't certain would be kept? These men needed something firm to grasp or they'd spin out of control. "Ned, it's not going to be pretty, but you won't lose your arm."

CHAPTER 5

At noon, Natasha sat alone at a table in the Nitty Gritty Café waiting for Zol. They'd agreed to debrief here in their usual spot after she'd met with Mrs. Patel. She flipped through her notepad and jotted in the margins, thrilled that her visit with the widow had mined a vein rich in helpful details. She couldn't wait to share them with Zol.

Marcus, the café's proprietor, reserved this isolated table at the rear of his establishment for the staff at the health unit. The café was a block and a half along Concession Street from the unit, a perfect location. The subdued lighting and eccentric South American décor, along with Marcus's homemade sticky buns and exotic coffees, softened even the most heated debates. The stipulations of legislation, the concerns of an anxious population, the scarcity of funding, and the demands of self-serving politicians almost always forced contentious interpretations of the bare scientific facts. Marcus's pastries increased the palatability of the discourse and the creative decisions that had to be made.

"Hi, Dr. Zol," Natasha said as her boss approached. His eyes had lost their sparkle. "Is something wrong?"

"Just need a latte." He pulled off his winter coat and hung it on the rack that screened their table from the others.

"I ordered one," she said. "You can have it when it comes."

"No — I can wait for mine."

Marcus appeared like a red-haired genie bearing two frothy glasses on a polished tray. He wore his white apron over a black T-shirt and trousers. "Here you are, Dr. Szabo. Just in time, by the look of you."

"Thanks, Marcus. You've got that right." He took three sips from his glass. White foam clung to his bare upper lip, making him look more endearing to Natasha than ever. Especially today with that cast of anxiety troubling those deep green eyes.

Natasha sipped at her latte, doing her best to avoid a foamy moustache. She had enough difficulty with the real one that had to be waxed every three weeks. She stared at the menu without reading it. She found it awkward starting a conversation with a man. According to her mother, it was fine for a woman to mention the weather or small domestic matters, but a girl had to leave it to the man to initiate the meat in a conversation. Her mother was hopelessly old-fashioned but she was also shrewd, adept at turning the world to her bidding while appearing delicate and helpless. Natasha dabbed her lips with a serviette and studied the list of familiar menu offerings with greater intensity than it needed. "Do we have time for a sandwich?"

"Sure. Let's order and then you can tell me about Mrs. Patel."

As Marcus strode toward the kitchen to prepare their lunch, Zol took a long swallow of his coffee and wiped his mouth with the back of his hand. "Okay. I'm all ears."

Natasha skipped the details of arriving at the Patels' two-bedroom apartment in a respectable but aging high-rise where the superintendent put no priority into vacuuming the lobby carpet. She didn't tell her boss about her embarrassment at the strong smell of curry that burst into the hallway when Mrs. Patel answered her door. Nor did she talk about her irritation that Indian homes were too often cluttered with family photos and tacky knickknacks — tassels and elephants and gaudy statuettes of Hindu gods. She much preferred the spare apartment of Bjorn, her stockbroker boyfriend — it gleamed Scandinavian chic and never gave off any cooking smells.

"The Patels — that's Mr., Mrs., and their son, Nikhil — came to Canada eight years ago from England. They lived in Leeds for twelve years — from 1983 to 1995. They're Hindus, from Gujarat state."

"Have they been back to India?"

"Just once. Five years ago. I gather money has always been tight."

"He was a car salesman, right?"

"Yes. A frustrated one, according to Mrs. Patel. He studied engineering at university in India and worked as a factory supervisor in Leeds, but no one would accept his qualifications here in Canada."

"Yeah. It's a familiar story," said Zol, lifting a slice of sesame flatbread from the basket on the table. "We open our immigration doors to qualified professionals, but once they get here we slam the doors of opportunity." He snapped his bread with both thumbs. "For some," he continued, his jaws working, "it might be better to start with a clean slate and no expectations."

"I suppose," she replied without conviction, thinking of her own father, a pediatrician with a thriving practice in downtown Hamilton. He'd immigrated at a time when Canada gave full opportunity to good doctors from all over the world. Things were different now. She shuddered at the thought of her gentle father behind the wheel of a taxi cab.

Zol dabbed his lips. "Anyway — back to Mrs. Patel."

Natasha enumerated Danesh Patel's negative checklist of CJD risk factors: no family history, no brain surgery, no corneal transplants, no growth hormone injections. Never a blood transfusion. The Patels never ate even a sliver of meat; Mrs. Patel had never allowed it in her home. Whenever she and her husband dined out, it was always at the homes of friends and relatives or at Indian restaurants that prepared proper vegetarian meals.

"What about her husband's lunches when he was at work?"

"She usually packed them. But she did say there's a Sub Haven near his work. He would get a veggie sandwich there when he'd forgotten his lunch."

"Now, remind me — where was he run over?"

"Outside the car dealership. Mrs. Patel showed me the news-paper reports. She's kept a file of them. The police claimed he just walked blindly into the traffic on Upper James. Killed instantly by a woman driving a minivan. It wasn't her fault. But it was a hit and run. The woman turned herself in the next day when her kids spot-ted blood on the front bumper."

Zol grimaced. "I remember the story. But why did he wander into the traffic? Was it suicide, like the dentist?"

"No. Not that Mrs. Patel would admit. But he hadn't been him-self for a while."

Zol's eyes brightened. He finally seemed interested in the details she'd spent all morning harvesting. "Yeah? Since when?"

"Mrs. Patel couldn't say exactly. Since sometime in April or May."

"And when was he killed?"

She checked her notes. "June twenty-eighth."

"So he hadn't been himself for two or three months before he died. Just like Dr. McEwen."

"Sorry?"

"Dr. McEwen underwent a change in personality about three months before he committed suicide. Hamish Wakefield met with his widow this morning. McEwen had become distractible, angry, and tearful."

"I don't know about angry or tearful, but Mr. Patel did become forgetful. He forgot to pay the phone bill for three months in a row, and the company cut off their service."

"Do you suppose he walked into those busy lanes of traffic purely out of distraction?"

She shrugged. "It's possible." She stared at the crumbs on her plate. They almost formed the image of the Mesha Rashi from her mother's favourite astrological chart — Passion and Determination. Not that Natasha actually believed all that stuff. "Um," she said, biting her lower lip, "there's one more thing. I'm not sure it's worth mentioning. But . . ."

Zol raised his eyebrows. "Shoot," he said, spinning his hand in that keep-going gesture she knew so well.

"I had the distinct feeling that Mrs. Patel was holding back about something."

"What do you mean?"

"It wasn't during the formal part of the interview. She was very helpful while I was taking notes. Tearful at times, understandably. But as I was getting ready to leave I made an innocent comment, and her manner changed."

He put down his latte. "What happened?"

"I'd noticed a framed photograph that seemed to have a place of honour on a table. It showed a recent likeness of Mrs. Patel with a much younger man. At least, he didn't look forty-nine. Jet-black hair, smooth skin, not a single wrinkle on his face. I asked if the man was her younger brother. That's when she began to look anxious, as though she had something to hide.

"'No,' she said. 'That's my husband. On our twenty-fifth anniversary. We celebrated it this year.' She sobbed and admitted how very proud he was of his youthful appearance. 'To be successful in the business of selling automobiles,' she said, 'you must look young — no grey hair, no wrinkles.'"

"Sounds like he dyed his hair," said Zol. "That's no big deal these days. Lots of men do it. I don't think it's linked to CJD."

"But she did seem to be hiding something. And feeling guilty about it."

He tapped his chin and looked into the distance. "A little pearl for us to keep in mind." He wiped his hands with his serviette then spread his fingers. "Look, Natasha — I know we agreed to visit Bernard Vanderven together this afternoon. But there've been two more streptococcal deaths at Shalom Acres, and I have to meet with the director. The staff and families are feeling guilty and angry. For us, that's a dangerous combination." He looked at his watch. "I'd like you to go spend a few minutes with Vanderven. On your own."

Oh, no, thought Natasha. He must be kidding. She hadn't finished with the outbreak at Shalom Acres. It wasn't fair. Bernard Vanderven wouldn't have any patience with an underling. Especially a brown-skinned woman under thirty. She'd never get anything out of him. "Please, Dr. Zol, shouldn't I keep —"

"No, you've done a wonderful job at Shalom Acres. All you can. Today it needs politics, not epidemiology."

The troubled look returned to Zol's eyes. He glanced again at his watch. "I know it's a lot to ask, and I'm sorry. But Vanderven won't eat you alive."

This was no time for Natasha to argue. "Yes, Dr. Zol. Of course I'll go."

"Thanks, Natasha. I can always count on you. He'll be expecting you at three thirty." He forced a smile. "The man is going to be brusque. But you can handle him."

Shortly after three o'clock, Natasha settled into a seat in the sumptuous reception room on the top floor of Kelso International's shiny glass building. She'd given herself plenty of time to drive from the health unit to Bernard Vanderven's head office in the industrial park on Nebo Road. Her appointment was for three thirty.

She passed the time by checking and rechecking the list of questions she'd prepared and rehearsed after meeting with Zol at lunchtime. When she was unable to study her lists any longer, she looked at the décor of the overstuffed room. The reception area had the feel of an English manor-house parlour she'd seen in *Architectural Digest*: Oriental carpets resting on darkly stained hardwood, loveseats and wingback chairs upholstered in complementary brocade, large paintings of hunting scenes in gilt frames, heavy drapes of ruby velvet arranged in three layers.

"Come this way," said a thirty-something secretary wearing a bias-cut silk dress in rich purples. Natasha thought the woman spoiled the overall effect with too much eyeshadow. The secretary's heels, which matched the dress and the eyeshadow, clicked against the hardwood. "Mr. Vanderven will see you now. But he's only got a few minutes."

Natasha took a deep breath and slipped her papers into her briefcase, glad she hadn't brought her down-market nylon backpack. Her knees felt insubstantial as she stood, but they didn't fail her. She followed Miss Aubergine Eyeshadow through an oak door marked Bernard Vanderven, CEO.

"So where's Dr. Szabo?" asked Bernard Vanderven from behind his desk after Natasha introduced herself. He didn't stand at her approach. "Your boss said he had to meet with me urgently. Today. So where is he?"

"I'm sorry, Mr. Vanderven, but he got called away on another matter. He asked me to come in his place. I — I have just a few questions to ask, and I promise not to take much of your time."

He lifted the French cuff of his white shirt and glanced at his watch. "Let's get going. Have a seat."

She started off with a brief condolence on the death of his wife. Vanderven dismissed it with a wave of a giant hand, the amber gem on his cufflink catching the late afternoon sun streaming through the picture window behind him. Natasha used the opener she'd used with Mrs. Patel, that his wife had suffered an unusual form of encephalitis.

"Encephalitis? What are you talking about? It was her heart."

"Yes, Mr. Vanderven, your wife suffered a cardiac event. But a detailed examination of her brain showed she also had encephalitis. Inflammation of the brain."

"Why the hell are you bothering me about this now?"

"The health department needs to be sure that it wasn't contagious, that other people aren't at risk."

"For God's sake, girl. That was five months ago. If it was contagious, you people are a bit late."

He was right. Five months was way too long to be tracing encephalitis contacts. But CJD had an entirely different time frame. She had to ignore Vanderven's contempt and press on. She opened her notepad. "Can you tell me about her illness? What was it like?"

"Her heart stopped. She died in her sleep. That's it."

"But was she not unwell for some time before that?"

"What are you implying?"

She'd have to frame the poor woman's mental symptoms diplomatically if she wanted to get anything out of the husband. "Was she feeling stressed? A little forgetful, perhaps?"

He snorted through pursed lips. "Joanna had nothing to be stressed about."

"Was she becoming forgetful?"

Vanderven's gritty face softened a little. "Well, yes."

"In what way?"

"She was a fashion model when I married her. But for the few weeks before her death she no longer cared about her appearance. When she left the house without putting on her cologne or her eye makeup, I knew something was wrong."

"Did you notice anything else?"

"She'd go shopping and not remember where she'd parked the car."

Natasha reckoned it might be safe to smile, to relax the conversation just enough to squeeze a few more details from this icy man. She smiled, nodded, and ventured: "I've done that, too."

"But not every time you take the car out."

"Oh dear. I see." She paused. Her eyes caught a painting on the wall — hounds goring a fox. She gripped the hem of her skirt, pulled it straight, and looked at Vanderven. "When did you become aware of these things, Mr. Vanderven?"

"For God's sake. I don't know. I'm a busy man." He stared at the office door, as though expecting someone important to walk through it. After a moment, he frowned, as if joggled out of a distraction. "Look — she was fine in Rio. That was February. Carnivale. It must have been after that when she started forgetting things."

Now that he seemed prepared to provide a few answers, Natasha went quickly through her checklist. Where did Joanna grow up? Oxford, England. Where did they meet? Milan. When did she move to Canada? Three years ago. Was Joanna vegetarian? Certainly not; not even when she was a model.

When Natasha asked where they purchased their food,

Vanderven's bull neck flushed above his shirt collar. "Christ. How the hell should I know?"

Natasha's cheeks burned, and her eyes stung with tears. She gripped her pad with both hands, stared at the polished brass carriage clock on Vanderven's desk, and swallowed hard. Her cheeks stayed dry.

"All I can tell you," Vanderven said, "we ate a lot of pork and Angus beef."

He must have seen something in her face. Determination? Anger? Vulnerability?

"Joanna was big on salads," he continued, a hint of softness in his voice. "I hate chicken. Get too much of it at dinner meetings."

The telephone rang. He grabbed it before the second ring. "Yeah? Who? That guy from Detroit? Good, I've been expecting him. Park him on hold for a sec." He pulled a business card from the desk drawer, scribbled on the reverse, and thrust it toward her. "Show this to my housekeeper at this address. She'll let you in and tell you everything you want to know."

He picked up the phone, pressed a button, and started talking auto parts before she had time to stand.

CHAPTER 6

A half-hour later, Natasha had typed and printed her page-and-a-half report. "Mr. Vanderven didn't give me much to work with, I'm afraid," she said, handing the two stapled sheets to Zol.

"I'll say," he replied after scanning each line. As usual, he found her wording concise, her points crystal clear. "Not nearly enough to get Trinnock off my back. I'm dreading him getting wind of this CJD business before we've made some decent headway."

"I'm hoping to find something more useful tomorrow at Vanderven's place."

Zol's phone began to flash on his desk. He picked it up.

"It's Dr. Trinnock," said Anne, "calling from Huntsville."

Zol scowled. The moment of truth had arrived. He'd been counting on Trinnock being too distracted and too well-oiled by his cottage-country blab-fest to pester him for a day or two. He took a deep breath as Anne transferred the call. "Hello, Peter," he said. "Having a good meeting?"

"It's okay, but too cold for golf." Ice cubes clinked in a glass, then Zol heard a burst of baritone laughter. "And you?" Trinnock said. "Anything exciting happening down there?"

"Couple of things we're still sorting out."

"Look, it's all a bit hush-hush," Trinnock continued, "but rumour has it there are two or three cases of variant CJD somewhere in southern Ontario. Tell me they're not in Hamilton."

Zol's stomach tightened. His hands turned cold. Had Banbury squawked? "Well, actually . . . yes. We had three cases reported to us . . . yesterday." Technically, it was yesterday. Hamish had called so late on Tuesday night it counted as yesterday.

"Three? Yesterday?" Trinnock sounded apoplectic. "For God's sake, man. Why didn't you call me immediately? I'm going to look like an idiot, ignorant of what's going on in my own patch."

"I'm sorry, Peter, but until a few minutes ago, there really wasn't much to say. Natasha's only just returned from interviewing the family of the third case. And it's good news."

"What do you mean, good news, for Chrissake?"

"All three cases lived in England at the height of the mad cow epidemic there. We're pretty sure that's where they contracted their CJD." He shot Natasha a sheepish look: *What else am I going to say to him at this stage?*

"I damn well hope so."

"We're still checking the details."

"I don't want a horde of satellite trucks descending on us like that goddamn Lassa fever fiasco."

"Yes, Peter."

"There'll be hell to pay if this blows up in our faces. I'll give you the weekend to get it sorted out. Quietly." Trinnock cleared his throat. "And keep in mind — that promotion of yours isn't a done deal."

Zol ended the call and gazed into the darkness that came all too quickly on November afternoons. "Oh, Natasha," he sighed. "Life is one damn deadline after another."

She nodded and bit her lower lip, then went back to her office.

He closed the door behind her and set the lock. He reached into the inside pocket of his blazer and pulled out a slip of paper. The note trembled in his hand as he pondered what was written in his own scrawl: the name and phone number of a private investigator recommended by his lawyer friend, Dave Hatala, earlier this afternoon. Dave had sworn that a PI's alternative approach could be a lifesaver, especially when a matter needed absolute discretion.

There was no way the health unit could be seen to have a private eye on its staff. But Dave insisted that this particular one could slip invisibly in and out of anywhere, public and private. She used unconventional methods but she didn't break the law. And what was the problem if she helped crack the case, saved hundreds of lives, and Trinnock never found out? When it came to paying her, Zol could call her a consultant. The unit hired many consultants every year, and the accountants seldom asked questions.

Zol fingered the paper. Yes, he'd phone her. Dave said she screened her calls, so Zol should leave a message. He looked at his watch: five forty. He had to get Max to soccer by six fifteen. He'd leave her his cell number.

Sweat trickled down his neck as he dialled. He couldn't quite believe a regular guy like him was phoning a private eye.

"Colleen Woolton is bright and feisty," Dave had said. "You'll be pleased with her service. And one last thing...." He'd coughed or chuckled, Zol couldn't be sure which. "Don't be put off by her height."

Natasha arrived at Zol's house at nine fifteen the next morning to collect Ermalinda on the way to Vanderven's mansion. Zol had suggested it might help to have Ermalinda along because she and Vanderven's housekeeper had long been friends, and they attended the same Filipino Catholic church. Perhaps Letty would feel more comfortable opening her pantry cupboards to a sympathetic compatriot.

As Ermalinda sat smiling shyly in the front seat, her mittened hands folded in her lap, Natasha mused about what her father had once said about Filipina women being housekeepers to the world.

From Hong Kong to Helsinki, Dallas to Dubai, families were cod-
dled and vacuumed and laundered by millions of gracious, nearly
invisible women who had developed personal service to an art
form. What power they could wield if they organized and shared all
the secrets they'd witnessed in the bedrooms and bathrooms of the
global elite.

Natasha pulled her Honda to the sloping curb and set the handbrake. Vanderven's three-storey mansion dominated a cul-de-sac at
the edge of the Escarpment. It looked like a brand-new French
château, right out of the box. The slate roof alone would have cost
more than an average Hamilton house. Natasha clutched at the
gaping collar of her coat and picked her way up the long flight of
front steps, Ermalinda two steps behind her. There was no handrail,
and the shards of ice that had escaped the gardener's shovel made
the fashionable fieldstone treacherous. An icy wind howled through
the cedars screening the back garden.

"Good morning," Natasha said to the small woman who
cracked open the front door. Dark, almond eyes squinted in the
burst of unexpected sunshine that leapt from behind a bank of
heavy clouds.

The wind whipped across the vulnerable spot between the hem
of Natasha's skirt and the tops of her boots. "I'm Natasha," she said,
shivering, "from the health unit."

The housekeeper, her jet-black housedress and frilly white apron
ironed to perfection, ushered the visitors in. Ermalinda completed
the introductions. Natasha, who had never thought of herself as tall,
towered over the two Filipina women. She was struck by how gentle
they were, how slowly they spoke, how carefully they moved.

Letty took their coats and led them into a sun-filled room at the
rear of the house. Most other families might have furnished such a
space with a pair of loveseats, a plump armchair, pastel colours, and
wicker accents. The Vandervens had crammed it with stiff faux
Versailles: French-provincial settees and matching hardback chairs,
porcelain vases sprouting silk flowers, gilded bowls stuffed with wax
pineapples and pomegranates. The formality reminded Natasha of

the reception area at Vanderven's office and sparred with the California windows that stretched to the vaulted ceiling on three sides. The effect was no less tacky than Mrs. Patel's Gujarati kitsch.

Natasha chose a chair and pulled her notepad from her briefcase. "Thank you for meeting with us, Letty. I hope we won't take too much of your time."

The housekeeper lifted a plate of home-baked gingersnaps from the coffee table. "You like a cookie?" There was sadness and uncertainty in her eyes, as if to say, *This is a lonely place — I don't know how I'm supposed to help you — I'm afraid I'll make a mistake.*

Natasha took a cookie, placed it on a napkin, and wiped her fingers. She had no intention of eating the gingersnap. She never ate on the site of an outbreak investigation. "I'm not sure what Mr. Vanderven has told you, but we think Mrs. Vanderven ate something that made her sick."

Letty's hand leapt to her mouth. "You mean," she cried, "I . . ." Tears filled her eyes, and her shoulders heaved.

Ermalinda jumped from her chair and sat beside Letty on the loveseat, her arm around the sobbing woman. "It's okay, Letty, dear. Don't worry. It not your fault. Miss Sharma not saying it's your cooking."

"I'm sorry, Letty," Natasha said. "I didn't mean to . . . Ermalinda's right. It's not your fault."

Ermalinda dabbed her friend's cheeks with a tissue. The two women held hands while Letty sobbed, wrapped in a grief so intense one would think Joanna Vanderven had died last week, not five months ago. Letty blew her nose and stuffed the tissue into her sleeve. She stared at her shoes and looked like she would never open her mouth again.

Natasha felt like an idiot. She'd treated Letty like a witness instead of Ermalinda's friend, and now Letty had clammed up. Natasha forced herself to pick up the cookie and bite into it. Barely tasting it, she washed it down with a swig of orange juice. "These cookies are delicious. I wish I could bake," she said, hoping Letty would look up from her shoes, or at least stop sobbing. She took another bite, surprised that the gingersnap actually was tasty. She told Letty so again, this time with genuine conviction.

Letty stopped sobbing, pulled the tissue from her sleeve, and wiped her cheeks. Ermalinda squeezed her friend's arm and handed her another tissue. Then she looked at Natasha as if asking for permission to restart the questioning. Natasha raised her eyebrows and nodded quickly, glad of any help.

"Dr. Zol need to know about the meat," Ermalinda said softly.

"What meat?" Letty whispered between sobs.

"Well," Ermalinda said, "maybe something wrong with the meat Mrs. Vanderven used to buy."

Letty placed her palm on her chest. "But I never use bad meat. I never . . ."

Natasha made her voice sound as soothing as possible. "We don't mean your cooking, Letty." She took another cookie from the plate. "We need to know where the meat came from."

Ermalinda nuzzled closer to Letty. "She worry something hidden in it."

"Hidden?"

Natasha smiled, glad of Ermalinda's well-chosen words. "That's right. Something so tiny that nobody could see it." She was itching to have a look in the pantry and kitchen cupboards of this impressive mansion, but there was no way she was going to rush Letty. "I'd like you to tell me where the Vandervens bought their groceries."

Ermalinda handed Letty a glass of juice. She sipped it slowly.

Natasha smiled as sweetly as she knew how and added, "Did Mrs. Vanderven do the shopping herself?"

Letty put down her glass. "Yes. She like shopping."

"You can tell Miss Sharma, Letty," said Ermalinda. "Mrs. V., she like Kelly's SuperMart."

"And Four Corners," Letty said.

"The gourmet-foods place on Concession Street?" Natasha asked, looking at Ermalinda. Her pen was poised. "What's its full name?"

"Four Corners Fine Foods," Ermalinda said, her voice confident.

CHAPTER 7

At eleven o'clock that Thursday morning Hamish hunched in his laboratory at Caledonian Medical Centre. It was impossible to put the CJD business out of his mind, but he had to review the results of the latest batch of research experiments performed by his technician. He could save scores of lives every day, but if he didn't get his research published in the right journals every year, his career would be toast. The dean would see to that.

He was working on one of those ironies that added to the complexities of medical practice: antibiotics, the drugs meant to kill bacteria, sometimes had the opposite effect. In the presence of antibiotics, a species of bacteria called *C. difficile* released toxins that torched the lining of the bowels. Elderly patients often died within hours, their dignity stolen and their beds soaked in blood and excrement. No one knew where the bacteria came from or how antibiotics incited such a storm of inflammation. As Hamish saw it, the key to the puzzle lay in locating the exact source of the offending *C. difficile*. During an epidemic, when the disease marched along the corridors of a hospital from patient to patient, the source seemed obvious. But where did the first person in an outbreak pick up the *C. difficile*? Hamish reckoned the microbes must lurk somewhere in the food chain, in the form of barely detectable spores. He proposed to develop a reliable method of finding those spores.

Several papers in the food-science journals had captured his imagination. While searching the Internet one evening, he'd discovered that scholars were abuzz with a new approach to identifying specific animal DNA in food. They'd commercialized a test that could detect chicken, beef, pork, horse, sheep, and even cat in any food sample. Using a polymerase chain reaction — the technique for determining which culprit's blood was on the murder weapon, made famous on television crime shows — food scientists could identify what they called "species-specific mitochondrial DNA." They admitted the name was a mouthful but claimed the method was so accurate that Jewish and Muslim caterers could test all-beef sausages to be certain they were free of pork. Fast-food restaurants could make sure their beef patties were free of horse meat. But why a kit for detecting cat meat, Hamish had no idea until he read the manufacturer's package insert. It said the test had been developed to "preserve the integrity of the food supply across the global village," code for keeping cat meat out of take-out curried lamb and mu shu pork.

Hamish knew that the mitochondria inside the cells of every mammal shared a common ancestry with bacteria, back to the time when all life on Earth was a soup of microscopic ocean creatures. He figured that a food-science test for animal mitochondria could probably be adapted for detecting free-living bacteria. After all, mitochondria and bacteria were close cousins. And if his test turned out to be accurate and easy to perform — and not too expensive — he might even revolutionize infectious-disease practice.

He'd optimistically purchased several of the food-testing kits for his technician to evaluate. The test had turned out to be more finicky than expected, and these latest results were disappointing. Hamish decided he would try repeating the experiments himself tomorrow, Saturday. He wasn't on call, so he'd have the whole day free. In the meantime, he had Ned Krooner and a dozen in-patients to see before lunch and then an afternoon clinic's worth of outpatients. He hung up his lab coat, washed his hands, and headed for the elevator.

A few minutes later he stepped to Ned Krooner's bedside. The tips of Ned's fingers poked from beneath a bulky white bandage that extended all the way to his shoulder. Ned's face had changed since yesterday. His eyes glowed above his grizzled cheeks with a brightness they had lacked before the surgery. "Good morning," Hamish said. "How's the pain?"

"Better," Ned said. He pointed to a bag of intravenous morphine hanging on the pole above his head. "That stuff is working good."

Hamish reached for the chart at the foot of the bed. Ned might be enjoying the effects of the narcotic, but it was the timely surgery and the correct choice of antibiotics that had made all the difference. Ned's temperature had come down; his urine output was normal; the morning's blood results were good, too. The infection seemed under control and hadn't damaged his kidneys. "Glad to hear it," Hamish said. He was relieved to see that Ned still had all his fingers. Dr. Blayne had noted in the chart that the fasciitis hadn't damaged any muscles or tendons but that Ned had lost a great deal of skin from his forearm. In a couple of weeks a skin graft procedure would be needed to fix the gaping wound.

"Hi, Doc," said a deep voice. Lanny Krooner entered the room carrying a large plastic bag and a brighter face than yesterday. "Doing not too bad, eh?" He slid a pizza box from the bag and placed it on Ned's table. The smell of cheese and tomato sauce filled the room. A change from yesterday's sweat and manure.

Lanny unzipped his leather jacket and extended his hand to Hamish. "Like you said, Doc, he didn't lose his arm." His grip was a bit too firm. He released it too slowly.

"Yes, yes, things do look good," Hamish said, his mouth suddenly dry. "But we're not done yet."

Lanny stiffened. His amber eyes glowed. "What?"

"I mean . . . I mean, Ned's got a large wound that's going to take some time to heal."

"But he's still gonna keep his arm, eh?"

"I expect so."

"He better." Lanny handed Ned a piece of pizza, then lifted a small package from the plastic bag. "Ned wanted me to give you this."

A red and white packet slid into Hamish's hand. He turned it over and saw a half-dozen sausages lined up on a polystyrene tray beneath a plastic wrapper. The label said Escarpment Pride Viennese Pork Sausages.

"His biggest seller," Ned said in a chirpy voice. "Four Corners can't keep 'em in stock. And they charge big bucks for them in that fancy store o' theirs."

"You mean . . ." Hamish said.

"Yeah. He makes them hisself. On the farm. He's a butcher, eh? We got the farm to ourselves ever since our parents passed away. I do the mink, Morty tends the hogs, and Lanny does the books and his sausages." He looked at Lanny as if apologizing for saying too much then stuffed his mouth with pizza. A spark of humour flashed in his eyes as he licked tomato sauce from his lips. "Haven't found no women to take us on."

It was awkward accepting gifts from patients, particularly food. You never knew the condition of the kitchen it came from or whether it had been properly stored. But these sausages did look professional, as though they'd come straight from a grocery-store display case. If they stayed wrapped and frozen in the laboratory freezer until he took them home, and if he cooked them thoroughly, Hamish reckoned it might be okay to try them.

"Gotta ask you, Doc," Lanny said. "Will Ned be on any pills when he goes home?"

"I expect so. He may need to take antibiotics for a couple of weeks after he's discharged, maybe longer."

Lanny slid out of his jacket and looked around as if to be certain no one else was listening. "We don't have a drug plan, eh? Being self-employed and all. So I'm gonna get you to put Andy Krooner's name on the prescription. He's our cousin. Works at the Ford plant. Got a great drug plan."

Hamish slid his thumb across the slippery packet in his hand. The sausages suddenly felt tainted, no longer a gift but an obligation. He swallowed hard. "I'm sorry, Mr. Krooner. I can't do that. I'd lose my licence."

The defiant glare returned to Lanny's eyes. Acid burned the back of Hamish's throat as Lanny studied his face, memorized his features. Lanny turned to the pizza and tightened his fist, the muscles of his back and shoulders rippling beneath his T-shirt.

CHAPTER 8

"Extraordinary," said Colleen Woolton, private investigator, from behind her desk at two thirty that afternoon.

Zol had just given her the ten-minute gist of the CJD story.

"And yes," she continued, her hazel eyes sparkling, "it would be my pleasure to help you with your investigation."

Zol couldn't quite place her accent. Australia? New Zealand? No, probably South Africa. That would fit with the photo on the wall behind her — a lioness and two cubs in a sundown standoff with a wildebeest and her calf. Her voice was controlled but soothing, just like her face. Freckles sprinkled her nose, and she had a warm smile that seemed to come straight from the heart. Even in her shoes she was only about five feet tall. Her head and body were perfectly proportioned and her demeanour attractively feminine.

She swept her thick, loosely braided ponytail off her left shoulder. Its strands of copper and gold glinted in the rays streaming from the bank of halogen pot lights in the ceiling. "I must tell you — if we're going to work together, I need to be kept abreast of all the details of the investigation as they emerge." She opened her hands and spread her fingers in reassurance. "Only so that I can help you by supplying the missing pieces others might have difficulty snagging by, shall we say, more traditional means?"

Zol rubbed his sweaty palms against his thighs, embarrassed at feeling this nervous in the presence of such an attractive woman. "Sure," he said. "At the health unit, I always insist we work as a team."

She pulled a scribbler from a drawer and picked up her pen. "Do you have time to give me the details of what you've got so far?"

He took his notes from his briefcase and proceeded line by line through the three cases. Colleen seemed to follow every word, took detailed notes, and appeared more at home with the medical jargon than he had expected.

After half an hour, Zol stood, stretched, and removed his blazer. It was sweltering under the pot lights. He felt awkward towering over Colleen's tiny frame and sat down immediately. "You're very good at the medical terms," he said. "Have you —"

"Handled a medical case before?" She shook her head. "Not as a PI. But I did manage my husband's practice." Her gaze dropped to her hands. "Until he was killed."

"Oh. I'm sorry." He tugged at his collar, his neck slippery with sweat.

She waved dismissively. "It's been five years."

"What was his name?"

"Liam. Liam Woolton. I doubt your paths would have crossed. He was a general internist."

"Oh? Where?"

"Saskatchewan. When we first arrived from South Africa he took a post in Yorkton. I don't suppose you've been there."

Zol shook his head.

"To a girl from a city like Cape Town, it felt like Timbuktu." She looked guilty for a second, as though she'd spoken out of turn. "But good people," she added. For several moments she rubbed at a stain on her desktop. "After four winters we couldn't take minus thirty any longer. Picked up and moved to Ontario's sun parlour — Leamington." She looked up. Though her eyes were dry, tears didn't seem far away. "But Liam was killed before we actually established the practice."

She turned and reached into a small fridge, then handed Zol a glass and a bottle of water, both frosted with condensation. "Enough about me," she said. "You look like you could use a drink."

Zol didn't bother with the glass. He drained half the bottle before putting it down.

His cellphone vibrated against his belt. With the ringer turned off, he'd been ignoring the buzzing of incoming calls ever since he'd left his office. This time he excused himself, flipped open the device, and answered it.

"Dr. Banbury's looking for you," Anne said, clearly frustrated. "He says it's urgent."

"Sorry. I've been tied up. Did he say what he wanted?"

"Just for you to call him back as soon as you can. I'll give you his number."

Zol tore a sheet from the message cube on Colleen's desk and jotted down the number. "Thanks. I'll call him now." He turned to Colleen. "That was our secretary," he said as he ended the call. "The brain pathologist I was telling you about, Julian Banbury, he's been looking for me. It sounds urgent."

"You make the call, and I'll pour us a little Amarula. It can always be counted on to steady the nerves."

Banbury picked up on the third ring. "About time you called me," he said. "Got some news for you, old chap."

"Yes?" Zol said, his pulse throbbing at his temple.

"Just finished another batch of autopsies. Found four more cases of CJD."

Zol felt the blood drain from his face. He closed his eyes and leaned forward. "Did you say four?"

"Yes. Just like the others. In fact, exactly like the others." Banbury sputtered as he tried to clear loose phlegm from his throat. "I reviewed every slide, and there is something curious about all this."

"Yes?"

"The pattern of the amyloid plaques in this whole set of brains is unique. All seven have a configuration that's not like anything that's been reported before."

"What do you mean?"

"The British cases have a daisy-like pattern. The plaques I've discovered are denser and more elongated. More like tulips."

"Tulips?"

"That's right. Tulip plaques. That's what I shall call them when I post this on ProMed."

Oh God, thought Zol, *he's not going to broadcast this on the Internet already.* "What — what does this mean?"

"Heavens, man. What do you bloody think it means? We've got something new and exciting happening. Right here in Hamilton."

Zol gripped the edge of Colleen's desk and stared absently at the poster of the lioness and the wildebeest.

"Dr. Szabo? Are you still there?" asked Banbury.

"Hmm."

"Sounds like you've got yourself a whole new cricket match. Seven cases of homegrown CJD and maybe more to come. Do this right, and you'll be famous."

"More likely infamous."

"Hunt down the prions, get this sorted, you'll be a hero."

"You kidding? Even if I found the prions tomorrow, the press would say I dragged my feet and put lives at risk by masterminding a cover-up. And whatever lobby groups get involved — cattle ranchers, meat packers, God knows who else — they'll accuse me of reckless grandstanding, making wild suppositions without benefit of a meticulous investigation."

"Come, come, my good fellow. It won't be that bad. Not when the facts come out."

"Maybe. But in the meantime I get tarred and feathered by all sides. Like the MOH in Walkerton — he did a perfect job of handling their E. coli water tragedy and still he got crushed in the stampede of a panicking public."

"You're exaggerating."

"Not by much." Zol grabbed the water bottle and finished it off.

"Look, I need you to give me some wiggle room — a few days before you post this on ProMed."

"Come, come. I've already been through this with Hamish Wakefield. I'm not going to sit on something this big for long. It will take me the weekend to do some special stains and review a few more slides. Then two or three days to write my report. I shall be ready to make my ProMed posting sometime early next week."

Less than a week! They'd never be able to find the source of the outbreak that quickly. "Can you at least call me before you make any announcement? I don't need to tell you what's going to happen when this gets out."

"I can assure you, this is the real thing. Not like that ridiculous Lassa fever fiasco. But yes, I shall call you first. Would you like the names of the latest cases now, or shall I fax them to you?"

Anyone could read the printouts as they rolled out of the fax machine at the health unit; it was as good as publishing the whole damn story in the *Spectator*. "No, no. Please don't fax them. Not to my office."

Colleen caught Zol's eye, pointed to her machine, then flipped him her business card, the fax number circled. Somewhat calmed by her self-possessed manner, he nodded and read out her fax number, his voice feeling not quite as strained.

Two minutes later, the machine beeped and fired out a hand-written list of four names with their occupations and birth dates. As Zol scanned the sheet, he was shocked at the sight of the second name: Delia Smart, Shakespearean actress, fifty-eight.

Suddenly, his mind flashed back a dozen years, and he pictured his favourite customer glowing in the candlelit corner she always favoured at The Bard's Table in Stratford. He could almost hear that commanding voice, that perfect diction gushing over his beef Wellington. A career ago.

An iceberg of guilt floated in Zol's chest as he drove to the health unit from Colleen Woolton's office. Twelve years ago he'd been an apprentice, a mere underling at The Bard's Table. But he'd known about the uninspected steaks and chops the owner brought in on a regular basis from a dodgy butcher. The owner had insisted the animals had been a little lame, but healthy, and perfectly good on the table at half the price. But what if the animals had been lame not from injury, but from mad cow disease? What if he'd had a hand in infecting Delia Smart with prions? How could he live with himself? More than ever, he had to hunt down the source of the prions, to prevent further cases. Only then might there be a melting of his icy guilt.

Two aspects of Banbury's discovery suggested this cluster was unique. First, there was the unprecedented appearance of so many variant CJD cases in one city within such a short interval. Second, there was the brand-new microscopic pattern of prion damage in those brains, Banbury's tulip-shaped plaques. Yesterday, while Zol and Natasha had been staring at Hamilton's three known cases of variant CJD, Natasha had speculated they might represent a new variety of human CJD, something homegrown without any connection to British mad cows. Now that they were facing seven cases, and at least one of the people had eaten uninspected beef here in Ontario, it was almost certain Natasha was on to something. Her sixth sense for epidemiology was impressive. Maybe, just maybe, Natasha's intuition could give this investigation a fighting chance.

Zol turned in to the parking lot behind the health unit and caught sight of Mr. Wang's wheelbarrow in the yard outside his restaurant across the street. The wheelbarrow lay on its side like a bad omen, its metal sides dented and rusted, its wooden handles splintered, its wheel-fork twisted. A garden hose lay coiled beside it, beneath an outdoor water tap. A century and a half ago and an ocean away, the legendary Dr. John Snow had traced the source of epidemic cholera to a water tap in London, England. Had that landmark discovery dawned on Dr. Snow after months of plodding through the mucky streets of London, or had he been seized by a flash of brilliance one fateful weekend while he was jammed against a deadline?

Natasha gripped the phone on her desk. "Of course it's important, Mamaji." Dr. Zol had only just left her office after breaking the news of the four additional cases of CJD and the tulip-shaped plaques in all the brains.

Natasha continued her carefully worded explanation to her mother. "It's a project we need to finish by Monday." It was all she could do to keep from explaining she'd be missing Friday night supper with the family because she and Dr. Szabo had a public-health emergency on their hands. If Natasha even hinted about tackling a crisis, her mother would soon have it known all over Hamilton that her daughter was single-handedly defending the city against Armageddon.

"But Tashu, we always count on you for Friday supper. I'm making your favourite, *dahi besan kadi*. And your brother is bringing Deepak, that nice young doctor."

Natasha rolled her eyes and fingered the curls at the back of her neck. "He's not a doctor, Mamaji. He's a drug rep. He sells anti-biotics and birth control pills."

"Well, almost same thing. He works with doctors every day."

"For heaven's sake, what —"

"He's so nice-looking. Beautiful teeth. And almost vegetarian. He only eats a little chicken."

What did only eating a little chicken have to do with being a good husband? She was surprised her mother hadn't mentioned the light colour of his skin. Perhaps she was finally learning a little Canadian political correctness. "If he's such a nice guy, I'm sure you'll enjoy his company without me."

"Why don't you come just for an hour? I'll have everything ready."

"No, Mamaji."

"But you have to eat, Tashu. I think you're working too hard. You'll get wrinkles before we find you a husband."

Natasha wouldn't take the bait this time. "I'll be fine."

Dr. Zol had asked her to come to his house at six thirty to review all seven cases. Dr. Wakefield would be there, and supper would be ready. She figured the meal would be delicious, if what she'd heard about her boss's kitchen prowess was even only half correct.

"But what about me?" continued her mother. "I haven't seen you all week. My West Nile virus could return, and you'll never see me again."

"Come on, Mamaji, that all happened almost two years ago. And you never had West Nile. The tests for it were negative. You weren't even that sick."

"I could have died. The doctor said so."

Natasha shook her head and tapped her fingers against her desk. The doctor had said it was a good thing it wasn't West Nile — just an infection with Coxsackie virus, a relatively harmless form of viral meningitis. All her mother chose to remember was the doctor saying that a more serious form of meningitis could have killed her.

"Sorry, Mamaji. I have to go. I'll call you tomorrow. Save me some of the *dahi besan kadi*."

She looked at her watch: four fifteen. She'd have to hurry if she was going to get over to health records at Caledonian before five. The charts of the four latest CJD cases were essential for their meeting at Dr. Zol's.

CHAPTER 9

Natasha and Hamish arrived on Zol's front steps that evening within seconds of each other. Their arms laden with bulky packages, they nodded shyly at one another and introduced themselves in the semi-darkness. Natasha was clutching Joanna Vanderven's Louis Vuitton bag and a bundle of hospital charts. The slippery folders slid precariously in her arms and nearly escaped before she hitched them into the crook of her elbow. Hamish juggled five plastic bags brimming with a complete Italian dinner from Four Corners. He pulled off a glove with his teeth and reached for the doorbell. As his finger made contact, one of his bags crashed onto the veranda and rolled down the steps. It left a gory trail of tomato sauce and mushroom pieces. Zol had conceded that this was no night to be disdainful about a decent meal arriving packaged in cardboard and plastic. He might have second thoughts when he saw the extent of the mess tomorrow in the light of day.

Zol answered the door, scooped the charts from Natasha's arms, and helped his guests stow their winter paraphernalia. As they passed the living room and stepped into the kitchen, Natasha raised her hand to stifle a wide-eyed *Wow.* Zol responded to the enthusiasm on her face and explained that the place had been both restored and expanded.

It had started as a plain centre-hall with two tiny bathrooms, Zol explained as Natasha ogled. The builder had modernized the plumbing and the roof-lines, redesigned the veranda, and added a state-of-the-art kitchen leading to a sunroom that embraced a view over the Escarpment. Natasha stroked the restored oak mouldings and tapped her toe against the patina of the hardwood flooring. As usual, Zol kept to himself the small matter of the lottery jackpot that had allowed him to quit the restaurant business, graduate debt-free from medical school, and purchase a home that really was stunning.

Hamish apologized for spilling tomato sauce on Zol's porch as he tucked the soiled container into the garbage bin and ran his hands under the tap. Zol shrugged and laughed, then assembled the contents of the remaining packages into a respectable meal.

Natasha wandered through the adjacent rooms. Though she didn't know how long Zol had been divorced, she could tell that a woman had never settled here. The dining room wasn't graced by the softness of flowers or ceramic figures arranged on a sideboard. There wasn't the cozy clutter of lifestyle magazines scattered on the coffee table or piled in a basket in the sunroom. The living room's dark twill drapes needed a brighter touch, red or yellow shantung perhaps, and some contemporary zip in their arrangement. The uninspired artwork was decidedly masculine: a huge Robert Bateman print of a bear catching a fish, a cluster of moody lake-country landscapes, and that famous van Gogh self-portrait.

The meal from Four Corners turned out to be tastier and fresher than Zol had expected. "We've got a fair bit to cover, so we might as well get started," he said, helping himself to another piece of garlic bread from the basket on the table in front of him. "How are you fixed for water, Hamish?"

Hamish covered his mouth with his fist, swallowed, and tried to clear his throat. "I'm fine," he said, whispering through the scars in his voice box.

Zol caught Natasha's eye. "Will you take notes as we go along?"

She nodded and pulled her notepad toward her. "I'm all set."

Zol gestured to the pile of charts between them. "I suppose you didn't get much chance to look at these newest cases?"

"I flipped through them and scribbled a few notes," Natasha said.

"Can you give us a summary before we focus on the details?"

She glanced at her notepad. "Three women and one man. They range in age from twenty-seven to fifty-eight. All have Hamilton addresses. And they died within twenty-one days of each other."

Hamish opened his mouth in surprise. "Three weeks! Quite a tight cluster."

Zol suppressed the image of Delia Smart cutting into a serving of his beef Wellington. "If we're going to find a common source," he said, "the tighter the better."

Hamish sipped from his glass, then reached for another helping of tomato-mozzarella salad. "When did they die?"

"The first one, six weeks ago," Natasha said. "The last one, three weeks ago."

Hamish rolled his eyes. "Julian Banbury didn't waste any time looking at their brains. No point in stalling when you've got a once-in-a-lifetime crack at fame."

"What do you mean?" said Natasha.

"He's looking at seven cases of a brand-new form of CJD," Hamish explained. "Unlike the other forms, it's got a short incubation period, and from what you told me on the phone, Zol, a distinctive pathologic pattern in the brain. Tulips, was it?" Hamish smirked as if to say he thought the term was eccentric, even comical. "He must be counting on this variant being named after him."

"Hmm," Zol said. "Banbury Disease." He raised his empty fork and poked the air with it. "But we don't know for certain about the incubation period, eh? It might not be so short."

Hamish speared the last nugget of mozzarella from the serving dish. "I think it has to be. Seven cases, right out of the blue and simultaneously? They must've contracted those prions quite recently."

Natasha dabbed her lips with the corner of her serviette. "How recently, Dr. Wakefield?"

"Hard to say. But I'd estimate no more than two years before they first started showing symptoms."

"Are you sure? Only two years?" cautioned Zol. What Hamish was proposing was a major departure from common doctrine about Creutzfeldt-Jakob. "That's very short for CJD."

"Well, no, I'm not sure. But I doubt it could be much longer."

"Let me get this right," said Zol. "You're saying we should look for possible shared sources of prions no more than a couple of years before the first case started showing symptoms?"

Hamish shrugged. "We have to start somewhere."

Natasha smiled. "Yes," she said. "Sometimes you have to start with a hunch."

Hamish aligned his knife and fork on his emptied plate, inspected their arrangement, then shifted them slightly. "I think we should look at these four latest cases in chronological order." He lifted his serviette from his lap, folded it into a perfect square, and placed it on the table.

Zol cocked his head toward Natasha. "Okay then. Who was the first to show mental changes?"

"Delia Smart, the actress. She became ill four or five months before the others."

Natasha extracted the woman's chart from the pile beside her and extended it toward Zol.

"Zol!" Hamish said sharply. "Be careful. You're going to get tomato all over the charts."

Zol grabbed his serviette and looked pointedly at his hands, which had grazed the sauce on his plate. "Sorry." He made a show of wiping away the oily film from his fingers. He held up both hands for Hamish to inspect. "How's that?"

"Fine."

Natasha stared at her plate. Though her eyes were hooded, her lips formed a tight, perceptive grin.

Zol took the chart and dropped it on the table beside his plate. He stared at its cover; his fingers hovered over it.

"Dr. Zol, are you okay?" She'd noticed the tremble in his fingers. She leaned toward him and lowered her voice. "Was she a friend of the family?"

Zol closed his eyes and drew in the scent of sandalwood that enveloped her. At such close range he found it especially warm and comforting. "You're very perceptive," he said after a long draft from his water glass. "She was a regular customer at the restaurant where I worked in Stratford. A really fine lady. Always went out of her way to compliment the staff. It's awful to think of her mind dissolving into nothing."

Natasha held his gaze. Her expression said she understood his pain.

Hamish was unperturbed. "Did she act at the Festival?" he asked. "My mother used to drag me there every summer."

Zol fingered the spoon beside his plate. "She was one of their stars. Portia, Lady Macbeth, Cleopatra."

Hamish lifted his glass in a mock salute and chuckled. "It was so long ago that we don't need to suppose you poisoned her, do we?"

Zol's shoulders stiffened, and his cheeks burned. He stared at his plate. Hamish could be so damned insensitive. His digs were all the more biting because they were accidental. Over the years, Zol had learned to deal with bullies. Restaurant kitchens were full of them. But how did you handle the thoughtless gibes of a lonely scholar who was socially awkward? About a year ago, Zol had returned one of Hamish's tactless volleys, and the guy pouted for a month.

Zol held his tongue. He couldn't risk sending Hamish into a funk.

"How should we do this?" Natasha asked, her face still anxious. "Should we each take a chart, spend a few minutes with it, then present a summary?"

"But there are four charts," Hamish said.

"That's okay," Natasha said. "I've had a head start. I'll do two."

Zol placed Natasha's empty plate on top of his and moved the dishes to the far end of the table. He didn't dare touch the Zenlike arrangement Hamish had created at his place. Natasha passed Hamish a chart, and for the next few minutes the room was quiet except for the rustling of paper.

When he'd judged that Natasha had finished reviewing the last page of her second chart, Zol said, "Are we ready?" Seeing the others nod, he patted Delia Smart's chart with his palm. "Delia was the first to develop symptoms. I should lead off."

He started with a story that had caught his eye a year ago. Delia Smart had withdrawn abruptly from the preliminary rehearsals of her role as Gertrude, Hamlet's mother. It was rumoured she was unable to learn her lines. In her chart was the consultation letter from the neurologist who assessed her at the time and made a diagnosis of early onset dementia consistent with Alzheimer's disease. Eight months later, in August, Delia spent a day in Emergency with a bladder infection. The nurses' notes described her as weak, mute, and bedridden. She died at home on October tenth, having lost at least fifty pounds. The surprise in the autopsy was the evidence of cjd, not Alzheimer's, and Banbury's tulip-shaped plaques in her brain, concentrated in the amygdala.

"What's the amygdala?" Natasha asked.

"Two almond-shaped structures deep in the brain," Hamish explained. "One in each hemisphere."

Natasha looked puzzled.

"Sorry," Hamish said. "I keep forgetting you didn't get into med school."

Zol's hands flew up as he leaned into the table. "Hamish. What the ..."

Natasha looked at Zol, then lifted her eyebrows and shook her head, the gestures almost imperceptible.

Without missing a beat, Hamish raised his teaching finger and continued, "The brain, actually the cerebrum, has two sides, each called a hemisphere. And each has an amygdala. In the temporal lobe." He pointed to the hospital chart in front of him. "My guy's tulip plaques were concentrated there, too."

"My cases, as well," Natasha said, her eyes bright and alert. "Both of them."

"Did they have memory problems?" Hamish said.

Natasha nodded.

"The amygdala plays a role in memory and regulates emotions, especially fear," said Hamish.

Zol shrugged and held up his palms. "I don't mind admitting I slept through neuroanatomy, but we're getting ahead of ourselves. Tell us about your case, Hamish."

Hamish swept his hand over his flat-top, then summarized his case.

Owen Renway, age forty-two, had worked for the Canada Revenue Agency as a delinquent-accounts officer. He died on October nineteenth, nine days after Delia Smart. He'd been on sick leave since May. The hospital chart contained only the barest details of his illness because he was never admitted to the hospital and not evaluated there as an outpatient. He must have seen a doctor at another clinic. On the evening of his death he vomited at home, choked until he turned purple, and was found without vital signs when the paramedics arrived.

"All attempts to revive him on the scene and at Caledonian's Emergency Department were unsuccessful," said Hamish, closing the chart.

"Did the autopsy confirm the cause of death as suffocation after aspiration?" Zol asked.

Hamish made a face. "Yes, his lungs were full of vomit."

"And his brain?"

"Same as the others."

"All right," said Zol. "Now it's your turn, Natasha."

"I'll start with Rita Spinelli, age thirty-eight. She owned the Sunroom Boutique, an expensive dress shop on Concession Street. She died almost exactly like Danesh Patel."

"How so?" Hamish asked.

"Hit by a truck when she wandered into four lanes of traffic." Natasha explained that after three days in intensive care at Caledonian Medical Centre Rita was declared brain-dead. Her husband wanted to donate her organs, but the consulting neurologist in ICU put a stop to that upon learning she had memory problems, a change of personality, and hadn't been able to run her business since August. He couldn't rule out CJD. As it turned out, he was correct.

"Can you imagine if she'd donated her organs?" asked Zol. "We'd be looking at half a dozen more cases at least."

Natasha closed her eyes, took a deep breath and let it out slowly.

"When you're ready, Natasha, tell us about the fourth case," said Zol.

"This one is really sad. She was only twenty-seven."

Tonya Latkovic, a high-school math teacher, had been referred to Caledonian's psychiatric clinic during the summer because of depression and forgetfulness. Except for a history of migraine headaches, she had always been healthy and vivacious. She showed no response to antidepressants, and when she couldn't face returning to her classroom in September she was put on stress leave. In the middle of the night of October thirty-first she wandered off from the home she shared with her parents. The next day she was found dead at the bottom of the Escarpment.

Natasha fingered the iridescent black opal pendant she wore every day. Its teardrop shape seemed to glow of its own accord. "The *Spectator* published an interview with the woman who found the body while she was walking her dog. I remember reading it and thinking . . ." She clutched her arms to her chest.

Hamish shifted his chair closer to the table. "What did the autopsy show?"

"A fractured femur," Natasha said. "She bled to death from a fractured femur. I didn't know that could happen."

Hamish raised his index finger to its professorial position. "Oh, yes," he said, "it's *classic.*"

Natasha looked at Zol and held his gaze, then lifted her eyebrows again as they covertly shared their understanding of the quirky young professor. "And of course," she continued, "it showed CJD with tulip plaques, just like the others."

The phone rang in the kitchen. Zol hoped it was Max or Ermalinda saying they'd seen their movie and were on the way home. No such luck. It was Peter Trinnock.

"So, Zol, how are things on the CJD business?"

Zol cleared his throat. "Banbury has just reported four new

cases. We're reviewing them now. Planning our strategy for the weekend."

"You'll have to do a lot more than plan. And who's *we*?"

"Natasha and Hamish Wakefield."

"Natasha who? Oh yes, the new girl. Why do you have her on the case? Why not Gibson? He's got a lot more experience."

"She's got the nose for this sort of thing. Remember the E. coli at that Croatian wedding? It was Natasha who —"

"I hope you know what you're doing. It's all gonna be on the line on Monday afternoon. My office. Four o'clock."

Trinnock hung up, and Zol leaned his head against the kitchen wall.

Damn. How was he going to find a watertight lead in three days? And was it going to lead straight to The Bard's Table?

He plodded back to the dining room. He'd have given almost anything for a double Glenfarclas at that point, but he couldn't take the chance that it might dull his grey cells.

"Dr. Zol," Natasha said, the whites of her eyes radiating her concern. "Bad news?"

"That was Dr. Trinnock. He's mad as hell."

"He's got nothing to be mad about," Hamish said. "We didn't plant these cases. We're only trying to solve them."

"But if we don't do it fast, Toronto will be all over him. Ottawa, too."

Hamish looked puzzled.

"The Canadian Food Inspection Agency."

"Of course. Prions in the food chain are a federal responsibility."

Restless, Zol stood behind the chair he'd been sitting in and gripped its back. "We've got three days to come up with the lead that will take us to the finish line."

Hamish scowled, puffed his chest, then let out a long, loud tsk. "That's ridiculous. He can't expect . . ."

Natasha turned to a fresh page on her notepad. "I'm sure Dr. Trinnock doesn't expect complete closure by Monday. Just a strong, plausible hypothesis for us to spend the next week nailing down."

Zol wished he could share Natasha's optimism. "Whatever way we look at it," he said, "it's going to be a hectic weekend." Still standing, he rocked his chair on its back legs. A rattling sound came from a large leather bag that sat on the seat. "What's this?" he asked.

"Sorry," Natasha said, "I put it there. I meant to give it to you earlier. It was Joanna Vanderven's. Her housekeeper gave it to me this morning."

"It's a Louis Vuitton," Hamish said. "*Very* expensive. Unless, of course, it's a knock-off."

Zol looked at Hamish. "How do you —" At any other time he could have made hay out of this one at Hamish's expense. But not now. Not tonight. "What's in it?"

"All her medications," Natasha said. "Her housekeeper kept them hidden after Joanna died."

"But why did she give it to you?" Zol asked.

"I don't know. Perhaps she trusted me, saw me as a friend of Ermalinda's."

"We should have a good look at them," Hamish said. "Remember — the toxicology lab found all those drugs in her blood."

"But it's not our business," Zol said. "For God's sake, we've got enough to worry about."

Again, a raised finger from Hamish. "At this point, isn't everything about these people our business?"

"Okay, you take the bag, Hamish. It's now officially your baby." Giving the man no chance to respond, Zol turned toward the kitchen. "I'm putting the coffee on."

He had only taken three steps when the doorbell rang. He could see Colleen Woolton standing on the veranda, cradling a parcel.

Her bright gaze darted around the hallway as he led her in. "I suppose I've missed most of the meeting. It took longer than I expected to wrap up my other case. But it's settled now." She placed a hand on his arm and looked into his eyes. "You seemed to enjoy the Amarula this afternoon." She pressed a brand-new bottle of the African liqueur into his hand and gave his arm a steadying squeeze. "Looks to me like you could use it right now."

Seeing Colleen standing there looking fresh and confident, and remembering her sure-footed approach in her office this afternoon, Zol was sure he'd been right to bring her into the inner circle of the investigation. How else was he going to dig up tangible answers for Trinnock by Monday afternoon? If Hamish got uppity about Colleen's involvement, well, too bad.

He pulled a hanger from the closet. "Here, let me take your coat and then . . . and then I'll introduce you to Hamish and Natasha."

She'd noticed the hesitation in his voice and shot him a puzzled look as she handed him her scarf and gloves.

"To be honest," he admitted, "they're not exactly expecting you. I didn't know how to tell them I'd hired a private eye. Hamish can be a bit touchy."

"For heaven's sake, Zol, you make me sound like an ill-mannered ex-cop out of a paperback novel."

"Tell Hamish about your *New England Journals*. You'll melt his pedantic little heart."

CHAPTER 10

The next morning Zol arose feeling anxious and impatient. Anxious about having to face Douglas Matheson, Delia Smart's husband. Impatient to get the interview over with and perhaps clear the pall hanging over The Bard's Table and its dodgy meat. He dispatched Max to the TV room for a festival of Saturday-morning cartoons as soon as their last mouthfuls disappeared from their breakfast cereal bowls. He put the cartons of milk and juice in the fridge, picked up Dr. Osler's Parker, and tried to jot down a list of questions for Douglas Matheson.

He found himself too distracted by thoughts of Colleen to concentrate on his task. When she'd stepped into the living room last evening, scented with jasmine and armed with a bottle of African Amarula, Hamish had greeted her with a frown. He was barely civil when Zol introduced her as a private investigator who would be consulting on the case. Hamish didn't say it, but it was clear that he considered their CJD cluster strictly a medical matter, not the purview of a private eye better suited to photographing wayward husbands cavorting with their mistresses. But Hamish started to come around when Colleen explained that she once managed her husband's internal-medicine practice; he softened when he heard she hadn't had the heart to cancel her husband's weekly subscription to the *New England Journal of Medicine*; he sat agape when she told him that she still read the editorials and the abstracts before placing every issue in Liam's former study. Anyone in possession of a decade's worth of *NEJM*s neatly ordered in a personal library secured Hamish's immediate respect as a kindred spirit. Colleen had been quick to admit that she couldn't explain the biochemistry of prions, but she proved to be fully aware of the infectious link between British cattle falling sick and the kingdom's smouldering epidemic of human CJD. Yes, she was definitely going to be an asset to this case.

"Would you like a coffee, Dr. Szabo?" Douglas Matheson said to Zol an hour later as Matheson led the way to his living room in Dundas, the crunchy-granola town that huddled next to Hamilton and liked to think of itself as a Victorian village housing Caledonian's professors and patrons of the arts. "I've learned to become quite independent in the kitchen since Delia took sick."

Zol had drunk enough caffeine for one day. He didn't need to add to the jitters he already felt. It was going to be tough to sift through the domestic details of a much-celebrated life he'd once seen as untouchable. The chore would be all the more complicated if Douglas Matheson recognized him from The Bard's Table.

"Thank you, no," Zol said. "Unless you happen to have decaf."

"That's all I ever drink. I'll be back in a jiff."

While the silver-haired gentleman padded off to the kitchen, Zol stole the moment to review his plans for the day. Too bad Ermalinda wasn't free to mind Max the entire day; she had some sort of pressing commitment for the afternoon. After this visit with Douglas Matheson, he had to be home in time to give Max his lunch and get him to his swimming lesson for two thirty. Then they had to complete their weekly marketing at Four Corners Fine

Foods before it closed at five. It was never a quick trip because Max liked a say in everything they would be eating for the next week. At seven thirty the group would reassemble in Zol's sunroom to spend the evening, and possibly the whole night, dissecting all the information they'd gleaned separately today. Hamish would be meeting with Owen Renway's partner, Kenyon Cheung. Rita Spinelli's husband was expecting Natasha. Colleen would visit the parents of Tonya Latkovic. With luck, a common thread would materialize, a tantalizing lead that would satisfy Trinnock. Zol knew what would happen if Trinnock pulled the plug before Zol and his team were given half a chance to solve this case themselves. The blood roared in Zol's ears at the thought of a flock of pompous, media-hungry epidemiologists descending from Toronto like vultures onto his investigation.

Zol looked around the living room. Photographic incarnations of Delia Smart watched him from all sides. From the piano, from the rolltop desk, from the mahogany side table: Ophelia the broken-hearted maiden, Catarina the endearing shrew, Cleopatra the sultry empress. Within a paired set of frames angled on the mantel, Delia Smart the ingénue gazed at quite another Delia whose facial creases spoke not of aging but of wisdom. There were no photographs showing Delia at The Bard's Table, but Zol could picture her there all the same, seated in her favourite spot, radiant, her spoon poised over one of his special crème brûlées.

Matheson returned with two coffees on a tray. He handed Zol a mug, peered through the window, and grumbled about the blustery weather. "Hamilton has always been our winter home. It's supposed to have less snow than Stratford. But you just can't beat Stratford in the summer. . . ."

Zol let Matheson prattle on for another minute, then offered condolences and thanked his host for agreeing to meet on such short notice. He pulled a notepad from his briefcase and forced himself to begin the dissection of the celebrated life. "Perhaps we should start with . . ." He cleared his throat and started again. "Please, tell me how and when Miss Smart started showing signs of her illness."

Matheson put down his mug and focused into the distance. "It's hard to say exactly," he said. "At first she just started forgetting little things, like leaving her sunglasses on the counter at the bank. I didn't think anything of it. But when she couldn't remember our grandson's name, I knew something was wrong." His fingers trembled as he ran his hand through his thin white hair in a practised motion that suggested he once had a much thicker mane. "I took her to the doctor, but he said she was just overtired." Matheson slapped his palm against his thigh. "I knew it was more than that."

"When was this, sir?"

Matheson looked at the ceiling. "Let's see. I took her to the doctor the day after her birthday. Late November." He inclined his head toward his nicotine-stained fingers, steepled against his belly. "Everything came to a head not long after Christmas. She wore a shamrock-green dress instead of her tartan shawl to the Robbie Burns dinner on January twenty-fifth, insisting to everyone that the beloved poet was Irish." He looked at Zol, his eyes wide with dismay. "I can't tell you how embarrassing that was. That doctor of hers is an idiot." Matheson jabbed at his forehead with his forefinger. "Overtired, my eye. She was ill, for God's sake."

Matheson began a cough that barked and rattled relentlessly, like a freight train. His eyes watered, his cheeks flared, his lips turned blue. Zol rose to fetch a glass of water from the kitchen, terrified he might be required to perform CPR, but Matheson came out of it. "Sorry. Bad lungs," he croaked, patting his breastbone. "Old before their time."

Into Zol's mind flashed the shades of the summers he'd spent helping his father with the tobacco harvest, the truckloads of leaves dispatched from their farm to the brokers and the cigarette factories. He suppressed the images before they could fully take shape. "Please take your time. Do you need a glass of water?"

Matheson shook his head, wiped his eyes, and blew into his handkerchief. "Water doesn't help." He looked at Zol and dipped his eyebrows. "Where was I?"

"You were telling me how you first realized that your wife was having problems with her memory."

"Oh yes. Well, the week after the Robbie Burns fiasco her director phoned me from the rehearsal hall. Said I had to come right away, that Delia was in a terrible state."

"What was wrong?"

"He'd just cancelled her role as Gertrude — Hamlet's mother — because she couldn't remember her lines. He said she would never be ready for opening night."

"That must have come as a shock."

"She was off her head with fury. But by the next day she'd forgotten all about it." His face darkened by sadness, Matheson cast a hand at the array of portraits that surrounded them. "The theatre had always been her life."

"I'm so sorry. Do you mind telling me what happened next?"

Matheson explained that he was finally able to get his wife to see a neurologist. The diagnosis was early onset Alzheimer's disease, which made sense in a fifty-eight-year-old woman whose parents had both died of the disease before they were seventy. She went rapidly downhill, deteriorating faster than her parents had, according to her brother. Nurses and homemakers were brought in around the clock, and by mid-September she stopped chewing. After that, she couldn't even swallow.

"I didn't force-feed her, you know. She'd always been adamant that I'd never feed her through a tube or put her on life support."

Zol shifted in his chair. "Had she worried about that?"

"She'd seen the indignities imposed on her parents and vowed they'd never be inflicted on her."

"I understand. Did she slip away at home?"

"Yes, on October tenth. Five days after her last sip of water." Matheson closed his eyes. His shoulders heaved as he sobbed.

A lump caught in Zol's throat. Douglas described his beloved Delia with such tenderness. When Zol recalled the stormy relationship he'd endured with Francine, their constant bickering and her numerous fits of dish-throwing rage, he was suddenly envious of the man sitting on the chesterfield, tears streaming down his bloated cheeks.

Matheson collected himself. He seemed relieved when Zol shifted the conversation away from Delia's illness and toward mundane questions about where they'd purchased their food. Delia shopped mostly at Kelly's SuperMart and Four Corners Fine Foods. When Zol asked about I and W Meats, the butcher shop where Joanna Vanderven had been a loyal customer, Matheson replied that he'd never heard of the establishment. A few minutes later, Zol found packages of frozen sausages and lamb chops bearing the Four Corners pricing label in Matheson's freezer, but no wild game, no British bangers, no vials of growth hormone.

"Don't know why a beautiful woman would need growth hormone," Matheson grumbled when Zol asked about it. "But she did get regular injections. Cortisone for her knees — you can't be limping all over the Stratford stage. And Extendo-Tox for, you know . . ."

Extendo-Tox, now the hottest brand of Botox anti-wrinkle therapy, had recently taken the market by storm. Ads for it were popping up everywhere. "I suppose that's not surprising, really," said Zol. "These days it's just part of being a model or an actress over thirty-five."

"Well, I didn't like it. She was beautiful the way God made her. Besides, she only had tiny wrinkles. Not worth noticing, and certainly not worth injecting with some sort of toxin."

Zol continued with his checklist. Delia had never lived anywhere but Ontario. She'd visited Britain many times but only for short stays. She usually ordered lamb, fish, or vegetarian when they ate out. "Except," Douglas Matheson said, "at a place called The Bard's Table. It's in Stratford. They do a terrific beef Wellington."

Was Matheson going to recognize him without a chef's hat covering most of his head?

"Do you still go to The Bard's Table?" Zol asked.

"Well, not since Delia . . . lost her memory. Up until then, we went once a month during the Festival season."

CHAPTER 11

It was noon when Hamish pulled his Saab into a visitor's spot in front of Heritage Towers, the condominium where Kenyon Cheung lived. The seven-storey tower dwarfed the leafy Hamilton neighbourhood of tiny brick houses built for veterans returning from the Second World War. Hamish turned off the ignition and sat for a moment, fingering his keys. Up close, gay men made him nervous. Not when they were his patients, distracted by their health concerns. Not when they appeared on television or in the movies. Not even when he observed their jubilations from the sidelines of Toronto's gay pride parade. In fact, when viewed from a safe distance, gay men fascinated him. They quickened his pulse and stiffened his manhood. He wished he could join them. But in social situations they terrified him, reminding him of the day he had overheard his father shouting at his mother: "If that goddamn church singing turns my boy into a queer, I'm going to smother him with a pillow."

Hamish was certain that at close range any gay man could see that he was queer and, given half a chance, would announce it to the world. His rational side knew that in Canada, in the twenty-first century, it was acceptable to be gay. In fact, gay men were often celebrated — in bars, in city halls, even in some churches. But it was his irrational side that was the problem. It governed his bedtime compulsions to straighten every book on the shelves in his study and align every shoe on the floor of his closet. And it consumed him in an overriding fear that the world would fall apart the instant it was known that trim guys with crisp haircuts turned him on.

In response to Hamish's buzz at the panel in the vestibule, Kenyon Cheung released the front door lock. Hamish stepped into the lobby and rode the elevator to the seventh floor. He found Kenyon's door, straightened his jacket, and ran a hand across his haircut.

"Be right there," said a muffled voice in response to Hamish's knock.

A young Asian man opened the door and offered a firm, dry hand.

Though Hamish's stomach felt inside out, he found it a welcome change to greet another man eye-to-eye. Kenyon also stood five-foot-five. On recognizing the handsome manliness in Kenyon's smooth, square jaw, Hamish stroked his own with a nervous hand. Though they both possessed enough clean-shaven whiskers to attest they'd gone through puberty, it was clear that neither could grow the sort of beard that would satisfy a lumberjack. When the two men stood on either side of the threshold and passed their palms in automatic unison across their salon-perfect flat-tops, a flash of understanding passed between them, and they smiled into one another's eyes.

"Owen loved to eat," Kenyon said to Hamish once they'd settled in the kitchen. "And I like to cook. So we were a good match." The tentative smile faded from his face and he stared at his hands resting on the glass tabletop.

"Again, I'm sorry to intrude on you like this," Hamish said. "It must all be so fresh. It's been only a month since Owen . . . you know . . ."

"It's all right, you can say it. He choked to death on too much steak and Burgundy. The old Owen would have enjoyed the irony."

Kenyon was making this much easier than Hamish had expected.

"Where would you have bought that steak?"

"It was nothing special, so I must have picked it up at Kelly's."

"Did you shop anywhere else?"

"Oh yeah," Kenyon said, and proceeded to count the stores on his fingers: "We hit the Bombay Market for Asian stuff, Botticelli's for Italian, I and W for their sausages, and Four Corners for everything else you can't find at Kelly's." He smiled and rolled his eyes at Hamish's discovery of their guilty indulgences. "Yes, we made the rounds."

"I'm not much of a cook, but I've been to Four Corners once or twice. I hear they've got great chocolates."

"Every kind you can think of — Lindt and Godiva, Rogers' and Walker's. And special Swiss ones with fantastic creamy centres."

That sounded like the chocolates Brenda McEwen had told him her husband was addicted to. "Yes," Hamish said, "don't they come in kiwi and a few other fruits?"

"Our favourites are mango and passion guava. Owen doesn't let a week go by without . . ." Kenyon closed his eyes and massaged his forehead with his fingertips. His lips quivered, but there were no tears.

Hamish wanted to reach out and pat Kenyon on the shoulder, an action that came easily when his elderly patients struggled with painful memories. But he just could not be that forward with a man his own age. He was afraid of the response he'd provoke. Recoil or reciprocation: either would be mortifying. "I'm sorry. This really is a bad time. Perhaps —"

Kenyon opened his eyes. "No. It's okay." He ran his hand over the dark, luxurious bristles of his flat-top. "You're here on a Saturday, for God's sake. This must be important. Just ask me all your questions, and I'll get through it."

Hamish scanned the list he'd prepared. "Did you and Owen ever eat game?"

"You mean moose and deer?"

"Yes."

"Never at home." Kenyon straightened the crease in his blue

jeans. "Don't know any hunters. Besides, Owen would never eat Bambi." He gazed at the ceiling as though trying to jog his memory. "I've had venison at restaurants. Owen did try bison a few times. They do a nice job of it at The Bard's Table. That's in Stratford."

"I know," Hamish said. "A colleague used to work there," he continued, jotting down reminders of the connections he'd discovered already: Owen with Miss Smart at The Bard's Table; Owen with Hugh McEwen and the Swiss chocolates at Four Corners. After he'd exhausted his questions about their diet and filled three pages of his notepad, he was ready to probe the next topic on his list. "Did you do much travelling overseas?"

"Only cruises. Eastern seaboard and the Caribbean. Usually from New York. Owen was afraid to fly, so we'd drive to the ship, take the cruise, and drive home."

"Did he ever get to Europe?"

Kenyon shook his head. "We did drive as far as Lauderdale a couple of times. Non-stop, except for gas. That was brutal. But a whole lot better than Owen clicking his tongue and grunting next to some mouthy jock in economy."

"Sorry?"

"Owen had Tourette's. Not too many signs of it at home, but when he got upset, he'd grunt like a porker. It worked like a charm on his income-tax defaulters. If they got the least bit huffy with him he'd start working his jaw, blinking his eyes, and grunting like a wild boar. The feds would get a cheque within a week."

Hamish smiled. "Talk about inheriting lemons and making lemonade."

"Yeah, well, he had to. The grunts got a lot less noticeable after they started injecting his vocal cords. About two years ago. The treatments made him a bit hoarse, but he was pleased at the improvement. I was, too." He pulled a tissue from his pocket as his eyes began to glisten. "And then this latest thing hits him. Jesus."

Hamish sipped his tea. He was about to clear the constant tickle from his throat but he found he didn't need to. The tickle had disappeared. This tea was working wonders. "Perhaps you can tell me how it all started," he said, delighted at the strength of his voice.

"You mean the memory loss?"

"Yes, and perhaps he had other signs of encephalitis."

Kenyon's shoulders tensed. "Encephalitis. That's a brain infection. Owen had a brain infection?"

"Um . . . That's what his autopsy showed."

"Wait a minute. All those questions about meat and butcher shops and travel." Kenyon's face flooded with alarm. "He had mad cow disease, didn't he?"

Hamish stared at his cuticles. He didn't know how he was going to phrase his answer. He'd promised Zol he wouldn't reveal anything as specific as prions and CJD; Zol had gotten so angry when he thought Hamish had revealed too much to the dentist's widow. But Kenyon's question was so direct, and so insightful, that it demanded an honest answer. Hamish couldn't lie. Not to a man with whom he felt such a strong connection. He paused and waited for a blast of inspiration.

Kenyon's lips grew pale, his pupils huge. "Come on. You owe me an explanation."

"Look — we don't know *exactly* what it is. To be honest, it's something so unusual that . . . that Owen was among the first to come down with it."

"What? You mean there are others?" When Hamish didn't answer, Kenyon stood and walked toward the window. He turned slowly and planted his feet. He jabbed his hands onto his hips and glared. "Look, I've been a trial lawyer for nine years. I'm a pro at reading faces, and yours says you're hiding something." He took his seat at the table again and lifted his teacup. He stared into it, swirled it slowly, and stared again. After several moments he put down the cup and rested a hand on Hamish's wrist. He squeezed lightly.

It was a rush to feel the warmth of Kenyon's palm against his skin. And amazing how right, how natural it felt.

Kenyon's scowl had disappeared. "You're facing other cases, aren't you?" he said, his tone empathetic, the aggression gone. "And you guys don't know what it is."

"We're doing everything we can to figure it out."

Kenyon removed his hand. "Oh my God." He bit his lower lip and gazed into the distance as though imagining a chaotic future. "You're an infectious-disease specialist. That means you're probing an epidemic."

"Let's not go that far."

"But there could be a lot more cases unless you guys figure out where it came from."

Reluctantly, Hamish nodded. "Yes."

"So get out your pen and paper and let's get on with it." The cups and saucers rattled as Kenyon cleared them from the table. "I assume we've got to retrace Owen's steps," he said. "When do you think he contracted whatever it was that killed him?"

"We don't know for sure, but we're looking back two years from the first signs of illness."

Kenyon set the dishes in the sink and leaned against the counter. He frowned, as if working to recall everything that could be important. "Owen had viral meningitis a couple of years ago. His doctor said it wasn't dangerous, just damned unpleasant. He got that right." Kenyon wiped the table with a cloth, which he folded and placed on a rack under the sink. "The fever and headache lasted a week and the tiredness another few weeks after that. He was back to his old self before Christmas."

"So he recovered completely? No after-effects?"

"None," he said, returning to his seat. "For the next few months he was in great shape." Kenyon swept the thighs of his jeans with his palms. He pulled his chair closer to the table and rested his smooth, pale forearm only millimetres from Hamish's. "Things didn't start going bad until the spring. The first time I noticed anything, we were getting ready to go out for my birthday."

Hamish had to force himself to concentrate. The warm touch of Kenyon's palm still lingered on his wrist. "What was that about your birthday?"

Kenyon flashed a quizzical look that hinted he'd caught Hamish daydreaming. "As I said, it was the first time I saw Owen acting strange. My birthday, May fifth. He put our whitening toothpaste under his arms instead of deodorant. Ruined his favourite shirt."

"And then he started losing control of his emotions and having memory problems?"

"You really are on top of his case, aren't you? I'm glad I pushed for the autopsy."

Hamish's heart raced like a Lamborghini, but neither angst nor fear had its foot on the gas.

CHAPTER 12

"Watch me, Dad," Max called from the far side of the swimming pool at three thirty that afternoon. "I'm gonna do a really huge one." With that, Max sprang from the diving board and made a large cannon-ball splash.

The pungent smell of chlorine peppered Zol's nose and stung his eyes as he watched from the poolside bleachers. Every minute of discomfort was worth it to watch Max having such fun in the pool. "That *was* a huge one," Zol said with a clap of his hands after the small body popped to the frothy surface. "Good for you. Now let's see the butterfly you've been working on."

The weekly lessons, the free swims afterwards, and Max's natural enthusiasm had turned him into such a nimble swimmer that you had to look closely to see that his left arm didn't straighten completely at the elbow. In all the rippling and splashing, the knot of crooked fingers in the left hand disappeared. Here, Max was as whole and as agile and as perfectly created as any other boy.

Day to day, Max didn't seem to notice the spasticity of his arm or the compromised function of his hand. But still, it was a worry. His pediatrician said the spasticity in Max's fingers was certain to worsen as he got older. And so would the teasing. His classmates in grade two only showed wholesome curiosity at the special way Max held his game gadget. They cared nothing about cerebral palsy, did not even know the term to use it as a label of derision. Zol ached to think of those same seven-year-olds transformed into a huddle of taunting preteen bullies.

The pediatrician had referred Max to a neurologist, Dr. Margolis, at Caledonian Medical Centre. Margolis pronounced that Max would be an excellent candidate for a new treatment of the muscle stiffness that had disabled Max's arm since birth. Extendo-Tox, a derivative of the botulinum toxin first made famous as the de-wrinkler of Hollywood's aging faces, was said to be working wonders at relaxing the cramped-up limbs of children affected by CP. By partly paralyzing overstimulated muscles, Extendo-Tox made crooked joints straighter and clawed fingers nimble. And because this new extended-action version of the toxin had been bioengineered to last for twelve months at a time, there were very few injections compared to the old formulation that had to be painfully repeated at least four times every year.

The hitch was that Dr. Margolis had a long list of children waiting for the Extendo-Tox injections. Margolis was the only pediatric neurologist in the two hundred kilometres between London and Toronto. His partner had left for greener pastures in the U.S.A. where MRIs and PET scans were available almost instantly at the swipe of a credit card. Zol still couldn't stop feeling resentful that the earliest Dr. Margolis's secretary could book Max for the procedure was the third week of January. So much for watching Max unwrap his Christmas presents with a rejuvenated left hand.

At the sound of four toots of the lifeguard's whistle the free swim was over for the week. In the changing room, Max slipped off his bathing suit, gave himself a cursory wipe with his towel, and put on his clothes as Zol handed them to him, piece by piece, so they wouldn't fall onto the wet floor. When he still had his socks, shoes, and sweater to put on, Max planted his bare feet and cocked his head. "Daddy, I'm wondering."

"What are you wondering?"

"Will Cory go to heaven?"

"Cory? He seems fine to me. I don't think he's going anywhere. Here — dry your feet and put on your socks."

Max didn't budge. "But when Cory dies, will he go to heaven?"

"I don't know, Max. I've never thought about it."

"Michael Thornley said cats aren't allowed in heaven."

"How does he know? Has he been there?"

"No, silly. Once you go there, you can't come back. Like Uncle Joe."

Zol smiled, lifted his son by the armpits, and plunked him on the bench. "I'll think about it while I'm drying your feet."

"I'd miss Cory too much if I never, ever, ever saw him again."

Zol lifted Max's foot, wiped between the toes, and pulled on a sock. "Well then, I'm sure you'll see him in heaven." He stroked the back of Max's neck, nuzzled him, and closed his eyes. He slipped his arm around Max's waist and drew him tight. "But you won't be going there for a very long time."

"How do you know, Daddy?"

He looked straight ahead into the bank of lockers in front of them, where Max couldn't see the graffiti of emotions on his face. A shiver shot across his shoulders.

"Dad?"

"Yes, Max?"

"How do you know I'm gonna see Cory in heaven?"

He shoved Max's sneaker over his sock and pushed at the Velcro tabs. "Well, heaven is supposed to be a perfect place. It's got everything you want to make you happy."

"Even video games?"

"Definitely," said Zol. "And if it would make you happy to have Cory there, he'll be waiting for you." He wiped Max's other foot and pulled on his second sock. "How does that sound?"

Max smiled and gave the thumbs-up sign with his right hand. "Are we going to Four Corners now?"

Zol yanked Max's sweater over his curly head and popped it across his nose in a motion that always made the youngster laugh. "Yep."

"Goodie. Can I have a super-duper sausage dog?"

Zol winked and returned the thumbs-up. "Maybe I'll have one, too."

At five thirty Zol set a bowl of partially prepared brownie batter on the kitchen table. "Okay, Max. It's almost ready for you to start stirring," he said. "Have you got the wooden spoon?"

Max nodded and held up his hand, spoon ready, his eyes as wide as the solar system. They'd been that wide at Four Corners while he was scarfing a Viennese pork sausage, slathered with corn pickle and ketchup, followed by a handful of sickly sweet Swiss chocolates.

Clutching the spoon with his right hand, Max hopped onto a chair, perched on his knees, and reached for the half-filled mixing bowl.

"Wait just a sec," said Zol, lifting the hot saucepan from the stove. "Let me pour in the butter and chocolate." He swirled the thick dark liquid over the white mound of flour, sugar, and baking powder. "Okay. All yours."

Max held his spoon high and motionless above the bowl, like a conductor not quite ready for his orchestra to begin. "Daddy . . ." Max cocked his head and fired a teasing look that said Zol had made one of the dumbest moves ever. "You forgot something."

"What?"

"Can you guess? They're yellow."

"Yellow?" Zol stared into the bowl for a moment and tapped the cleft in his chin. "What a goof," he said, slapping his forehead. "I forgot the eggs."

Zol cracked two eggs into the bowl and steadied it while Max, the tip of his tongue clamped between his lips, whisked the batter with the force of a professional.

"Can I have one as soon as they're done?" Max said, hunched over the bowl, stirring with gusto.

"Don't tell me you've still got room in that tummy of yours. Haven't you had enough chocolate for one day? How many did the lady give you at Four Corners?"

"Only three."

"These brownies are for my guests tonight. You get to have popcorn at the movies."

Zol watched Max's smile fall like a sponge cake removed too soon from the oven. The boy's enthusiasm with the spoon quickly faded.

"Come on there, Mr. Chef," Zol said, "put some muscle into it. We've got to get these into the oven so they're done and cool enough for you to cut and test before the show."

Max's face bunched in confusion, then brightened. "You mean . . . ?"

"Isn't it your job," said Zol, "to test all brownies baked in this house to be sure they're delicious enough to serve to company?"

At six thirty, Zol wiped most of the chocolaty crumbs and smears from Max's hands and chin, and dressed him in his boots, winter coat, toque, and mitts. Max was peeking through the glass of the front-hall window when a minivan pulled into the driveway. "They're here," he shouted and ran ahead down the steps.

Ermalinda climbed out of a rear door of the vehicle. Her sister smiled and waved from the front passenger seat.

Zol descended the steps and shivered as the frosty air raised goosebumps on his skin. He crossed his arms and clamped them to his chest.

The driver, Ermalinda's French-Canadian brother-in-law, rolled his window halfway down. Vapour billowed from Jean-Guy's lips as he called, "*Allô*, Dr. Szabo. The night, it is cold. You should be putting a jacket."

Zol shuddered then slapped his hands against his shoulders. "Max is excited about the movie. Thanks for taking him."

Jean-Guy pointed at two small, bright-eyed bodies bundled and strapped into the seat behind him. "Our two, they are excited. And us, we are having a good time."

Max was too excited to wave goodbye as he skipped down the sidewalk. Zol felt a pang of emptiness as his son ducked into the third-row seat without even a backward glance. As soon as the rear door clunked closed, Jean-Guy tapped the horn and backed into the night.

A few minutes later, Colleen Woolton rang the doorbell — an hour early. As Zol threw open the door, her eyes crinkled; her mouth opened in a warm smile. Behind her in the driveway, her silvery Mercedes-Benz sedan glinted under the street lamps.

"I know I'm early," she said, "but I was doing a little surveillance job not too far from here. There didn't seem much point in driving home and right back out again."

"Hmm . . . bad guys in my neighbourhood, eh?"

"Afraid so." She unbuttoned her coat and undid her scarf. "I run into villains almost anywhere. This one's not violent, but he'll get his comeuppance. Not to worry."

"I'm amazed to hear you talk about bagging bad guys. You seem so . . ." He felt foolish instantly and wished he were better at keeping his mouth shut.

Colleen shrugged. "Short? Yes, I *am* small. Some might say too petite to handle brutes. But —" She tapped her temple with her forefinger. "This job takes mostly brains. I can hire brawn when I need it."

As he placed Colleen's scarf and coat on a hanger, a wonderful fragrance wafted from the silk and sheepskin. By force of habit, he began to identify the components — gardenia, citrus, vanilla, and a hint of jasmine — that the perfume maker had blended with such skill and subtlety.

Zol had always been a sucker for jasmine activated by the warm glow of a woman's skin. His high-school English teacher used to say that Shakespeare's heroes were wooed by their eyes, while his heroines were wooed by their ears. For Zol, the wooing came through his nose.

While Colleen busied herself with her winter boots, Zol faced the open closet with his hand on her coat. He closed his eyes and breathed deeply, struck again by the yearning that surfaced wherever he expected it least: in an elevator, in a supermarket, in a video store. The lesser part of this yearning was purely biological, akin to hunger, and could be satisfied discreetly in a private moment. The greater part was more profound. It was a loneliness of spirit that he feared might last a lifetime, deepening when Max grew into an independent teenager. His yearning intensified as he fumbled with the coat and the hanger and wondered why no woman had proven equal to the promises conveyed by her scent.

He swallowed hard and guided Colleen and her captivating fragrance ahead of him into the kitchen. He manoeuvred himself to the opposite side of the counter before the private detective he'd hired to unravel a complicated problem could spot what was developing inside his jeans.

"Have you eaten?" Zol asked, by way of a diversion.

Colleen inclined her head and bit her lower lip. "Actually not," she said, then added, "but I didn't come early so you'd have to feed me."

"Do you like Campanzola? I was going to make myself an omelette."

She pulled up a bar stool and climbed onto it. "Sounds delicious." She rested her elbows on the countertop, her tiny ankles hugging the legs of the stool.

Zol pulled ingredients from the fridge and peeled an onion. His eyes stung, and the physical intensity of the earlier moment eased, leaving in its wake a pleasant excitement. He hadn't felt this good in ages.

Colleen's gaze fixed on his hands at the chopping board. "It's extraordinary how you do that," she said.

He paused and looked up from his task. "The first thing we learned in cooking school."

"Chopping onions?"

"Chopping everything but our fingers." He held up his hands and fanned his digits. "See, still got all ten."

"There's quite an art to it."

"I suppose." He made a show of chopping a green pepper. "It was the first thing that impressed my family. More than the taste of my cooking."

"Oh, come on."

"No, I'm serious. They still prefer my mother's meals. She gets a bit huffy if I make more than a peanut butter sandwich in her kitchen."

He continued preparing the ingredients for the omelette and for a mesclun salad to accompany it. Colleen seemed content to watch the process without having to natter. He enjoyed feeling comfortable in the silence of another's presence. She seemed to like it, too.

As he combined the ingredients for a quick vinaigrette, Colleen lifted her nose and lowered her eyebrows. "Is that walnut oil I smell?"

This captivating woman had a fabulous sense of smell. Zol hoped it matched a discriminating palate. "You've got a great nose," he said, and passed her the unlabeled glass bottle in which he stored the walnut oil. "Do you think it's okay? Walnut goes off pretty quickly. Even in the fridge.

"Smells just fine to me. But I'm no expert." She sniffed again, gave a smile of satisfaction, and placed the bottle on the counter. "The first thing I notice about things is the way they smell." She clasped her hands, separated them, then took a deep breath as if to say something, but hesitated. She fiddled with the clasp of her watchband.

Zol busied himself with the baby greens until Colleen finally took another deep breath. "You know," she said, "what struck me first about this house was the oil of bergamot." Her cheeks coloured as she continued, "Not that it's overpowering, and perhaps I shouldn't mention it, but every now and then it wafts through the air. Like a signature — of you and your home."

The final nail in the coffin of his doomed marriage had been Francine's complete lack of sense of smell. Day after day he had come home to Max's dirty diapers left rotting in a pail, filling the house with a terrible stench. Francine had shown no interest in the subtleties of his cooking, and she'd drenched herself in far too much cheap cologne because a girlfriend suggested it, not because she could appreciate it.

But here was a woman who understood — and seemed to share — his passion for aromas. His pulse raced in his throat. He couldn't trust himself to say anything rational or coherent, so he hunched over his cutting board and minced the hell out of the peppers and salad greens.

Colleen lifted the flask of walnut oil and appeared to study it. She set it down and raised the bottle of balsamic vinegar from the counter and examined its label.

"Look," she said, breaking the awkward silence, "I've offended you. And I'm sorry."

He stopped chopping. Was she playing him? "No," he said. "Not at all." He could feel himself beaming as he studied the golden glints in Colleen's hazel eyes. "In fact, I'm thrilled. Yes, totally."

He opened the fridge, reached into the back where he always kept a bottle of bubbly, and poured out two flutes before either of them said another word. He lifted his glass. "To all the wonderful scents in the world."

Colleen leaned in close and clinked her glass against his. "And to oil of bergamot," she said.

Her delicious scent rose from her skin and caressed his nose. "And jasmine," he said, inhaling from behind his glass. "But only just a hint."

Colleen cocked her head just like Max did when he was puzzled. She sniffed her champagne and paused without taking a sip. "Green apples on warm toast," she said. "Lovely."

Yes you are, he said silently.

When they'd finished their supper, Zol brought out his notepad. He'd rather have taken Colleen on a tour of his house, showing her the restorations. But he knew that if he flirted any longer she'd think he was an ass. Retreating to emotionally safer ground, he said, "I'd like to hear about your visit with that girl's parents."

"The Latkovics." Colleen took a sip of water, then set her glass on the table. "It's all very sad. I can give you the exec-sum before the others arrive."

"The what?"

"The executive summary. The short version."

"You PIS are as bad with your lingo as doctors." He smiled and flipped his pad to a blank page. "I'm all ears."

"They live in a tiny bungalow in that older neighbourhood off Upper Wentworth. The houses all look the same except for how they've been painted and had new porches added."

Zol had learned about the so-called victory houses in school. They'd been put up by the hundreds across Canada in the forties and fifties to house returning veterans and their families. "Modest folk in that part of town."

"The Latkovics seem the salt of the earth," Colleen continued. "In their late fifties, I'd say. He works for the steel company, she's in the hospital laundry."

"At Caledonian?"

She nodded, and her earrings glinted in the candlelight. "They're Yugoslavian. Crosses on the walls and no Cyrillic script anywhere, so I'd say they were Croatian. It was a bit of a strain to understand their accents. They both sobbed quite a bit, which made deciphering their words quite a challenge. But I don't think I missed anything important."

"How forthcoming were they?"

"Very. I think they'd do anything to discover why their daughter lost her mind."

"Is that how they put it? She lost her mind?"

"Sums it up, doesn't it?"

Colleen summarized Tonya's life in a few sentences — born in Canada twenty-seven years ago, high-school mathematics teacher and basketball coach, good general health, never travelled anywhere except to Mexico on holiday and to New York and Pennsylvania for basketball competitions. "And you know," she said, lifting the last few bits of lettuce from her plate, "Tonya was a strict vegetarian — since she turned fifteen. Her parents were emphatic about that, and I gather not too pleased."

"Hmm . . . That makes two of them who didn't eat meat — Tonya and Danesh. Complicates things a bit."

"How so?"

"Those prions must be well and truly hidden — somewhere we might never think of looking. Not in any of your regular steaks, chops, or bologna."

"We shall just have to work by the PI's motto."

"Which is?"

"Keep your eyes peeled and your mind open to any possibility, no matter how extraordinary, how shocking, how contemptible."

Colleen put down her fork. "Tonya's migraine headaches were rather a plague. She'd had them since childhood. Her father complained about the cost of the injections she was taking for them. Her drug plan didn't cover them. Do you know what they would be?"

"Sumatriptan, I would guess. Costs about twenty dollars a shot and sometimes it takes a couple to settle one bout of migraine. Drug plans limit the number of injections they'll pay for."

"I don't get headaches, but I gather certain foods and wines can bring them on."

"Yeah. And chocolate," he said. Francine used to get migraines from chocolate, but she'd eat it anyway. Then she'd spend two days in a darkened bedroom expecting Zol's mother to drive an hour back and forth from Brantford and coddle her like an injured princess.

"I *thought* chocolate was bad for migraines," said Colleen. "That's why I found it extraordinary when I saw an opened box of chocolates on the desk in her bedroom."

"It was still there, a month after her death?"

"Believe me, her room is like a shrine. They've touched nothing. The rest of the house is spotless, but that bedroom hasn't even been dusted."

"I guess you didn't sneak a chocolate."

"Of course not."

"It wouldn't do to eat the evidence."

Colleen threw back her head and laughed. Her coppery-blonde ponytail swayed with a natural beauty. "Besides," she said, "I don't like creamy centres."

"They weren't those Swiss ones they sell at Four Corners, were they?"

"Swiss? I didn't notice. And there was nothing on the box to say where they'd been purchased. But wait a sec." She opened her scribbler and scanned her handwritten notes. "I did write down the name of them: Lorreaux Chocolate Fruit Explosions. The logo is the cutest little bird with black wings, a yellow breast, and —"

"A long curved beak."

He felt sick.

"Zol, you're as white as a salt pan." She held out her glass to him. "Here, have some water."

He took three gulps and gave his head a shake.

"What's wrong?" Colleen asked.

"Max eats those chocolates every week. He loves the little bird, the honeycreeper, on the box."

"You get them at Four Corners?

"Yeah, our Saturday ritual."

"I see." Colleen patted his forearm with her hand then rested it there. She looked serious for a moment, then her face lightened. "But really, I don't think there's a problem."

"What do you mean?"

She pressed the warmth of her palm into his forearm. "Six degrees of separation."

"What?"

"Hamilton's not a huge city."

"And?" he said.

"We all must be connected. At least to some extent. As it turns out, I shop at the same Polish deli as Tonya's mother."

He gulped another mouthful of water. "But we've linked two of our cases — Hugh McEwen and Tonya Latkovic — to those very chocolates."

Colleen leaned forward and held his gaze with hers. "Tell me —

can you actually get CJD from eating chocolates?"

"Well, maybe. In theory, anyway — if they're made with gelatin produced from the bones of infected cows."

Colleen released his arm and sat back in her chair. "Well, let's not panic," she said. "The others will be here shortly, and we shall soon see how far this connection goes." She folded her serviette and placed it on the table. Her eyes crinkled as she flashed a nurturing smile. "I'm guessing that this time Monday you'll be laughing at the notion of chocolate CJD."

CHAPTER 13

At seven forty-five, Zol asked the assembled threesome — Colleen, Hamish, and Natasha — to bring their notes and join him at the table in the sunroom. Through the open shutters overlooking the Escarpment, the black expanse of Lake Ontario held its mirror skyward. Ever punctual, Venus was casting her eye over the orange plumes shooting from Hamilton's lakeside steel mills. Mars would come later to guard the sweaty backs of the midnight shift as they stoked the flames of prosperity.

While the men in the mills roasted beside their molten furnaces, the souls around Zol's table smouldered with their own private irritations. Hamish, still frustrated that an early summons to the ICU had prevented him from running any mitochondrial experiments in his laboratory, rubbed his hand across the bristles of his flat-top. A clump of freckles at his wrist caught his eye, and he smiled at the remembered warmth of Kenyon's palm.

Natasha's anger at having to break her dinner date with Bjorn had cooled to disappointment. It could be worse — she could be at her parents' bored to cinders by the anxious patter of a pharmaceutical salesman with too much gel in his hair. Besides, her date wasn't broken, just postponed until the club scene started hopping.

Serene composure may have been Colleen's hallmark, but she was struggling to maintain it. She felt as though she were on probation — every time she opened her mouth, Hamish replied with a little edifying lecture. And since Liam's death five years ago, she'd never been attracted to a man with the strength of what she was feeling for Zol. It frightened her that it was happening so quickly. A man with a son posed a bundle of complications she didn't need, but she felt drawn to Zol, complications and all. And she hadn't even seen Max yet, just peeked into his bedroom. If he were anything like his father, she knew he would be a sweetie.

Zol, of course, was steamed on several fronts. His tensions flared as his mind wandered to thoughts of Max, the chocolates, and Trinnock's ridiculous deadline. He pulled the one-dollar coin from his pocket and weaved it through his fingers with a practised hand. The fluid tango of coin and fingers slowed his pulse.

After the others had settled, Zol pocketed the loonie and asked that they start with thumbnail sketches of the seven victims. He nodded toward Natasha in deference to her talents as an epidemiologist, and suggested they build the foundation of their investigation — the epidemic curve — by presenting the cases in chronological order.

He led off with Delia Smart, stage actress, age fifty-eight. She had first shown signs of forgetfulness a year ago. Eleven months later she slipped into a coma and died at home, shrivelled almost to nothing.

Natasha followed with the case of Joanna Vanderven, socialite and former model, age forty-three. She began forgetting things in March and died unexpectedly in June — a disturbance of the heartbeat.

Then Natasha recited the case of Danesh Patel, car salesman and former mechanical engineer, age forty-nine. His memory problems started in April. At the end of June he walked into high-speed traffic and died instantly.

Hamish raised his hand and related the story of Owen Renway, accountant and tax collector, age forty-two. He became forgetful in

May, stopped going to work in July, and choked to death on a steak dinner in October.

Colleen gave the details of Tonya Latkovic's death. The twenty-seven-year-old math teacher became tearful, restless, and moody a few weeks before the end of the school year. She wandered off on Halloween night without putting on her winter coat. Her body was found the next day at the bottom of the Escarpment. She had bled to death from a fractured femur.

Hamish continued with the case of Hugh McEwen, the dentist, age thirty-four. In June, he started becoming tearful, his behaviour erratic. In September, he committed suicide by taking an overdose of morphine and nitrous oxide.

Natasha wrapped things up with the case of Rita Spinelli, age thirty-eight. She owned a popular dress shop and was well-known for her vivacious personality. In mid-summer, she lost interest in her business and was easily provoked to anger and tears. Like Danesh Patel, she wandered onto a highway. Only three months separated the onset of her symptoms and her death.

The collective weight of the cases descended on the group. No one spoke. Zol fingered the loonie in his pocket. His stomach tightened as he pictured Max in the darkness of the cinema. Hamish gazed through the window. Colleen folded her hands in her lap and closed her eyes, pondering the fiery crash that had consumed her Liam.

The only sound at the table was the scratch of Natasha's pencil completing a graph on her notepad. She held it for the others to see. She'd drawn seven stars to mark the dates the victims first showed symptoms. One star sat in November, March, April, and May; there were two in June and a final one in July. Moons marked the timing of the deaths. There were two in June, one in September, and four crowded October.

"Thanks, Natasha," Zol said, impressed with the clarity of her impromptu graph. "It's pretty clear we're dealing with a cluster."

"You mean an epidemic," Hamish said, the strength of his voice an unexpected presence at the table. "We might as well call it what it is."

"I hate that word," said Zol. "It stirs everyone up."

Natasha's head bobbed in agreement. "And then we have to un-stir them."

"But you're right," Zol said. "It *is* an epidemic, with a new case every month since March."

"And we might as well face it," said Hamish, pointing his finger toward the window. "There must be cases out there we don't know about. I'm sure it won't be long before another turns up on Banbury's table."

Natasha gasped. "More cases?"

Hamish shrugged. "Bound to be."

"We'd better get busy," Zol said. He looked at Natasha. "You've brought your laptop?"

She reached for the briefcase on the floor beside her chair, lifted out the computer, and placed it on the table. "I've got a template database ready to go."

While the computer warmed up, Zol looked around the table. Hamish's untouched water glass caught his eye. "By the way, Hamish," he said, "what's happened to your voice? It's so clear."

Hamish's cheeks glowed. "Green tea." He stroked his neck and looked at his glass, clearly uncomfortable at his voice being the focus of attention. "Ken — Kenyon Cheung — served me some when I was at his place today. It started working right away."

"Really?" Zol replied. "You should market it."

"Well, I did buy —" His voice cracked and faded. He forced a cough before an embarrassed smile hit his face. "I did buy some."

Zol heard sounds of scurrying at the front door. Two sets of winter boots clacked against the slate floor, and muffled voices murmured from beyond the kitchen. A moment later, Max burst into the sunroom leaving a wake of discarded mitts, toque, scarf, and parka. He threw his arms around Zol's neck, squeezed hard, and blurted at the top of his voice, "Any brownies left?"

Zol laughed, then sniffed at Max's sweatshirt in imitation of a bloodhound. "Hey, you smell like a popcorn factory. Did you even watch the movie?"

Max pulled a face but his eyes still danced with glee. "Daddy. Of *course* we saw the movie."

"How was it?" Zol asked him.

Max released Zol's neck. "Awesome." He surveyed the table as though looking for brownie crumbs. He was in luck. The entire batch — less the two he'd already eaten — was still on a plate in the kitchen.

"Did they find Nemo?" Natasha asked.

Max danced on one foot and then the other, fidgeting. "Yep." He turned toward Cory, who'd crept into the room and was purring at his feet.

Zol grasped his son by the shoulder. "Max — I want you to meet our guests. You know Dr. Hamish. And Natasha from the office. And this is Mrs. Woolton."

Zol watched Colleen's face as she extended her hand. She gave Max the same nurturing smile Zol had found so appealing that first day in her office. "Please, call me Colleen," she said in a voice that was soft but not patronizing.

Max held his tongue between his teeth and stared at Colleen's long, golden braid. "Um . . . hello," he said, shaking her hand. His eyes swept the table a final time, then he leaned down, scooped up the cat, and skipped out of the room with Cory in his arms.

Zol followed him to the front hall, said goodbye and thanks to Ermalinda, and locked the door behind her. When he returned to the sunroom, Natasha, Colleen, and Hamish sat huddled around the computer. Like wide-eyed youngsters at a Ouija board, they were peering at the screen and pointing in a dozen directions.

"Looks like there's lots to keep you guys busy," Zol said. "I'll leave you to it while I get Max settled."

Three hands waved in cursory acknowledgement, but no eyes lifted from the screen. Natasha's fingernails clicked against the key-board. As Zol strolled from the room he wondered whether anyone else saw the irony — a small team of brains racing to find that spot in the universe where deadly prions had ambushed seven other brains, and maybe countless more.

"How's it going?" Zol asked when he returned to the sunroom half an hour later. He'd let Max have one more brownie, helped him brush his teeth, read him a bedtime story, then tucked him under his Star Pirates duvet and handed him two CDs in place of a second story. Max made a face, but quickly lost himself in music that only a seven-year-old could enjoy a thousand times over.

"Max is a sweetie," Colleen said. "And he's settled already?"

"Hope so," said Zol, aching with pride. His heart swelled whenever adults took to Max, but with Colleen the stakes had risen higher. He craved her approval of his son, her acceptance of Max's crooked arm, her affirmation that Zol was a good dad.

"Natasha's database program is extraordinary," Colleen continued. "You can put all kinds of things in and it organizes them. Instantly."

Zol leaned over the table and breathed in the lingering citrus of Colleen's scent. "Coffee will be ready soon. Find a hot spot yet?"

"Nothing striking," said Hamish.

"We haven't really looked," Natasha said. "We've only just finished inputting the data."

Colleen threw back her shoulders and stretched her arms. "Coffee would be great. Thanks."

"Do you want to see what we've got so far?" Natasha asked.

"Sure," Zol said. "Let's plug the laptop into the TV." He retrieved a cable from a shelf below the television and handed one end to Natasha. "This works with mine. It should work with yours."

At the press of a button on Zol's remote, the image of the database bounced from the laptop to the wide-screen TV. "Make yourselves comfortable," he said, pointing to the wicker armchairs and loveseat.

Hamish moved to the loveseat. Colleen took one of the chairs, Zol the other.

"We've organized the data into tables," Natasha said from her place at the computer. "This might be a good time to read them. Some connections might pop out at us."

"Sure," Zol said, "sounds great. Natasha, it's your baby. You start."

Natasha adjusted her chair, cleared her throat, and read aloud from the screen.

Demographic Characteristics	
Sex:	3 men, 4 women
Age:	Range 27 to 58, Median 42, Mean 41.6
Ethnicity:	Anglo-Saxon 4, Italian 1, Slavic 1, South Asian 1
Wealthy:	Joanna V, Dr. McEwen, Rita S, Delia S, Owen R
Modest Income:	Danesh P, Tonya L

Hamish turned to Zol. "When we looked at their addresses, we discovered that three live right here in your part of town." He raised his hands, palms up. "They're practically your neighbours."

"You can't call Vanderven my neighbour, Hamish," Zol said. "He's at the far end of Scenic." There was no way he was going to let Hamish connect him with the victims. It was bad enough that Max had been eating the same damn Swiss chocolates as McEwen and Latkovic.

Colleen beamed Zol a reassuring smile and indicated the list of addresses. "Owen Renway and Tonya Latkovic were practically neighbours, as well, but farther east."

Zol leaned into the soft down of the cushion at his back. "That leaves the Patels on their own in the far northeast, and Delia Smart over in Dundas," he said. "Does this first table hint at anything?"

Three foreheads crinkled at him.

"No? Okay, what's next?" Zol asked.

Natasha clicked, and the TV flashed three columns.

	Occupation	Spouse/Parents Occupation
Delia S:	actress	retired lawyer
Joanna V:	former model	auto-parts millionaire
Danesh P:	car salesman	homemaker
Owen R:	tax collector	lawyer
Tonya L:	teacher, basketball coach	steelworker, hospital laundry
Dr. McEwen:	dentist	homemaker
Rita S:	dress-shop owner	lawyer

Hamish pointed at the screen. "Three of the spouses are lawyers." His clear voice was a surprise every time he opened his mouth.

"Do they work together?" Colleen asked.

"Kenyon Cheung gave me his card," said Hamish. He pulled his wallet from a pocket and read from the card. "Sherman & Mac-Intyre, Barristers and Solicitors, ninety-nine Concession Street."

Natasha flipped through the pages of a notepad dense with her handwriting. Her eyes filled with worry as though she'd lost something. "I'm sure it's here somewhere," she mumbled. "Yes. Yes, here it is. Rita Spinelli's husband is with Delancey, Spinelli, and Munro. Hey. I thought the address sounded familiar. Same building, ninety-nine Concession."

Zol's stomach tightened. "I think I know where that is," he said, forcing himself up from his chair. "Let me check the phone book."

He pulled the directory from a kitchen drawer and turned to the Fs. At the sight of the address, he leaned against the counter and swore under his breath.

"What's wrong?" asked Colleen when Zol entered the sunroom a moment later.

He ran his tinder-dry tongue against his teeth. "Ninety-nine Concession is the Escarpment Professional Building." He swallowed hard. "I thought I recognized the number. Four Corners Fine Foods takes up half the ground floor."

"But why look so glum?" said Hamish. "I thought the whole idea was to find connections."

"Not with the grocery store where Max and I go shopping

every week. And where the ladies feed him chocolates."

Natasha dropped her eyes.

"Remember," said Colleen, "we're bound to find we've got things in common with these people." Her bright eyes searched for consensus around the room. "But we can't let it get to us."

Zol gripped the back of Colleen's chair with both hands, his heart racing. "I know, I know," he said without conviction. He sensed the glow radiating from her body and stepped away from it. At that moment, he just couldn't handle it. "What's next?"

Natasha clicked and read again from the screen.

Past Surgery	
Cholecystectomy:	Joanna V, Owen R, Rita S
Appendectomy:	Owen R, Dr. McEwen, Tonya L
Fractured Leg:	Danesh P
Hysterectomy:	Delia S

"The most recent surgery was Danesh Patel's," said Natasha. "Four years ago. They put a pin into his fractured tibia."

"But none had neurosurgery," said Zol. "And no organ transplants. Any blood transfusions?"

Hamish raised his tutoring finger. "Hard to be certain without an exhaustive review of charts in several different hospitals. But not to the knowledge of family members."

"I guess it's not that important," Zol said. "So far, CJD has never been linked to blood products."

Hamish's finger remained stuck in tutoring mode. "There can always be a first time."

Natasha coughed discreetly and moved on to the next screen.

	Recent Health
Delia S:	arthritis in her knees (cortisone injections); wrinkles (Extendo-Tox injections)
Joanna V:	depression, anxiety, severe heartburn; several meds including antidepressant
Danesh P:	perfect health until memory problems
Owen R:	longstanding Tourette's syndrome
Tonya L:	migraines (sumatriptan injections)
Dr. McEwen:	swallowing difficulties, puréed diet, esophageal manipulations
Rita S:	perfect health until memory problems

"Delia and Danesh worried about aging," Natasha said. "Delia was getting Extendo-Tox for wrinkles, and Danesh dyed his hair." She dropped her gaze and studied her hands for a moment. "My mum knows the family. It's an open secret that Danesh fooled around."

Colleen removed a stray thread from the fabric of her skirt. "Joanna and Rita were both in the fashion industry," she said. "What did they do to keep looking young?"

"Joanna saw a dermatologist regularly," Natasha said. "Her housekeeper said she got quite anxious before each visit. And Rita made a weekly trip to her favourite spa. Hair and nails." Natasha's ruby nails glowed against her yellow notepad. "I know the place. I've been there, as well." She hid her hands beneath the table as crimson blotches sprouted at her throat. "Oh my gosh! Bright Day Spa. It's on the second floor of that same building."

Four pairs of eyes stared at the television. No one mentioned the aroma of fresh coffee wafting from Zol's kitchen.

"Isn't it ironic," said Colleen, "how preoccupied they were with the appearance of the outside of their skulls, while a time bomb ticked away on the inside? You wonder what decisions they would have made if they'd known."

"Indulged their vanity more intensely," Hamish said, a cynical scowl clouding his face. "More hours of pampering, knowing they wouldn't have much longer and might as well spoil themselves."

"According to my mother, Danesh didn't have the money for anything more expensive than hair dye," Natasha said.

Zol paced behind the loveseat. "Really?"

"He was the most successful salesman at the dealership," Natasha said, "but always crying broke. My mum could never understand it."

Zol tapped his chin with his forefinger and squinted at the TV. "Maybe he had a few expensive habits his wife didn't know about."

"Were there needle tracks on his arms at autopsy?" Hamish asked.

Natasha shook her head emphatically. "No."

"We'll have to pay a visit to ninety-nine Concession to see what's going on there," said Zol. "But let's move on to your next screen."

Country of Birth	Regions Visited	Lived in England?
Delia S: Canada	Caribbean, Europe, UK	No
Joanna V: England	Americas, Asia, Europe, UK	Yes
Danesh P: India	UK, USA	Yes
Owen R: Canada	Caribbean, USA	No
Tonya L: Canada	USA	No
Dr. McEwen: Canada	Caribbean, UK, USA	Yes
Rita S: Canada	Caribbean, France, Italy	No

"Staying close to home didn't protect Tonya," said Hamish. "And this makes it clear we can't blame a diet of English beef."

"Yeah," said Zol, "Owen, Tonya, and Rita never set foot in England."

"And remember," said Colleen, "Danesh and Tonya were vegetarian."

"Any chance they weren't all that committed to it?" asked Hamish.

"Mrs. Patel is a tyrant in her kitchen," Natasha replied. "I'd say Mr. Patel would never have dared eat meat."

"And Tonya's parents said she was very strict about her diet," Colleen said. "Keeping fit for basketball."

Hamish rolled his eyes. "Basketball?"

Colleen turned to Hamish. "Yes, she led St. Adele's senior girls to the Ontario championships."

Hamish scrunched his lips and shook his head in disgust. "What does keeping fit have to do with not eating meat?"

Colleen shrugged. "Just part of her routine, I suppose." She glanced at Zol, her eyes betraying her frustration at Hamish's negative attitude.

Again, Hamish rolled his eyes. "There's just no science behind it," he said. "And she was a math teacher, for heaven's sake. Supposed to be the epitome of a logical thinker."

"Just goes to show you," Zol said, in his role as peace broker, "there's logic on paper, and then there's . . ." He looked at Colleen, inviting her to finish his sentiment.

"All those frailties that make us human?" she said.

Zol smiled inwardly at her perfect response. "And keep us all in business," he added.

"I suppose," said Hamish. "Tobacco, alcohol, and plain stupidity — infectious-disease practice would be pretty quiet without them."

Colleen brushed a strand of golden hair from her cheek and sniffed the air. "That coffee smells awfully good, Zol."

"Let's stretch for a minute. Max and I made a batch of brownies this afternoon. He says they're delicious."

Colleen ran her tongue over her lips. "Sounds perfect."

Zol loved the way she purred it: *purrrh-fect.* He poured the coffees at the kitchen counter then they all returned with their mugs to the sunroom. As he placed the plate of brownies on the coffee table, it was all he could do to restrain himself from asking Hamish to take Colleen's chair so he could sit beside her on the loveseat.

Natasha took a bite of brownie. Her whole face smiled in satisfaction. She wiped her fingers with a paper serviette and tapped at the keyboard. "And this brings us to the food — my favourite part of public health."

Grocery stores

Kelly's SuperMart (4 outlets)
All seven victims

Food Bargains
Danesh P
Tonya L
Rita S

Botticelli's
Owen R
Rita S

Bombay Market
Danesh P
Owen R

I and W Meats
Joanna V
Owen R
Dr. McEwen

Four Corners Fine Foods
Delia
Joanna V
Owen R
Dr. McEwen
Rita S
(Tonya L)

Several moments passed while they read from the screen and drank from their mugs. Between mouthfuls of brownie they praised Max's kitchen prowess, and Zol confessed that the extra chunks of chocolate had been his son's idea.

Hamish wiped the bottom of his mug with a serviette and steadied it on his knee. "There's an awful lot on this slide."

"Sorry," said Natasha. "Too much at once?"

"No, it's fine," Zol said. He pointed at the screen. "I notice they all shopped at Kelly's."

"But so does practically everyone in the city," Hamish said. "They've got four big stores,"

"Yeah," said Zol. "If the prions are coming from Kelly's, God help us."

"Four Corners might be more manageable," said Natasha. "Smaller shop, only one outlet, and five or six of the seven cases shopped there."

"Why the parentheses around Tonya's name?" Zol asked.

"Because we're not absolutely positive she was a customer," said Colleen. "I found a box of Lorreaux chocolates on the desk in her bedroom. It's only an assumption she bought them at Four Corners."

Zol sighed and nodded. "Max will tell you that's the only place around here you can find that brand — his favourite." He realized the silliness of suggesting his seven-year-old was a connoisseur of fine chocolate. "I mean . . . not that he actually buys them."

Natasha smiled then clicked at her keyboard. "Well — if we include Tonya, that means eighty-six percent of the cases are linked to Four Corners."

"That *is* a strong correlation," said Hamish.

"But don't we have to have one hundred percent of the victims linked to one perpetrator?" Colleen asked.

Zol shook his head and swallowed a mouthful of brownie. "As long as —"

"Even the most successful epidemiological investigations," Hamish said, his voice strong, his face intense, "rarely reveal a one-hundred-percent correlation with the contaminated source." He raised his professorial hand. "For a variety of reasons, the link is missed or unapparent." He counted out the reasons on his fingers: "One — people don't realize they shared the source. Two — they've forgotten. Three — they're afraid and won't admit the connection. And four — they lie."

Zol buried his nose in his mug and forced himself to control his guilty smile at yet another Hamishism. He looked up and caught the expression on Colleen's face, which left no doubt she thought his friend could be overly pedantic. With time, she'd come to appreciate the big heart beneath all that brain.

Zol turned to Natasha. "What was the percent linkage of the E. coli cases to your Croatian wedding sausages?"

She lowered her gaze and paused. Zol was sure she was searching the depths of her prodigious memory. "Seventy-one point four," she said, wiping a spot of chocolate from her fingernail.

"And in that case," Zol said, sneaking in his own bit of professorial tone, "we were able to prove that the E. coli came from the sausages. They were undercooked, and culture-positive for the toxic strain."

"So," Colleen said, "we look for signs of a strong connection that's not necessarily universal. And then we investigate for supportive details?"

"You got it," said Zol.

"Any ideas," Colleen asked, "about what all of them might have purchased at Four Corners?"

"Zol," said Hamish, his voice its old harsh whisper, "what sort of chocolate did Max add to those brownies?"

They all gazed at the plate of half-consumed chocolate brownies on the coffee table.

Hamish's hand flew to his mouth. "Not those Swiss ones he likes so much?"

"Nothing so fancy," said Zol. "Just baking chocolate. But are we all thinking what I've been afraid to say? Everything is connected to those Lorreaux chocolates?"

"Looks like it," said Hamish, again counting on his fingers. "One — there's McEwen, who was addicted. Two — Owen bought them every week. Three — Tonya had them on her desk."

"And Joanna Vanderven makes four," Natasha added. "She ate them to calm her nerves."

And look," said Hamish, pointing at the screen, "Delia Smart shopped at Four Corners. She might have picked them up there, too."

"I saw them in Rita Spinelli's living room. You can't miss that box with the black-and-yellow bird," Natasha added.

Zol raised a palm. "Hold on," he said. "Do we actually know that Rita Spinelli ate them? Maybe it was just her husband. And he's not sick."

"I didn't ask," Natasha said. "But it would be easy to find out." She glanced at her watch. "I can call him right now."

Zol stared through the window. All he could see was the vast blackness of the sky hanging above the lake. He was afraid of Spinelli's answer, but there was no avoiding it. He pointed toward the kitchen. "Phone's on the wall beside the microwave."

Two minutes later Natasha returned, picking her way across the scatter of rattan mats on the hardwood. She took her seat and wiped her face with a tissue. It was obvious she was feeling the collective weight of everyone's gazes. "Yes," she said, "Rita ate them. A lot."

Hamish uncrossed his legs and brushed crumbs of brownie from his trousers into his palm. "Okay," he said brightly, "including Rita, but not Delia Smart or Danesh Patel, the rate of correlation with those chocolates stands at . . . ?"

Natasha's shoulders slumped as she answered. "Five out of seven. That's . . . seventy-one point four percent."

"Well then," Hamish, said. "Same as the wedding sausages."

CHAPTER 14

Zol heaved himself out of his chair and plodded to the kitchen to phone Delia Smart's husband. By the ninth ring it was clear that Douglas Matheson wasn't going to answer. Not tonight.

The enthusiasm for the investigation dissipated from the sunroom as soon as Zol left a message on Matheson's machine and put down the phone. Natasha presented her final slides, but her voice sounded flat and tired. The others made only a few half-hearted comments. They buried themselves in their notes and promised to spend the next day hunting down assorted data missing from their assigned cases. No one lingered, not even Colleen. After he helped her into her coat, she fixed him with her gaze, squeezed his arm, and followed Hamish and Natasha out the door. Zol tipped the remaining brownies into the garbage and poured himself two fingers of Balvenie. The house, now utterly silent, felt like a mausoleum.

The next morning, without the energy to shave, or dress, or retrieve the *Sunday Star* from the front porch, Zol stared into his half-eaten bowl of cereal. He watched Max from the corner of his eye, terrified what might be lurking in the boy's future. When the phone rang, he just sat and let it ring.

After about a dozen rings, Max shot Zol a quizzical frown,

dropped his spoon, and ran to the phone. "Dad," he said, singsonging the word in exasperation, "it's for you."

A minute later, Zol felt like soaring. Tears were stinging his eyes, and Max was giving him a look that said parents are impossible to figure out. But Zol couldn't remember when he'd last felt this good.

Delia Smart hadn't eaten a single chocolate for four decades. Matheson's call made that clear. Delia had been allergic to all forms of chocolate since childhood. It gave her headaches and palpitations. She never touched it. Not even a nibble.

And then he remembered Natasha's remark last evening about cracking the case without proving that *every* victim was linked to a single source of prions. He tossed the juice carton into the fridge and slammed the door. Natasha was wrong. And so was Hamish. All the victims *had* to be linked to a single source. Of course they did. There were only seven CJD victims, all sick within a tight time frame, and all living in Hamilton. Something out there had infected all of them. And that something wasn't the chocolates. Whatever it was, they were going to find it.

Forty-five minutes later, Zol signalled his turn into the parking lot of the Escarpment Professional Building, half a kilometre west of the health unit, at 99 Concession Street. When he checked the mirror he saw Max in the back seat, clicking away at his game gadget. The blue-and-white Four Corners logo beckoned from above Max's favourite window. Would he sense the familiar territory before Zol turned off the ignition? Santa's elves and reindeer were dancing around a castle built from stacked tins of Christmas pudding. Hundreds of chocolates, spilling from the top of a giant Christmas stocking, were begging to be gobbled by the handful.

Zol took Max by the hand as they skipped across the parking lot. After a detailed examination of the window, and much speculation about the flavours in the centres of the candies, they pulled open the door of the building. On a Sunday morning the vestibule was as far as they could get. Four Corners stood locked and in darkness. The adjacent pharmacy glowed brightly but was closed until tomorrow. Three elevators sat in the lobby with their doors open and their lights off, out of bounds until Monday.

Zol ran mentally through the histories of the CJD victims. He had reviewed them again this morning after Matheson's call. At least five had shopped right here at Four Corners, including two whose lawyer spouses still worked in this building. Natasha had said the vitamins, remedies, and medications in Joanna Vanderven's fancy bag had been mostly purchased here. Across the street, Hugh McEwen had operated his dental office in the same renovated house as Rita Spinelli's dress shop.

When he added it up, there was little doubt that this building was the centre of the epidemic. But what bound it all together? The building itself? Something trapped between its walls, soaked into its carpets, dissolved in its water supply? No. None of the victims had worked here. Anyone spending their workdays in a blighted building would have been the first to get sick.

Zol cast his eyes up and down the building's list of offices and businesses. The prions had to be contaminating something sold or administered right here. He copied down the names of every enterprise, all six floors of them.

On the way home, he phoned Colleen on the cellphone. He asked her to come help him sift through what was surely a treasure chest of leads. When he offered lunch, she laughed and said he was always preparing food.

"Well, sure," he replied. "Cooking helps me think. It's amazing what brilliant connections you come up with while you're whisking egg whites."

An hour later he was assembling their sandwiches while Colleen looked on. "If you'll take these in to Max and his friend Josh," he said, "I'll put ours on the table." He handed her two turkey-breast sandwiches, each dressed up with a dill pickle, a handful of potato chips, and a candy cane. "Between these and the video games, the boys will be happy for an hour or two."

"If we're lucky," she said over her shoulder.

He set to work on their plates. He spread the bread with Dijon and topped the turkey with caramelized onions and goat cheese. He added a garnish of kalamata olives but felt too shy to plunk a handful of greasy potato chips onto their plates.

"Don't we get any chips?" she said with a look of dismay as she took her place at the kitchen table.

"You really want some?"

"Of course."

He filled a wooden salad bowl with potato chips and placed it on the table. "Help yourself. But you haven't earned a candy cane yet."

He turned his ear toward the noises spilling from the computer room. The closed door kept the volume down but the proximity to the living room and kitchen meant he and Max remained connected. Separate but connected — the sort of relationship a father was supposed to have with his son. Waves of reassuring beeps and laughter squealed through the door.

Zol took a seat and bit into his sandwich. His eyes met Colleen's, paused, then darted away. For a minute or two, conversation was impossible as they chewed on the crusty slices of sourdough bread.

Colleen put down her half-eaten sandwich and licked her lips. "Delicious," she said, and plucked an olive from her plate. "I love these." She popped the glistening orb into her mouth and sucked on it as though pondering the complexity of its flavours. "I phoned Mrs. Latkovic."

"And?"

"Those chocolates *did* come from Four Corners."

"The ones on Tonya's desk?"

"Hey, don't look so glum."

What did she expect? His son had eaten cartloads of those chocolates, and now she'd confirmed that six of the seven CJD victims shopped at Zol's favourite grocery.

"For goodness sake, Zol, buck up." She picked up her sandwich, then pointed to his fountain pen. "That looks like an antique. Can I try it?"

He didn't like the look of all that oil on her fingers. "It's, um, a very special keepsake. Belonged to William Osler."

"Look, I'm wiping the oil off my fingers. I know about Osler. And those nodes he made famous — painful lumps on the fingers. A sign of infection inside the heart."

This woman was full of surprises.

She raised an eyebrow. "Surprised you, didn't I?"

That was one of those questions it was better for a guy not to answer.

She looked distant for a moment. "I learned a lot typing Liam's consultation letters." She uncapped the Parker and wrote her name and address. "Mmm . . . Slides like velvet. But hey, it's leaking." She handed him the pen and wiped her ink-stained thumb with her serviette. "Enough about Osler. What about that treasure chest of leads you promised?"

Zol showed her the list of offices and businesses from 99 Concession.

She tugged at one of her glass-beaded earrings as she studied the list. The colours in the bauble matched the complex hazel of her eyes. "Well, there are three law firms. We knew to expect at least two."

Zol pointed to Delancey, Spinelli, and Munro. "Rita Spinelli's husband must be a partner at this one. And Owen Renway's partner works here, at Sherman & MacIntyre. And here's a holding company."

"With only a number for a name. If there's some fishy business going on there, it's with money, not prions." She pointed to a family practice with two doctors, and then tapped her finger on the name of a dermatologist, Dr. James Zupanzik. "Why is he familiar?"

"His ad's in the newspaper every day."

"Yes, of course. Rejuvenation something-or-other."

He read from the page he'd ripped from yesterday's *Spectator.*

"Light rejuvenation, cosmetic laser, and botulinum-toxin therapy."

"He's into wrinkles in a big way."

"And he's got the entire third floor of that building."

"Any prions there, do you suppose?"

"Not in his lights or lasers," Zol said. "But he probably injects collagen or other stuff that comes from animals."

"Perfect. Our first suspect."

Zol drew an arrow beside Zupanzik's name, then pointed to the listings for the fourth and fifth floors. "There are a lot more outfits here worth starring — three naturopaths, three chiropractors, two massage therapists, a reflexologist, a herbalist, and an acupuncturist."

"Goodness," Colleen said. "That's a ratio of . . . eleven alternative therapy practitioners to just three medical doctors."

"Millions across the country have no access to a family doctor, but there's no shortage of . . ." — he made a face and drew quotation marks in the air with his fingers — "*holistic* practitioners."

"Happy to take half your paycheque for extract of echinacea and eye of newt."

Francine had spent five thousand dollars in a single year on bogus immune-system boosters. Her naturopath had sprinkled a carload of potions onto the fertile ground of her already unstable personality. The junk science, the ridiculous jargon, the outright deception, and the wasted money still made Zol fume.

"Yes," she said, "the 'It must be good, it's natural' spiel used to drive Liam crazy."

"Bring your credit card to the desk but leave your common sense at the door."

Colleen chuckled and tossed her braid. "But realistically," she said, crinkling her brow, "what could they be dispensing that causes CJD? Don't they just use herbal stuff?"

"Except for the rhinoceros horns, the antler fuzz, and the tiger oil. Holistic medicines are unregulated, you know. The government ignores them because it doesn't classify them as drugs. At the health unit, we can confiscate herbal remedies, or clear them from the shelves, only if we can tie them directly to an outbreak. Like the

Salmonella they traced to the black-bear gallbladders a herbalist was dispensing in Toronto."

She shook her head. "Good grief." She took another olive and chewed it slowly, then pulled its pit from her lips and set it on her plate. "But what makes you think our cases patronized any of these practitioners?"

"Look how many associations we've discovered between our cases and this building." He turned to a fresh sheet on his notepad and started a new list. "Six out of seven shopped at Four Corners. Most of Joanna Vanderven's prescriptions were purchased at the pharmacy on the ground floor. Two spouses worked at law firms in the building. We know that Delia Smart was getting Extendo-Tox injections, and Joanna made frequent visits to a dermatologist. Maybe both of them were patients of Dr. Zupanzik."

"We can find out from their husbands," Colleen said.

"But how about all those alternative outfits? We can't go skulking around their offices without some strong suspicions."

"Why not? You're the health unit, for heaven's sake — public safety and all that."

"The law is specific. Our job is to hunt down and interview the contacts of people known to have contagious infections. And we're supposed to delve into situations where there's danger to the public — like epidemic diarrhea in a daycare. But if we don't have a compelling reason, we can't force private practitioners to give us unrestricted access to their medical records."

Colleen frowned and spread her palms to show she'd never heard of anything so ridiculous. "Six cases of CJD linked to that building isn't compelling enough?"

"But we'd have to explain exactly what we were looking for."

She took a deep breath and looked ready to speak, but closed her mouth. After a moment her eyes flashed. "I get it. If we told them we suspected prions in their potions, the shit would hit the fan."

"Exactly. We'd have the press on our backs in a second, not to mention Trinnock. And the mayor. And every other politico who expects us to hand them a solution the instant there's a whiff of a problem."

She pursed her lips. "So," she said with a sidelong glance, "we have to be creative."

"That's where you come in."

She frowned and shook her head. "I don't break into offices."

"That's not what I meant."

"What *do* you mean?"

He could feel himself blushing. He'd already asked Hamish to more or less lie, and now he was thinking of asking Colleen to do the same. Good God. This was going to end up as a terrible mess, with a pink slip slapped into his hand as a souvenir.

"You could call the offices one by one and play a little loose with the truth," he said, unable to look Colleen directly in the eye. "Tell them you're from the Ministry of Health. In Toronto."

"What am I calling about?"

He thought for a moment. Shalom Acres glared from a headline on the page he'd ripped from the *Spectator.* "You're investigating the flesh-eating epidemic at Shalom Acres."

"And what's that got to do with these alternative practitioners?"

"You're concerned about the safety of their staff and their clients."

"And?"

"Um . . . You need to know if any of the people on your list — our seven victims — ever visited their offices."

"I suppose," she said, her voice a little brighter. "And if it looks like I've scored a connection, the receptionist might be so frightened about flesh-eating disease she'll tell me everything we want to know."

"And if none of the names rings a bell, she'll soon forget you called." Zol scooped a handful of chips from the bowl and let them soften in his mouth. He could feel his face tighten. He chewed and swallowed, then asked, "What if a receptionist panics at the mention of flesh-eating disease? What if she calls the families? I can see it now: Rita Spinelli's lawyer husband fuming to my boss about government intrusion. Trinnock will know it was me who ordered the calls."

Colleen fingered an olive pit and looked up. "No, he won't. I'll say I'm just checking a list of contacts generated by the Ministry's computer, and we always follow up these things no matter how innocuous they are. We at head office know it's better to be safe than sorry." She nodded. "And I'll thank them on behalf of the Ministry for the valuable holistic service they contribute to their community."

He started to smile, but his worries still outweighed his confidence. "What if they look at phone records and trace the calls back to you?"

"They won't."

"You sound so sure."

"I'll drive to Toronto. Sherway Gardens. They have a bank of pay phones in a quiet spot at one end of the mall."

His shoulders relaxed as he told himself that Colleen had done this before.

She was brilliant.

The plan sounded brilliant.

But would it work?

CHAPTER 15

That evening, Hamish's stomach launched a rebellious rumble that echoed in the stillness of his laboratory. He gave his abdomen a perfunctory rub and lifted his eyes from the bench, suddenly aware of the piercing glare of the fluorescent lights. The clock said nine twenty. He hadn't eaten since noon; little wonder he felt shaky and light-headed. And he'd quaffed so many cups of green tea he must have downed quite a hefty dose of caffeine.

It had been a frustrating Sunday, tinkering with the test for species-specific mitochondrial DNA. If he were going to use it to find diarrhea-causing *C. difficile* bacteria in food samples, he needed to see how the test reacted to traces of unexpected DNA and to chemical food additives.

The test had worked perfectly last week when he'd spiked samples of pork sausage with the thigh muscles of two euthanized mice and a cat, all no longer required by research colleagues down the hall. The kits had identified the pork and the cat tissue, and ignored the mouse they'd not been designed to detect. But today, when he'd added commercial barbecue sauce — to see how the test performed in the presence of the chemicals added to everyday foods — he'd been given no reading whatsoever. One or more of the nineteen flavourings, dyes, and stabilizers in the sauce must have interfered with the reaction. If the process could be disrupted so easily by a household condiment, then maybe the test wasn't the silver bullet he was looking for.

He rubbed at the kink in his neck and squinted against the light. He would try one last run tonight. He opened the fridge and found he'd used up all the meat he'd bought at Kelly's SuperMart, but he spotted the packet of Escarpment Pride Viennese sausages from Ned Krooner's moody brother. He set it on the counter and chuckled at the satisfaction of knowing, within the hour, whether Krooner's meat was one hundred percent pork. It would be a comfort to know it was free of prions from mad cows before he took it home for dinner.

If he were going to get the test to work, he'd have to dissolve away the inhibitory chemicals in the barbecue sauce. Ethyl ether might do the trick. He decided to run Krooner's sausages in duplicate before calling it a day: one sample plain, the other spiked with barbecue sauce and treated with ether. He still had some cat muscle left; it had worked well before. He would use it as a control.

He set up his samples, taking care to wash his hands between each one, and loaded them into the DNA amplifier. He patted his pocket to be sure he had his wallet and keys. The machine would cycle automatically for the next fifty-five minutes. In the meantime, he might as well go downstairs to the vending machines.

On the ground floor, he inserted coins into slots and pulled out a flaccid turkey sandwich and a can of cranberry juice. He dropped into one of the hard plastic chairs at the rear of the deserted, dimly lit cafeteria and stared at the pallid Sunday dinner balanced on his knees.

Growing up, he'd never had Sunday dinners. Not any that he could remember. Until he'd left home for university, he had to sing at church every Sunday. For the entire day. Nine o'clock matins, eleven o'clock Eucharist, five thirty evensong. As he recalled the weekly gropings of the choir director at remedial practice after evensong, his temples pounded with fury. At age fourteen he'd kicked the horrible man in the shins with his first pair of brogues. That had stopped the fondling, but not the revulsion, nor the penetrating images that could still disturb his sleep. The man had been a criminal, not "just affectionate," as his mother had insisted. When Hamish had summoned the courage to tell her as many of the details he reckoned she could handle, she set her jaw, narrowed her eyes, and refused to believe a word. That was when the trust poured out of their relationship.

He ached with envy when he thought of the ties that linked Ned Krooner and his brothers. Admittedly, Morty said so little Hamish could only guess what was going on inside his head, but Lanny was the fiercest advocate a man could ask for. He protected Ned like a guard dog. As a child, Hamish had prayed in vain for a sibling, someone to understand his torment when his dad called him a sissy for singing in the choir and his mother locked herself in the bathroom until he promised not to quit. After he left home, he had yearned for a partner, someone who would know him inside out. Even delight in his foibles.

He inspected his sandwich. Life as the only child of bickering parents had been as desolate as the slice of shrivelled turkey between his fingers. He thought of Max. Zol made his son popcorn, took him swimming, and poured his apple juice into a wineglass. Max was one lucky kid, and all that warm attention from his father hadn't made him mouthy.

Hamish finished his sandwich, tossed the empty juice can into the recycling bin, and made his way back to the lab. He washed all the traces of mayo and mustard from his hands — and with them the pointless reflections that crept up on him whenever he was too exhausted to keep such thoughts at bay. What could not be changed had to be endured, like all those Sundays wasted trying to please his melancholic mother. He donned his white coat, and approached his workbench to complete the DNA detection. As he picked up a pipette, he felt the wave of adrenaline that always rose with the final steps of an experiment. He never knew when a late-night result would turn into a dazzling revelation.

He steeled himself for a peek at the readouts. His thumbs went up. All three tests had given a clear and proper reading, even the sample spiked with barbecue sauce. The ethyl ether had dissolved away the inhibitor. Wonderful. This project just might turn out to be fruitful after all.

His head spun with the groundbreaking possibilities the test might bring to diagnostic laboratories — in hospitals, in agriculture, in the food industry. But frustration swamped him when he took a closer look. Hell's bells. He'd mixed up the specimens. He'd consumed so many cups of green tea his shaky hands must have spilled one sample into another. What else could explain finding cat tissue in all three of them?

Could he have contaminated the test tubes? Surely not. He'd prepared each one separately and washed his hands in between.

He sat at his desk and rubbed his head. It was late, he was exhausted, and a jackhammer pounded at his temples. But there was no way he was going home until he straightened out this mess. He opened his binder and reviewed the operating procedure step by step.

He'd followed the instructions exactly. No doubt about it.

He looked again at his results.

The sample of cat muscle showed only cat. *Good*.

The Krooner sausage, spiked with barbecue sauce and treated with ethyl ether, gave a clear reading. *Great*. But the sample was positive for both pork and cat. *Not good*.

The Krooner sausage that had no sauce also gave a clear reading. *Good*. But it, too, was positive for both pork and cat. *Terrible*.

While his heart raced and the turkey sandwich somersaulted in his belly, he retrieved Lanny Krooner's remaining sausages from the refrigerator. The red and white packet with its bold logo and smartly printed label looked entirely professional. He had opened it himself and was sure it hadn't been tampered with. But there was no doubt about it: now, in the lab, those "pure pork" sausages contained traces of cat meat. He pictured Lanny standing in his kitchen, carving up the bloodied corpses of stray kittens and dropping them into his sausage machine.

He clenched his teeth, triple-wrapped the sausages in biohazard bags, and returned them to the refrigerator. He flooded his hands with disinfectant soap, scrubbed, rinsed with a lakeful of water, dried carefully, then donned a pair of heavy rubber gloves and spent almost an hour scouring the sinks, the benches, and all his equipment.

When he was satisfied that everything was as clean as humanly possible, he dialled Brenda McEwen's number. She answered cheerfully, and their chat was brief and enlightening. He hung up and checked the clock. Nearly one o'clock. He was exhausted, but there was no point in going home to bed. He'd never fall asleep.

He stared at the phone. Should he call Zol? Now that Brenda had confirmed his suspicions, surely it wouldn't be right to wait until morning to break the news to Zol? Brenda hadn't minded the late hour. Neither would Zol. With tomorrow's deadline looming, he'd be thrilled at these developments.

Zol picked up on the fifth ring and answered with a grunt.

"Hi, it's Hamish. I found another link. It could be the one."

"Let's have it." The sleepy tone disappeared from Zol's voice.

"Remember the sausages Natasha listed on her computer? Escarpment Pride, pure pork? She found a package of them in Vanderven's freezer. And in Rita Spinelli's. Kenyon Cheung told me that he and Owen bought them all the time. I don't know about Delia Smart." He paused to give Zol a moment to process before he charged on. "And the best part? I just found out that Hugh McEwen ate them, too. Brenda forgot to mention them before."

"You called his wife — at *this* hour?" Zol asked.

"She didn't mind. Doesn't sleep much these days."

The line was quiet except for a strange, low-pitched rumble. Probably the cat on Zol's bed, purring next to him.

"I'm not going to let you twist me up any more," Zol said. Hamish could hear him rubbing the stubble on his chin and cringed at the noise. His father used to scratch at his five o'clock shadow and make that same sandpapery sound whenever he was angry.

"First it was the chocolates," Zol continued, clearly steamed, "and now it's these sausages. There are no damn prions in either of

them. For God's sake, Hamish, Danesh Patel and Tonya were vegetarians. And pigs don't get CJD."

"But, Zol, those sausages are . . . are tainted."

"With what?"

"Cat meat."

"You mean chicken gizzards and pigs' cheeks? Not exactly poi-
sonous."

Hamish held his breath, then spoke distinctly into the phone:
"Not cat *food*, cat *tissue*. I'm talking muscle, lymph nodes, maybe
even bone marrow." His eyes strayed to the refrigerator where the
sausages lay triple-bagged in heavy plastic. He hoped he'd secured
them well enough. "They're made up near Campbellville by the
brother of a patient of mine. He gave me a package the day before
yesterday. They're called Escarpment Pride Viennese sausages."

"I know the ones. A hot item at Four Corners. But what makes
you think — at one in the damn morning — that they're tainted?"

"I used them in a mitochondrial DNA test I'm developing for bacterial diagnosis. They're pork sausages all right — but laced with cat
meat. I just completed the latest run in the DNA amplifier and —"

"I'm too sleepy to understand how you could ever find cat tissue
in pork sausages when you're looking for bacteria. But it can't be
relevant. Not to our investigation. Two of our cases were vegetarians. And cats don't get CJD."

Cory purred into the telephone.

"You can't be sure of that," Hamish said. "Sheep, elk, and other
animals get prion brain disease. Why not cats?"

"If those sausages contained prions, half of Hamilton would
have CJD by now. Your theory is ridiculous."

Hamish froze as that awful word boomed in his ear. His father
used to say he looked *ridiculous* in his choir gown with its frilly
collar. The passing years had not diminished the sting.

"I can't tell Peter Trinnock," Zol continued, "that we've traced
our CJD to a yokel up in Campbellville making sausages out of stray
cats. He'd think I'd lost it completely. Besides, it looks like I've
found the prions."

"Where?"

"Too early to say."

The rejection hit Hamish like a punch in the stomach. "I thought," he said, trying to catch his breath, "I thought we were a team."

"And look where it's got us. Sausages made out of cats, for God's sake. For sale in Hamilton's finest gourmet supermarket. No, I don't buy it." Zol scrubbed again at his stubble. "I've got Colleen working on a lead that makes a lot more sense."

Flames of humiliation scorched Hamish's throat. Anger stiffened his jaw. Colleen? What did a private investigator know about basic science and field epidemiology? Only science was going to solve this case. He tried to speak, but all his larynx would release was a croak. When he tried again, out came the old grinding whisper. "Then stuff your investigation. It's . . . it's none of my business anyway."

It made him seethe — his research ridiculed, his larynx seizing again, thousands of lives hanging in the balance because Zol was besotted by that woman.

Hamish hung up and coughed into his fist. What time did trial lawyers go to bed? Kenyon Cheung knew first-hand what was at stake. Could they share a nightcap?

Never mind. He was not going to risk a second rejection tonight.

On his way out the door the next morning, Zol fished two packages of Escarpment Pride sausages from the fridge and tossed them into the garbage bin. He'd bought them only two days ago at Four Corners. It seemed like a waste of perfectly good meat. But there was no way he could face them, even though Hamish's idea about cat meat mixed in with pork sausage had to be one of the most outlandish things Zol had ever heard. He did have a nagging feeling there was something waiting to be discovered at Four Corners Fine Foods. He decided to stop there on the way to the office.

He paced up and down the aisles of Four Corners, inspecting the shelves he knew by heart. He started with the stacks of apricot and cherry jams imported from the emerging economies of Slovenia and Croatia. Did those jars contain prions? A qualified no. What about the panettone from Padua, the apple cakes from Amsterdam, the shortbreads from Scotland? Surely not, unless the baked goods contained beef tallow instead of the butter promised on the labels. He examined the coffee beans from Brazil, Kenya, and the South Pacific. Papua New Guinea was famous for its *kuru*, a form of CJD transmitted by cannibalism, but surely it was safe to drink their coffee. Wasn't it? How about the tinned beef from Argentina, the cocktail sausages from Poland, the duck-liver pâté from France? If prions were running loose around the planet, they'd be impossible to trace.

The eagle on a packet of Escarpment Pride sausages glared at him from the meat cooler as though guarding a secret. He leaned in to read the fine print on the wrapper and his cellphone vibrated against his hip. He jumped backward and grabbed the phone from its holder.

The incoming call carried an unfamiliar area code. From somewhere outside North America. He considered pressing *Ignore* to cut off the call, but thought better of it. "Zol Szabo here."

"Hello Zol."

Damn. If he'd known it was Francine, he wouldn't have answered. She was the last complication he needed right now.

"Zol?"

"Yes, Francine. Isn't it early for you to be out of bed?"

"What do you mean? It's three o'clock."

"Three? Where are you?"

"Spain."

"Oh."

She was probably at another ashram. She'd lived at a string of them for the last six years, since Max was ten months old.

"I'm coming to Toronto and I wanna see Max."

"When?"

"A couple of weeks."

"That doesn't give me much time to make any arrangements."

"Swami Sivananda said that time is just a figment of the narrow mind."

Whatever.

"I'm gonna stay at my friend Allie's. Max can come to her place. Give you a break for the weekend."

"I don't need a break. Not from Max. And he doesn't do sleepovers."

"For Chrissake Zol, I'm his mother. I wanna see him. It's been friggin' ages."

The ashrams and the yoga hadn't done much for her mouth. "More than three years, Francine."

"That's not my fault."

Nothing ever was.

"You can have a supervised visit for six hours, just like you're entitled to."

"That's not fair."

He stared at a display of leeks, asparagus, and artichokes at the far end of the aisle. From that distance it looked like a patchwork portrait, the bearded face of one of her swamis. "That's what the judgement says."

"I don't care about that," she said.

"I'll have to contact a social worker and book a supervisor for the visit." It had been so long, he couldn't remember exactly whom to call.

"I don't need a goddamn supervisor to see my own child."

"Tell me when you'll be in Toronto and I'll make the arrangements."

"I told you. A couple of weeks."

"I need to know the date."

"Don't be such a tight-ass. I don't do dates. Swami said they inhibit the fluidity of the human spirit."

He rolled his eyes. "Does Allie know when you're coming?"

"She's cool."

"Have her call me." He cleared his throat. "Anything else?"

"How's Max's arm? Is it still, uh, you know?"

"Yeah, it's still spastic, Francine. Cerebral palsy doesn't go away."

She had always hated the distortion of Max's arm and would never touch his hand.

"He doesn't mind," he added. "And neither do his friends." At least not at this stage amid the innocence of grade two. And maybe the Extendo-Tox would help when Max finally got in to see Dr. Margolis.

Zol's resentment flared. He was facing the case of a lifetime and a looming deadline, but he kept getting ridiculous calls that threatened to derail him. First Hamish, then Francine. "I gotta go," he said, and ended the call.

If he did hear from Allie, he'd tell Max about the visit and arrange for a supervisor. If not, he'd know that Francine had cashed in her ticket for a few hundred grams of dope.

CHAPTER 16

Zol drummed on the top of his desk while his coffee grew cold beside a jar stuffed with pens and paper clips. His notebook was crammed with a thousand facts that amounted to nothing. He'd scrounged the Internet, then trolled the stacks at the university's medical library, skimming every reference he could find on gelatin, prions, and CJD. He found editorials speculating that prions could make their way into gelatin from the boiled-up bones of mad cows. But in every study, gelatin came up clean. And no scientist had ever linked CJD to candies or confections of any kind.

How could you get a prion disease without being exposed to meat, gelatin, or animal by-products? At first, the meat-free diets of two of the CJD victims had seemed to complicate the puzzle. Now they felt like a godsend. Even if Hamish was right about Max's favourite sausages being spiced up with cat meat (Zol couldn't help but picture Cory's cousins on the chopping block), sausages of any kind couldn't be the source of the epidemic. Tonya and Danesh would never have touched them. He fished two loonies from the top drawer of his desk and weaved the coins through his fingers. What other source of prions might be lurking in the fridges and cupboards of Hamilton? The source wasn't animal, and not likely to be mineral. Was it vegetable? How safe were peas and corn, carrots and eggplants?

He breathed deeply, calmed just a little by the cadence of the coins moving in symmetry across his fingers. His hands froze in mid-air. The loonies teetered between his fourth and fifth digits.

Where did Four Corners get the asparagus he'd seen on display that morning? Certainly not locally, not in November. Asparagus was a spring crop. It must have come from a country where the seasons were reversed, maybe Chile. How much did he know about Chile? How trustworthy was their government these days? Was it honest enough to report every case of BSE over a territory stretching hundreds of kilometres at the bottom of the world? Thousands of mad cows could be pooping all over Chile, and the rest of the world might never know it. Farmers could be spreading prion-infected manure onto their cash crops — artichokes, asparagus, potatoes, even zucchinis. Zol began to imagine prions swarming over his dinner plate, swimming in a glass of his favourite Maipo Valley red. He looked up with a start at the sight of Anne at his door.

"Mrs. Woolton's here, Dr. Szabo. Should I show her in?"

He slipped the loonies into his blazer pocket and ran a hand through his hair. "Um . . . sure," he said, straightening his blazer as he rose. "Of course."

"It was easier than I thought," Colleen said once they had settled at a small round table by the window. "It always amazes me how people reveal the most personal details to a perfect stranger on the telephone."

The jasmine on her skin had lifted his spirits already. "We were due for a break," he said.

She flipped through her notepad. "Excuse the scribbles. I didn't take the time to make picture-perfect notes like Natasha's. But the information is all here."

"No problem," he said, pulling his pen from his pocket. "I'll tabulate while you talk. Shoot."

"I'll start with the family practice — two women, Dr. Isabelle Graham and Dr. Patricia Brunton. Only one of our cases is on their books — Rita Spinelli. She last saw Dr. Brunton on August twelfth. Was diagnosed with depression and prescribed medication — fluoxetine. The receptionist already knew that Rita had been killed in a traffic accident, and volunteered that the woman was otherwise well, came in for her Pap tests, was allergic to penicillin."

"Good going. You must have sounded very official."

Colleen's eyes danced at the compliment. "As soon as I mentioned a strep outbreak at Shalom Acres, she opened right up. Told me three times that Rita had never been diagnosed with strep throat."

"Was she alarmed?"

"No. I reassured her that strep has a two-week incubation period, so Rita's last visit in August put them in the clear by twelve weeks. She seemed satisfied with that."

"Perfect. But did we learn anything?"

"A good practice run before calling the dermatologist."

"Dr. Zupanzik?"

"I'll get to him later. Let me tell you about the naturopaths and chiropractors."

"You got through to them? Great."

Colleen shook her head. "Not so great. Joanna had six sessions with a Dr. Boonstra. I couldn't get his office staff to tell me what herbs and medicines she'd been given, but the receptionist was quick to assure me that everything they prescribe is one hundred percent organic and natural."

"So is cyanide."

"Too true." She held his gaze in a way that said she was with him completely, then continued. "Next was Tonya, who visited the acupuncturist for her migraines. Seven sessions. Ending last May."

"Were those the injections her father was talking about? Not that expensive migraine drug — sumatriptan?"

"Acupuncture just involves needles, doesn't it? They don't inject anything."

"No drugs. Just the right sort of flick of the fingers," he said, rubbing his thumb against his forefinger, "and a little electrical buzz on the needles." He looked at his sheet. "Anything else?"

"Only Joanna Vanderven's weekly appointments with her massage therapist."

"You mean that's it? Nothing more from all those alternative practitioners?" He shrugged out of his blazer and swung it over the back of his chair. "I need to get this straight," he said, doing his best to diffuse his frustration by unbuttoning his cuffs and rolling up his sleeves. "You called every alternative practitioner in the building, they all answered, and the only people they recognized from our list were Joanna Vanderven and Tonya Latkovic?"

"Don't put away your notepad. Dr. Zupanzik has a chatty receptionist — who, it turns out, is pregnant."

"What's that got to do with anything?"

"She got very concerned about her baby as soon as I brought up the strep cases at Shalom Acres. When I mentioned flesh-eating disease — it was difficult to sneak that one in quietly — she peppered me with questions and fed me with answers left, right, and centre."

He shifted in the hard wooden chair and fingered his pen. "You struck gold?"

"Not exactly. But I did confirm that Delia was getting Extendo-Tox injections from Dr. Zupanzik."

"I knew that already. Her husband didn't approve. Thought it went against life's natural order."

"But get this. Zupanzik was also injecting Joanna, Rita, and Danesh."

"Danesh Patel? With Extendo-Tox?"

"Don't look so surprised. Men are just as vain as women."

He waved his hands in apology. "Of course. You're right." He tapped his chin as he thought for a moment. "Natasha had a feeling Patel's wife was hiding something. And we know the family was often short of cash despite Danesh earning top dollar at the dealership."

Colleen nodded. "Extendo-Tox isn't cheap. Empties the bank account as quickly as it melts away the wrinkles. And it could explain Joanna's nervousness before her appointments with the dermatologist. I'm guessing she didn't like needles."

Zol drew his chair closer to the table. "Exactly when did these four start getting Extendo-Tox?"

"Remember," Colleen said, straightening her back, "I was just supposed to be interested in the Shalom Acres Streptococcus outbreak, asking if any people on my list had visited the office recently. I couldn't get too nosy or I'd blow my cover."

"Sorry. It's just that you seemed to be onto something."

"I can't be sure, but it sounds like they all had at least two shots of it. The receptionist was some proud to tell me that with Extendo-Tox you only need to be injected about once a year — its effect lasts ten or twelve months."

Zol nodded. "It has a much longer duration of action than the original toxin."

"It was developed here in Hamilton, I gather."

"By a biotech outfit with ties to the university. A huge local success — scientifically and financially."

"Did you buy any shares?"

"No. I should have, though. Rumour has it that Extendo-Tox made millionaires out of several investigators and their backers at Caledonian."

Colleen looked at her notes. "Delia was scheduled for a repeat injection last February but cancelled."

"Too sick by then to care about wrinkles."

"The receptionist was aware that Delia and Joanna had died. I had to use my most nurturing voice to reassure her their deaths had nothing to do with strep or flesh-eating disease."

"Is anyone going to make a fuss, call the health unit with a bunch of searching questions?"

Colleen shook her head. The golden flecks glinted in her hazel irises. "It's okay," she said. "The receptionist settled right down when she realized it had been nineteen months since Delia Smart's last visit to the office. Same for Joanna."

"I put you in a tight spot with this line about strep and Shalom Acres."

"Not to worry. I do tight spots for a living."

He gazed at the November sky, grey and dull as pewter. The trees across the street were so bare they looked dead. "If Delia's third Extendo-Tox dose was to be last February, and there were ten or twelve months between doses, we can estimate when she got her first dose. There's a calendar in my desk. Somewhere." He pulled open several drawers then dug an agenda from the bottom one and brought it to the table. "If we count back twenty months from last February, we come to . . . June the previous year."

"Delia's husband first noticed her forgetfulness a year ago — November the following year."

"That means," Zol said, counting out the months on his fingers, "she received her first dose seventeen months before showing any symptoms. That's a very short incubation period for CJD, but Hamish would say it fits our tight cluster."

Colleen uncrossed her ankles and leaned over the table. "We need to clarify a couple of things."

"What?"

"We don't know enough about Owen Renway, Hugh McEwen, and Tonya Latkovic. Unless they were getting Extendo-Tox, maybe none of this matters."

"But it's still a fantastic teaser for Trinnock. Four cases of CJD after contact with a new biological agent that has neurotoxic properties? It's enough to get him to admit we're on to something and extend our deadline past four o'clock this afternoon." He saw the expectant look in Colleen's face. His mother used to do that — raise her eyebrows and purse her lips whenever he forgot something important. "What?" he asked.

"Is it scientifically possible for Extendo-Tox to contain prions?"

He sensed the bubble about to burst. "We better look it up in the CPS. If Extendo-Tox is totally synthetic, maybe you're right — it can't contain prions."

"I wouldn't know. I'm not the scientist. I just help string the evidence together. It's up to you to decide whether we've strung pebbles or pearls."

He lifted the electric-blue *Compendium of Pharmaceutical*

Specialties from the bookshelf and turned to the Canadian drug bible's Extendo-Tox monograph. He read: "Synthetic Botulinum Toxin, modified to resist degradation, provides an ultra-long biological effect on the myoneural junction, free of animal and bacterial proteins."

He looked at the flawless skin around Colleen's eyes and couldn't imagine her ever needing Extendo-Tox. This investigation, on the other hand, was in desperate need of a facelift. "So it's synthetic," he said. "Created entirely in the lab. Paralyzes muscles just like the natural toxin, but with a longer-lasting effect."

"Sounds ideal for the patients."

"But throws a wrench into our theory. Unless I'm missing something, *synthetic* and *free of animal proteins* means no prions. End of story."

Colleen riffled through her notepad and scribbled a set of hieroglyphics into its margins. When she'd finished, she tapped the back of Zol's hand with her pen. Her face was a lantern of enthusiasm. "It's still worth digging a little more," she said. She lifted her arm to glance at her watch, and another wave of jasmine swirled through the air. "And there's enough time before four o'clock today to find out whether Owen, Hugh, and Tonya ever had their wrinkles treated."

"But Tonya was only twenty-seven," Zol said, closing the heavy pharmaceutical reference. "And Hugh was under forty, having too much trouble with his stomach and esophagus to worry about wrinkles. Looks like we're going to get a string of pebbles out of this one."

"Don't be too sure."

He made a mental note to call Dr. Margolis and cancel the Extendo-Tox injections for Max's spastic arm. No matter how miraculous those treatments sounded for cerebral palsy, no one was going to give that stuff to his son until Zol was sure it was absolutely safe.

CHAPTER 17

It was lunchtime when Hamish found himself gazing at a sparkling new Accord in the showroom of the Honda dealership on Upper James Street.

"I bet you wanna take one for a spin," said a salesman who seemed to appear out of nowhere. Hell's bells. He'd chosen this quiet corner so he could gather his thoughts, get the lay of the land before asking questions about Danesh Patel.

It had taken him ages to fall asleep after Zol had ridiculed his test results. Hamish had made up his mind to drop the case and let Zol stew in his own misguided investigation. But the plight of the victims haunted him all night like an anxious ghost, keeping him awake until he pledged to pursue his investigation. He'd fallen asleep with a mental image of himself handing Zol the prions on a platter and Zol's condescending sneer dissolving into boundless, sheepish gratitude.

"It's turned out to be an okay afternoon," the salesman continued, undaunted by Hamish's lack of response. "I'm Jim Robinson." He extended his hand. "Glad to know you."

The man's grip was rough and dry. His spectacles, askew on his beefy face, needed a good cleaning. Dandruff dusted his shoulders.

His large belly, incompletely covered by a red plaid vest, looked wrapped for Christmas by amateur hands. "Roads are dry," he said, "and that awful wind, eh? It finally died down."

Hamish peered at the sky through the showroom's picture windows. The clouds pressed dark and heavy. Not a day to try out the sunroof featured on the Honda's sticker. "A friend of mine said he was thinking of an Accord," Hamish said, "so I thought I'd have a look at the new ones."

"Be my guest. But you can't judge a car just by looking at it." Jim tugged at the bottom of his vest, which didn't budge. "You've gotta drive it, feel its spirit."

"Is it fully loaded?"

"Sure is. Got ABS, side airbags, and a terrific new sound system." Jim turned and coughed. "If your friend is interested in a fantastic deal, we still have a few of last year's models on the lot."

"He's really into sound," Hamish found himself saying. *If I'm going to tell a lie, I might as well embroider it.* "He's been waiting since last summer for the new model."

Hamish stepped to the rear of the vehicle and made a show of examining its tail lights while his predicament spun in his head. How could he bring the conversation seamlessly to the topic of Danesh Patel? Natasha had hinted about a secret life. Drugs? Prostitutes? The horses? If Danesh had been at the racetrack, secretly eating Krooner's sausages laden with prions, that would show Zol whose ideas were ridiculous.

He sipped from his water bottle, let out a quiet cough to clear his unpredictable voice box, and looked into the wide, toothy smile of the salesman. "My friend was speaking with Mr. Patel."

Jim's face darkened, and he stared at his unpolished shoes. "Sadly, Dan is no longer with us."

"I know," said Hamish. Then, without thinking, he added, "I was his doctor."

Jim looked up. His face, still solemn, was tinged with hope, as if Danesh's doctor might finally explain why the man had wandered into four lanes of fast-moving traffic.

ROSS PENNIE

"So you knew him?" asked the salesman, coughing again. "It was a terrible shock. I still can't understand . . ." He wiped his mouth with the back of his hand, then tugged again at his vest. His eyes brightened a little. "Dan was a great guy. Full of stories of when he was a boy in India. Did you know that his father was a train conductor? Dan used to ride with his dad, shining shoes and running errands for pocket money — his education fund."

"Sounds like Dan was more than a colleague."

"His wife had him on a tight leash, so we never went out after work. But we ate lunch together. Every day." Jim leaned forward and cupped his hand next to his mouth. "Our lunches were his secret vice," he said softly. "None of that veggie crap he got at home." He patted his belly. "Good, honest Canadian food that sticks to your ribs."

"Oh?"

The salesman stepped back. "Maybe I shouldn't be telling this to his doctor."

Hamish leaned forward. "It's okay. I had a feeling he wasn't a strict vegetarian."

Jim chuckled. "He told you about the meatball subs at Sub Haven?"

"Not exactly. But he told me he occasionally ate meat at lunch."

"Occasionally! He *was* a good storyteller. He ate meat every day. Either ham or turkey from Sub Haven or those little meat pies from I and W across the road."

"Yes?"

"The pies reminded him of when he lived in England. Funny name, but they taste great." Jim's wide face flared. "They have a letter K on top. Made out of pastry." He looked away for a moment and cleared his throat. "Dan always peeled it off, dipped it in mustard, ate it first."

Delighted — and more than a little surprised — at the success of his subterfuge, Hamish excused himself with a promise to return for a test drive on a sunny day. He left his car in the lot and walked half a block to the traffic lights. Upper James seemed more like a highway than a city street. Even at noon, three lanes of cars and tractor-trailers whipped by in each direction. Danesh hadn't had a chance in the middle of all this. Hamish stood well back from the curb and shuddered at the pathologist's post-mortem description of the poor man's shattered brain.

Hamish looked up to catch the light turning green and spotted the butcher shop in the strip mall across the street. The sign above the window said Inverness and Westphalia: Purveyors of Fine Meats. A Scot and a German. The sparks would fly when those two disagreed.

The rank smell of cold blood hit him in the face as he entered the shop, and the whine of an electric saw filled the room. A woman wearing white coveralls and a hard hat, her jaw set and her eyes focused, guided a carcass through the high-speed blade of a band saw.

While the butcher concentrated on her noisy task, Hamish examined the refrigerated case beneath the counter. Steaks, chops, and chicken breasts lined the shelves at one end. In the middle, rashers of bacon in orderly rows, mounds of ground meat in neat trays, piles of sausages in earthenware dishes. At the far end, past the hams and salamis, commercial packages with bright logos: cheeses, pâtés, sausages, meat pies.

Krooner's red-and-white labels caught his attention, and he spotted the sausages and slabs of coarsely minced Escarpment Pride Head Cheese; it looked nothing like cheese, and he blushed to remember Zol's laughter at his assumption that head cheese was a dairy product. The same logo was fixed to a half-dozen attractive little pies garnished with a pastry letter K. The label said "Krooner's Melton Mowbray, 100% Ontario Pork." *Yeah, sure.*

The whining stopped. The woman pulled off her hard hat and hung it on a hook near the back of the shop. As she approached the counter, Hamish noticed the delicacy of her features with surprise. Her soft curls were more ginger than auburn, and her nose and cheeks were sprinkled with freckles. A smile danced across her face.

"It's been a grand morning, so it has," she said, wiping her fingers on a tea towel imprinted with a Saint Andrew's cross. "What can I get you today?" She sounded like she'd never left Scotland.

Hamish stared into the display case. "Um . . . I'm not sure." Out of nowhere, he was seized by three sneezes in rapid succession.

"One's a wish, two's a kiss, and three's a disappointment," the woman recited, still smiling. Seeing the puzzlement in Hamish's face she added, "Well, that's what we say back home."

"Oh," he replied, wiping his nose and feeling no further ahead.

"What do you have in mind? We've got butterfly pork chops on special offer."

He pocketed his tissue and pointed to Lanny Krooner's Melton Mowbrays. "I think I'd like to try one of those meat pies. But can you tell me what's in them?"

"They're a pork pie, sir. And right fine. Made locally here in Escarpment country. Near Campbellville. Very popular, they are."

"Do they need to be cooked?"

"They're fully baked, so you can eat them cold. But if you prefer," she said, lifting a pie from the case, "you can warm them up. Pop them in the cooker — fifteen minutes at three-fifty."

"Do you sell a lot of them?"

"Mr. Krooner makes them by hand, so he can only provide us with four dozen a week." She returned the pie to the case and pointed toward the window. "Ach, he's just been. You've missed him by a few minutes. He delivers about this time on a Monday, and his pies are always finished by a Thursday."

"I see he makes sausages and head cheese, as well."

"Ay. And again, everything is made by hand."

"Let me take a pie, a package of his sausages, and a small piece of head cheese."

"Are you new to head cheese?"

"Um . . . well, yes. But a friend of mine has eaten a lot of it. Said yours was delicious."

"We don't make our own. We just sell Mr. Krooner's. Will you be taking a wee piece for your friend?"

"Sadly, he passed away recently. He was a dentist. Maybe you remember him."

She paused. "Dr. McEwen?" A shadow passed across her face. "A great chap, to be sure. And one of our most regular customers. It was sad to be seeing the announcement of his death in the paper."

"Did he have any favourites besides the head cheese?"

"I'm proud to say he particularly enjoyed our own British-style sausages. Sometimes he took home a package of Mr. Krooner's Escarpment Pride Viennese sausages, but I think they were a wee bit spicy for him."

"Let me have six of your bangers, then," Hamish said, proud at sounding familiar with the term.

The woman nodded and grabbed the tongs from her work table. "You'll be familiar with bangers, then. But mind, ours are a little different from what we used to make back home. My husband adds a little of his German flare to the recipe. There's nothing quite like them."

Hamish pulled a twenty from his wallet and handed it to the woman, then slipped the change into his pocket. As he reached for the plastic shopping bag, his hands trembled. He paused and closed his fist. Krooner's packets might be crawling with prions. He should have asked the woman to double-bag his order.

Restless energy seeped from Zol's pores all afternoon. He dialled Hamish's number half a dozen times but was always greeted by the stilted voice of the answering machine. He paced the carpet, almost counted the seconds left before Trinnock's deadline. Zol had nothing to give his boss. Trinnock was going to shake his head, fidget with his glasses, and call in some self-important expert from Toronto. Zol yearned to have his own team solve the case. Maybe that was small-minded of him, but he did have an excellent staff, and it would be such an affront to be eclipsed by Toronto, just for want of a bit more time to fit the puzzle together.

Over and over he hoped to hear Colleen's musical accent on the line, confirming that Owen, Hugh, and Tonya had received Extendo-Tox injections, just like the others. But each phone call brought only another complaint. Goose poop fouling the city's parks. Stachybotrys fungus contaminating an elementary school. Soap missing (again) in the toilets of a Lebanese restaurant.

He looked at the clock for the umpteenth time and wondered why Natasha hadn't reported in. Was she in trouble, or on the brink of cracking the case? Perhaps she was just stuck in traffic.

He needed some fresh air. He grabbed his coat and buzzed Anne, told her to hold all calls except those from Colleen, Natasha, and Hamish. Theirs he would take on his cellphone.

He shivered at the thought of the resentment Hamish must be harbouring. Hamish hadn't answered any of Zol's messages, hadn't even responded to his beeper, despite his obsession for answering pages within a seven-minute window. Losing his cool last night had cost Zol an ally at a crucial moment. Had it also cost him a friendship? Hamish was unnaturally tidy, clumsy at small talk, and too often tactless. But the way he listened with his eyes made Zol feel he was the sole focus of Hamish's impressive intellect. He was interested in everything Zol said. Most guys cared more about themselves and their exploits than about their buddies.

Zol nearly collided with Natasha as she rushed through the front entrance of the building.

She looked exhausted, dwarfed by her bulky winter coat. Her hair hung limp, and her shoulders were hunched. "I don't care if I never go grocery shopping again."

"Long day?"

"I'll say. I've been up and down every single aisle at Food Bargains, Bombay Market, Botticelli's, and all four branches of Kelly's SuperMart."

"What'd you find?"

"Nothing."

"Not even a whiff?"

She tugged at her long woolly scarf and shook her head. "I'm sorry."

"I was hoping for a miracle. That you'd trip over a fantastic lead."

She stamped the slush from her boots. "I'm really sorry, Dr. Zol."

He touched the shoulder of her coat. "For heaven's sake, Natasha. It was an impossible task." He'd sent her searching for the one perfect golden thread that united the lives of all seven victims. As much a fantasy as the tale of Rumpelstiltzkin.

Her eyes widened with desperation. "But all the cases have to share a common source. They just *have* to. Will Dr. Trinnock give us a little more time to find it?"

"We'll know in twenty minutes," Zol said, and started toward the door.

Natasha pulled off her mittens and bit her lower lip. Her demeanour changed from fatigue to apprehension. "There is one thing I'd better tell you. I was at I and W meats yesterday. It's the butcher shop where Joanna Vanderven had a standing order. Owen Renway used to shop there as well."

"Go on."

"I had brunch there yesterday. In the café next door. They call it a tea shop, and it's run by the same family." She glanced at the clock above the elevator doors, frowned, and gave Zol a look that said, *I'll be quick, please hear me out.* "The butchers don't work on Sundays, but the woman in the café said the deli section was open and she could sell us any of the packaged meat from the display case. Well, I had a good look around and I saw the head cheese — the same brand as the sausages I found in the freezers at the Vandervens' and the Spinellis'. You couldn't miss that logo — a vicious-looking eagle on a red-and-white background." Red blotches bloomed across her throat as she unwound her scarf. "We know Dr. McEwen liked to eat head cheese. If he bought that same brand of deli meats as Joanna Vanderven and Rita Spinelli and Owen Renway and . . . and . . ."

Zol knew what was coming. "And who?"

Her eyes got bigger as they brimmed with tears. "You and Max."

His stomach churned at the image of Max chomping through an Escarpment Pride sausage, his fingers smeared with ketchup and mustard. Zol couldn't bring himself to tell her about Hamish's cat-meat theory. It was too outrageous. And besides, it was more disgusting than dangerous; he'd never heard of cats getting infected with prions. Until he could speak with Hamish face-to-face, he was going to do his damnedest to put those Campbellville meats out of his mind. "Four Corners wouldn't purchase anything from an unlicensed vendor," he assured her. "Escarpment Pride meats must be fully government inspected. And Grade A."

CHAPTER 18

At four o'clock, Zol stopped and took a breath outside Peter Trinnock's office door. The folder of notes tucked under his arm gave him little comfort. He ran a hand through his hair, checked his fly, and straightened his belt buckle. His ears still ached from the arctic blasts that had bitten at him during his short walk along Concession Street. Colleen had phoned at five to four, and he'd ducked into a doorway, straining to hear her voice against the roar of wind and traffic. But he needn't have bothered. She'd turned up nothing. Brenda McEwen had answered neither her phone nor her doorbell; Tonya Latkovic's mother had never heard of Extendo-Tox; Owen Renway's partner, Kenyon Cheung, had been incommunicado the entire day, secluded in a courtroom.

"Come in," Peter Trinnock called in response to Zol's rap. His forehead glistened in the light of his desk lamp. His pale eyes, small and round, peered like prisoners from behind his glasses. "Have a seat."

Zol sat stiffly in the chair in front of Trinnock's desk. He tugged at his collar, swallowed hard, and swept his thighs, silently cursing the moisture on his palms. He always found it so difficult talking to Trinnock: there was an extraterrestrial look to those pale grey eyes, set too close together and diminished by thick lenses.

Zol rested his folder in his lap and began the synopsis he'd memorized. He started with Hamish's call last Tuesday night. At first it had looked like three isolated cases of variant CJD. All three had lived in England and had probably acquired the infection there many years previously — serious for them, but manageable from a public-health perspective in Ontario.

So far so good.

But when Zol got to Julian Banbury's call reporting four more identical cases, Trinnock pierced him with his piggy-eyed gaze. The veins on his cheeks flared like a tangled nest of spiders. "You should have called me immediately."

Zol looked at his hands. "I did, but you were at your conference in Muskoka."

"I wasn't stranded at the North Pole, for God's sake. You could have found me if you'd actually tried."

"But I had so few facts to tell you. I wanted to —"

"You wanted to prove you could solve a big case on your own."

Trinnock was right. "I'm sorry."

"Tell me what you've turned up so far. It better be good."

"It's tricky. Two of the cases are strict vegetarians."

Trinnock narrowed his eyes and shook his head. "Impossible."

"The British have found the same thing. And they've never explained it. I think it means we have to look for prions in unexpected places."

"Like where?"

"For a while, we suspected a certain brand of Swiss chocolate."

"Chocolate? Come on. That's ridiculous."

"Not entirely," Zol said quietly but firmly. He was treading a fine line between continued humility and enough professional assertiveness for Trinnock to take him seriously. "Not if it's made with gelatin."

"Gelatin? You mean boiled-up bones from infected cows?"

"That was the idea. But we've ruled out the chocolate. We can't link it to all the cases."

"Good thing. It sounds pretty far-fetched. And there's no point in upsetting the Swiss without a bloody good reason." Trinnock opened his hands. "So what else have you got?"

"The most promising lead we have so far is taking us to Extendo-Tox, the anti-wrinkle —"

"I know what it is." Trinnock wiped a slick of sweat from his brow. "But . . ." He stopped and stared out the window, pondering some notion far beyond the naked trees lining the Escarpment. "But it can't possibly have prions in it. It's synthetic. I've read the prospectus from cover to cover."

Zol pictured the Porsche Trinnock had bought last summer. Only room enough in it for Trinnock's golf shoes and a brand-new set of Callaways. He must have invested heavily in Extendo-Tox. He would be counting on another windfall when Extendo-Tox hit the American marketplace next year.

"It *is* a neurotoxin," Zol said, choosing his words carefully. "And relatively new on the market. Four of our cases got injected with it regularly."

"But it's been given to thousands with excellent results. They use it all over Europe, in Australia, even Japan. It'll be huge in the States once we finally get the FDA to approve it."

"Maybe we're just seeing the leading edge of a huge wave of similar cases. After all, it was developed at Caledonian and marketed here a good few months before anywhere else."

Trinnock wagged a reprimanding finger. "I'm surprised at you, Szabo. You're usually so level-headed. But now you're talking about an apocalypse. Based on — how many cases?"

"Four."

"That's only half your victims." Trinnock stabbed at Zol's notes. "What about the others, the ones who never got Extendo-Tox? Hell, your investigation is pathetically incomplete. And your theory's ridiculous."

Zol couldn't speak. A vice of shame gripped his throat. He knew that Trinnock was right: his investigation *was* incomplete. Extendo-Tox had made for a tantalizing theory, but even the chocolate could be linked to more of the victims. If only he'd had more time.

Trinnock pulled off his glasses. His fingers trembled as he polished the lenses with a handkerchief. He replaced the glasses and leaned back in his chair. "Well? You must have other leads by now."

Zol was too embarrassed to mention his unsubstantiated theory about Chilean vegetables tainted with prion-contaminated cow manure. And he couldn't bring himself to tell Trinnock about Hamish's cat-meat story. He knew that Trinnock would laugh him right out of the office. Besides, four of seven CJD victims consuming Larry Krooner's products didn't constitute any more credible a lead than the Extendo-Tox.

"No," Zol said, fingering one of the loonies in his blazer pocket. "That's all we've got so far."

"Well then, I'll have to call Toronto." Trinnock peered at his watch. "It's not four thirty yet. Someone will still be in Elliott York's office. They'll have to send us an investigator. A proper field epidemiologist. We just cannot be seen to be dragging our feet."

Zol moaned silently: here it came, a heavy hitter from Toronto who would play to the headlines and confuse the investigation by ignoring local knowledge, a big snout wired to the national television news, hogging a sensational story and making slop of the solution by jumping to outlandish conclusions. Zol again remembered the Lassa fever fiasco of two years ago: the glare of the spotlights, the whir of the cameras, the chaos in the wake of Dr. Wyatt Burr. Overnight, the man had transformed a simple case of malaria into international bedlam.

At eight fifteen the next morning Wyatt Burr swaggered out of the elevator onto the fourth floor of the health unit. He was not sporting Levi's or a ten-gallon Stetson, but he did wear a bolo tie and had just ridden in from Toronto on a Ford Mustang. Anne had the honour of greeting him. Without so much as a good morning, he demanded immediate access to a private office with a high-speed

Internet connection, an uninterrupted supply of coffee, and the promise of a pepperoni pizza delivered at twelve thirty sharp. Anne ushered him through a door marked Maggie Baldwin RN, Vaccine Coordinator and flicked on the light; she invited him to make himself at home then quickly taped a Do Not Disturb sign to the door, feeling guilty at keeping Maggie out of her own office.

A minute later Anne pushed Zol's door open after a brief knock. He was hunched at his computer, lining up the day's agenda, still undecided whether he felt relief or disappointment that Trinnock's deadline had come and gone. In a way, he was glad Toronto was running the investigation. Let them take the heat.

He looked up from the screen. Anne's pinched face had more colour than usual, and there was a rare unruliness to the salt-and-pepper of her hair. She looked like she'd run three city blocks.

"God has arrived," she said with mock gravity. She fingered the cameo pendent nestled against her steel-blue twin-set. "And he doesn't seem too pleased."

Damn. They'd sent Dr. Bolo Ties. The man had the confidence of Zeus and the subtlety of Cyclops. "What's he unhappy about?"

"Nothing in particular."

Burr never needed a reason for a scowl or an excuse for a slur, especially in front of an audience. "Where is he?"

"I put him in Maggie's office." Anne glanced anxiously at the doorway, then checked her watch. "Oh dear, I better put on the coffee. Then it's downstairs for a carton of half-and-half. He said to be sure he had a non-stop supply of double-cream-no-sugar."

Zol pulled a ten-dollar bill from his wallet. "Here. I'm happy to buy as many litres of half-and-half as it takes to keep him from barking too loudly."

Anne smiled and accepted the bill. "Keep your wallet handy."

He followed her down the hall to Maggie's office where he found himself staring at the side of Wyatt Burr's shaved head. Burr had commandeered a computer and was peering at the screen, cursing under his breath. Despite all those double creams, his facial bones jutted above hollow cheeks and a skinny neck.

Zol extended his hand. "Good morning, Dr. Burr. I'm Zol Szabo, the associate MOH working on the CJD file. We met a couple of years ago."

Burr swivelled in Maggie's chair and accepted the handshake. His eyes showed no glint of warmth or recognition. "Wyatt Burr. Toronto General." He withdrew his hand and punched twelve digits into the phone. He growled into the receiver, "Shit, Gretta, you screwed up my schedule already and it's not even eight thirty. I told you to move Skolnic and Bagley to Thursday, not Wednesday." He slammed down the phone and scowled at Zol. "Holy crap, this is a hell of a time for you guys to drop the bomb of the century on me. I'm already up to my eyeballs."

Zol fidgeted with the loonie in his pocket. Burr's face was almost a fixture on television, fronting for the Ministry, Health Canada, and the Canadian Food Inspection Agency. It was nerve-racking to stand inches away from that face in the flesh, to feel the brunt of its energy. "Well," Zol said, "we're hoping another pair of eyes will see what we've missed." He lifted Maggie's papers from her desk and replaced them with the stack of files he'd carried from his office. "Here are the charts of the seven cases and the detailed notes of our fact-finding interviews with the families. We've created a reasonably comprehensive database. And we've come up with a few links between the cases. I'll send them to you electronically in a couple of minutes."

Burr waved his hands dismissively. The beak of the eagle on his bolo tie gaped in the glare of the computer screen. "No," he said. "Nothing but the medical charts and the raw details of the family interviews. I wanna find the links myself, draw my own conclusions." He grabbed the top chart from the stack, his eyes narrowing as he absorbed the front sheet. In an automatic motion, he lifted Maggie Baldwin's empty coffee mug to his lips. As he tilted back the lipstick-stained stoneware, his eyes widened. His arm froze. He glared at the cold mug and screwed up his face, then wiped his mouth with the back of his hand and slammed the mug onto the desk.

Zol heard nothing from Trinnock or Wyatt Burr for the rest of the day. The case had been torn from his hands, and they felt empty. He couldn't even share his feelings with Hamish, who was obviously having one of his pouts. Two desperate phone calls from Shalom Acres quickly reminded him that there was lots to keep him busy at the beleaguered nursing home; their strep epidemic continued to blaze out of control. He sent Natasha to spend the day there, interviewing the staff and poking through the cupboards. They agreed to discuss her findings tomorrow and then make a joint expedition there after lunch.

At four thirty the following afternoon Zol returned to his office from Shalom Acres. He still had to tackle a long list of emails, which accumulated with disheartening speed. Though at this point, almost any diversion, even email, was better than fretting about CJD. He'd enjoyed the two hours he'd spent at the nursing home, staring down the nurses' anger at his declaration — phrased as diplomatically as he could manage — that the staff had played a role in transmitting invasive strep from resident to resident. He'd been able to announce, with great relief, that the investigative team (Natasha, of course) had successfully tracked the deadly path the bacteria had carved through the facility. Its point of origin: the fingers of a personal support worker, a shy Somali refugee whose tender hands, raw with eczema and teeming with bacteria, had been shaving and bathing the elderly elite of her adopted country. He worried that dealing with her shame would be more difficult than eradicating her pathogens.

He clicked Send on an email and answered Anne's buzz — Trinnock wanted him in his office. Immediately.

What did Trinnock want this late in the day? Zol had given Wyatt Burr all his notes. Was the man finally going to ask for his impressions of the case?

"Come in and join us," Trinnock said in reply to Zol's knock. "Dr. Burr has completed his investigation. He's going to give us a preview of his report."

Zol's glow at the nursing-home success vaporized under Wyatt Burr's dry-ice gaze. Surely, the man couldn't have solved the case. Not already. There was so much data — he couldn't have sifted through it all. He couldn't single-handedly have found the prions after only two days. He was smart but not superhuman.

Burr eyed Zol's entrance with a blank stare then strode to the picture window. He rolled down his sleeves and buttoned his cuffs. Shielding his eyes, he peered through the glass as if straining to make sure the Toronto skyline still beckoned from the distance.

The stench of Wyatt Burr's lunchtime pizza — tortured tomato, burnt cheese, and soggy cardboard — filled the office. Zol knew how much Trinnock despised take-out pizza. The boss must hate the cloying smells oozing from the box defiling his Chippendale desk.

Trinnock nodded like an obsequious waiter toward the honoured guest from Toronto. "Dr. Burr has worked efficiently. And taught us a thing or two about field epidemiology."

"It wasn't all that difficult," Burr said. He lifted his ballpoint from Trinnock's desk and tucked it into his shirt pocket. "I've tackled worse."

"We're grateful for your expertise," said Trinnock.

Burr held his pose as he drank in the praise. "Julian Banbury's description of the amyloid plaques was the tipoff," he said. "Those tulip formations in the brains — arranged in a pattern never seen before — meant you had to look for a source of seriously distorted prions."

"Good thinking," Trinnock said, adjusting his spectacles. "But distorted how?"

"Some sort of process that kept them infectious but changed them radically."

"Something more complicated, I presume," Trinnock added, "than cutting steaks and filling sausages."

"Correct," said Burr. He cut the air with a stroke of his hand. "This has nothing to do with meat. The prions are too misshapen. Besides, two of the victims were vegetarian."

Zol knew there were vegetarians among the British cases of variant CJD, but Burr was making it clear there was no room for discussion.

Burr tapped his polished forehead. "Anyway, field epidemiology is all about finding the unexpected link that cracks the case."

Zol eased into a chair near the door and sat on his hands.

Trinnock looked pointedly at Zol then turned to Burr and said, "So, Dr. Burr, what was it that my staff missed?"

"The chocolates."

Before he could stop them, Zol's hands were flapping like crows' wings. "No," he said. "We ruled them out." Zol turned to Trinnock for support but saw only stone.

Burr thumped his foot on the hardwood and folded his arms across his chest. His Adam's apple bobbed above the eagle on his bolo tie as he glanced at Zol then held Trinnock's gaze. "Are you people interested in the report I'll be sending to the Ministry?"

The tangled veins on Trinnock's cheeks blazed like lasers. "Of course we're interested in your report, Dr. Burr. Extremely. Please, have a seat."

Burr sat down and recrossed his arms, his eyes piercing like daggers.

Zol tucked his hands under his thighs.

"Every one of your cases," Burr began, "is linked to a single brand of gourmet chocolates." He stopped and looked at Trinnock then back at Zol, as if expecting to be interrupted. He sniffed, clearly pleased by the rapt silence of his audience. "They've got gelatin centres and they're imported from Switzerland. The exact name is . . ." He lifted his pad from Trinnock's desk. "Lorreaux Chocolate Fruit Explosions." He paused, raised his eyebrows, then continued. "I called the head office in Geneva and verified they do contain gelatin from European sources."

Trinnock leaned forward in his chair. "And you say *all* our cases ate those chocolates?" He flashed a sideways scowl at Zol that conveyed a lecture full of anger and disappointment at Zol's recklessness in missing the target.

"Yeah." Burr waited a moment before continuing. "Before I got here, your staff had linked them to five of the seven victims. It took a few phone calls for me to verify that the remaining two ate them as well."

Zol's cheeks filled with heat. "But we —"

Trinnock lifted a cautionary hand then turned to Burr and forced a smile. "And the gelatin in the chocolates comes from cows with BSE?"

Burr smirked. "You got it. Boil up their bones and you get gelatin — laced with prions."

"The prions are distorted by such processing?" Trinnock asked.

"Exactly." Burr looked at Zol as if to say, *At least your boss gets it.*

"Would that be British cows?" Trinnock asked.

"Shouldn't be," Burr replied without hesitation. "Not these days. The Brits are very careful about what parts of the cow they eat. They stay well away from the bones. Incinerate them before they can get into the food chain. Other countries aren't always so careful. There's a fair bit of BSE amongst the herds in France and Switzerland."

"Where do we go from here?" said Trinnock.

"I'll call Elliott York right now and fax him my preliminary report. With something this big he'll call a press conference this evening. He'll issue a public warning and get those chocolates off the shelves. Immediately."

"And," said Trinnock, polishing his spectacles, "we've got to stop people from eating any they've already purchased. Are you going to call Health Canada?"

"Elliott knows how best to work with the feds. He'll call Ottawa." A smile lit his face for the first time. "Those desk-bound nerds at the Canadian Food Inspection Agency are gonna drool all over themselves. This is their case of a lifetime. They'll issue the official product recall and make sure it's carried out across the country."

A minute later Zol slipped out of Trinnock's office and shuffled to the rear of the building, to his office overlooking the garbage cans and Mr. Wang's cluttered yard. He dropped into the chair and leaned his elbows on the desk, his head heavy in his hands.

Wyatt Burr had to be mistaken about Danesh Patel and Delia Smart eating those Lorreaux chocolates. Natasha had spoken with Mrs. Patel again on Sunday. Danesh never ate chocolate. He hated it in any form. And Delia's husband had been clear about her chocolate allergy.

What line of questioning had Wyatt used to change their stories? He must have cross-examined them so roughly they'd buckled and given him everything he wanted to hear. Mrs. Patel would have been an easy target. Against an aggressive government official, a recently widowed immigrant wouldn't stand a chance. She would agree with anything Burr said to keep herself on the right side of the law.

It defied credibility that Wyatt Burr could finger the chocolates so quickly. Only two days reviewing something as important, as complex as this file, and he was going public with his findings? Just like he'd done with Lassa fever. A superficial look and a snap decision. And while the authorities were stumbling down the wrong track — for who knows how long — the public was going to keep gobbling up those prions. Damn it to hell. How many more people were going to lose their minds thanks to Dr. Bolo Ties?

Zol scratched at the stubble on his chin and stared at the gathering darkness outside the window. The only way to get back on track was to patch things up with Hamish.

CHAPTER 19

Later that Wednesday evening Zol swore at the screen as he watched the CBC ten o'clock news. Elliott York, Wyatt Burr, and the provincial minister of health were announcing the lethal danger of the Lorreaux Chocolate Fruit Explosions. From chairs aligned behind a broad table, the three officials told the country to head straight for their kitchens. Destroy everything that might contain gelatin: yogourts, puddings, sauces, jelly beans. Turn every refrigerator and cupboard inside out. But: do not panic.

To make matters worse, Burr, who had obviously never made jam, confused fruit-derived pectin with animal-derived gelatin and told the entire country to throw out every jar of jam, jelly, and marmalade in their possession. He spouted that ridiculous "better safe than sorry" creed. When a reporter, his voice rising, asked Elliott York how best to dispose of these foods without contaminating the water supply, all three officials stared blankly at the camera. Zol could almost hear the minister of health counting the number of votes she was going to lose in the next election. Then Wyatt Burr chimed in with the assertion that grocery stores would take everything back. Zol pictured the chaos in the parking lot at Kelly's SuperMart. He saw the artistic displays at Four Corners demolished by patrons jostling for attention, their arms loaded with boxes overflowing with syrups and sauces, chocolates and frostings, pumpkin pies and Turkish delights.

The health minister, her hands gripping the table, promised that the chocolates would be checked for prions in a government laboratory in Winnipeg. It sounded like a sensible start until she declared that teams from the Canadian Food Inspection Agency would spread across the country the next day, investigating the safety of all foods containing gelatin.

Zol knew that was impossible. A small group of boffins couldn't accomplish such a Herculean task. The public would realize that in a day or two when the minister couldn't give their kitchen cupboards the all clear.

Then a camera captured the Swiss embassy in Ottawa, dark and silent except for the front lobby, where a frightened-looking man with a five o'clock shadow waved a mop at a reporter and said, "No speak Engleesh."

No matter what Wyatt Burr had written in his report, Delia Smart and Danesh Patel had not contracted CJD from eating Lorreaux chocolates. Zol was certain they'd never eaten them. And if those confections were laced with prions, tulip CJD would be popping up in every country that sold them. No, Wyatt Burr had stumbled upon the chocolates, cooked up a solution, and forced the facts to fit. Scientific blindness had been around for centuries. Look how the Catholic Church had humiliated Galileo.

Zol shook his fist then flipped a loonie through his fingers as the news faded to a commercial.

A few minutes later, Hamish walked into the lobby of Heritage Towers. He leaned into the intercom and pressed a button on the front panel. "Hello, Kenyon," he said as a light came on. "It's Hamish Wakefield."

He was bursting to tell someone about his latest results on the samples from I and W Meats. There was no way he was going to risk another icy rebuff from Zol. And Julian Banbury gave him the creeps. The man's bulging eyes, crooked teeth, and English accent reminded him too much of his old choirmaster. Sharing the results with Kenyon seemed the natural thing to do.

"Hamish," Kenyon called out in reply, "I've just been thinking of you."

Was there a catch in Kenyon's voice or was it just the tinny speaker system? "Really?"

"It's been all over the TV news."

"What?"

"Come on up. Seven-oh-two."

After the elevator let him out, Hamish rapped on the door of 702. A piano concerto, Rachmaninoff, faded slightly, and a moment later Kenyon stood in the doorway. Dark circles smudged his lower lids. He wore a black T-shirt and matching pyjama pants. He squeezed Hamish's arm.

It was clear they'd passed the formal nod and handshake stage. Hamish couldn't quite believe his sense of pleasure — for the first time barely touched by anxiety or guilt — in the presence of a warm and handsome man. But why was Kenyon so upset?

Ice cubes clinked in Kenyon's glass as he stepped back from the threshold. "Did you see tonight's news on TV?"

"No. Been in my lab since five."

"Big announcement about your CJD thing. They've cracked the case. Didn't take them long."

They couldn't have, thought Hamish. Unless . . . Had Zol gone up to the Krooners', discovered the sausage operation, taken samples, tested for prions — all in two days? Impossible. "They couldn't have. Not that fast."

"They say it's the gelatin in those chocolates."

"What chocolates?"

Kenyon pointed to the box on the coffee table. A black-and-yellow bird stared from the cover. Kenyon drained his Scotch in two gulps. "Our favourites."

"No. We excluded them. Categorically. Two of the victims never ate them. Never ate *any* chocolate."

Kenyon rubbed the back of his neck. "Jesus, Hamish. I'm gonna lose my memory, my mind. Just like Owen." He stared at the wall as if his eyes could see a future filled with horror.

"No, you're not. Kenyon, listen."

"Stop calling me Kenyon; only my mother calls me that. The name is Ken."

"Look — it's not the chocolates. It can't be. By now there'd be hundreds of CJD cases all over the world — wherever they get shipped."

"That's not what they just said on the news."

Hamish swallowed to clear the tightness in his throat. His eyes swept the room. "Have you got any of that green tea?"

"Sure. There's some in the fridge. Okay if it's iced?"

A minute later, Hamish took the tall, frosty glass from Ken and settled into one of two armchairs in the living room. "Never mind the chocolates. I've discovered something. I think it's important and I need your help."

"My help? I'm no good to anyone right now. Can barely bring myself to open my kitchen cupboards. They must be loaded with prions. Besides, I know nothing of the law covering scientific discovery and intellectual property."

Hamish flicked his hand. "I'm not looking for a lawyer. But I have to warn you. You're going to need a strong stomach when you hear what I've got to say."

Ken took a swallow from a fresh measure of Scotch.

Hamish placed his tumbler on a coaster and steepled his hands. "You know those Escarpment Pride sausages you buy from Four Corners?"

"Yes, they're made up near Campbellville. Pork, I think. Can't place all the spices." Ken's eyes widened. "Don't tell me I can't eat *those*."

"Well . . . some of that spicy flavour is cat meat."

Ken sputtered into his drink. "What?" An ice cube bounced from his glass onto the coffee table. It rolled off the edge and skittered across the hardwood into a far corner. "You're not serious."

Hamish said nothing. He didn't know how else to put it.

Ken uncrossed his knees and yanked at the legs of his pyjamas. "You *are* serious," he said. "You're telling me I've been eating bits of pussycat?"

"Only small amounts."

Ken screwed up his face. "Jesus. That's positively revolting." He dropped his shoulders and stared into his Scotch. After a moment he swigged his drink.

"I might as well complete the story."

"Oh, shit."

"There's also cat meat in the head cheese and pork pies from the same Campbellville butcher."

"Not the Melton Mowbrays!"

"Afraid so."

"Jesus. How do you know?"

Hamish explained how his research into antibiotic-triggered diarrhea had led him to the meat-testing kits and Lanny Krooner's sausages. "And after I stumbled onto the cat meat in the sausages, I did a little shopping at I and W Meats."

Ken's face was bone white. "Tell me the truth. Am I going to get CJD?"

"I didn't come here to frighten you. I don't even know if there's anything wrong with the cat meat."

"That's not an answer."

"There is no answer. At least, not yet."

Ken ran his palm across his flat-top. "You sound like a lawyer."

Hamish's academic puzzle had taken on a personal dimension he had never experienced. "I'm sorry, I really am."

They sat for a few minutes, motionless, listening to the melancholy tones of Rachmaninoff. When the music paused between movements, Ken spoke. "You said you needed my help?"

"Maybe my tests are wrong. Maybe Lanny Krooner is a flawless sausage maker. We'll never know unless we inspect his place." Hamish lowered his voice; from the first sip, the iced green tea had made it strong and clear. "An *unofficial* inspection, that is."

. "But don't the authorities check his operation on a regular basis? You know, those official notices you see on the front doors of restaurants?"

"I'm betting Krooner's been pretty wily," Hamish replied. "He could've covered things up the moment the inspectors arrived."

"We've been eating his pies and sausages for a good couple of years. He must have passed at least a few inspections."

"His farm's not far. I think it's on the Escarpment. Close to Rattlesnake Point."

"How do you know?"

"His brother is a patient of mine. Has a mink farm on the same property. He's in hospital with a bad infection — one of his mink chewed up his arm."

"And you think we can just saunter up there and see what's cooking in their kitchen?"

"Yes," Hamish replied. He stared for a moment at the lint on his socks. "Dumb idea, eh?"

Ken slowly stroked his chin. There wasn't the harsh, raspy scrape Zol made when he scratched at his face. "Can you make it look like a house call?"

"No. My patient will still be in the hospital."

"Well then, we'll just have to take a hike toward Rattlesnake Point. On the Bruce Trail." Ken looked toward the rolltop desk in the corner. "I've got a map. Walking on the trail was the one bit of exercise Owen didn't balk at. Well, he used to balk but . . ."

Hamish sensed Owen as an awkward presence in the room. He stared at his iced tea. As he opened his mouth to speak, Ken raised his hand pre-emptively. "Do you know exactly where the farm is? The trail can be pretty mucky this time of year."

"The address on the hospital chart is vague — only a rural route."

"That's okay. Ontario's land-registry records are available on the

Internet. Real-estate lawyers check the database all the time. I'll get the exact location."

"Do you think we can look like a couple of hikers who just happen to drop by?"

"You got hiking boots?"

"I suppose I could buy a pair."

"You'll need them." Ken's eyes darkened. "I hope it doesn't seem too much of a coincidence that you're their doctor. Is the butcher the suspicious type?"

Hamish pictured Lanny's coyote face. But bolstered by his new-found spontaneity, he shrugged and raised his open palms. "Sort of."

"I suppose we could show up at the farmhouse and ask to refill our water bottles."

"Are you free tomorrow?"

Ken laughed. "I wish. Another long day in court." He paused and looked up, as if running through his schedule in his mind. "The judge is taking Friday off. You free then?"

"Sounds good. Hospital visiting hours aren't until the afternoon. Lanny should be at the farm in the morning. We'll need him there to show us around. Can I meet you here at nine?"

CHAPTER 20

The next afternoon, Natasha's favourite sandwich shop was deserted
when she walked in to pick something up for lunch. Three bored-
faced employees, fidgeting behind the counter, were folding waxed
paper into frogs and airplanes. The place usually buzzed like a mad-
house, but barely a soul in Hamilton was trusting restaurant food
today.

Natasha made her purchases, returned to the office, and dropped
her lunch onto her desk, then typed her password into the computer. While the Internet browser started up, she removed the
wrapper from a turkey sandwich. She leaned back in her chair and
closed her eyes, relieved to have a few quiet moments to herself.

She lifted the sandwich and gave it a thoughtful squeeze. The
warm bun gave off that wonderful yeasty smell of freshly baked
bread. Inside, the shreds of lettuce appeared harmless enough, but
the slices of turkey looked too perfectly oval to have come from an
actual living creature. Low-fat garlic mayonnaise oozed from
beneath a single slice of mozzarella cheese. That mayo was sure to
be full of MSG and thickened with gelatin. Was she a fool to eat it?

She took a deep breath, shrugged at the mayo, and bit through
all the layers of the sandwich. She licked her lips at the zesty tang

of the sauce. If it contained a little gelatin it didn't matter. She was confident that Dr. Bolo Ties was all wrong about the gelatin in the Chocolate Fruit Explosions.

This morning at eight o'clock she'd visited Four Corners at opening time. She'd spoken to the strained-faced manager, who looked like he hadn't slept all night. He told her the store was only open to employees until the shelves had been inspected and cleared of everything containing gelatin. It could take days, he added. She explained that she was from the health unit and asked him to check his invoices for Lorreaux Ltd. He shuddered and led her to his office. His records showed that in the past two years the store had received six shipments of Lorreaux Chocolate Fruit Explosions — ten different lot numbers. She had gone back to the office and phoned Lorreaux's head office in Geneva before it closed for the day. A prim-sounding woman, impressed that Natasha was calling from a government agency in Canada, verified that chocolates bearing those ten lot numbers had also been shipped to distributors in the United States, Japan, and five countries in the European Union.

Natasha chewed a mouthful of sandwich and stared at a blank spot on the wall. Four Corners had received the same lots of Lorreaux chocolates as shops in countries all over the world. There was nothing unique about the shipments sent to Hamilton, yet tulip CJD had shown up here and nowhere else.

The chocolates couldn't be the problem. Not by themselves.

She toyed with the crumbs on the wax-paper sandwich wrapper. She'd been over this a dozen times and still could see no other way to look at it: the prions causing this localized epidemic must be hiding in something prepared and consumed, perhaps injected, right here in Escarpment Country.

Injected. *Injected.* She dropped the sandwich, licked sauce from her fingers, and opened her scribbler. She tapped on her keyboard and called up the database they'd constructed in Zol's sunroom on Saturday night. She'd updated it by adding Colleen's discovery that Rita, Delia, Joanna, and Danesh all had received Extendo-Tox anti-wrinkle treatments from Dr. Zupanzik. And her own discovery that Joanna, Rita, Owen, and perhaps Dr. McEwen had all eaten Escarpment Pride ground-meat products.

She typed "injection" into the word-finding function of the database. The cursor jumped to the Extendo-Tox injections. She clicked the mouse, and the cursor jumped again, to Delia Smart — cortisone injections for arthritis in her knees. Next, it jumped to Tonya — injections for migraine. Natasha scanned the page. Listed farther down were medical details: Owen Renway — experimental treatment for Tourette's; Dr. McEwen — esophageal manipulations for achalasia.

Five of the seven victims had been injected for a variety of conditions before they'd shown signs of CJD. What if Owen and Dr. McEwen had also received injections? The Indian newspaper her aunt sent regularly from Delhi had run a story about unscrupulous companies repackaging discarded needles and syringes without sterilizing them. Had such a scam made its way to Hamilton?

She called up Google on the computer and typed "injection," "Tourette," and "achalasia" into the search box. In less than a second, a list of links filled her monitor. Five titles almost jumped from the screen. Just what she'd suspected: injections *were* used in the treatment of both Tourette's and achalasia. The injections used in both diseases almost hit her in the face. Synthetic botulinum toxin, otherwise known as Extendo-Tox.

Her fingers trembled as she typed in three new search terms: "injection," "migraine," and "botulinum toxin." She waited a millisecond for her answer: neurologists from Hamilton's Caledonian University had reported the successful treatment of drug-resistant migraine with injections of Extendo-Tox.

She peered at the screen and guided her eyes with her index finger to be sure she was reading every word correctly. She did the same with the previous screen. She double-checked the hand-written notes in her scribbler. Four of the CJD victims had received Extendo-Tox from Dr. Zupanzik. The remaining three — Tonya Latkovic, Owen Renway, and Dr. McEwen — had medical conditions that were sometimes treated with it. She reached for her cardigan and drew it over her shoulders.

The more she thought about it, the more plausible it seemed. Extendo-Tox, the pride and joy of Hamilton's medical establishment, was teeming with prions. In her mind she heard that speech the mayor made at every opportunity: "Extendo-Tox is the triumph of an exceptional government-university-industry partnership, the envy of the world."

Her arms hugged her chest as she shivered inside her sweater.

The epidemic was only just beginning.

When Zol returned to his office after a trip to the bank machine down the street, he was surprised to see Colleen seated at his desk. Her scent, a youthful blend of jasmine and tamarind, filled the room.

"Have you seen the signs in the windows up and down Concession Street?" he said. "Our Products Do NOT Contain Gelatin. Even Marcus has one."

Colleen bobbed in agreement. "Whoever heard of gelatin in a latte, for heaven's sake? That Dr. Burr has done a bang-up job. Extraordinary."

Zol stuffed gloves into pockets, then hooked his coat on the rack. "And there's nothing I can do about it. First I have to sit back and let Wyatt Burr hijack our investigation. Then I have to sit and watch while he announces his ridiculous *solution*." Zol's mimed quotation marks with his fingers then searched his pocket for the comfort of a loonie. "You'd think Burr was Moses with the Ten Commandments, the way he's got the ears of every official, even the federal minister of health."

"We'll just have to keep plodding."

"Trinnock flatly forbids any pursuit of the Extendo-Tox angle. You should have seen him Monday afternoon when I started to tell him about it. Those veins on his cheeks nearly exploded." He jabbed at his scribbler. "Anyway, it looks like Extendo-Tox is a bust. We can only link it to four of the cases, and it's synthetic — can't contain prions."

"You might change your tune when you hear my latest tidbit."

"It better be freeze-dried and vacuum-packed. Trinnock will have my cojones for soup if I ever mention Extendo-Tox again."

Colleen's dimples winked. "You told me he was retiring."

"I don't want to think what this week's done for my chances at the Oval Office." His hands gestured out the window at the parked cars, the battered garbage cans, the scattered mounds of cigarette butts. "I might be stuck looking at *that* for the next decade. Never mind. What's your tidbit?"

"Tonya Latkovic's injections weren't sumatriptan."

"No? What, then? Acupuncture?"

She ran the tip of her tongue along her upper lip. Her eyes sparkled with mischief. "Extendo-Tox."

"You're kidding."

"I spent the morning with her mother. Face-to-face, her English is pretty good. Better than my Croatian."

"So, she knew all along about the Extendo-Tox?"

"No. Not a thing. We telephoned her neurologist together. From her kitchen. He was a real stickler — his nurse refused to give out any information over the phone. Wouldn't even admit Tonya was his patient."

"Not like those receptionists you finagled in those offices at ninety-nine Concession Street."

Colleen rolled her eyes. "He made us come in person, bring Tonya's death certificate, and sign a release."

"But he gave you the info?"

"Squeezed us in between patients. I think his receptionist took pity on us. Mrs. Latkovic was quite a sight. A smidgeon shorter than me and eyes that looked like they hadn't stopped crying since Tonya went missing on Halloween night."

"What did he tell you?"

Colleen paused. She stared at the wild loonie weaving through Zol's fingers.

Zol returned it to his pocket. "You were saying?"

"Tonya had been getting Extendo-Tox for about eighteen months. Then she stopped turning up for her appointments."

"About the time her depression set in?"

"Exactly. Her last Extendo-Tox was in May. She was due again in July but didn't show up."

"And was dead before November." He shifted his chair. "How many shots did she get?"

"Quite a few."

"But I thought the whole idea is that Extendo-Tox only needs repeating once a year or so."

"Except with migraine. According to the neurologist, it's trial and error. You don't know exactly where to inject. Every case is different. Tonya had ten sessions, and the results were disappointing."

"No wonder her father complained about the cost."

"Yes. Seven hundred and fifty dollars per session. And not covered by drug plans."

"Hmm. Because it's still considered experimental."

There was a knock at the door. Natasha peeked into the office. "Oh, sorry, Dr. Zol. Anne said it was okay. But I see you're busy."

"Colleen dropped in with some interesting developments."

Red blotches coloured Natasha's throat below her pinched face. "Should . . . should I come back later?"

Zol beckoned her in. "Have a seat." He lifted an empty chair from the far end of the room and placed it next to Colleen's. Natasha didn't budge from the doorway. He could see that her eyes had lost their lustre since her triumph yesterday afternoon at Shalom Acres. "What's wrong?" he asked her. "Something happen?"

Colleen reached down and grabbed her purse by its strap. "Perhaps I'd best slip out," she said to Natasha. "Give you a moment with Dr. Szabo."

"I'm okay," Natasha said. She clutched her opal pendant for a moment, then looked at Colleen. "I think you'd better stay. You'll want to hear this as well." She closed the door until it clicked, then cleared her throat and looked anxiously at Zol. "I was bothered by all the injections."

"What injections?" he said.

"Tonya's migraines, Delia's knees, and all those Extendo-Tox sessions with Dr. Zupanzik. So I went online, did a little searching, and found out that Tourette's, achalasia, and migraines are all treated with Extendo-Tox."

Colleen leaned forward in her chair and clapped her hands. "We're with you there, Natasha. I was just telling Zol how I visited Tonya's neurologist today. He injected her with Extendo-Tox. For a year and a half."

Natasha fidgeted with the collar of her cardigan. "That makes it five confirmed with Extendo-Tox exposure."

"Extraordinary," said Colleen. Her broad smile said she was pleased with her morning's contribution.

"And you're suggesting," Zol said to Natasha, "the final two might have been treated with it as well."

"This is scary, Dr. Zol. There must be thousands out there getting Extendo-Tox."

"Thousands with wrinkle-free faces and brains on the verge of dissolution. I hate to have to tell you this, but Trinnock doesn't want to hear anything more about Extendo-Tox. Or it's my head on a platter. I can't go to him, or anyone else, with this Extendo-Tox thing."

Natasha looked stricken. "But Dr. Zol —"

"Not until we wrap it up tight. No holes. Every angle covered."

"Isn't that how it should be, anyway?" Colleen asked.

"Exactly," he said. "Brainstorming is an essential part of our business. But we do it behind closed doors. If it leads to something highly suspicious — or even better, a firm conclusion — *then* we tell the public. We can't go spouting wild theories the moment a problem lands on our doorstep."

Colleen closed her eyes, as if picturing theories running wild all over Escarpment Country. "One can only cry wolf so many times," she said. A mischievous grin lit her face as she held Zol's gaze for a moment. "Someone should have made that clear to Wyatt Burr."

Zol's brief contentment evaporated. He patted his shirt pocket and lifted out his antique Parker. "You know what Dr. Osler used to say about pompous guys like Wyatt Burr?" he said, holding up the pen. "The greater the ignorance, the greater the dogmatism."

"And if they'd had television in his day," Colleen added, "he would have said something clever about the addictive power of the TV camera."

He uncapped the pen and turned to Natasha. "So, what do we do next?"

"Are we allowed to explore the possibility that Owen Renway and Dr. McEwen got Extendo-Tox?" Natasha said.

"Of course," he said.

"And Dr. Trinnock's command?"

"We work discreetly. We don't mention Extendo-Tox outside this office until we've built a Trinnock-proof case. That has to be clear." He looked at one woman and then the other, collecting a solemn nod from each.

He wrote "Renway" and "McEwen" on either end of the top line of a blank page of his notepad and drew a vertical line between them. "These two are Hamish Wakefield's cases but . . ." A tickle of shame lodged itself in his throat. He tried to clear it by coughing into his fist. "He must be away." He coughed again. "I haven't been able to get hold of him for four days. Any suggestions how we might approach the partners without it looking like a health unit inquiry?"

Colleen picked up her ballpoint. "Mrs. McEwen should be easy enough to approach without arousing suspicion."

"Maybe," he said. "But she must have a lawyer by now, poised to sue Lorreaux Chocolates for millions. Her husband ate them by the truckload."

Colleen brushed a stray hair from her cheek and tucked it behind her ear. "Better not involve either of you two, then. She'd tell her lawyer the health unit was interested in Extendo-Tox, and —"

Zol thrummed a riff against his desktop. "It would get back to Trinnock faster than we could say synthetic botulinum toxin."

"So let *me* approach her," Colleen said, "as Dr. Wakefield's colleague."

"Which is true," Natasha said with a quiver in her voice. She was clearly anxious about any hint of subterfuge. "And you could remind her of their university connection."

"Good idea," Colleen said. She patted the sleeve of Natasha's cardigan and cocked her head toward Zol. "Not to worry. I'm not going to get this guy into trouble."

"Owen Renway's file is going to be a lot more difficult to crack," he said. "He was never a patient at Caledonian Medical Centre, so his chart is bare except for the day he arrived by ambulance, vital signs absent. We'll have to approach his family or his partner."

"Another lawyer," Colleen said, rolling her eyes.

"There was no mention of any family in the chart," Natasha said. "Just his partner, Kenyon Cheung."

"How about a family doctor?" Zol asked.

"I think there's a GP's name on the autopsy report," said Natasha, as she stood up. "The charts are in my office." She hurried toward the door. "Back in a sec."

"She's keen, isn't she?" Colleen said.

"Better than most doctors at this investigational stuff."

"Commitment without ego." Colleen paused, examining her polished nails. "Like you," she added.

"Careful, you'll make me blush."

"I'm serious. You remind me a lot of Liam."

"I trust that's good."

"Very."

"Here we are," said Natasha, scurrying into the room. "The autopsy report is being sent to Dr. Elizabeth Hammill. Her office is in Dundas." She waved a yellow Post-it note. "Here's her phone number."

"Who's going to call her?" Zol asked.

Colleen looked at him. "You, of course. You won't have to

mention Extendo-Tox. Just ask for the details of Owen Renway's therapy for Tourette's."

Zol shrugged and took the number from Natasha. "I guess I can be as discreet as either of you."

He dialled, then stared into his notepad feeling the weight of the women's eyes upon him. After eight rings, a live voice answered. Zol explained who he was, then was put on hold with the promise that the doctor would be with him shortly.

"Yes?" said a woman's voice, clearly anxious and harried.

"Dr. Hammill? This is Dr. Zol Szabo. I'm the Associate MOH at Hamilton-Lakeshore Health Unit."

"Look, as I told the inspector yesterday, the man's coming on Monday to fix our fridge. Most of our vaccines are in Dr. Nishio's office down the hall. They're perfectly safe there. I just have a few doses here in a cooler. I'll use them up today. I don't see what's the big deal."

"Actually, I'm not calling about your fridge. And thank you, it sounds like you have everything in hand." It was against the rules to store vaccines in a cooler where the temperature could not be properly maintained or monitored, but he needed her on his side.

"Oh. So what's this about?"

"I'm hoping you can help us. One of your patients died recently, and we're investigating the cause of his death."

"Who would that be?"

"Mr. Owen Renway."

"I can't divulge any information about my patients. Not without them signing a release."

"Mr. Renway has passed away."

"But —"

"It's okay. When it comes to matters of public health and safety, the law provides for you to give me, in good faith, any information pertinent to my inquiries. Especially in the case of a reportable disease like encephalitis. Everything you tell me is kept in confidence."

"I understand," she said above a background of screaming infants.

"If you would prefer, you can call me back. That way you'll

know you're connected to the health unit and everything is above board."

"No. I haven't got time for that. What do you need?"

"Can you tell me anything about Mr. Renway's general health? I understand he was undergoing treatment for Tourette's syndrome."

"Goodness. You don't die of Tourette's."

"Quite right. But we're looking at his life and death from a variety of angles."

"Oh . . . Then you should be more interested in his dementia. What a terrible thing that was." She gasped. "Don't tell me . . . he got that prion disease from those chocolates they're warning everyone about?"

He paused, wondering how much he should tell her. She was bound to get the autopsy report in a day or two. "I'm afraid I know nothing about the chocolates," he said, "but we've been advised he had a form of CJD, a prion encephalitis."

"Oh my God. I knew he was a gourmet cook and loved to eat, but . . ."

It sounded like triplets wailing in the background.

"You were going to tell me about his Tourette's."

"Oh yes. That's easy. The treatment was working wonders."

"And what did it involve?"

"That new stuff. Injected into his voice box. Very effective."

Zol's pulse quickened. "Do you have the name of the medication?"

"Sure. It's what all the dermatologists are using these days. Extendo-Tox."

Zol gave Colleen and Natasha a thumbs-up. "How long had he been getting the injections?"

"I don't remember. He went to Toronto for them. Started about a year ago, maybe longer. I'd have to check his chart."

"That won't be necessary. But let me take just one more minute of your time, then I won't need to bother you again." He kept the smile in his voice and asked a few more questions about Owen's general health. He thought it best to deflect the focus of his inquiry away from the Extendo-Tox. He thanked her again and wished her a pleasant day.

He turned to the women. "Well, there you are. Extendo-Tox number six. Good work, Natasha."

The look of alarm returned to her face. "But now what, Dr. Zol? We've got to get the stuff banned as soon as possible."

He shook his head. "We have to do our homework first."

"I'll do my best to speak with Brenda McEwen today," said Colleen.

Natasha fidgeted with her cardigan. "But —"

"There's no way around it," Zol said, fishing the loonie from his pocket. "We have to prove our case. I'm not going to go on national television and pull a Wyatt Burr."

Natasha shivered. "Even if all seven cases did get Extendo-Tox," she said, "how do we prove it caused their CJD?"

"For that we need an expert. I'll talk with Julian Banbury. He must be having a field day with these cases. He might even welcome our Extendo-Tox wrinkle." When Colleen groaned at the pun, he opened his palms and shrugged.

He saw the two women out of his office and returned to the desk and opened his PDA. It contained the phone number of a specialist who was far more important at that moment than Julian Banbury: Dr. Margolis, the pediatric neurologist who was set to inject Max's spastic arm with Extendo-Tox. With what Zol knew now, he was not going to let Margolis shoot any of that stuff into his son.

Margolis's answering machine came on with a click. Zol flipped the loonie between his fingers as he listened to an interminable spiel about office hours, street address, scope of practice, and prescription renewals. When he finally took a breath to leave a message, the female voice advised, "This machine does not take messages. If this is a medical emergency, call nine-one-one or go to your nearest Emergency Department. Otherwise, call back on

Monday between ten and eleven in the morning or between two and three in the afternoon."

He crashed the receiver into its cradle, then calmed himself and glanced at the calendar. There wasn't really a problem. Max's appointment wasn't until January. There would be plenty of time in the next six weeks to cancel the injection.

CHAPTER 21

Friday morning's glint of sun promised a reasonable day for a hike. Ken gripped his Bruce Trail map like a talisman while Hamish sped the Saab northwest from the city on Highway Six. The late November countryside lay ragged and colourless. An undulating quilt of barren fields and leafless woods. To Hamish's relief, the slush had vanished from the roadways thanks to three days of above-freezing temperatures. He'd not paid a visit to the car wash for forty-eight hours, maybe a record for this time of year.

Hamish steered off the highway and onto the country road Ken said would take them to a spot on the Bruce Trail a couple of kilometres from the Krooner farm. Ken's Internet search of Ontario's land-registry records had revealed the exact location of the Krooner property — Swytt Road, just beyond the hamlet of Kilbride. The farm backed onto the Escarpment and the Bruce Trail, so it seemed like a straightforward matter to start hiking along the adjacent section of the trail, build up a credible sweat, and drop in on the Krooners.

As the familiar bustle of the suburbs faded behind them, and increasingly more snow filled the ditches, Hamish's anxieties flared. They hadn't formulated much of a plan. He and Ken had only a vague idea of what they would do, what they would say, once they arrived at the Krooners'. The farmhouse might be a long way from the Escarpment trail or on the wrong side of a ravine. And there was no way around it, Lanny Krooner was an unstable creature.

Ken pointed through the windshield. "Turn to the right, there."

"You've got to be kidding," said Hamish, pulling a face. "That's not a road. That's just a strip of muck."

"Of course it's a road."

Hamish winced. "We're going to get stuck."

"Hikers drive up here all the time."

"In November?"

Ken waved away Hamish's fears. "We'll be fine. See that sign?"

A black-and-white arrow, nailed to a tree, pointed into a thicket. Below it, a small white notice said simply, *Bruce Trail.*

Hamish shook his head. "You mean this is it? All that hype about Canada's longest public footpath, and not even a parking lot?"

"What did you expect? A McDonald's? Valet parking?"

"Very funny." He peered around. "It doesn't look like a United Nations heritage site to me. Where's the delicate ecosystem? There's nothing here but trees and rocks. And far too much mud."

Hamish drew onto the verge beside the primitive roadway and set the handbrake, then turned off the engine and opened his door. His shoulders slumped at the sight of the mud on the side panels. He could hardly wait to get back to the car wash. He grabbed his backpack and retied the laces of his hiking shoes. The woman at the camping store had told him these were perfect for the Bruce Trail — lightweight with hefty, non-slip treads.

At the edge of the thicket, he stopped and read a notice nailed to an evergreen tree. *Bruce Trail Users' Code.* It said to leave only thanks and take nothing but photographs. That would be easy; what would anyone want with a bunch of twigs and stones?

Ken pointed to the left and headed onto what looked like a track between the trees. Frankly, it was hard to tell. All Hamish could see were rocks, soggy leaves, and the occasional patch of grimy snow.

After twenty minutes, it was apparent that the woman in the camping store had never hiked this mucky trail in November. Certainly not after three weeks of intermittent snow and rain. Hamish's shoes were so clotted with mud they hobbled him like shackles. Ken's natural pace soon had him well in the front.

When Ken's lead had grown to seventy-five paces, Hamish's chest began to tighten. He leaned against the nearest tree and tried to calm his breathing. It was no use. His chest constricted rapidly into full-blown wheezing. He hauled his inhaler from his pocket. Three puffs of salbutamol. A minute later, three more. His mouth was as dry as a sandbox but he was too exhausted to pull a water bottle from his backpack. His heart raced, spurred by the heavy dose of asthma medicine. He looked around, desperate for somewhere to sit. All he could see was mud. Not even a log to squat on. He slumped against the tree trunk.

He called for Ken, but the effort was wasted: his voice box emitted only a pathetic croak.

Finally, Hamish saw Ken turn, shielding his eyes against the low, late-autumn sun and peering impatiently. "Come on," he called. "Hurry up. Two klicks to go."

Still gasping, Hamish drew a hand across his throat.

Ken threw up his arms. He scuffed the soles of his boots against the root of a tree. "What's wrong?" he called.

There was no way Hamish could respond.

Ken started trudging back. He scowled in alarm as he approached, then gripped Hamish's arm and peered into his face. "What's the matter?"

"Asth — ma."

"Jesus. You should have warned me."

"Didn't — know — this — heavy-going."

"You gonna be all right?"

"Used — puffer."

"Is it working?"

Hamish shrugged, then nodded.

Ken peered through the trees and out over a meadow strewn

with boulders. "No signs of a farm." When Hamish made a face, Ken mimed *stay cool* with his hands and said, "Catch your breath, then we'll go to Plan B."

Half an hour later, Hamish handed Ken the car keys and pitched heavily against the trunk of the Saab, grateful that the long trek was over. He gulped from his water bottle, then dropped into the passenger seat and struggled to pull off his shoes. They fell to the ground. That's where they could stay. He was not going to let them mess up the Saab.

Ken slipped into the driver's seat. "You gave me a scare out there. You sure you're okay?"

Hamish sucked back the last mouthful of water and checked his pulse. Strong and regular, and below one-twenty. "I'm just out of breath." He felt like a fool for having forced the termination of the hike. He looked straight ahead through the windshield. "I told you. I'm too young for a heart attack."

"You look like shit."

"Good. I won't have to fake it at the Krooners'."

"Forget Plan B. I'm taking you straight home."

"No way," Hamish said. Sweat stung his eyes. "Hell's bells. I didn't just walk an hour through quicksand so I could go home empty-handed." He pulled a Kleenex from his backpack and dabbed his face. "We'll just drive to the Krooners' and tell them we're lost."

"Then stop wiping the dirt off your face. You'll need to look convincing, not pretty."

Hamish stuffed the tissue into his pocket and pulled his door closed. He didn't have the strength to slam it.

Ken frowned. "And you're really going to leave those shoes behind? They'll be fine when they dry out."

"Forget it. Do you know where you're going?"

Ken patted the map on his knee. "It should be just up the road." He started to turn the ignition key, but hesitated. "What are we going to say when we get there?"

"Like we agreed — we got lost."

Ken ran his tongue around his lips. "And we're thirsty." He started the car and gently revved the engine.

Hamish stiffened. This was his first time in the passenger seat. "Don't forget to adjust the rear-view mirror. You sure you know how to drive a standard?"

"My Accord's a five-speed."

"But watch the clutch. It's touchy. Grips fast."

Ken looked over his shoulder then eased the car onto the roadway. "Just relax."

A few minutes later, Ken brought the Saab to a stop beside a battered mailbox. Hamish squinted at the faded letters across its side — KROONER. A long gravel driveway led two hundred metres to a farmhouse. It seemed a lot farther from the road than any of the neighbouring houses. Several buildings clustered beyond it.

Hamish scrunched his nose. "Smell the pigs."

Ken pointed to a distant barn with a curved roof, its walls shiny, like aluminum. "Over there."

"How do you know?"

"Well, see how it's built a long way from the house? And look, no grass around it. Just mud."

"Please, I've had enough mud for one day." Hamish pointed to four long, low sheds. Each stood open-sided and protected by an overhanging pointed roof. "Those look like cages under there. Must be for the mink."

Ken let out the clutch and turned into the driveway. "Here goes."

They were halfway to the farmhouse when a Rottweiler with a massive head and huge shoulders bounded toward them, barking. With its teeth bared, it looked fierce enough to rip the bumper off the Saab.

"So much for Plan B," said Hamish as Ken inched the car toward the house.

Ken stopped behind a pickup truck. "We'll soon see if anybody's home. No one could miss that commotion." He killed the engine.

The dog worked its jaws, looking as if it itched to jump through Hamish's window.

After a few long moments, a male voice shouted from the right side of the house. The dog looked over, stopped barking, and sat on the gravel beside Hamish's door. Its back muscles quivered; its teeth looked as dangerous as ever.

Lanny Krooner appeared, holding a shovel. He wore a plaid jacket and a pair of tall rubber boots. He drew his lips tight across his teeth and stooped to peer into Hamish's window. "You lost or something?"

Hamish rolled the window down a crack. He swallowed hard. "Hello, Lanny. It's Dr. Wakefield. From Caledonian."

Lanny stepped back. It was impossible to tell whether he was angry or horrified. "Jesus Christ," he said, shaking his head, wiping his mouth with his hand. "It's Ned, isn't it? Going to get that amputation after all."

"No, no," Hamish said. "He's fine. Really. He's fine."

"Then what are you doing here?"

"We were hiking on the trail and — and we must have made a wrong turn on the way home. Saw your name on the mailbox and . . ."

Lanny rapped the hood of the Saab. "No GPS in this machine?"

"No."

"So you wanta get back to town?"

Hamish nodded. On his home turf, and with that shovel in his hand, Krooner looked more forbidding than Hamish remembered him. No carefully gelled hair, no razor-pressed jeans, no stylish loafers.

"Dead simple. A left, a right, then left and right again, then left."

"Sorry?"

"That'll get you back to Highway Six."

The dog was panting beside Lanny and wagging its tail, which meant it was probably safe for Hamish to power his window down a bit farther. But the second he put out his head to look back along the driveway, the dog bared its teeth.

Lanny patted the animal's massive head. "Easy, Millie."

"You mean we turn left here?" asked Hamish, eyeing the dog,

his finger hovering by the electric-window button.

"Then right, then left and right and left. No sweat." Lanny stepped away from the car. He was going to let it go at that. No offer of a drink. No tour of his operations. No samples of his sausages.

"Hamish," said Ken, his tone all business. "You'd better call the hospital. You were supposed to check in by now. That man with malaria?"

Hamish threw Ken a puzzled frown. There was no man with malaria.

Ken pointed to the farmhouse. "Since your cellphone isn't working," he enunciated loudly, "you need to use the phone — in the house."

Hamish turned to Ken and whispered, "Forget it."

"But Hamish, the hospital *expected* you to call half an hour ago."

Hamish rolled his eyes at Ken. Then he coughed and grabbed his empty water bottle. "Okay, okay," he said. He called through the crack in the window, "Lanny, can I use your phone? My cell isn't working, and I need to call the hospital."

Lanny shrugged. "I suppose."

Hamish's heart raced. His throat tightened. He couldn't bring himself to open the door.

Lanny dipped his eyebrows. "Are you gonna come in or not?"

Hamish pointed to the dog.

"It's okay. Jake's out the back with Morty and the hogs. And Millie here won't bite." He threw a stick ahead for the dog to chase, then chuckled. "Not unless I turn my back."

Outside the car, Hamish made the introductions. He felt vulnerable standing in the farmyard in his stocking feet, Lanny towering over him.

"What happened to your shoes?"

"Lost them in the mud. On the Bruce Trail."

Lanny shook his head and mumbled something about city slickers. His mouth tightened into a smirk as he studied Hamish's face. "Excuse my French, Doc, but you look like hell. Lose your water bottle, too?"

"No."

Ken nudged Hamish. "But it *is* empty."

Lanny led them to the back door. Piles of dishes towered in the kitchen sink on the other side of the window. "I'll open a couple of brewskies," he said, pulling off his boots.

"Could you make that a Coke?" asked Hamish.

"What's wrong with you, Doc? Beer too strong for you?"

Hamish stiffened. He looked at his filthy wet socks and hesitated.

"Now what's your problem?" Krooner asked, opening the door.

A blast of warm air, heavy with the smell of cooked cabbage, poured from the doorway. Hamish stepped into the kitchen.

Lanny pointed through an open swinging door. "If you wanta use the phone, there's one in the dining room."

The phone was sitting on a large metal safe beneath a window. A television blared to an audience of empty armchairs in the adjacent living room.

Lanny watched from the kitchen as Hamish dialled the number. It felt as if the farmer was making sure Hamish didn't try to crack the safe. It took ages for the hospital switchboard to answer, and even longer for someone in the intensive care unit to pick up. Lanny lost interest and swung the door closed. When a nurse came on the line, Hamish inquired about a patient he'd been following and ordered a new set of blood cultures. He ended the call and returned to the kitchen.

Ken and Lanny were sitting at the table, each holding a bottle of beer. Hamish took a can of Coke from the table and gulped it gratefully.

"Ken, here, knows my sausages," Lanny said. For the first time, his eyes looked friendly, civil. "Says he buys them all the time at Four Corners." He drained the bottle and set it on the badly marked tabletop — not a coaster in sight. "Have you tried the ones I gave you?" Lanny asked.

Hamish's stomach twisted. "Not yet. Been too busy to cook this week."

Lanny looked disappointed. "Hope you froze them."

"Oh, yes."

Lanny opened the refrigerator. "Another beer?"

Ken's bottle was still two-thirds full. "I'm good with this one." He smirked and pointed to Hamish. "I'm driving this guy's car." He raised an eyebrow. "You still look pretty dry, Hamish. You better have another Coke."

Lanny set a fresh Coke on the table and pulled on his second beer. "I was telling Ken, here, how you guys missed all the excitement by just a couple of days."

As far as Hamish was concerned, there had been more than enough excitement over Ned's arm.

"Yep," Lanny continued, "the pelting's over for another year. The Mexicans are gone, the pelts are all sold, and most of the carcasses are in the compost." He scraped his thumbnail across the label on his bottle. "Sold them to your people, I figure," he said to Ken.

Ken leaned forward. "Sorry?"

"Hong Kongers. Bought the whole damn lot this year. Fifteen thousand pelts. Usually we sell to a broker in Montreal, but this year they all went straight to Hong Kong. Gave us top dollar."

Ken smiled as though fascinated by the notion of his relatives purchasing all of Lanny's pelts and turning them into expensive garments. "Those would be the mink sheds we saw as we drove in?"

"Yep. Most of them're empty now. Just our docile breeders left. Got rid of all the crazy biters like the one that got Ned." He drained his beer, smacked his lips, and drew the back of his hand across his mouth. "Mating starts again in February."

Ken poked Hamish's shin under the table, then said to Lanny, "What do you do with the carcasses?"

"Used to send them to a rendering plant. They turned them into chicken feed and pet food. But not anymore. Against the law now. Ever since mad cow." He shook his head as if frustrated by the vagaries of governmental bureaucracy. "Gotta compost 'em or burn 'em." He took a third beer from the refrigerator and swigged a couple of drafts. "Besides, mink's got a strong taste — on account of the scent glands." He studied his bottle and chuckled to himself, a private joke. "A little goes a long way."

Ken ran his finger around the mouth of his bottle. "You really put fifteen thousand mink carcasses in the compost? Sounds like a terrible waste of meat."

Lanny leaned on his elbows. "Well, I save a few, eh?" He cupped his hand to the side of his mouth. "For the dogs, and on the QT for the neighbours. Mixed with Morty's leftover pork — well, I mean, it's a real delicacy." His eyes clouded as he ripped a strip from his beer label. "Like I said, just for the dogs."

Ken turned to Hamish and ever so slightly dropped his jaw. With a flick of his eyes and a subtle jerk of his head he made it clear he wanted out of there. He coughed into his fist. "What time do they expect you back at the hospital, Hamish?"

Hamish checked his watch. "Oh, look at that. It *is* time we got going."

They swigged their drinks, thanked Lenny, said their goodbyes, and headed toward the car.

Back in the Saab, neither of them said a word until they reached the end of the driveway.

Ken groaned, "Oh my God."

"I know."

Ken turned left, gunned the engine, then swerved to miss a rabbit dashing across the road.

"Hey, take it easy," said Hamish, gripping his shoulder belt. "This isn't your Accord, you know."

"I was wrong."

"What?"

"I told you I'd heard everything. You know, from working in the courts?" Ken glanced in the mirror. "That was until today."

Hamish wiped the sweat from the back of his neck. "And I was wrong about the sausages," he said. "Not a scrap of cat meat in them. No wonder those tests were only weakly positive. They were picking up *mink* meat."

"As soon as he started talking about the mink, he got that guilty look. I can spot it a mile away."

Hamish wiped his palms against his thighs. "I can't believe it."

"Dog food, my ass. He's concocting the ultimate delicacy — ground pork enhanced with fine Canadian ranch mink." He thumped the steering wheel. "And he's flogging it at Four Corners. I'll never be able to look at a Melton Mowbray again."

Hamish took one last look at the farm. The massive hog barn sparkled in the sun. "I bet he's mixing mink into the head cheese, as well."

"So now what? You going to phone Zol Szabo this afternoon?"

"You must be kidding. This all sounds crazier than the cat meat. I've got to prove it before I say anything to Zol. Got to get Krooner's stuff tested for mink mitochondria."

"Mink might-oh what?"

"That test I've been fiddling with. For detecting bacteria. If they've got test kits for pork and beef and elk, they must have one for mink."

"But won't that take a while?" Ken's face crumpled. His hands trembled on the steering wheel. "You've got to shut this guy down right away. Owen's dead. I've eaten a tonne of those pies and sausages. And people are snapping them up every day at Four Corners."

A spray of gravel clattered against the undercarriage as the Saab's rear wheels fishtailed on the shoulder.

Hamish gripped Ken's arm. "Watch it!"

"This car can take it."

"No. Pull over. I've got to tell you something."

Ken sighed noisily, then geared down and drew the car to a stop. He stared straight ahead. "What?"

"I know you're worried about getting CJD, but there's a really good chance you're *not* going to end up like Owen."

Ken turned and fixed Hamish with his eyes. "Come off it, Hamish. A really good chance doesn't cut it. I ate more of those pies than Owen ever did."

"Not everyone is susceptible to prions. To get CJD, you have to have both the prions *and* the gene that codes for susceptibility."

"Owen had the gene?"

"He must have. That's why he got CJD. But there's every chance you don't have it."

Ken's eyes pleaded. "What makes you so sure?"

"Look at you. You ate the same food and you're fine. Perfectly well."

Ken buried his face in his hands and muttered into his palms. "Jesus. I haven't slept a wink since Wednesday, since you told me about the cat meat." He lifted his head, then rubbed his eyes and the back of his neck. "Anything else?" he asked, his voice flat.

"There's a guy at the University of Guelph who's been helping me with my mitochondrial project. He's got colleagues at the university who are experts on prions."

Ken's eyes brightened. "We could get to Guelph in half an hour."

"But the samples of Krooner's stuff are back in my lab."

"You think they'll test them for you?"

"Don't see why not."

Ken slapped the steering wheel and threw the Saab into gear. "We're going to put that bugger away. Forever."

CHAPTER 22

Four Corners brooded in darkness that Friday afternoon — doors bolted and blinds drawn. As Zol drove by, posters in every window declared Closed For Inventory. No mention of when they expected to reopen, their shelves cleared of Wyatt Burr's demon gelatin.

Several blocks along, the parking lot at Kelly's SuperMart buzzed with panic and anger. The past three days had seen so much honking, revving, and squealing that a team of Hamilton's finest had been installed to corral the mayhem. The officers' hand-waving and whistle-blowing made little impact on the bedlam. Pickup trucks and compact cars stuffed with groceries jousted for the smallest patch of pavement, a beachhead from which to unload every prion-infested item the rumour mill had condemned. Three television vans, their antenna cranes extended, their satellite dishes gleaming, surveyed the rowdiness as they broadcast the city's humiliation to the world.

The morning's paper had run photographs of similar commotion in Geneva and Montreal. This scene was replicating itself across the country and around the globe. Panic was infectious and, thanks to television news, its transmission more efficient than any prion. And all for nothing. The Swiss had opened their books and their factories to the experts of the World Health Organization and the American Centers for Disease Control. As permanent hosts of the WHO, and conscious of their nation's synonymy with perfection, the Swiss showed proof they'd tested every batch of food-grade gelatin before releasing it for consumption. Despite this assurance, Wall Street had suspended trading in the stocks of the food-processing giants on both sides of the Atlantic. Overnight, the makers of comfort foods and treats had become pariahs, their products shunned like poisons.

Where was Wyatt Burr going to hide when the experts found no prions in any Swiss products, including Max's favourite chocolates? He wouldn't need to hide, of course. He was such an expert on doublespeak that even when the bare facts proved him wrong he made it sound like he'd executed every move with perfection. It still puzzled Zol that no one else remembered how just two years ago Burr had hijacked the international media for a week and convinced the world that Hamilton was the epicentre of a Lassa fever outbreak. When the tests had come back negative, the story fizzled, the media moved on, and no one bothered to explain that the patient had nothing more than a case of malaria.

Sitting tall in his minivan, his fingers drumming on the steering wheel, Zol felt the thrill of the hunt. Hard on a trail far more promising than chocolates and gelatin. He was on his way to Caledonian for a rendezvous with Julian Banbury. Colleen had called with the fantastic tidbit she'd gleaned from Hugh McEwen's GP. As Natasha had suspected after searching the Internet, a specialist in Toronto had been injecting Hugh's esophagus with Extendo-Tox to relax the overactive sphincter impeding the flow of food into his stomach.

That made it seven victims out of seven.

Julian Banbury peered at Zol from his laboratory doorway, his shirtsleeves rolled to the elbows, showing his spindly arms. His legendary eyeballs, moist and bloodshot, bulged from their sockets as he scanned the corridor with his lizard-like gaze. It was common knowledge he had the worst case of exophthalmia anyone at Caledonian had ever seen.

He beckoned Zol inside and closed the door, then heaved a jumbled stack of papers from the only chair in the room. He half-sat, half-leaned against the anarchy of his cluttered desk. Decades of scribbled musings, printed data, and neurological journals stood in piles two feet high on the desk. A dozen paper coffee cups, bearing various stages of scum and mould, wobbled atop the unstable columns. A framed photograph, propped against the desk lamp, showed a falcon chick teetering on the ledge of a tall building, contemplating two tractor-trailers on the street below. An inscription along the bottom said, *Peregrine Baby Jackson and the Hamilton Naturalists' Club thank you for supporting Falconwatch.*

Banbury motioned Zol to have a seat. "Now, what's all this about Extendo-Tox and CJD?" His Adam's apple bobbed above the pale scar of his thyroidectomy.

The chair lurched as Zol sat down. It was missing a rear caster, forcing him to hunch forward and balance on the three good legs. "As I mentioned on the phone, Dr. Banbury, all seven of our victims underwent Extendo-Tox injections."

Banbury swept back his unruly mop of grey hair. "Bloody hell. How certain are you about that?"

"Very."

He drew a handkerchief from his pocket and wiped the spittle from the corners of his mouth. "When did they receive them?"

"About eighteen months before their symptoms started."

"And you actually think Extendo-Tox caused their CJD?" He squeezed his handkerchief and balled it in his palm. "Come now." His lips formed a patronizing smirk.

The room felt freezing cold. Zol tugged at his lapels and closed the gap in his blazer. "Well," he said, losing his balance as the chair dipped with a jolt, its shortened leg grating against the floor. "It *is* a neurotoxin."

"My good man, you should have done your homework.

Extendo-Tox affects the *peripheral*, not the *central* nervous system." Banbury ran a finger along the inside of his forearm from his elbow to his wrist, as if tracing the path of the median nerve. "It targets only motor nerves. It doesn't affect the brain."

Zol studied the floor. Between the rickety chair and Banbury's smirk, he felt like a schoolboy up for a reprimand in the principal's office.

"Furthermore," said Banbury, "your time frame is too bloody short. Too short by far."

"For regular CJD, yes. But you said yourself, this isn't regular CJD. It's something new. Maybe it has a much shorter incubation period."

Banbury's eyes strayed to a photograph on the wall beside the desk. It showed him standing beside a podium, shaking the hand of a well-groomed man in a business suit. Behind them a banner said, *Extendo-Tox: Harnessing a Natural Wonder.* "Highly unlikely," Banbury said, crossing his arms. "Anyway, your Ministry friends have found the culprit."

The notion that Wyatt Burr was a friend or colleague was nauseating. "Do you honestly believe that?"

"Why not?" Banbury glanced again at the photo. "Better than falsely implicating one of our finest achievements."

"But why is this cluster showing up only in Hamilton?"

"It's the job of you food-inspection people to figure that out. I don't speculate — I just report what I see." Banbury crossed his shins and puffed his chest. "I trust you saw my posting on ProMed?"

Zol raised his eyebrows, then slathered butter onto his voice: "You took the world by surprise." He hoped his smile looked at least vaguely sincere. "And created a lot of buzz among the experts."

Banbury's lips tightened in a grin as he gazed toward the far wall.

Zol allowed the man to revel in a private moment of self-satisfied fame, then rose carefully from the wobbly chair. "If the gelatin in those chocolates were loaded with prions, your tulip CJD would be popping up all over the world." Zol's fist tightened inside his pocket. Banbury and his Extendo-Tox chums were not a bunch of choirboys. They had their gold mine to protect. "And the British have been testing their gelatin for years and never found any prions in it. If England's is clean, Switzerland's must be, too."

"Hmm." Banbury ran a hand through his mop of hair. "I suppose the Brits ought to know. The blighters have had most of the world's mad cows grazing in their fields."

Zol let Banbury ponder the tribulations of his homeland for a moment, then said, "So, Dr. Banbury, could you help me at least explore the Extendo-Tox connection? Your expertise, your inside knowledge would be invaluable."

Julian looked away. "I can't. I signed a confidentiality agreement with the company before working on the project. I'm forbidden to tell you a bloody thing about Extendo-Tox except what's public knowledge."

"But seven people are dead. The brains of hundreds more could be in the early stages. And more people are getting Extendo-Tox injections every day. You can't just —"

Banbury scowled and stepped toward Zol. "You can't waltz in here and tell me what I can and cannot do." His breath blew hot and stale in Zol's face. "And from what I've seen on television, this matter is out of your hands. Toronto is holding the reins. You have no business —"

"This is still my community. And I care about the people in it."

Banbury's bug-eyed face turned crimson. "What are you insinuating?"

His heart racing, his cheeks burning, Zol stared at the web of blood vessels in Banbury's eyes. He lifted his Parker from the inside pocket of his blazer and rolled its ebonite barrel between his thumb and forefinger. The heat gradually left Zol's cheeks, his heart rate settled, confidence seeped into his chest. "Let me ask you this," he said, still anxious but in control, "is it remotely possible that Extendo-Tox could be contaminated with prions?"

Banbury shook his head, his gaze fixed on the antique pen. "Extendo-Tox is completely synthetic. That's public knowledge. It's bacteria-free, egg-free, animal-free, even human-free. As it says in the product monograph, it's an artificially synthesized protein. It cannot possibly contain prions. And as you said about the gelatin, it's in use all over the world." He paused, then his face began to soften as though a crack of doubt were opening in his mind. "Why would Extendo-Tox cause CJD only here in Hamilton? There aren't even any cases in Toronto. They've got four or five times our population and, I understand, plenty of dermatologists who use it."

"Because it was developed here. The first human subjects came from Hamilton. Our local doctors were the first to popularize its use."

The blood deserted Banbury's cheeks. He jerked backwards, then steadied himself against his desk. "Bloody hell, man, do you know what you're saying?"

"Yes, sir, I do. And that's what has me scared. Extendo-Tox has only been on the market in Europe since the spring. Not long enough for CJD to make itself obvious over there. And the drug's not licensed yet in the U.S."

Banbury's tongue flitted across his teeth. "No, you're talking madness. It's simply not possible."

Julian Banbury was the keystone of any Extendo-Tox connection. The man had to be steered past his ego. Past all his shares in Extendo-Tox, Inc. Zol eased back into the wobbly chair and braced himself with the toe of his shoe. Desperate for a whisper of inspiration, he fixed on Dr. Osler's Parker as he wove it through his fingers. The embryo of an idea began to grow. "Prions are a type of protein, right?" he asked, fighting his anxieties and doing his best to sound collegial.

"Correct."

"And . . . and they work by folding in a certain way?"

Banbury nodded.

"And," Zol continued, "they cause brain damage, CJD, by folding in an *abnormal* way and recruiting zillions of similar proteins to fold in the same harmful pattern."

"That's more or less correct."

"Then maybe Extendo-Tox is acting like a prion and causing a new form of CJD — your tulip pattern."

Banbury lost his footing and slumped against his desk. He tried to speak but his tongue only flitted across his lips. With the shifting of his weight, a pile of books and paper cups toppled to the floor. A slick of coffee shot across the linoleum. He stared at the mess and wiped his face with his handkerchief.

Zol motioned to the chair. "Here, why don't you sit down?"

"No. I'm all right." Banbury's eyes flickered with guilt. This couldn't be the first time he'd had misgivings about Extendo-Tox. Zol found a mug that looked fairly clean and filled it from the sink in a corner of Banbury's office. Banbury took a sip. "You realize the significance of that theory of yours?"

"So do you, Dr. Banbury." Zol held the older man's gaze. "And a mind like yours is itching to put it to the test."

Banbury cradled the mug and stared into its tea-stained bottom for several moments. "I'll have to think about it."

"But you've sparked so much interest on the Internet, you can't stop now."

"My good man, it would be very difficult to prove. In point of fact, virtually impossible. I would need to isolate and characterize the prions in the brains of our seven victims. But no lab in Canada can test human tissue for prions. Guelph has a superb prion lab, but it's licensed only for samples of food and specimens from animals."

"What about Atlanta — the CDC?"

"And let the bloody Americans —" Banbury coughed the remainder of that thought into his handkerchief. "We must keep this under our hats," he said.

Zol stiffened at the suggestion of a cover-up. He straightened his back.

"But of course," Banbury added briskly, "just until we've got it sorted."

CHAPTER 23

Zol's weekend dragged like a slow-cooking osso buco with the salt and spices missing. A dreary stew of angst and apprehension. Hamish was still avoiding him. Banbury was thinking about testing for Extendo-Tox in the victims' tulip CJD. Wyatt Burr was expounding on every channel about his grand revelation, still predicting a global prion plague and an international catastrophe.

By Monday morning, Zol was glad to get back to the distractions of the office.

"Dr. Szabo! Am I ever glad to see you," Anne called as he passed her desk on the way in. Anxiety creased her face, and she pointed to Trinnock's door. "The team from CTV has been setting up in there for half an hour, but Dr. Trinnock's not coming in."

Zol threw her a puzzled frown.

"Asthma. Sounded pretty wheezy when he called."

"But what's CTV doing here?"

"*Canada AM*. They're supposed to interview Dr. Trinnock at eight fifteen."

"Live?"

"Yes."

A bright light flooded through the partly opened door, and an electrical cord slithered on the floor like a black snake.

Zol shrugged. "Well, they'll just have to pack it all up and find some other crisis to meddle in."

Anne tucked a silvery strand of hair behind her ear. "Dr. Trinnock says you're to do the interview." She assumed her mothering look and extended her arms. "Give me your coat."

"Forget it."

Her fingers beckoned for his coat. "Dr. Trinnock made it very clear. He wants you to do it."

Zol loosened his scarf but went no further. "No. I shouldn't be doing this."

"Why not?"

"I'm not involved. It's Wyatt Burr's show. Let him and the rest of them justify their own horse sh— their own horse feathers about contaminated gelatin."

Anne glanced sideways at the reporter standing in the open doorway.

"Dr. Szabo?" he boomed. "Only twenty seconds to air."

Zol's face tightened. He ripped off his coat and tossed it to Anne. As he headed into Trinnock's office, the glare of halogen almost blinded him. The reporter, reeking of aftershave, checked his watch and adjusted a gadget in his ear. Before Zol realized what was happening, a cameraman had clipped a microphone to his lapel, and the reporter's perfect teeth were barking into his face.

"What's it been like, Dr. Szabo, to discover you're at the centre of an epidemic that's on its way to destroying brains all over the world?"

Zol's heart rate shot up. He'd expected some sort of easy warm-up question, not this sucker punch. Maybe, he thought, they were not yet on the air. Maybe this was just some sort of sound check. "I . . . I don't think that's going to happen. I mean —"

"But Doctor, we understand those chocolates have been shipped to thirty-seven countries — and counting. And we're told that's not the end of it. The Canadian Food Inspection Agency reports that contaminated gelatin might have made it into all kinds of foods and consumer products." The man stared at Zol, his eyes dark and unyielding. "Won't that make for a global epidemic?"

This was obviously no sound check. Where was he supposed to look? At that large freckle on the reporter's chin? At the camera lens? At the red light blinking above the lens? He fixed on the reporter's chin, and out came the dilemma that had been plaguing him all week. "No one is certain that anything is actually wrong with the gelatin."

"That's not what we've been hearing from Ontario's health minister and the federal food inspection people. They've told us to avoid those Swiss chocolates and everything else that contains gelatin. Even certain medications, including painkillers."

"But there might not be any prions in those chocolates. There's a good chance they're perfectly harmless."

The reporter gaped. His oversized chin dropped. "That's quite a statement, Dr. Szabo, considering the strength of the warnings from the authorities."

At the sound of his name being broadcast across the country — virtually in the same breath as the minister of health and the CFIA — his knees quivered. He stepped backward, and his thighs bumped against Trinnock's antique desk. He was trapped.

The unyielding mouth in front of him wouldn't let up. "You must be in possession of information that government agencies are not aware of."

Prickly sweat streamed down Zol's cheeks as the lights bore down on him. He pictured Julian Banbury, scurrying bug-eyed inside his cluttered lab, fussing over the latest data on Extendo-Tox. Of course Zol had information the Ministry hadn't heard about. He thrust his hands into his pockets and balled his fists. "All I know is that the tests on the chocolates have not been completed. We have no proof they contain prions."

"So, you're saying that the public warnings about contaminated gelatin have been a waste of time? To use your own words, just horse feathers?"

"I didn't say . . ." But, of course, he had. Outside the office, off-camera. And the reporter had heard him. As his cheeks flared like lanterns, he could feel the guilt plastered all over his face.

The reporter lunged for the kill. "It seems you take exception to the information coming from Chantal Ferguson's office. You think the minister and the CFIA acted too hastily."

"Well, it's not my place to contradict the minister of health; it's just that —"

"Have you got a theory of your own, Doctor?"

Zol nodded, then tried to take it back with a quick shake of his head.

The reporter lifted his eyebrows and smiled like an old salt sensing that a good-size fish had grabbed his hook. "Tell us about it, Dr. Szabo."

"Let me just say that . . . that I'm pursuing another lead."

"But Doctor, lives are at risk all over the world. In the interest of public safety, let us in on your concerns."

Zol felt the edge of Trinnock's desk press into his thighs. He couldn't back away, and he wasn't going to shrug the questions off like an arrogant so-and-so. Yet he couldn't breathe a word about Extendo-Tox. Not at this stage. To announce it now would end his career; Trinnock and the health minister would see to that. And the lawyers who worked for Extendo-Tox would have a heyday suing him into homelessness.

But he couldn't keep staring into the camera like a ninny while all of Canada watched. He had to answer with something truthful even though he knew it wouldn't set him free. He gulped a breath of the stifling air and fixed his eyes on the camera lens. "I'm hoping to have something more to say in a few days. For now, that's it." He grabbed his lapel mike and yanked it off.

The reporter scowled, then set his massive jaw as the camera eyed his perfect teeth. "There you have it, Canada," he said in a tone that made it clear he was never short of answers. "The official who uncovered the epidemic that's destroying brains in an upscale Ontario community says his government has mishandled the investigation. Dr. Zol Szabo says we've all been handed a load of horse feathers. It's clear that this story, one of global proportions, is far from over. Dr. Szabo will have more to tell us later this week. Stay tuned." The reporter cupped his hand over his electronic earplug and smiled into the lens. "Now back to you, Vanessa."

The spotlights clicked off; the reporter removed the gadget from his ear; the cameraman swung his equipment to the floor. Coloured spots swirled before Zol's eyes. He fumbled for the door, his stomach roiling with anger and humiliation.

The reporter stepped forward with his hand extended, his lips forming a grin not mirrored in his eyes. "That was great, Doctor," he said. "Thanks very much."

Zol recoiled, refused the outstretched hand.

The reporter turned on his heel and swooped his hand into the inside pocket of his jacket. He pulled out a sheet of paper and studied it. Probably his day's agenda. A hit list of other lambs he was preparing to sacrifice.

"For God's sake, man," Trinnock said as Zol responded to the ringing of his office phone two minutes later. "Horse feathers?" Trinnock blustered between wheezes. "Have you lost your mind?"

Zol dropped into his chair as his ear filled with the raspy crescendo of Trinnock's coughing.

"What were you thinking?" Trinnock continued. "You were only supposed to give them harmless local colour."

"I got broadsided. Half a minute's warning and I'm on national television — interviewed by a Rottweiler."

Trinnock's gasping accentuated his ferocity. "The minister's going to be furious."

Zol's stomach tightened at the thought. "I know, but —"

"But nothing." Zol pictured his boss's face, purple with rage and lack of oxygen, his tiny eyes watering. "And — I can't protect you," Trinnock said.

Couldn't or wouldn't? And how much protection would Zol need if the tests showed that the prions were in the Extendo-Tox and not the chocolates? Who knew? The actions of politicians weren't guided by logic.

Trinnock gasped again. "Hold on." His phone clattered onto a hard surface. There was a whoosh-and-suck, whoosh-and-suck as he puffed at an inhaler. And then a pause before he continued, "What's all this about a new lead? You damn well better not be chasing after Extendo-Tox."

Trinnock didn't really want the truth, so Zol wasn't going to give it to him. Not today, anyway. "Just a foolish hunch," Zol replied. "I won't trouble you with it."

"Out with it, Szabo. That's an order."

Zol stroked at the cleft in his chin. What could he tell Trinnock? He had to say something to get Trinnock off his back. He lifted his pen from his pocket and rolled the barrel between his thumb and forefinger. His mind filled with an image of the bustling aisles of Four Corners before the store had been forced to pull down its blinds and lock its doors. He saw shelves of bundled Chilean asparagus.

Trinnock let fly a wheezy cough. "Szabo — you still there?"

Zol winced. "Yes, still here, sir."

"So?"

"Chilean vegetables."

"What?"

"I'm worried about the manure they use in Chile. You know, on their cash crops. If it's cow manure, it could leave a residue of prions on the vegetables they ship to us."

"What vegetables?"

"Things that grow close to the ground. Asparagus, for instance."

"For God's sake. They don't have mad cows in Chile."

"Can we be sure?"

"Prions in manure? Hell, that's lunacy."

Trinnock was taking the bait. "Like I said," Zol replied, "maybe it's a foolish hunch."

"Well, for God's sake keep it quiet. The Swiss are hopping mad about their chocolates. We can't have the Chileans gunning for us as well." Trinnock was hit by another fit of coughing, then recovered and added, "I've decided I want you off this case completely. I'm serious, Szabo. If I find you within a mile of this investigation, I'll have you out on your ear. For good."

Half an hour later Zol stepped out of the lunchroom with a mug of steaming coffee. At first, he'd retreated to his office behind the locked door. He'd stared out the window at the litter and the garbage bins. He'd made up his mind to take the rest of the day off, then realized that brooding would do nothing to cool his anger. Hiding out at home would merely delay the inevitable embarrassment of encountering colleagues abuzz with the story of his TV performance. It was better to face them today, get the initial awkwardness over and done with.

As he headed along the corridor from the lunchroom, he spotted Natasha walking toward him. When their eyes met, she dipped her gaze to the carpet.

"I see you heard about the horse feathers," Zol said as she reached him. He tried to chuckle, but it fell flat.

Natasha stopped, looked up, then hunched her shoulders like a distressed rabbit. "Oh, Dr. Zol, Anne said they put words in your mouth."

"Kind of. But it was my own fault. They must have heard me ranting outside the door before we got started." He beckoned toward the empty lunchroom, and a wave of coffee slopped from his mug. "Damn. Can't do anything right today," he said. He slurped at his overfilled mug, then raised his eyebrows. "At least I didn't let anything slip about the connection with you-know-what."

Natasha's face brightened a little. "Any news from Dr. Banbury?"

He put a finger to his lips. "Hunting for prions is a slow business. I don't expect to hear anything until later this week."

"Oh my gosh, that seems like a century." She fidgeted with her pendant and looked around to be sure no one was listening. "I heard about another case."

"What?"

"I guess I'm not really supposed to know. Well, not yet, anyway."

"What do you mean?"

"My cousin works on the neuro ward at Caledonian. She's nursing a woman the neurologist said might have variant CJD."

"Does she fit the profile of our other cases?"

Natasha nodded. "So far. But I didn't think I should be pumping for details. Not without your permission." She scuffed at a bare spot on the carpet. "The patient is a young woman. Some sort of VIP. My cousin said I would recognize her name." Her eyes widened. "She didn't divulge it, of course."

"Why would your cousin mention it to you?"

"Because I work at the health unit and the story's all over the news." Her hand flew to her mouth. "Oh, Dr. Zol," she said, her face crumpling, "my family has no idea what I actually do here."

"I know," he said, cradling his mug with both hands. "Keep me posted."

As he approached his office, he could hear the phone ringing.

"It's the mayor on the line," Anne said when he lifted the receiver.

"He only ever speaks to the boss. Can you get him to call Dr. Trinnock at home?"

"It's you he wants."

"Oh, no."

"Yes. And I better warn you — he's upset."

"Heard about the horse feathers, eh?"

"He was watching."

Zol pulled a face. "Great."

"Take a deep breath," Anne said, "and I'll put him through."

There was a pause, then, "Szabo? Who the hell do you think you are? Certainly no expert on brain diseases."

"Sir?"

"But there you are, embarrassing us all on national television."

"I'm sorry, sir." There was no point in going into the details — Trinnock's sudden illness, the blazing video lights, the pummelling questions, that he'd been thrown to the lions. "I got broadsided."

"Bullshit. It was *you* doing the broadsiding. You went out of your way to make us look like bumpkins."

"I was doing my best, Your Worship, to answer the questions honestly."

"Hell, you don't give the media honesty. You give them the goddamn party line. What rock did you just crawl out of?"

"I've learned my lesson, sir. Next time I'll be better prepared."

"Next time? There isn't going to be a next time. Not for you. When we get Trinnock out to pasture, I'm gonna see that we get someone *competent* heading our health unit. Someone like that Dr. Wyatt Burr. Now there's a man who knows what he's doing."

CHAPTER 24

At four forty-five on that most miserable of Mondays, the trill of Zol's office phone nagged at him for the umpteenth time. Whoever it was would have to damn well call back tomorrow. He'd been bashed around enough for one day. And more important, he didn't want to be late for his date with Colleen. Was it really a date? No, he decided, just a drink after work.

As soon as the ringing stopped Anne's buzzer blared. "I think you better take this call," she insisted. "It's Dr. Banbury, and he sounds exasperated."

Zol took the call.

"Dr. Szabo," said Julian Banbury, "I did as you asked. I looked for Extendo-Tox in those brains. It was a massive job. Bloody massive."

"What did you find?"

"Nothing. Absolutely nothing. Immuno-staining for botulinum toxin was negative in every brain."

"Oh."

"Yes. 'Oh.' In point of fact, chasing that wild goose of yours consumed my entire weekend."

Zol rubbed at his temple. "But don't you agree? The link with Extendo-Tox appears to be irrefutable."

"I grant you, it may seem so on paper. But in reality? Not a trace of that toxin in any of those brains. Not even in the densest amyloid plaques."

Damn. "Now what, sir?"

"You must keep hunting for another source of those prions. Animal by-products. Poultry. You'd even be wise to consider fish or seafood." Banbury cleared his throat. "Yes. A new prion emerging from an unexpected source must be responsible for my tulip pattern."

"Are you going to send a sample of Extendo-Tox to the prion lab in Guelph?"

"That would be a complete waste of time."

"But isn't there a remote chance it's contaminated?"

"Good heavens, man. Not bloody likely. Have you forgotten? Extendo-Tox is completely synthetic. I'm certainly not going to risk my reputation making wild allegations against the biggest biotech breakthrough Caledonian's ever accomplished."

Despite the dusk and lengthening shadows, Zol could still see Mr. Wang's water tap across the street. How much ridicule had Dr. Snow endured when he'd exposed the community tap in a London slum as the source of a deadly outbreak of cholera? Had Snow's boss threatened to fire him if he announced his findings? Whatever the circumstances, the man had done the right thing.

"But Dr. Banbury, this is way bigger than our reputations."

"My good man, I'd say you've got yourself into enough trouble already — or should I say horse feathers? I'd be watching my step, if I were you."

Zol ended the call, and with it the workday. Although this had probably been one of the worst days of his life, it wasn't as bad as that day Francine had called him at the hospital. He was a surgical resident at the time, gowned and gloved and assisting at a hysterectomy. She told him that in five minutes she was leaving their marriage, their son, and the country. Max was asleep in his crib; she figured he'd be okay in the house on his own for a while, but he'd be wanting his lunch soon and Zol had better come home and feed him. As Francine's taxi sped toward the airport, Zol raced home, still dressed in his blood-spattered scrubs. When he burst through the door, Max was asleep and the house cluttered by the tempest of Francine's reckless exit. While his ten-month-old son sat in a high chair flinging his lunch at the kitchen walls, Zol called his program director at the Faculty of Medicine. They agreed it was next to impossible for one man to be both a surgeon-in-training and a single parent. Zol transferred to a vacant training spot in the public-health program, where the working hours were predictable and overnight calls were never expected. He came to like public health, and found it worth giving up surgery to have Max all to himself and Francine out of his life. It was a year before she phoned. Collect, from an ashram near Bombay.

At the Nitty Gritty Café across from the health unit, Zol ordered a glass of Australian merlot from a harried barman. Patrons crowded the bar. Marcus had breathed unprecedented bustle into the place by revamping his menu and serving only Fair Trade coffee. He'd brought in milk and cream from an organic supplier, baked his own loaves from stone-ground grains, and found home-style jam that was certified gelatin-free. It was the only place around that anyone trusted to serve prion-free fare.

Zol couldn't remember the last time he'd had a drink before five o'clock, but he wanted one now. He kept his eye out for Colleen. He needed a good dose of her nurturing smile, her delicious perfume. Funny how he was attracted to her common sense. He used to run from it in a woman. That was how he'd ended up with Francine, whose quirky charm soon devolved into recklessness.

Just after five Colleen rang on his mobile to say she was tied up and couldn't join him. She would call him later in the evening. And not to worry that every radio station had played that horse-feathers sound bite all day long. He'd spoken the truth, and sooner or later he would be vindicated. Just hang in there. Her advice was much harder for him to swallow than a third glass of merlot.

He took his drink with him to the men's room. The liquor laws didn't allow people to take alcohol into the washrooms, but no one cared about such trivialities these days. He locked the door of the tiny lavatory. After the hubbub around the bar, the quiet john felt like a haven.

The job of a public-health specialist had turned out to be more about sweating over the public's wrath than protecting its health. As a trainee, he'd been shielded from the harangues of the press and the politicians for five years. But today, less than two years on the job, he'd managed to become a clown in a media circus. If Wyatt Burr took over Trinnock's job, it was clear that Zol would not be staying in Hamilton; he'd either be posted to the rocky wilds of Moose's Testicle or forced right out of public health into some hot, greasy roadhouse kitchen where food was served not by its taste but by its weight. Hell.

He wondered what Hamish thought about all that had happened after their last powwow in the sunroom. It had been a week since they'd spoken, and in that time their orderly investigation had turned into a maelstrom fuelled by accusations, edicts, and fear. Zol knew he'd been too sharp with Hamish on the phone. But what had Hamish expected, calling after midnight, waking a guy up with such an outlandish allegation?

What did Hamish think about Wyatt Burr's brouhaha over the gelatin? Perhaps he was so miffed about the sausages he didn't care. By now, Zol thought, Hamish could see that Public Health had bungled things completely; probably he was staying well away, leaving them to their idiocy.

Since the day he had first stepped into a health unit, Zol had felt the tension between physicians in practice and doctors in public health. Both sides wanted to do the right thing. Clinicians erred in favour of individual preoccupations, the public-health docs in favour of political correctness. Too bad they seldom worked hand-in-hand. Zol swirled the merlot and dipped his nose deep into its bouquet — cherry and cedar overlaid with a hint of wood smoke. He remembered Hamish fussing over the wine he'd brought for dinner. Despite his prissy quirkiness, Hamish was a good guy. He wasn't called the Whispering Warrior for nothing.

Zol gulped the rest of his wine and set the empty glass on the counter by the sink. He pulled his cellphone from his pocket and dialled Caledonian Medical Centre.

"Hello." Hamish's voice rang strong and clear. He must still be drinking his green tea.

"Hi, Hamish. It's Zol."

"I see that."

"What? Oh yeah." Call Display. Should he apologize about the other night or just plunge ahead? He felt the buzz from the merlot and plunged. "What's new?"

"Quite a bit, as a matter of fact."

"Anything you'd like to share?"

"Only with someone who doesn't believe my research is ridiculous."

"Look, Hamish, I'm sorry I snapped at you. I was sound asleep. And . . . and — well, I'm just sorry."

Hamish said nothing, did not even cough or clear his throat by way of an answer. Zol forced himself to continue. "I must have called you half a dozen times to apologize, but you never answered."

"I know." Several silent moments passed until Hamish sighed noisily and clucked his tongue. "You have to admit, all this business about the gelatin, it's a bunch of bull." His tone was clipped, but at least he was talking.

"Don't you mean horse feathers?"

"I suppose." Hamish sounded puzzled. "But hell's bells, it's more like bullshit."

"Where have you been all day, Hamish?"

"In my lab and on the wards. Why?"

"You haven't been watching TV or listening to the radio?"

"Of course not. It *is* a workday, Zol."

"Right. It's just that, um, never mind. You were about to tell me what's new."

"As a matter of fact, I'm expecting the final word in thirty minutes."

"Really? What word?"

"A guy in Guelph is sending me a fax. Going to break your case wide open."

Hamish was still working on the case? Zol hardly dared get his hopes up. "And send Wyatt Burr into a corner licking his wounds?"

"It better."

A volley of crackles threatened to break the connection. Just as it seemed the line had been severed, Zol could hear Hamish's voice loud and clear. "So are you *remotely* interested in hearing about it?"

Zol's cheek's burned from the wine and the verbal slap. "You bet," he replied, keeping his voice as bright as possible. The bathroom door handle rattled, and Zol heard a deep voice grumbling on the other side. He imagined a phalanx of glaring faces, growing longer by the second. "But look, I'm on my cell. In an awkward spot."

The room filled with the boom of impatient knuckles banging against the door.

"What was that?" Hamish asked.

"Tell you later. How about dinner? Tonight, my place. We can talk."

"Do I have to choose the wine again?"

"Not this time. If you've cracked this case, there's a bottle of champagne in my fridge with your name on it."

Zol paid the taxi driver who drove him home, went in, and pulled off his winter gear in the front hall. The merlot still whirred in his head. He said goodbye to Ermalinda and closed the door.

Max stood with his hands on his hips, his face serious. "But *why* didn't you drive the car home, Daddy?"

What was he going to tell Max? That the car had broken down? The battery had died? No, he wouldn't lie. Not to his son. But as he'd learned this morning, telling the bald truth could really dump him in it. He patted his belly. "Because I drank something that didn't agree with me."

"Are you going to throw up on the carpet? Like on Christmas when I got poisoned?"

Zol chuckled and rubbed Max's curly head. "No one poisoned you, Max. You just caught a germ."

Max stood his ground, his arms crossed against his chest. "Grandma said I got poisoned. Like Snow White. 'Cept I didn't fall asleep."

"Okay. We'll call it food poisoning." Zol gripped the door jamb as he was struck by the image of Wyatt Burr's rodent face telling the nation to stop eating gelatin. In any shape or form. "But no one did it on purpose."

"But where's the car?"

"At the office. Don't worry. I'll drive it home tomorrow."

Max lifted Cory from the floor and headed toward the kitchen.

The air hung heavy with the smells of burnt tomato, charred garlic, and overheated olive oil. Ermalinda, bless her, struggled as an uninspired cook who believed that the hotter the stove, the tastier the food. "What'd you have for supper?" Zol said. Maybe there were still the makings of a meal he could throw together.

Max plunked the cat down by his half-eaten dish of fishy mush. "Spaghetti," he said. Cory sniffed the cat food and slinked away, his tail held high. Max grabbed his game gadget from the table and poked at it. After a moment he looked up, a wide smile lighting his face. "Can we play NASCAR Speed Marvels?"

"Dr. Hamish is coming for supper. We have to talk about work," said Zol. As Max's mouth dissolved from toothy delight to firm-lipped dejection, Zol was stabbed by pangs of guilt. This CJD business was eating into their time together. "But look — if you get into your pyjamas and brush your teeth while Dr. Hamish and I are eating, I'll play NASCAR with you when we're done."

"Maybe Dr. Hamish'll wanna play, too."

Zol smiled at the image of Hamish punching the buttons on a video joystick. "Why don't you tell me what you did at school today and I'll see if I can revive Ermalinda's spaghetti."

CHAPTER 25

Hamish padded into Zol's kitchen in his stocking feet an hour later. Zol knew without looking that his shoes would be perfectly aligned by the front door.

"Here you are," said Zol, pressing a thick piece of garlic toast and a Chardonnay spritzer into Hamish's hands. "You got the fax?"

"Most definitely."

"And?"

Hamish put down his wineglass and licked his fingers. "Let me put everything into context." He wiped his hands with a Kleenex, dragged a stool to the counter, and settled himself on the seat. Then he began to recap the saga of the Krooner brothers.

After several minutes of listening to details he mostly knew, Zol couldn't contain himself any longer. "But Hamish, what about the big news from Guelph?"

Hamish took a deep breath. "You know how I said there was a touch of cat meat in Lanny's pork sausages?"

Zol concentrated on the bubbles breaking the surface of his club soda. "How could I forget?"

"Well . . . I was wrong."

Zol looked up. His friend's cheeks were flushed, his eyes narrow, his gaze dipped in embarrassment. "Oh?" said Zol.

"It's *Mustela*. A genus of furry mammals in the ferret family."

That didn't sound good.

Cory padded in and stood by his dish, waving his tail. His amber eyes glowed expectantly, and his whiskers twitched as he let out a meow.

"But what's that Krooner guy doing with ferrets?"

"There's another member of the *Mustela* genus," said Hamish. A smirk brightened his face. "Until a week ago, the Krooners had twenty thousand mink on their farm. They just finished slaughtering most of them for their pelts." He lifted a fine, light-coloured hair from the rim of his wineglass. He picked two more hairs off the counter and folded them into a tissue.

Zol gulped at his soda water. "Don't tell me."

Hamish smiled. "I don't think I need to." He picked up the printed fax. "It's all right here. Krooner's sausages, head cheese, and pork pies are all positive for pork *plus* tissue from an animal of the genus *Mustela*. It must be mink. Lanny as good as told Ken and me when we were up there last week."

"You went to his farm?"

Hamish shrugged and nodded.

"For God's sake. The guy sounds like a whacko. If you'd gone snooping in the wrong place . . ."

"We pretended we got lost while we were hiking," Hamish said, helping himself to another piece of garlic toast. "Had a drink in his kitchen. And from a distance, saw the hog barn and all those mink cages. Lanny let it slip that he added mink meat to his dog food. He called it a tasty delicacy. Said a little went a long way."

Hamish raised his professorial finger. "This means we've found the source of our prions," he continued. "Mink get a disease called transmissible mink encephalopathy. It's a prion brain disease, like mad cow. It was first described in Wisconsin, in 1947. Likely started by feeding mink the meat from lame dairy cows who had unrecognized BSE." He paused and swept the lint from his sleeve. "Ned Krooner's arm was a terrible mess. The mink that bit him was deranged, off its head."

Zol set his elbows on the countertop and rubbed his cheeks with his palms. Oh, God. How many millions of prions had he eaten in Krooner's Viennese sausages? Max, too. Jesus. The thought of Max staring into oblivion, moaning, gob drooling from his mouth . . . Zol shuddered. What if he lost his marbles before Max started losing his? He couldn't let Max watch while he turned into a goddamn vegetable. Would he even know CJD had hit his brain? Would he know he was losing his memory? Or would he keep forgetting he had a problem? His mum and dad would have to move in, look after both of them. What if they got sick, too? Had he ever served *them* those sausages? "Oh my God," he said, "everyone who's eaten Krooner's products is going to get CJD. Max, me, and half of Hamilton."

"That's what Ken said. He's eaten a tonne of Lanny's pies and sausages."

"That's no goddamn comfort."

"I beg to differ."

Zol lifted his head. "What do you mean?"

"There've been only seven cases so far —"

"Plus an eighth in the hospital that Natasha's cousin seems to know about."

Hamish's eyebrows went up. "Okay, maybe eight. But the woman behind the counter at I and W Meats said Krooner's stuff flies off the shelves. With sales that good there should be *hundreds* of cases."

"Wonderful. And we're all in the early stages, waiting for the rot to set in."

Hamish folded his hands and relaxed his face. He looked like a different person, one who'd never known an anxious moment in his life. "No, Zol, you're fine. And you're going to stay that way. I'm sure of it." His opinion came across as a brilliant diagnosis delivered by an expert — measured, sure-footed, and surprisingly comforting. "There have to be many other factors at play," he said. He caught Zol's gaze and wouldn't let go. "The British experience is that almost everyone in the country has ingested prions, but only a tiny group has come down with CJD. Genetic susceptibility seems to be crucial." He unfolded his hands and tapped his chin with his finger. "But I don't think it can be the only factor."

Zol clutched at Hamish's words like a drowning man gripping a life buoy: *only a tiny group has come down with CJD.*

"I'm thinking," Hamish said, his voice still mellow, "there has to be something else affecting the brain. Something working simultaneously with the prions." He picked up his glass and stared into it as though it might contain the answer. "Could be a neurotropic virus, like West Nile. Or an enterovirus, like Coxsackie." He drew a fingertip through the puddle of condensation left by the wineglass. "Or," he said, his face brightening, "maybe a neurotoxin we haven't considered — something in the food supply. Ciguatera contaminating a salmon farm? Mussels poisoned with domoic acid?"

Zol shook his head. He'd have been the first to know if the health unit had been notified of any seafood shipments poisoned by toxins or algal blooms. He hauled his voice through the sand in his throat, wondering if he'd been handed an answer to his prayers. "What about Extendo-Tox? All seven cases received it."

Hamish grabbed the counter. His pupils dilated so completely that his eyes turned from baby blue to almost black. "What? Why didn't you tell me . . ." His face clouded. His feet shifted. He studied his toes. The moment passed, and he shrugged as if to show that last week's estrangement no longer mattered. When he looked up, his eyes were shining. "That's amazing!"

"Banbury doesn't think so."

"All seven cases linked to the same neurotoxin? It has to be important." Hamish pointed behind Zol's shoulder and looked alarmed. "Look! Is that pot on fire?"

"Oh, the spaghetti," Zol said, jumping off his stool and dashing to the smoking pot. He turned off the gas and studied the pasta. The noodles had boiled dry, and half of them were stuck to the bottom of the pan. Those that weren't charred wouldn't exactly be *al dente*, but they'd do. He hit the buttons on the microwave where the tomato sauce was waiting. Zol didn't feel like eating, but

Hamish looked hungry, so he lifted two plates from the cupboard and took Ermalinda's coleslaw from the fridge.

Hamish rubbed at his flat-top. "This Extendo-Tox connection. It has to be our breakthrough. There's no way around it, Zol."

Zol pressed his fingers into the cramp in his neck. He wished he could share Hamish's enthusiasm. "Tell me again — what makes you think there must be other factors besides Krooner's prions causing our epidemic?"

"We've got a few things that don't fit with other reports of human CJD." He started counting on his fingers. "A focused cluster, a short incubation period, a new microscopic arrangement of the plaques in the brain. It looks like something is speeding up the prions. Making them go crazy. Something that works on the nervous system. A virus or a neurotoxin."

"Then Extendo-Tox does make sense?"

"Of course. Especially if it's linked to every victim."

"But," said Zol, "Banbury looked for Extendo-Tox in each one of those brains. Spent all weekend at it. No Extendo-Tox in any of them."

Hamish tapped his foot against the leg of his stool. He examined his fingernails, then looked up and raised a quizzical eyebrow. "What assay did he use?"

"I don't have a clue."

"Do you know what parts of those brains he examined?"

Zol spooned tomato sauce onto two plates of dried-out noodles. "He didn't say. Just that there was no trace of Extendo-Tox in any of the CJD plaques."

Hamish eyed the supper and sat at the table. "Maybe he missed it," he said, tucking a serviette into his collar. "He couldn't have looked in the right place."

"I never thought of that."

Hamish swirled a forkful of spaghetti onto his spoon. "The connection is just too good to pass up," he said, attacking his pasta with gusto. After several mouthfuls he held up his fork. "If the Extendo-Tox is an essential cofactor — but not a source of prions — it might be working at a site other than the actual CJD plaques."

Zol toyed with his dinner. He managed a little of the coleslaw, then put down his fork. "We're still not positive about the source of the prions."

Hamish's eyes shone bright and clear. "We will be soon. I've got a guy at the University of Guelph working on Krooner's samples. He's with the Food Safety Network. Can concentrate prions a thousand times on an RNA filter column and detect them with Western blot."

"How did you get hold of him?"

"Had a long chat with a helpful guy on Friday, when I drove the specimens up to Guelph." He turned his fork through the last of his pasta. "And just for the record," he added, "cats *do* get CJD — feline transmissible encephalopathy."

"Sorry. I should have known . . ."

"Listen," said Hamish, adjusting the alignment of his fork and spoon across his empty plate, "Julian Banbury was one of Extendo-Tox's key developers. He wrote the papers pivotal to confirming its safety. Without him, Extendo-Tox would never have been licensed."

"Watching it rocket to success must have been an unbelievable high for him."

Hamish nodded. "And if it ever takes a tumble, he'll be devastated." He yanked at his serviette and wiped his fingers. "So it's going to be up to *us* to shoot it down."

"Come in and close the door," Zol said to Natasha early the next morning as she strode into his office in response to his call. "Here," he said, clearing a spot on his desk, "you better put down your coffee."

Her face filled with alarm. "Dr. Zol. What's wrong?"

It had taken Zol ages to fall asleep last night. He'd called Douglas Matheson while Hamish was clearing the dishes and discovered that Delia Smart loved the Melton Mowbray pies with the letter K on the crust. After that, his mind had raced through images of Max flopped in his bed, his eyes sightless, his hands clenching a lifeless game gadget, the batteries long dead. At breakfast things hadn't seemed quite so bad as long as he forced himself to focus on Hamish's promise: no one could get CJD without exposure to a cofactor such as West Nile or Extendo-Tox.

He tried to force a smile for Natasha, but it wouldn't come. "There've been some significant developments," he said.

"With the CJD? That's great."

"Except I'm officially off the case." Zol's gaze dropped to the familiar clutter on his desktop. "Strict orders from Dr. Trinnock. After my fiasco on *Canada AM*."

Natasha's mouth gaped. The alarm in her eyes quickly morphed into anger. "That's completely unfair. You can't be off the case. Who else is —"

"Don't worry. I'm not giving up. But I do have to keep a low profile." He gestured toward a chair. "Have a seat." He paused and laced his hands together. "Tell me, do you ever eat pork pies or sausages?"

"No. We're vegetarian. Well, at least most of my family is. Sometimes I eat chicken."

"Then you can be objective."

"Sorry?"

"Hamish Wakefield came to my place last night." Seeing her eyebrows twitch, he quickly added, "Yes, we're working together again."

"That's good news. I really like Dr. Wakefield. Underneath all those brains is a caring heart."

"You took biology, didn't you?"

"My major."

"Then you're familiar with the genus *Mustela*?"

"Um . . . let's see . . ." She gazed at the far corner of the ceiling for a moment, pondered, then looked at Zol. "Ferrets, isn't it?"

He raised his eyebrows and held her gaze. The only way to get this out would be with a bit of drama. He waved his hands in a flourish. "The latest thing in gourmet meat pies and sausages."

"What?" She twisted her mouth. "Dr. Zol, that's disgusting. No one eats ferret."

"Not ferret. But it seems that some of us, Max and me included, have been indulging in a soupçon of . . . of mink."

Natasha clamped a hand over her lips. As Zol told her the story she sat stock-still, bracing herself with her arm against the desk. Her eyes grew larger by the second.

"And Hamish's contact in Guelph," Zol said, glad to be wrapping up the story, "will be able to give us a report about the prions sometime this week." He tucked his hands under his thighs and stared through the window. When he'd entered public health he'd never imagined anything like this would hit so close to home.

Natasha's eyes darkened. "This means hundreds will be affected."

He replied with his mantra, the notion that was keeping him focused, holding him together. "Hamish said not. He said mink prions require a cofactor to cause disease in humans."

"And that cofactor could be Extendo-Tox?"

"Exactly. We have to hope that only a limited number of people ate Krooner's products *and* received Extendo-Tox."

"But it still could be hundreds," said Natasha, pulling at the dark curls at the nape of her neck. "The same clientele that can afford Extendo-Tox also shops at Four Corners, where the prices are . . . well, you know." Her fingers hovered over her coffee mug, but she didn't seem game to take a sip. "So," she asked quietly, "now what?"

"We have to clear Krooner's stuff from the shelves of Four Corners and I and W. And from anywhere else he's been flogging it."

"We'll need a press release — radio, TV, and the *Spectator*. Everyone who has Krooner products will have to return them to the point of purchase."

"And not flush them down the toilet or feed them to their pets."

"Are we going to give a reason for the recall?" she asked.

Zol mulled that one. "We'll have to say something. It has to be the truth but we can't mention prions or CJD. I'm not pulling a Wyatt Burr and going off half-cocked about this. Besides, I'm still off the case."

"Shouldn't we notify the Ministry and the food inspection agency?"

"Technically, yes. But as far as the prions go, we're still only working on a hunch. And Trinnock will have a fit if I connect Krooner's sausages with CJD. I want to hear from the prion lab before we tell anyone what we've discovered. We can't go contradicting the party line with an incomplete case. We'd lose the public's confidence and there'd be chaos. And — I'd get fired."

"Oh, Dr. Zol, please don't say that."

"Our line will be that we're recalling Krooner's products because they haven't been properly inspected."

"The simple truth. Perfect." She shifted in her chair and crossed her ankles. "So, you'll contact the media?"

"After yesterday's horse feathers? No way."

She smiled briefly, then looked anxious again. Her neck and shoulders stiffened. "Dr. Trinnock, then?"

"Yeah. And we can't let him drag his heels. A few days from now we'll be announcing the prion results and revealing the full details of Krooner's mink-meat adulteration. The country's going to go ballistic. And the press will have a heyday scrutinizing our every move with their retrospectoscope."

"And if Dr. Trinnock says no to the recall and the press release?"

"He can't. He'll want to stick by Wyatt Burr and his gelatin, but he can't stop us recalling pork products that Guelph University's Food Safety Network has determined are laced with mink meat. So as long as we don't mention anything about prions, Trinnock will be okay with it."

"And who's going to slap that big red Failed Inspection notice on the Krooner premises?"

"That'll have to be me." Zol fished the loonie from his pocket. He wondered whether it would be safe to go up to Krooner's alone. No. Anyone passing dog food off as gourmet pies and sausages wasn't playing with a full deck. And being a farmer, Krooner would have a gun.

He'd talk to Colleen. She knew how to handle the Krooners of this world.

CHAPTER 26

"I can only give you a few minutes,"
Julian Banbury said, opening his laboratory door to Hamish's knock later that morning.

Hamish had already run the Saab through the car wash,
answered five emails, and signed off a dozen of the consultation letters he'd dictated the previous week. Correcting the letters had
taken longer than he'd anticipated, and he hadn't seen Ned
Krooner yet this morning. He planned to drop by Ned's room as
soon as he'd finished this meeting with Banbury. With luck, Lanny
wouldn't arrive until after the start of visiting hours this afternoon,
and Hamish wouldn't have to face him.

Hamish's stomach constricted at the thought of meeting Lanny
face to face. He wouldn't confront the snarly butcher over his
sausages, but one look into Hamish's eyes and Lanny would know
something was up. And there was no knowing what a guy like him
might do.

Banbury motioned for Hamish to come in. "I don't know what
more I can tell you," he said, his tongue darting back and forth
across his crooked yellow teeth. "As I explained to Dr. Szabo, there's
no botulinum toxin in any of those brains. Not in any form whatsoever."

Hamish cast his eyes around the laboratory. The cramped space churned with clutter. Glassware overflowed in the grimy sink. The curtains hung wrinkled and stained, as though Banbury had been drying his hands on them. How, Hamish wondered, could credible science emerge from such chaos? He crossed his arms tightly against his chest. "What sort of assay did you use?"

"I started with an immunoassay. It uses a polyvalent serum that targets all seven toxin serotypes, A through G."

"And you found no trace of toxin."

Banbury shook his head. "I was afraid your friend Szabo might be onto something with his folded Extendo-Tox theory." He dabbed his handkerchief at the specks of foam collecting at the sides of his mouth. "But it turned out to be science fiction." His tongue quivered. "Extendo-Tox can't possibly fold itself into a prion. Immunohistochemistry revealed nothing resembling botulinum toxin — folded or otherwise — in any of the amygdalas where the tulip-shaped plaques of CJD were concentrated."

"And you tested the brains specifically for Extendo-Tox?"

Banbury cleared his throat and looked away. "No. Extendo-Tox antiserum is too hard to come by. But it shouldn't matter. The polyvalent serum should detect Extendo-Tox just fine."

"Are you sure about that?" How sure could Banbury be about anything that came out of this shambles?

Banbury tightened his fists. His exophthalmic eyes strained in their sockets. "Look, young man. I've been researching neurochemistry for three decades. Since you were in diapers. I *do* know what I'm talking about."

Hamish ran both hands across the bristles of his flat-top, then pushed his fingers into the tightness at the back of his neck. He hated that age-equals-superiority bull. "Yes . . . of course you do, Dr. Banbury," he said, trying to sound contrite but knowing he was probably failing. "But I can't help wondering . . ." He scanned the room, but his eyes couldn't find anywhere to rest that was less chaotic than Banbury's face. "Is it possible to look for Extendo-Tox using a more sensitive method?"

"Well, there is a test designed to detect Extendo-Tox specifically. And it *is* particularly sensitive." Banbury wiped his eyes with his handkerchief and stuffed it into his shirt cuff. "I developed it myself, in point of fact."

"Really?"

Banbury smiled. "I used it to verify beyond a shadow of a doubt that Extendo-Tox doesn't bind to any tissue or receptors outside the peripheral nervous system. The developers didn't want it causing cardiac arrest when it was only supposed to paralyse simple muscle fibres."

"I understand."

"But I no longer have any of the test reagents. I returned them to the company when I finished the project. That is, after we assured ourselves of Extendo-Tox's safety."

"But you can get the reagents again, right? After all . . ."

Banbury stared through the window where a construction crane was lifting a girder toward the top of the hospital's new tower. "Not without a tremendous amount of paperwork." His shoulders sagged. "In point of fact, they'd insist on knowing exactly what I wanted it for and I'd have to sign a new confidentiality agreement that might keep the results buried for months, perhaps a couple of years if their lawyers were to get involved." He cleared his throat with a phlegmy cough. "Something tells me you don't want that."

"Certainly not."

"But to be honest, I don't see how Extendo-Tox can possibly be acting as a prion. Its link with the victims is just coincidental."

"Actually, I've never thought that Extendo-Tox was our prion."

"Our friend Dr. Szabo thinks it is."

"I look at Extendo-Tox as an essential cofactor, but not the only element in play."

"Now you're really complicating the issue." Banbury looked anxiously at his watch as if feeling pressed by his next appointment. "Why don't you let the government agencies do their job and find the prions for us? They know what they're doing."

Where, wondered Hamish, had this man been for the past ten

days? Perhaps he never went grocery shopping and hadn't witnessed the chaos created by Wyatt Burr's wild accusations. But how could he have missed the televised "updates" from the National Microbiology Laboratory in Winnipeg, devoid of any meaningful information? Every day they announced they were testing the Lorreaux chocolates for prions and promised that the results of their investigation would be available "shortly." When the tests did come back from Winnipeg, they were bound to be negative.

Hamish forced himself to hold Banbury's rheumy, pop-eyed gaze. "I've uncovered something that makes it impossible to overemphasize the importance of the link between the CJD victims and their Extendo-Tox injections."

Banbury coughed, looked again at his watch, and eased into the battered metal chair beside his cluttered desk. He swept his thick mane of wavy hair from his brow and rested his hands in his lap. "I sense there is something important you haven't told me about this prion business."

Hamish scanned the room for another chair; there wasn't one. He pulled a wad of tissues from his pocket then wiped the grime from the edge of the closest workbench and leaned against it. He decided he'd better tell Banbury the whole story, without checking with Zol. The old fellow seemed prepared to listen, but maybe only for the moment. If he were as pure a scientist as his cluttered lab suggested, he would be desperate to be the first to tell the neuroscience world how his tulip plaques had come about. But if that meant implicating his beloved Extendo-Tox, would he tell the whole truth?

Hamish worked at a crack in the linoleum with the toe of his brogue. It was essential that Banbury keep quiet about the mink in the sausages until the laboratory in Guelph finished assaying for prions. There was no telling what the Canadian Food Inspection Agency, the Ministry of Agriculture, Health Canada, the combined bureaucracies of three levels of governments, and the WHO would do if Banbury opened his mouth too soon. For starters, Zol would get fired.

"Dr. Banbury," Hamish began, "Zol Szabo and I think we're on to something. But we have to keep it quiet until we've got an airtight case. Can you agree not to say anything about it until Zol says we're ready?"

Banbury stared distractedly at the floor for a moment then raised his hand in a Boy Scout salute. "You have my word. Within reason."

Still leaning against the edge of the workbench, Hamish told Banbury about Ned Krooner's goring by a mink with probable transmissible mink encephalopathy, the discovery of mink meat in Lanny Krooner's products, and the link between Krooner's meats and six of the CJD victims.

At the end of the story Banbury coughed into his handkerchief and wiped his chin. He gazed at the mountain of books and journals on his desk as though recalling something hidden there. He opened his mouth, then looked at the door as if to be sure no one else was within earshot. He licked his lips and said, "Did any of the victims exhibit olfactory aberrations?"

"What do you mean?"

"I'm wondering about the state of their olfactory nerves," Banbury said. He then asked whether any of the victims had hallucinated about wonderful odours, or had complained of terrible smells that no one else noticed, or had lost their sense of smell altogether.

Hamish thought for a moment. Ken had said that Owen woke up one morning and began to hate the smell of coffee. He complained it smelled like vomit and refused to let Ken drink it in the house. That's when Ken switched to green tea. Brenda McEwen had said, only half-seriously, that she thought the fruity aroma of the Lorreaux chocolates made her husband high and fed his addiction to them. And hadn't Natasha mentioned that Rita Spinelli refused to bathe? Had she lost her sense of smell?

"Now that you mention it," Hamish replied, "at least two or three of the cases had problems with their sense of smell. Why do you ask?"

"Post-marketing surveillance of Extendo-Tox has uncovered a

number of recipients with olfactory aberrations. It's all very hush-hush and no one knows what to make of it, but . . ." Banbury stared at the floor as if harbouring thoughts he was not ready to reveal.

Hamish cast his mind back to his neuroanatomy class. It had been a difficult course crammed with minute details, all to be memorized for a final exam. One day the professor brought in a number of powerful scents and asked the class to describe their reactions as they sniffed them. Everyone was amazed how their minds were flooded with vivid details of events they hadn't thought about in years. The professor had then explained the strong bond between memory and the sense of smell, thanks to neural pathways linking the limbic system in the brain with the olfactory nerves in the nose.

Hamilton's CJD victims all had suffered memory difficulties. All had their prion plaques concentrated in their amygdalas, an essential component of the limbic system. "Isn't there a direct connection between the sense of smell and the amygdalas, Dr. Banbury?" Hamish asked.

"Of course. A veritable highway of nerve fibres leads from the odour-detecting receptors in the nose, through the olfactory bulbs tucked beneath the frontal lobes, along the lateral olfactory striae, and into the amygdalas."

"In words understandable to an infectious disease doc," Hamish asked, "what does that mean?"

"It means I must get out those brains, dissect out their olfactory bulbs, and examine them closely. As pathologists, we always ignore the bulbs at autopsy because they're almost never important. Not in determining the cause of death, at any rate."

"Is Extendo-Tox interfering with them?" Hamish asked.

Banbury studied his hands as though the answer were contained within his arthritic knuckles. "It wasn't designed to. But it seems that perhaps — just perhaps, mind you — it could be. At least, in some recipients." He ran his forefinger along his nose. "The nasal lining is so well supplied with blood vessels that negligible amounts of Extendo-Tox in the bloodstream could accumulate in the olfactory apparatus." He paused, his tongue quivering between his lips. His shoulders sagged and he seemed to wither on the chair like the desiccated spider plant on the windowsill beside his desk. "If . . . if Extendo-Tox exerts some sort of unanticipated effect on those olfactory bulbs and receptors, I suppose it's anyone's guess what the consequences might be."

Hamish pictured a text-book drawing of the two olfactory bulbs. They looked like miniature spring onions lying in parallel inside the skull, immediately above the nose. They connected the nose to the brain. If Extendo-Tox locked onto the nasal receptors that generated the sense of smell, it might migrate into the much-ignored olfactory bulbs and further concentrate itself there. And if it injured the bulbs, Extendo-Tox could open a pipeline between the bloodstream, the nose, and the brain, providing prions an expressway into the brain and its amygdala.

"What do we do next?" Hamish asked.

Banbury's chair pitched forward as he stumbled out of it. "We have no choice. We must perform the Extendo-Tox-specific assay on the olfactory bulbs."

"I thought you returned all the reagents to the company."

"Neil Rasmussen owes me a favour," Banbury said, rolling up his shirt sleeves, "and he's bound to have the reagents tucked away somewhere in a freezer." His eyes, red and bulging, half twinkled as he added, "He hasn't thrown anything out in thirty-five years."

CHAPTER 27

Just before ten o'clock that morning,
Zol turned in to his parking spot at
the rear of the heath unit and switched off the ignition. He turned
up the radio. While waiting for the news to come on, he watched
the sparrows huddling in the naked birches outside Mr. Wong's
back door. If they were looking for crumbs, they'd have a long wait
until the busboy put out the garbage sometime tonight. On the
street, the squirrels played a dangerous game of survival-of-the-
fastest against the stream of vehicles speeding down the road,
dodging the potholes and the puddles. How he hated the low
clouds and bitter drizzles that November inflicted on southern
Ontario. Without the sparkle of February's snow and the optimism
of March's strengthening sun, November offered only gloom, a
greyness that invaded the bones.

He told himself he shouldn't feel so glum. The visit he'd just
made to I and W Meats had been illuminating. The ginger-haired
woman behind the counter had coped with product recalls before.
The names of the microbes rolled off her Scottish tongue:
Trichinella, Salmonella, Campylobacter, E. coli. As Zol watched, she
tossed all of Krooner's "improperly inspected" products into a plastic garbage bag, secured it with a length of string, and placed it on

a shelf at the rear of her walk-in refrigerator. She promised not to touch the contents until she heard from the health unit later in the week. She was quick in her assurance that Lanny Krooner considered himself an exclusive supplier and sold his pies and sausages only to her and to Four Corners. And as for his head cheese, she was certain he provided it to no one else except Chef Heinrich at The Hungry Cuckoo. She forced a smile and wrote down the eatery's phone number and address, clearly anxious to redeem the sullied virtue of purveyors of processed meat. The Hungry Cuckoo wasn't open for lunch on Tuesdays, she explained, so Heinrich wouldn't be there until after one.

As Zol sat in the parking lot shaking his head at the latest update from Health Canada, a sticky note was sitting on his computer screen. It had been placed there by Anne some thirty minutes earlier. She wanted to be sure he saw it as soon as he returned. There was no urgency about it, so she hadn't bothered him with a cell-phone call.

"Good news," Anne's note began, "Ermalinda called. Dr. Margolis had a cancellation this morning. Max is getting his injection today! 10:15. On their way now."

At the end of the news, Zol stepped out of his vehicle and glanced up at his office window. The morning's crop of public-health dilemmas could wait a few more minutes. He needed a latte, a tall one in a proper glass with lots of froth. He locked the car and headed down the street to the Nitty Gritty Café. Perhaps Marcus could find him a quiet spot in a back corner.

He took his place in the lineup at the counter. The café was bustling with patrons, refugees from bars whose owners hadn't cottoned to Marcus's winning formula of gelatin-free organic fare. Zol breathed in the earthy aroma of fresh espresso and counted six heads dallying in the queue ahead of him. The young woman behind the counter was flirting with a youth in a baseball cap as he deliberated between a gingersnap and a brownie. The woman's eyes reminded Zol of Colleen's. They spoke of warmth and wisdom. Colleen should be calling back at any time. It had been two hours since he'd left a message on her mobile.

The irresistible fragrance of the coffee intensified as the line diminished ahead of him. When it came his turn, Zol smiled and asked for a latte. An extra tall one. The young woman asked if he wanted it to go. He paused and looked over his shoulder. So much bustle and noise, even in the back corner. He checked the time — almost a quarter past ten. He'd better get back to the office. Yes, he'd have it to go.

He strolled into his office and set the latte on his desk. He felt cheered when he spotted Anne's note and its promise of good news. A moment later his world fell dark. Dread consumed him. The walls pressed inward, and all he could see was the computer's screen saver — Max's drawing of birds and a rainbow over Niagara Falls. He'd been so proud to use every crayon in the box. Now the drawing sneered at Zol and mocked his fatherhood.

He ran his hands through his hair and pawed the wet from his forehead. He grabbed the phone, dialled the switchboard at Caledonian Medical Centre, and lived a millennium through more than a dozen rings before the operator answered and connected him with Dr. Margolis's line. And then the ringing started all over again. His watch said ten seventeen. Please God, may Margolis be like any other doctor — running at least a few minutes late.

A female voice chimed in that unmistakeable answering-machine tone: "We are in the office but on the phone at the moment, or helping other patients. If this is a medical emergency, call nine-one-one or go to your nearest Emergency Department."

His opened his mouth, his entire being frozen in concentration

and poised to leave a firm but simple message. Though far from
ideal, it might do for the moment. But six words came back at him
in the same flat tone, filling him with rage and panic:"This machine
does not take messages."

He stared through Max's rainbow on the monitor.

What could he do?

He could get in the car and storm Margolis's office. No. It was
a fifteen-minute drive to Caledonian's campus on Mud Street. Too
long.

He could tell Bell Canada to break in on the line. A public-
health emergency. No, he'd tried that before. He would have to
connect with three automated attendants, then speak with two
supervisors. And if the line were managed by a computer, he
couldn't break through anyway.

He looked again at his watch. Ten eighteen. He dialled the
paging operator at Caledonian. Lake Ontario could have drained to
nothing in the time it took an operator to answer.

Finally, he asked for Hamish.

"Dr. Wakefield is not on call, I'll put you through to Dr. Yang who
is the resident on call for infectious diseases. One moment pl—"

"No," Zol shouted. "I must speak with Dr. Wakefield. No one
else. Tell him it's Dr. Szabo — public health."

"You don't need to shout, sir. I'm just following procedure."

"Can't you just try his pager?"

"Dr. Wakefield is very particular. When he's not on call, he can
only be disturbed for a good reason."

"This is life and death."

The line clicked, and Zol heard a radio station; violins were
playing through an ad for a funeral home. He pictured himself
standing beside a junior-sized coffin in a carpeted room where
everything was suffused in grey. The music clicked off, and Hamish's
husky whisper scratched down the line.

"Thank God," said Zol.

"Hell's bells, Zol. What's up? I got paged Star One, that means
either cardiac arrest or a bomb threat."

Zol explained. Asked him to run over to Dr. Margolis's office. Do whatever it took to stop Max's injection.

"Be there in a flash."

Zol dashed down the stairs to the parking lot, chastising himself as he ran. How could he be so stupid? One way or another, he should have got hold of Margolis and cancelled Max's injection. At the very least he should have told Ermalinda he'd withdrawn his consent. That way, she would have called him about the last-minute appointment instead of following his previous instructions.

Shot or no shot, he had to be with Max, to hold him in his arms, breathe the green-apple smell of his hair.

The display on the phone said ten twenty as Hamish hung up. He strode to the door of the semi-dark viewing room. He'd been reviewing a CT scan in the imaging department when his beeper went off. His hand gripped the knob but stopped short of turning it. There was no use in dashing, blind and panicked, into the hectic, brightly lit maze of the department.

What was the fastest route to the children's care and research tower? Should he take the stairway at the end of the corridor, dash up one flight, then follow the elevated walkway? No, he had no idea which floor Margolis was on. Switchboard would know, but they took forever to answer. He could zip down three flights — or was it four? — and take the sub-basement passage. No. Too much running, too many stairs, too much time. He remembered the smoking terrace outside the cafeteria. That was it: two flights down, out the rear doors by the vending machines, across the terrace, and through the main door of Children's Care. A panel in the lobby listed all the docs and their offices.

Three minutes later, his legs seized with cramp, Hamish threw open the door to Dr. Margolis's office on the seventh floor of Children's Care. He leaned against the jamb, unable to take another step. His throat screamed for air. His heart pounded in his neck. He hadn't done flights like this since he'd carried the code blue beeper as a resident. And even then they insisted you walk, not run, to cardiac arrests.

All eyes in the waiting room turned in his direction. Mothers clutched their children to their laps, alarmed and annoyed at the red-faced madman wheezing in the doorway. He swept the room with his gaze — no sign of either Max or Ermalinda. Spasms clenched his throat in a grip too tight to launch a single word at the reception window on the far side of the waiting room. Still leaning against the door, he dug for the puffer in his lab coat. One pocket, then the other. Hell — he'd left it at his office.

As he gasped in the doorway, two crucial minutes evaporated. It tore him apart to see them wasted, but he had no choice. He could barely move, and he certainly couldn't speak. The receptionist eyed him from her wicket but said nothing. The incessant ringing of her phone kept her in her seat. The mothers stared, lips tight, feet planted, knees clamped. Their children squirmed over their colouring books and game gadgets. Hamish wanted to wave a hand as if to say, *Don't worry, I just need a sec,* but his embarrassment paralyzed him as much as the run up the stairs. His watch ticked to ten twenty-three. Had Max already had his needles?

When he figured he could manage a few words, he crossed the waiting room and slumped against the receptionist's counter. "Max Szabo? Gotta see him."

"Are you all right, sir? Your breathing. Should I call nine-one-one?"

He flicked his hand. "I'm okay — gotta see — Max."

"Excuse me. Are you a relative?"

"Friend — colleague."

"Then you'll have to take a seat. Max won't be long. In fact, Dr. Margolis is running early this morning."

Hamish clutched the edge of the counter as his stomach somersaulted. "His father sent me — must cancel injection."

"Cancel it?" said the young woman, clearly miffed at his intrusion into her ordered sphere.

He nodded vigorously.

"You can't just . . ." She looked at his name badge. There was a softening of the indignation in her face. Less authority, more respect. She rubbed at her ear. "I'm afraid you're probably too late," she said, the confidence now drained from her eyes. "But if you wait just a moment, I'll get the nurse." She rose from her seat and scurried into the hallway behind her desk.

"Hurry. Life 'n' death," Hamish croaked after her. He leaned on the counter. *Please God, wherever You are, spare Max that injection.*

Three clocks on the walls of the inner office said *Swiss Made* and ticked off the seconds, as if mocking his predicament. After thirty-seven ticks a scowling middle-aged nurse, her hips overfilling a pastel-blue pantsuit, opened the inner-office door. She motioned Hamish inside.

In her sturdy white shoes she stood three inches taller than Hamish. "What's going on?" she asked, clutching a clipboard to her ample chest.

"Dr. Szabo sent me." Though he felt like a schoolboy, he was relieved he could finally speak in sentences. "To stop his son's injection. We've discovered a problem. The Extendo-Tox. It might be lethal."

Her face stiffened. "Lethal? Heavens, no." Her hand massaged the wattle beneath her chin. "We've injected dozens of kids —"

"Has Max had his yet?"

She studied her clipboard. "Max Szabo? Oh yes. All done. Dr. Margolis is observing the effects right now." She scanned Hamish's name tag then searched his eyes. "You *have* to be mistaken about the Extendo-Tox."

"I must see Max."

The woman moved to the centre of the corridor, leaving no doubt that Hamish would have to push her out of the way to get any farther. "I can see you're upset, Dr. Wakefield. But the procedure was completed a good ten minutes ago, and it won't help Max if you barge in there now." She gave Hamish a confidential pat on the forearm. "And you know what doctors are like — very definite about how things are done." She looked again at her clipboard as if figuring out the best way to handle such a sticky situation. "Tell you what — I'll take you to Dr. Margolis's study. He'll join you there in a couple of minutes."

The hallway spun. Hamish steadied himself against the wall, managed a nod, and followed the woman down the hall to an oak-panelled den and dropped into a padded leather armchair. Ten minutes! The time bomb had begun ticking in Max's brain ten minutes ago. How long before the boy forgot which buttons to push on his game gadget? Dear God. If only Zol had called sooner. Hamish could have been the hero instead of the wheezing wuss, the useless fool who'd barged into a room jammed with people who couldn't wait to tell everyone about the crazy doctor. It would be all over the medical centre in a flash.

His ears burned.

He stared at a knot in the pinewood panelling and pictured prions and Extendo-Tox swirling deep into Max's brain.

As his head spun, a voice Hamish didn't recognize intruded into his thoughts. It spoke with conviction but without harshness. *Hell's bells,* the voice said, *what does it matter that those tight-assed mothers watched you gasping, red-faced and nearly barfing? Why should you give a shit how ridiculous you looked to them? Ten minutes from now those women will be telling their friends what they witnessed in the waiting room, but ten weeks from now they'll have forgotten all about it. But you, Hamish, maybe you won't forget this day. Not if it's the day you finally risked liberating yourself from your bogeyman, risked throwing off your self-imposed fear of criticism. It's time you put a stop to the tyranny of humiliation that makes you constantly look over your shoulder. Stop fretting that hints of disapproval are going to add to the warehouse of rebukes hurled at you in loneliness by your mother and harboured in bitterness by your father.*

At the approach of heavy footsteps, Hamish felt the tightness grip his chest again. Any second Zol would thunder into the room. What in God's name was Hamish going to say to him?

I did my best, but hell's bells, you should have called me sooner. Anyway, you should have cancelled the damn injection.

No. Not harsh candour.

Max is a great kid. You're strong. You can take it one day at a time.

No. Not platitudes.

Zol deserved the unembroidered truth, free of anger and recrimination.

I'm sorry, Zol. I'm so sorry.

CHAPTER 28

Max strode ahead through the parking lot beside the children's tower. If he wondered who'd been yelling in the doctor's office while he sat with Ermalinda in the waiting room, he showed it only in the stiffness of his gait. No skipping, no running, just the business of getting to the car with Zol's keys at the ready. He pressed the fob twice and slid open the rear door, then stared at his left hand. He held his tongue between his teeth and grinned as his palm opened, closed, opened again. He shuffled his feet and planted his toes, then plucked the keys from his right hand and tossed them with his left, yelping at the strength and precision of his throw.

"Terrific!" Zol forced himself to say as he caught the keys. He glanced at Ermalinda but got no response. She'd clamped her face into that neutral facade she wore whenever she didn't want to show what she was thinking. And she'd wrapped herself in a parka of worry. Or perhaps it was anger. Or was it shame? Of course she'd heard the shouting and noticed the tears bloating Zol's face. But in fairness, she had no idea what she'd done by bringing Max in for that needle. And why should she? She would have been thrilled when the nurse called from Margolis's office this morning with the offer of a last-minute appointment. Zol and Max had been talking about the needle for weeks; it was supposed to be a sort of Christmas present.

Zol leaned into the minivan and tousled Max's hair, then planted a kiss on the youngster's forehead. Max made a face and looked out to be sure no one was looking. Zol lingered there a moment. He needed a strong dose of hope more than anything, right now. Hope that there was substance to the promises the neurologist had made a few minutes earlier. Margolis had bristled when Zol and Hamish had exploded with their suspicions about Extendo-Tox. He'd insisted he knew of no childhood cases of CJD, not even in the United Kingdom where kids were mad for bangers and burgers. Kids' meals were loaded with more prions than anything else in the food chain, yet youthful brains were resilient, he'd said, like plastic. And resistant to CJD.

Zol wanted to believe him. But after Wyatt Burr, he'd lost his trust in experts.

Hamish dawdled through the corridors of the medical centre. There was no premium on the fastest route from the children's tower to his office, and he strolled through a fog. As he'd watched Zol, Max, and Ermalinda walk in sombre silence away from Dr. Margolis's office, he'd felt resolutely out of place. Excluded from the intimacy of the family circle. He'd done his best, but it wasn't enough. Not by a long shot. And where was he left when his best wasn't good enough? The answer was simple: tongue-tied, and alone.

His fingers unlocked the door to his office, his arms shrugged out of his lab coat, his hands hung the coat on the corner rack. His eyes strayed to his agenda. He shuddered. He couldn't imagine facing students this afternoon. What was the topic of their seminar? Congestive heart failure. Broken hearts. How fitting. The keys to the Saab beckoned from his desk, urged him to seek the noisy peace of the car wash.

As the Saab approached the entrance to its sudsy second home, his foot came off the accelerator. His toes hovered above the brake but refused to touch it. Obstinate, they jerked to the gas pedal, gunned it, and propelled the car into the stream of noontime traffic. His hands steered the vehicle into a right turn at the next traffic light, then through two dozen city blocks.

At the underground parking lot his right arm set the handbrake. His fingers pushed the button to call the elevator for the ascent to the fifth floor. His feet carried him toward the reception desk where a young woman was talking on the phone. It was clearly a personal call, and she managed to fit the word *like* into every sentence. Her hair hung partway across her left eye, and every few seconds she flicked the strands to the side with a toss of her head.

She put down the phone, tossed her head, and granted Hamish a look of utter boredom. "Help you?"

"Um, yes."

Although she didn't quite roll her eyes, it was clear she deemed him yet another pest in a long morning of nuisances. "Well?"

"I need to see Mr. Cheung."

She rubbed her thumb over a manicured cuticle. "Like, I have two Mr. Cheungs. The lawyer or the handyman?"

"Kenyon Cheung. The lawyer."

"What time's your appointment."

"Ah . . . actually, I don't have one."

"Mr. Cheung only sees people, like, by appointment."

"But this is an important matter. It's *medical*."

"Well," she said, tossing her head, "give me the file number and, like, I'll see what I can do."

"File number?"

Her shoulders heaved a dramatic sigh. "Like, every malpractice case has a file number. If you give me the number I can ask Mr. Cheung if he has time to discuss the case with you."

"This isn't malpractice." Not yet, anyway. "But it's urgent. And *personal*."

She seemed suddenly interested. She flicked the hair from her eye and studied Hamish closely. Swept him up and down. Her gaze was so piercing, so judgemental that it shook him out of his stupor.

His pulse quickened. What was she looking at? He inspected his tie. Was there something wrong with it? Was there something wrong with him?

Oh, no. She could tell he was gay. She would know that Ken was gay; he didn't hide it. She must be thinking Hamish had picked Ken up in a bar and was coming to tell him he'd got an STD. Oh God, was Ken into the bar scene?

He took another deep breath. *Remember,* he told himself, *what she thinks of you doesn't matter.*

The young woman waved her ballpoint. "Sir? I need your name."

"Sorry. Hamish Wakefield. Dr. Wakefield. From the health unit." Why had he mentioned the health unit? That was stupid. Now she was really going think he was here about an STD. "And, uh, I'm also at the university."

She shrugged, then lifted the phone. A moment later she motioned toward a plush armchair and a matching loveseat. "He won't be long."

Too restless to sit, he grabbed a copy of the *New Yorker* from the coffee table. An ad pictured an enormous chrome and granite kitchen. It was obscene and frivolous on the heels of the heartache in Margolis's office just minutes ago. Still, he found the magazine a welcome distraction. He'd only thumbed as far as the table of contents when he heard Ken's voice.

"Hamish. What a surprise." Ken's dark eyes sparkled as he shook Hamish's hand and added a reinforcing squeeze to his arm. "Good to see you. Come on in." He pointed to a brightly lit corridor lined with original oils. "My office is just down here." He shot a glance sideways and tightened his lips as he lowered his voice. "I see you met our Tiffany."

With the office door closed behind them, Ken patted Hamish's shoulder and asked, "So, what's up? Some breaking news about the case? I can't believe all the uproar."

"A lot of smoke and mirrors." The butterflies were having a heyday as they rose and fell inside Hamish's stomach. "But I do have two important things to tell you. The first one is easy, and . . ." Hamish looked at his brogues and noticed they could do with a polishing. "The second is more complicated."

"Have a seat."

Hamish found it easier to give important news — good and bad — standing up. He could pace away his nervousness and make a quick exit if he needed to. "I'd rather stand."

"You look anxious," said Ken. He forced a smile. "Maybe *I* need to sit down."

"No," said Hamish. "There's no bad news."

"Start with the easy part."

"You know how Owen used to get Extendo-Tox for his voice-box problem?"

"Sure."

"Have you . . . have you ever been injected with it?"

"With Extendo-Tox?" Ken touched his forehead, as if feeling for wrinkles. "Why? Do I need it?"

Hamish's legs felt weak, as if the only thing holding them up was the dread that — somehow, somewhere — Ken had been injected with Extendo-Tox. "*Please.* Tell me. Yes or no."

"No. Never. Not even close."

"Oh, I can't tell you what a relief that is."

"Why? What's all this about?"

Hamish scanned the room for a glass of tea, or even water. Nothing. He swallowed hard. "All seven victims got injections of Extendo-Tox."

"What?"

"It can't be a coincidence. Extendo-Tox is a toxin. It affects the nerves. It's not supposed to affect the brain but it must be causing the CJD."

"Wait a sec. What about the mink in Krooner's sausages? You said —"

"It takes both. The prions in the sausages *and* the Extendo-Tox in the injections. Together, they are causing rapid-onset CJD, I'm almost sure of it."

Ken crossed his arms, and his face grew pregnant with suspicion. "But I thought you said it's genetics that makes the difference. Owen's bad gene made him get CJD from Krooner's prions. You told me I'm okay because I have the good gene." He ground his foot into the carpet. "Are you changing your story?"

Hamish stepped back and clasped his hands in front of his chest. He felt sick, unnerved by Ken's unexpected skepticism. Ken should be thrilled at such good news. "No, no," Hamish pleaded, "I'm strengthening the scenario. In your favour. We've discovered that *both* agents — prions *and* toxin — are essential. It takes Lanny Krooner's prions *and* the Extendo-Tox to trigger this new form of CJD."

Ken narrowed his eyes. "Are you certain? Or is this just another theory?"

"We're waiting for a couple of confirmatory tests, but our data are watertight so far."

Ken shoved his hands into his pockets and looked toward the ceiling.

"Let me put it this way," Hamish continued, still pleading, "Extendo-Tox is essential to the case, not a coincidence." He reached forward and touched Ken's upper arm. "This time I'm willing to bet my career that you're in the clear."

Ken pursed his lips and let out a deep groan as he leaned heavily against his desk. He pondered the situation for several moments then pulled himself upright. "That's quite the ante," he muttered. "Between favourable genetics and this news about Extendo-Tox, you haven't left much room for reasonable doubt." He stepped forward, extended his arms, and folded them around Hamish. "I've been thinking about little else these past few days."

Hamish's shoulders stiffened at the unexpected gesture, but he quickly found himself savouring the wonder of Ken's male body, warm and firm, wrapped tightly around his own.

They broke their embrace, and each man showed the other an awkward, incomplete smile. "You said there were two things," Ken said, and stabbed at the corners of his eyes.

"Yes, Extendo-Tox by injection and prions in the sausages."

"I got that. But you started out by saying you had two things to tell me. You've told me the easy one. What about the complicated one?"

Hamish studied the patterns in the Oriental carpet at his feet. Birds, lilies, pomegranates all entwined on a tree of life. "I also came to tell you that . . . that . . . oh, this is so . . ."

"Tell me what?"

"That your friendship means a great deal to me." His eyes remained glued to Ken's face. If it scowled in disdain, he could be out of there in a flash.

A smile began to bud at the corners of Ken's eyes.

Emboldened, Hamish continued, "But no, that's not quite right."

Ken's smile stalled.

It was now or never. Hamish's heart pounded. His tongue grated like sandpaper against the roof of his mouth. "Let me put it this way — I've . . . I've fallen for you." He stepped back. "There, I've said it."

Ken's face beamed a fully ripened smile. He clasped Hamish's face and looked into Hamish's eyes as if peering into his soul. A long moment passed, then he pressed his lips against Hamish's. At first his touch was dry. It didn't feel like much. Then the softness of Ken's tongue found its mark inside Hamish's mouth. He couldn't believe what was happening, how wonderful it felt.

They pulled apart and studied each other's faces, both men smiling broadly. Ken locked the door. They embraced and kissed again.

"I was hot for you," Ken said, "that Saturday you first came to my place. But . . ." His gaze dropped, then found Hamish's eyes again. "It was too soon."

Hamish nodded and raised his index finger. "For both of us."

As Hamish stood there, drinking in Ken's presence, he realized he was basking in the thrill of a validation that had always eluded him. They said opposites were supposed to attract, but he knew he revelled in the similarities he shared with Ken. He took comfort not only in the equality in their heights but in the shared scent of their colognes and the firmness of their bodies. In the similarities in their haircuts, their clothing, their appreciation of order and neatness.

"You know," Ken said, "I love the way you raise your index finger whenever you're saying something important. It's so phallic."

Hamish dropped his hand to his pocket. "Oh God. You'll make me self-conscious. *Forever.*"

"No. Just let it be a reminder of me."

Hamish felt his cheeks blush, his ears burn. "I . . . I wasn't sure I should . . ."

"I'm so glad you did," Ken said, taking Hamish's hands. "But maybe I've got some convincing to do." He glanced at the agenda open on his desk. "I'm clear until three. How about you?"

Hamish told him about his seminar from two until five.

Ken checked at his watch. "We've got almost two hours. Fantastic. My place?"

"You mean . . . Now?"

"Absolutely."

Hamish shivered. Everything about this moment was bursting with freshness and uncertainty. "You'll . . ." He stared again at the carpet. "You'll have to show me the ropes."

Ken laughed. "No ropes and no chains. No leather, either." But when he sensed Hamish's anxiety at being misunderstood, he added gently, "Don't worry, Hamish. It'll be my pleasure. And yours, too. I'll see to that." He pointed to the bulge in Hamish's trousers. "Is that a box of condoms in your pocket?"

"No. I'm just . . . you know . . . happy to see you."

Ken laughed. "Good one. We'll pick some up on the way."

CHAPTER 29

Zol sank deeper into his living-room sofa, losing himself in Eric Clapton's chords. Max had returned to school; he couldn't wait to show off his brand-new hand. Zol had wanted to insist he stay home after the trip to the doctor, but what good would that have done? Max was a normal boy — at least for now — and of course he wanted to be with his friends. After he'd skipped away from the car, Zol sat in the school parking lot with the engine running, gazing at the red-brick wall until the crossing guard waved him off the property.

Now the CD player throbbed an endless loop of "Tears in Heaven" into the living room. He'd cried uncontrollably at first, sharing Eric Clapton's pain at the death of his son. Soon it would be Zol's turn to know such grief. Finally his tears were spent, and his cheeks stung as they dried. He stared at the cold, dark artificiality of the logs in the unlit fireplace. He couldn't imagine ever lighting it again.

A flicker of movement brushed the edge of his vision. He turned with a start to see Colleen standing in the living-room doorway. Worry and benevolence muted her face.

"I didn't mean to startle you," she said, then quickly added, "Ermalinda let me in." She opened her arms. "How *are* you, Zol?"

He paused the CD player and hauled himself off the sofa to accept her hug. His shoulders heaved as his sobbing started again.

"What's wrong?" she whispered.

He gripped her tight and sensed the iron strength of her tiny frame. "You've been talking to Hamish?"

"No. Ermalinda called me. Said you were upset but she didn't know why. Asked me to come over."

"So you don't know what happened?"

"Bad news?"

Zol released himself from the warmth of Colleen's body and dropped onto the sofa. When she started to sit in the armchair he touched the cushion beside him and said, "Please . . ."

He rubbed his palms on his thighs and swallowed hard. Despite the tightness in his chest the story poured out of him. It felt good to get it out.

"But it sounds like there's hope," Colleen said when he'd finished. "If the doctor said kids don't get CJD, it sounds like Max will be okay."

"But this is a different sort of CJD — no one has ever seen it before. And if the Extendo-Tox lets the prions in and speeds them through the brain, then it won't matter a damn that Max's neurons are more plastic than an adult's."

"You mustn't give up hope."

"It's not that easy."

"When that airliner crashed into the Atlantic with Liam on board, I spent three days hoping, hoping, hoping he'd be the sole survivor. That someone would find him floating on a piece of wreckage in Peggy's Cove." She squeezed Zol's arm. "I knew in my heart it was a ridiculous notion, but I felt I owed it to him. To give up hope was to abandon him to the icy waters."

"But this is different. It wasn't your . . ." Zol's chest tightened. He could barely get out the words. "It wasn't your fault that Liam died."

She put her arm around his shoulders and drew in close. "Zol. It wasn't *your* fault that Max got the Extendo-Tox. You tried to cancel it — you called two months in advance, for heaven's sake. It isn't your fault that Margolis's bloody machine doesn't take messages. And it wasn't anyone's fault that the doctor had a last-minute cancellation." Her palm stroked its warmth into the back of his hand. "Zol. You have to keep going. You have to prove the case against the sausages and the Extendo-Tox. You have to stop anyone else from getting CJD."

He closed his eyes and threw back his head. "I'm off the case. Trinnock said I'm fired if he finds me within a mile of the investigation."

"That's ridiculous."

Zol shrugged. "Trinnock's got me on a short leash. Wants to see me every afternoon. Make certain I'm behaving myself. But screw it. I'm not going back to the office today just so he can look me over."

"But you've got to tell him about Krooner's pies and sausages."

"The hell with it. He said I'm off the case."

"Zol, that doesn't sound like you. Besides, you didn't go looking for the information about Krooner and the mink meat. Hamish dropped it in your lap. And now that you know about it, you have to go public with it."

"I *was* going to tell him this afternoon."

"So — what's stopping you?"

"Not today." Zol pointed to his face. "Look at me. I must look a wreck. I can't face the office like this."

"When Liam's plane went down I wanted to hide in the house so no one would have to suffer the embarrassment of talking to me."

"You? In hiding?"

She nodded. "For three days. And then I remembered a poem we studied in school. Robert Frost."

"Robert Frost? You studied him? In South Africa?"

Colleen shrugged. "Of course."

"And what did he say?"

"'The best way out is always through.'"

"What?"

"'The best way out is always through.' Look, when you're paddling in the Zambezi, and you're suddenly up to your neck in crocodiles, you have to head for the closest riverbank, climb past all those teeth, and keep running until you're safe and dry. Or die trying."

At three thirty, as scheduled, Peter Trinnock waved Zol into his office. As Zol crossed the threshold, his gut tightened at the memory of yesterday's televised encounter right here in front of the Chippendale desk. But that was nothing compared to the ache in his heart over Max and the Extendo-Tox. He felt as though some misalignment in the universe had thrown his life into chaos. The random motions of all the molecules that up to then had given him a life of privilege and contentment were now aligned on a malignant path.

Trinnock, myopic, squinted and lifted his spectacles from his desk. He rubbed at them with a tissue. "It's been a bloody awful week," he said. His breathing showed no sign of yesterday's asthma. "My wife won't go near a grocery store, so we're down to rice and tinned corn. And the last of the four-pound Cheddar we bought in Balderson last summer." He huffed steam onto his glasses and worked at a defiant smudge. "How about you and Max?"

Zol wished the man would put on his bloody glasses and stop that awful pig-like squinting. "We're okay," he said. "Still lots of meat in the freezer, but Max says he's getting overdosed on pasta."

A smile almost formed on Trinnock's lips. Despite his brusqueness, he always had a soft spot for Max. What would he say when he found out about the Extendo-Tox injection?

"Look," Trinnock said, hooking the bows of his glasses over his ears, "it's safe to say we've both been distracted. Toronto and Ottawa raising hell on our turf, jockeying for butt-saving headlines. And the mayor and the minister furious about your horse feathers business."

Zol locked his face in neutral and fixed on the stripes on Trinnock's tie. That horse feathers thing was going to haunt him forever, stick to his reputation like porridge on a cast-iron pot. He held his breath while his fingers worried at the loonie in his pocket.

"It doesn't help," Trinnock continued, "that we haven't heard a peep from the prion boys in Winnipeg." He blew his nose and fired a look that said he expected a response. When Zol could only answer with a solemn nod, Trinnock straightened his glasses and said, "Well? There must be *something* new."

Zol took a moment to organize the jumble of thoughts in his head, then described how he and Natasha had tracked the Streptococcus outbreak at Shalom Acres to its source — the strep-infected eczema on the hands of the personal support worker. "But," he said to Trinnock's approving nod, "the mayor isn't happy. Tore a strip off me after yesterday's TV spot, then blasted me for not getting the Shalom Acres thing settled a whole lot sooner."

"Leave him to me," Trinnock replied. "The mayor is paid for his bluster. It helps in the polling booths."

Zol steeled himself again, knowing Trinnock's good mood would evaporate as soon as he heard about Krooner's sausages. "There've been some developments up in Campbellville you need to know about," he said, feeling as if he'd just pulled the pin from a hand grenade. "Only came to light in the past few hours."

Trinnock frowned and drew back. "Yes?"

"A small-time meat processor is . . . well, he's mixing mink meat into his pork pies and sausages." He told Trinnock about Hamish testing Krooner's samples and visiting Krooner's farm, then getting the *Mustela* results from the laboratory in Guelph.

Trinnock's face turned ashen. Even his hands went grey. "Jesus wept."

Zol was itching to spill his theory about the role of Extendo-Tox, but he held his tongue. Instead he said, "I need to talk to you about issuing some sort of press release before we get the prion results from the lab in Guelph."

Trinnock dropped his spectacles onto the blotter. "Bloody hell."

He rubbed at his tiny, alien eyes. "What are we going to say? Sorry folks, the gourmet chocolates aren't the culprit after all? It's really a madman up in Campbellville who's been spiking meat pies and sausages with contaminated mink meat?" Trinnock shook his head. "No goddamn press release. Not yet."

"But we've got to stop people from eating any more of Krooner's products."

"You said you already cleared them from the shelves."

"But just from the stores. What about people's fridges? Maybe he sells through outlets we don't know about."

Trinnock replaced his glasses. "A few more hours aren't going to make any difference. Not after all this time. We can't issue another alert without a proper investigation. The public won't stand us crying wolf again. And," he said, slamming his desk with his palm, "we've got to bloody well do the investigating ourselves. Look what happened when we got sideswiped by Toronto."

Zol did his best to keep a smirk off his face. "Am I back on the case?"

Trinnock peered over the top of his spectacles. "Looks like you were never off it."

Zol cleared his throat. "I think the first priority is an inspection of Krooner's place."

"Good idea," Trinnock said. "Have a look for yourself before we issue any press release."

Both men glanced out the window. In about half an hour the November gloom would descend into night.

"Scout out the farm in the morning." Trinnock raised a finger in warning. "Take a colleague with you. And don't push it. The proof of the pudding will be finding prions in Krooner's products. Are you sure Guelph is up to it?"

Zol nodded.

"Then as soon as we hear from them," Trinnock said, "we'll call the police."

CHAPTER 30

At eight forty-five the next morning Zol hovered with Colleen in the vestibule at the health unit. He frowned at his watch and cinched his scarf against the blasts that roared through the outside door every time someone pulled it open.

Where was Natasha? There'd been no answer when he'd phoned her apartment a few minutes ago. She was supposed to meet them here at eight fifteen for the inspection of Krooner's farm. It was Colleen's idea to have both women accompany Zol. Safety in numbers, she'd insisted, and the presence of two females would make the mission appear more like a matter of public safety than the first step in a criminal prosecution.

They checked their watches a final time and shrugged in resignation, then headed for Colleen's Mercedes.

Soon they were cruising north of the city on Highway Six, past the farms and fields that stretched to the horizon. The landscape undulated like a foreign state, a ramshackle republic of rolling hills blighted by bashed-up vehicles, twisted lawn chairs, and rusting appliances. Zol found it unsettling leaving the ordered hubbub of the brick-and-concrete city. Although farming country lacked the scars of the big-box stores and gaudy billboards, and looked pretty from a distance, the illusion stopped at the gates of the scrap-littered farmyards where pride of place took a back seat to expedience. To top it off, the biker gangs, chop shops, and rogue butchers like Lanny Krooner rendered the countryside no more secure than the dark alleys of the inner city.

Zol ran his fingers along the wood-grain panel covering the glove compartment of the Mercedes. Was he touching rosewood or something cooked up in a German chemical factory? He turned to Colleen. "It's just not like Natasha," he said.

Colleen looked thoughtful but not anxious. "As I said, there's bound to be a good explanation. I don't imagine there's cause for worry." She depressed the left-turn signal and guided the smooth-throated vehicle past a rusting jalopy.

"I'm not so sure. She's got an incredible memory, and she's never late."

The GPS on the dashboard displayed the most efficient route, via Carlisle and Kilbride, to the Krooner farm. It projected an ETA of nine fifty. They'd be there in twenty minutes.

"I shall have you back in your office before you know it," said Colleen. "And if there's still no sign of her, I'll ring my contact at the city police."

A lump cramped the pit of Zol's stomach. He shifted in his seat. "How do you think Krooner's going to react when we close down his shop?"

"Depends on how much we tell him."

He wondered how she could look so calm in the face of confronting a villain. "I wasn't going to mention the mink meat."

"Good thing," she agreed.

"He'd just deny it."

"It doesn't matter if he denies it. We don't want him going ballistic." She touched her hand to her chest. "Hold your cards close. We must keep Krooner on the defensive, uncertain how much we know."

Zol hauled a loonie from his pocket and weaved it through his right hand. "You're right. Trinnock will be satisfied if we have a look at Krooner's operation then serve the man with a temporary suspension of his operations." Zol palmed the coin and mimed quotations marks with his fingers. "Pending further investigation."

"You can shut him down? Just like that?" she asked, snapping her fingers.

"If he claims he isn't slaughtering animals, and he's processing meat that's already been inspected by the feds or the province, and he's just selling locally, *then* he comes under our jurisdiction." Zol flicked the coin skyward with his thumb and grabbed it in mid-air. "And yes, I can shut him down."

"Where do the feds come in?"

"They inspect all the kill floors preparing meat for transport out of province. They're especially fussy about international shipments."

"And the province?" Colleen's face showed the studious look he'd noticed whenever her brain was storing information for future reference.

"It controls the smaller guys — slaughterhouses that don't ship their products outside Ontario."

"Quite the assortment of regulations — the health unit, the municipality, the province, the feds. It all sounds so cumbersome. Small operations could squeeze through the cracks between the jurisdictions."

"Yeah. People are slaughtering animals on the sly all over the place," he said. "Barns. Basements. You name it." He recalled the headlines provoked by a Chinese restaurant in Toronto a year or two ago. "Even restaurants. Though they mostly just kill chickens."

"What do you mean *just* chicken?" Colleen wrinkled her nose as if she were wondering about the integrity of her last chicken curry takeout. "It must be impossible to prove unless you catch them red-handed."

"Inspectors don't get paid enough to confront a bunch of knife-wielding yokels in a back room somewhere."

Fifteen minutes later, after passing several road signs proudly proclaiming Niagara Escarpment Country, they pulled into the Krooner farm.

"Not sure I like the look of that," said Zol, pointing to a black-and-yellow sign nailed to a tree: *Private, Keep Out.* A second sign said, *Guard Dogs on Duty.*

A white vinyl-sided farmhouse, a dormer window perched on the upper floor, sat at the end of the gravel driveway. A pickup truck, black and shiny, was parked out front. Extravagant silver script decorated its side panels: *Escarpment Pride Fine Meats.*

Zol cast his eyes over the extent of the Krooners' operation: the mink sheds, the hog barn, a flat-roofed utility bungalow. Half a kilometre away, bordering a line of trees at the edge of the Escarpment, three mounds of earth jutted skyward, their peaks sharp as if freshly made.

Colleen glided the car to a stop behind the pickup. "Uh-oh," she said, tipping her head in the direction of the yard to the right of the house, "look who's on duty."

Zol stiffened at the sight of a pair of Rottweilers. "What are they up to?"

She shielded her eyes against the low winter sun. "One is licking the other. On the chest."

They stared transfixed by two hundred pounds of canine muscle.

"The one on the ground isn't moving," Colleen said.

A glistening darkness stained the earth in front of the downed animal's thorax. "That's blood," Zol said. "It's been shot." He wiped the sweat from his face with the back of his hand.

Colleen pointed toward Zol's side of the dashboard. "Open the glove compartment and hand me my mobile." He did, and she flipped open her compact cellphone and peered at the icons on its screen. "Two bars. That's fine." She killed the engine. "If we need help, we can call for it." From her purse she lifted a canister the size of an asthma inhaler.

"What's that?" Zol asked.

"Pepper spray."

At the click of her door handle, the standing dog raised its head and stared.

Zol's face tightened. "What are you doing? Let *me* get out first."

Colleen positioned the canister in front of her chest. "Don't argue." She eased the door open and swung her feet carefully out of the car, keeping her right arm extended, her weapon fixed on the animal. Her shoes crunched against the gravel. The dog's shoulders rippled. It aimed its gaze like a laser but kept its paws planted in the blood-stained earth. There was sadness, not hate, in the glow of its eyes.

Colleen rounded the rear of the Mercedes and opened Zol's door. The dog growled but didn't move. "So far, so good," she whispered. She led the way to the front door of the house, sidling between the Mercedes and the truck.

"Normally, I'd look around the yard before knocking on the door," Colleen said. "But we can't push our luck with our friend over there." She put a foot on the concrete stoop.

Zol gripped her arm and whispered, "We've got to rethink this. Krooner has a gun and he's obviously not shy about using it."

"He's a businessman," she said. "He's not going to pull a weapon on a government official."

Animated music chimed through the partly open front door. The artless sound of television. A commercial or a game show.

Colleen donned her leather winter gloves. She turned to Zol. "Put your gloves on. This could be a crime scene." The door opened to the pressure of her fingers.

Zol pulled on his gloves and followed her into a small vestibule. He crinkled his nose at the sickly tang of raw meat and warm blood. Was this where Krooner made his sausages? Or had he shot the dog in here and dragged it into the yard through a back door?

Straight ahead, beyond an archway, Zol could see two legs of a dining-room table. And a china cabinet with glass doors. Even from this distance it looked like the glass needed a good shot of Windex. This was no sausage factory, at least not one that would ever have passed inspection.

"We can't just sneak in," Zol whispered. "I can come unannounced, but I have to make myself known."

Colleen stepped to the archway, leaned forward, and peered

around the corner to the right. "Living room," she mouthed, pointing. "No one there. Just the TV."

Zol nodded. *"The Price is Right."*

Colleen rolled her eyes.

Zol shot her an inquiring look and mimed a knock on the door frame.

She nodded and motioned for him to go ahead.

He stepped beside her, planted his feet on the hardwood floor, and knocked on the wall beside the archway. "Anyone home?" he called.

No answer.

He called again. "Mr. Krooner. Are you home? Your door was open."

From the dining room something substantial clunked as it shifted on the floor. Tools, maybe. A low voice muttered, then shouted, "Stay right where you are."

Heavy footsteps brought a man into view. Thirtysomething, amber eyes like the Rottweilers'. And a shotgun cradled in his arms. "Can't you read?"

Zol glanced at Colleen. Her features were strong, resolute, but not hostile. He aimed for the same attributes in his voice. "We're with the health department." He put out his hand. "I'm Dr. Szabo and this is my colleague, Mrs. Woolton."

The man waved Zol's hand away with the gun. The sweat on his forehead glistened in the light streaming through the front-door window. "You're too late. Mink season's over. The pelts are all sold, and the carcasses . . . well, they're in the compost." His jugular veins bulged as he arched his neck to indicate the rear of the property. "All covered in dirt, just like they're supposed to be."

Zol recalled the tall mounds of fresh dirt he'd noticed when he and Colleen arrived. Had *all* of the mink carcasses been buried there? Or had Lanny Krooner kept a supply of them frozen for other purposes?

Blood smeared the man's knuckles and his shirt. It was sickening to think he must have just shot that dog and left it lying in the dirt.

Zol swallowed hard. "We're not here about your mink, sir. We'd like to inspect Mr. Krooner's meat-processing facility."

"Would you now?"

"Are you Lanny Krooner?"

"You got a warrant?"

"If you're selling food to the public, I'm authorized to inspect your premises without one. I'm sure you've been through this before."

"And always passed. Flying colours."

The overheated air pressed close. Zol yanked off his gloves and unzipped his winter coat. He forced himself to step forward and point over the man's shoulder to the dining room and the rear of the house. "Do you make your sausages in —"The words stuck in his throat, his tongue fat and useless. He stepped back, but he knew that the look on his face had betrayed him. The man was fully aware of what Zol had just seen. That much blood on the dining-room carpet, a pair of feet that size. You'd have to be blind to miss it.

The man raised his gun and hooked his finger on the trigger. His eyes glowed as fiercely as his dog's. "Okay. So you've seen Morty. You shoulda read the keep out sign. Shit. Now what am I gonna do with you?"

Krooner aimed his gun at Zol's face. Zol wondered whether he would hear it when it went off. Or would he find death a silent passage into nothingness? He sensed the woozy onset of a faint. He clenched his fists and rocked on his heels to force the blood up his veins and into his heart. As his heartbeat quickened, his vision cleared, and he saw Colleen's eyes seething with quiet anger.

Krooner waved his gun from side to side while seeming to work out a scheme to get rid of his unwanted visitors. "What's that you got in your hand, little lady?" he asked, pointing the shotgun at the cylinder cupped in Colleen's hand.

She didn't answer.

Krooner cocked his gun. "Throw it on the chesterfield."

She did.

Krooner scowled when he realized what it was. "Bitch. What

else you got in your pockets? Take off your coats. Both of you. Drop 'em behind you. Gloves, too."

They shrugged out of their winter things and let them fall behind them.

"Now, put your hands up and turn around — nice and slow — so as I can get a good look at you."

They did.

Krooner looked them up and down and noticed the ebonite cap of Dr. Osler's fountain pen poking from Zol's shirt pocket. "What the hell's that?" he asked. "Another goddamn dose of pepper? Hand it over."

Zol lifted the Parker from his pocket and held it out so Krooner could see it. "It's just a fountain pen," he said, not wanting Krooner to paw it with his bloodied fingers. "I . . . I can show you the nib."

"Stop right there." Krooner snatched the Parker and dropped it into the pocket of his shirt. "Know what?" he said. "We're gonna play Simon Says. Each time I step backwards I'm gonna tell you to step forwards. But I'm not gonna bother with the Simon-says part. Understand?"

Step by step, Krooner backed into the dining room, commanding them to follow on the point of his shotgun. When they reached the dining-room table, they could see the body lying on the floor. Astonishment filled Morty's sightless eyes. He'd been a hulk of a man with wild hair and a dark bushy beard. Like the dog outside, Morty had the front of his chest blown away. The walls, the drapes, the glass doors of the china cabinet weren't just old and soiled, they were sprayed with blood. Tipped on its side, next to the body, lay a can of barbecue lighter fluid.

Krooner backed beyond the table and stopped at a swinging door. He looked around the room, training the gun between Zol and Colleen. He would know he couldn't back through the door. He'd lose control. "Turn around. Both of you. Then you, little lady, step in front of your boyfriend. And keep your hands up."

As directed, they turned their backs to Krooner. Colleen stepped in front of Zol. He wished he could touch her, give her a sign of encouragement and get one from her. But he didn't dare.

"Okay. Doctor-guy, you listen good. Grab her wrists. One with each hand. Yup, like that. Now you're gonna walk forward. Around the table and out through this swinging door. To the kitchen. But no funny business. If you need any reminding, just look at Morty. He found out what this gun can do."

The three of them marched around the table in a slow lockstep.

Colleen halted at Morty's body lying like a felled oak across her path.

Krooner prodded Zol in the spine with his gun. "For Chrissake, keep moving."

Zol clenched his teeth against the pain of the barrel jabbing at his vertebrae. "But look — see what's in the way."

"I said, keep moving."

"I have to help her over . . . him."

"Then hurry up. And no funny business."

"Colleen," Zol said in a loud voice so Krooner wouldn't think he was plotting in whispers. "I'll lift you up."

"Right," she said.

He grabbed her by the arms and hoisted her over the massive corpse. Her shoes squished as she landed on the blood-saturated carpet.

Krooner jabbed again at Zol's spine. "Get going."

As they rounded the final corner of the table, Zol spotted an open safe, its shelves stacked with bundles of bills. A large suitcase lay on the floor, half filled with banknotes. Twenties and fifties. Compared to everything else in the room, the notes were pristine.

"Just keep going," Krooner growled.

One pace before the door, Krooner told them to stop. He directed Zol to let go of Colleen's arms and keep his own in the air. "Now, little lady, you push on that door, then turn around and hold it wide open with your ass."

Colleen kept her movements calm and steady, but not so slow as to make Krooner impatient. She held the door open exactly as Krooner had directed.

Krooner moved to the side for a moment and barked at Colleen, "Put your hands on your head. And keep them there. If you move, the doc will get a taste of lead." His gun trained on Zol, his fingers curled around the trigger, Krooner wiped his nose on the sleeve of his shirt. "Okay, Doc," he said, licking the sweat from his upper lip, "now you and me are going through. Nice and slow." He prodded Zol again.

Zol walked forward with his hands stretched high. As he passed under the doorway, he was tempted to grab the top of the doorframe, swing his legs backwards, and kick Krooner in the gut. But the steel barrel pressed so close to his spinal cord kept him from attempting anything so daring. Or so foolish.

Once all three of them had manoeuvred into the kitchen, Krooner marched them out the rear door and into the sting of the sunlight. With Colleen in front and Krooner barking directions from the rear, they crossed the yard and eased into the flat-roofed utility bungalow near the mink sheds.

Krooner flicked on the light as they entered what Zol recognized as an industrial kitchen. To the left, against the front wall, sat a large gas range and oven. Stainless steel counters, flanked by drawers, cupboards, and the two obligatory sinks, ran along the side wall. A work table and two metal chairs glimmered in the centre of the room. In a rear corner beckoned the emergency exit door, secured with a heavy bolt at eye level. A stainless steel double door at the rear bore the unmistakable handles of a walk-in refrigerator-freezer.

Krooner closed the front door behind him and paused with his back to it. "Sit down in them chairs." He waved his gun. "Pull up to the table. Like you was eating. And don't move."

CHAPTER 31

Natasha drummed her fingers on her office desk. Her mother had always been demanding. Exasperating. And a hypochondriac. But since her meningitis two years ago, she'd been more narcissistic, more histrionic than ever. And far more interfering. Natasha's dad blamed it on the change of life, but Natasha thought it was more intense than that.

Today, of all days, Mamaji had phoned at breakfast and claimed she was having a relapse of the viral meningitis that, as she put it, "nearly killed me." Hoping to zip in and out of her parents' house before meeting up with Zol and Colleen at eight fifteen, Natasha discovered her mother collapsed on the sofa, a wet cloth on her brow, her lips pale, her voice thin and shaky. No sign of Natasha's father; she assumed he'd left earlier for work. Natasha was on the point of calling 911 when Mamaji sat up, fanned the scowl on her face, and launched into a tirade.

A friend had telephoned to say she'd seen Natasha having dinner — an *intimate* dinner with candles and music — with a tall blond man. What was Natasha trying to do? Mortify her ailing mother in full view of her community? Soil the family's reputation and ruin her younger sister's chances for a respectable husband? Mamaji reminded Natasha she'd never liked the idea of her elder daughter moving into her own apartment. Look what it had led to. Intimacy with a man unknown to the family, of unknown pedigree.

The slur on Bjorn's pedigree had burned in Natasha's ears as she'd grabbed her coat and bolted from the house. If the people at the health unit, like Zol and Anne and Marcia, didn't notice the colour of the skin on her face and arms, why was her mother so aware of Bjorn's? Why had her parents worked so hard to get to Canada, to raise their kids in a land they saw had boundless opportunity, if they were going to hold their children in the shackles of prejudice? And now she was going to miss the most exciting day an epidemiological investigator could ever ask for. And she'd look like a South Asian woman whose family entanglements meant she couldn't be trusted in the final crunch.

She strolled to the lunchroom and put on the kettle. A cup of peppermint tea might help her feel less restless. As she stared distractedly at the kettle, listening to the water stirring toward the boil, she still fumed. Missing the date with Zol and Colleen gnawed at her like a fistful of chilies. She pined to be with them, snooping in Lanny Krooner's cupboards, finding the mink carcasses and pulling them from the back of the freezer in his sausage factory.

She scuffed her heels against the carpet as she trudged back to her office. She lifted the pile of mail from the basket. One by one she slit the envelopes open and tossed them in a heap. She sipped her tea. It was too hot to drink, so she extracted the first letter from the pile and unfolded it with a snap of her wrist. The Ministry of Health in Toronto. Head office wanted more details about the hepatitis A contracted by the produce manager at Kelly's SuperMart. She muttered under her breath. For heaven's sake, that case occurred three months ago, and she'd been over it a dozen times. There couldn't possibly be anything more they needed to know. The man had never become particularly ill, there were no secondary cases among his family or co-workers, no outbreak among Kelly's customers. No harm done. Just one man who probably got his infection from iced margaritas on his vacation in Cancun.

She dropped the letter and cradled her cup. She felt the soothing warmth seep into her fingers. Rita Spinelli's husband had held his cup like this when she'd visited him in his kitchen on that blustery Saturday morning. Had it really been only a week and a half ago? He looked so odd: a greying former football player, his barrel chest straining his shirt buttons, his enormous hands engulfing a delicate porcelain teacup painted with violets. He'd described how his wife came down with meningitis two years previously. It had hit her hard. Exhausted, she'd dragged about for weeks afterwards; for a couple of months she could only manage half days at her dress shop. And that was in November and December, the busiest months in retail. But she'd recovered and was fine for more than a year. Then came her depression and memory loss. Spinelli had always wondered if there was a relationship between his wife's meningitis and her depression. But Rita's family doctor had been emphatic — certainly not.

The taste of peppermint suddenly bitter in her throat, Natasha set down her cup. Her mother and Rita had meningitis about the same time. About two years ago. Had they both been infected with the same virus? Her mother's spinal fluid had grown Coxsackie virus. Her doctor had shown Natasha the report, figuring as a student of public health she'd be interested. As required by law, the result had been reported to the health unit, her mother's name added to the list of cases clustered in Hamilton. Was Rita Spinelli on the same list, or was it just an office diagnosis without laboratory confirmation? And hadn't Dr. Wakefield said that Owen Renway had meningitis in the year before the onset of his CJD symptoms?

She reached for the binder with the notes of all the family interviews. Yes, there it was: Owen Renway had viral meningitis two Christmases before the onset of confusion and memory loss.

What if all the victims had suffered meningitis from the same Coxsackie virus?

She turned to her computer and clicked on the RDIS icon for Hamilton-Lakeshore. As databases went, the Reportable Disease Information System was slow and awkward. But it was better than the alternative from the old days — rummaging at the back of dusty cupboards for slips of paper crammed into boxes. The information she needed was only two years old, and RDIS would have it, one way or another.

She typed in her password, waited for the program to accept it, then clicked on the search box. She entered the year her mother got sick, then *viral meningitis*. The cursor stopped blinking for a moment, but nothing else happened. She tried *meningitis* and *virus*. Still nothing. She typed *meningitis aseptic*, and pressed Enter again. The screen went blank, then flashed on, off, on, then went blank. The program was either hung up or deep in thought. She held her breath, her fingers motionless above the keyboard. Finally, the monitor sprang to life with a month-by-month listing under the heading: *Aseptic Meningitis*.

RDIS listed thirty-two cases of aseptic meningitis in the year her mother got sick: one in July, two in August, none in September, twelve in October, thirteen in November, four in December. RDIS gave no identifying data for any of them and no indication of the exact cause of their meningitis, just that the infection was viral rather than bacterial. RDIS revealed the age, city of residence, and date of symptom onset for each case. And no other information.

She studied the screen. Of the thirty-two cases in that year, twenty-nine occurred between October and December, about the time Rita Spinelli and Natasha's mother got sick; twenty-one were adults, and all lived in Hamilton or its suburbs. It seemed a fair-sized cluster, which should have provoked alarm at the time. But it hadn't; no one had ever said that her mother was part of a large outbreak. That's the way it went: some outbreaks didn't spark the public's interest, others caused a furor — like the flesh-eating disease at Shalom Acres.

From the top drawer of her desk, Natasha retrieved the keys to the filing cabinets in the library down the hall. The crucial details of every case of any illness reported to the health unit were locked away in there. Names, addresses, clinical summaries, detailed laboratory findings.

She jangled the keys as she mulled the significance of the twenty-nine cases of viral meningitis. To make it into the database, all those people must have had laboratory findings conclusive, or at least highly suggestive, of viral meningitis. But the disease was often not severe enough to warrant either a spinal tap or the special cultures needed to detect viruses in body fluids. Many people had fever and headache for a week or so without any doctor sending them to a hospital for tests. Dr. Zol had once told her that during an outbreak there were at least five times as many unproven, unreported meningitis cases as patients with laboratory confirmations. Twenty-nine reported cases would have been just the tip of the epidemic.

She strode down the hall to the library and unlocked the filing cabinet. She scanned the headings on the drawers: Bacterial meningitis, Chlamydia, Food poisoning, Influenza, Norwalk virus, Salmonella, Tuberculosis . . . Viral meningitis. Her heartbeat pounded in her throat as her fingers fished out the very last file from the back of the bottom drawer. She tucked the folder under her arm, locked the cabinet, and dashed back to her office.

She riffled the thirty-two pages in the file for the year her mother got sick, ready to spot familiar names. At the sight of the name on the fifth sheet in the pile, she froze. *Suneeta Sharma.* She covered the page with both hands, embarrassed to read her mother's personal details. She looked away, then swallowed hard and lifted her hands. The paper revealed nothing unexpected or embarrassing. Her mother had presented with fever, stiff neck, and severe headache; her spinal fluid had grown Coxsackie virus B5. Natasha squeezed her opal pendant and continued flipping through the pile of pages.

Her stomach tightened each time she spotted a familiar name. When she finished, she closed her eyes and mouthed a silent thank you that Max Szabo was not among them. She'd found five familiar names besides her mother's, all with Coxsackie virus B5 in their spinal fluid: Owen Renway, Rita Spinelli, Tonya Latkovic, Danesh Patel, and Kitty Ballyk, the host of *Good Morning Hamilton*. Could Kitty Ballyk be the TV celebrity her cousin was talking about, the VIP recently hospitalized at Caledonian with possible CJD?

She pondered. This was an epidemic, all right. Her mother, four CJD victims, Kitty Ballyk, and fourteen of the others diagnosed with viral meningitis were infected with Coxsackie virus B5 in October, November, and December of the same year. Natasha thought about the three remaining CJD victims: Dr. McEwen, Delia Smart, and Joanna Vanderven. Had they had clinical meningitis but never been diagnosed? Or had they been investigated in another jurisdiction and their culture reports never sent to Hamilton? Delia Smart had lived half the year in Stratford. Joanna Vanderven travelled almost constantly.

The public health laboratory, located in Toronto, performed the final identification of every Coxsackie virus isolated from anywhere in Ontario. Toronto would have the names of every Ontario resident from whom Coxsackie B5 had been cultured, no matter what hospital they'd visited. The Toronto lab wouldn't share that information with someone as low in the hierarchy as Natasha, but she was certain they would send it if Dr. Zol or Dr. Trinnock asked for it.

Her ears burned as she thought of Dr. Zol inspecting the Krooner farm, giving that whacko butcher what-for without her. Perhaps she could convince Dr. Trinnock to make a formal request for the information she needed. All he had to do was sign a form. Those piggy eyes of his gave her the creeps, and as far as she could tell he barely knew who she was. But he might do as she wanted, as long as she didn't mention Extendo-Tox.

CHAPTER 32

Lanny Krooner glowered beside the front door of his sausage kitchen, his feet planted wide, his gun cradled in his arms. As his thumb scratched at an itch on his chest, his eyes darted around the room as if he were weighing the methods of eliminating his inconvenient prey. Finally, he pointed the shotgun at Colleen and called across the room, "Little lady, stand up." He gestured toward a cupboard above the counter. "There's a roll of duct tape in there. Get it out."

Colleen stood and turned. Slowly. When her back faced Krooner, she looked calmly into Zol's eyes and mouthed, "Not to worry. We'll be okay."

As she lifted the roll from the cupboard, Zol noticed the checkerboard of light spilling through the window above the counter. Iron bars on a farm kitchen window? What else was Krooner up to in this place?

"Tape his hands together," Krooner shouted.

Colleen bound Zol's wrists in front of his chest, careful not to cut the circulation to his fingers.

"What are you doing, for Chrissake?" Krooner barked. "You should o' taped them behind his back."

A tiny smirk crossed her lips, but Krooner couldn't see it.

Krooner pawed the pockets of his jeans as if he were looking for something, then scowled. "Ah, to hell with it. Do his ankles. And make them good and tight."

She wrapped the tape around Zol's ankles, leaving enough wiggle room for him to keep his balance if he got a chance to stand.

"Now strap him to the chair."

When Zol's thighs were bound to the seat of the chair, Krooner said, "Sit up straight, Doc, so she can do your chest. I don't want you standin' up or nothin'."

Krooner inspected Colleen's handiwork, seemed satisfied, then waved his gun. "Now, little lady, you sit down. Gimme your hands." After he'd trussed her up he pushed their chairs tight to the table.

As Krooner headed for the door, Zol's pulse pounded at his throat. Keeping quiet, following Krooner's orders to the letter, had so far kept them alive — but had drawn them closer and closer to disaster. "So," he called, desperate to at least say something, no matter how lame it sounded. "What . . . what are you going to do now?"

"What do ya mean?"

"Going to leave us here forever?"

"'Til you rot?" Krooner laughed. "No. I decided you're gonna get the same treatment as the mink. Painless and —" he chuckled "— guaranteed humane."

"But what about Morty?" asked Colleen.

Krooner stopped, his hand on the doorknob. "Eh?"

"You can't just leave your brother on the floor in the dining room. He's got a hole in his chest you could drive a truck through. What would your mother say?"

"Shut up. Shut up about my mother."

"How did it happen, Lanny?" Colleen asked, her tone soft, motherly. "Why did you shoot him?" Colleen pressed, but gently. "Come on, Lanny, I know you'd like to come clean. Tell us why you shot your brother."

He leaned the gun against the door and rubbed his palms against his temples. His eyes filled with a mixture of hate and sadness.

"Because he's a big dumb asshole. And crazy as hell."

"I find that hard to believe."

"What do you know about it?"

"He made you angry, didn't he? And maybe scared."

"No shit." Several moments passed while Krooner looked out the window, stared into the distance. Sweat poured from his face. "He was going to burn the money. All of it. Every goddamn penny we earned."

"Why would he do that?" Colleen's tone was gentle, beseeching.

"I told you. He went crazy. Lost his friggin' mind."

"Lanny," Colleen continued, "Morty's a big guy. Pretty fierce by the look of him. Did he sic his dog on you?" With her hands bound together, it almost looked as though she were bestowing a blessing. "If you shot him in self-defence, that's not murder. Not even manslaughter."

"Shut up."

She pointed at the door with her steepled fingers. "Then why don't you take the money and run? That much cash will stretch a long way in Mexico. Or Central America. Get a head start. No one will find us for the rest of the day. You can be out of the country in a couple of hours. Take my car. Keys are in the ignition."

"What do you take me for, some sort of bumpkin? I might talk like a farmer, but I've been runnin' a million-dollar operation here. I'm gonna take the money and run, all right, but not 'til I've neutralized the two o' you."

Colleen raised an eyebrow at Zol, clearly exasperated at carrying the ball by herself.

He pictured Max alone at the breakfast table, toying with his cereal. "You bastard, Krooner. What are you going to do, turn us into sausages? Sell us at I and W Meats and Four Corners?"

Krooner lifted his gun and aimed at Zol's chest. "I bet you shop at Four Corners all the time and don't give a shit about their crazy prices. Ever try my sausages, Doc?"

Zol swallowed hard and stared unblinking into Krooner's wolf-like gaze.

Krooner stiffened. "That dame at I and W phoned me yesterday. Spoiled the damn good thing I had going. Told me she wouldn't buy no more stuff off me." He wiped his sweaty cheek with his shirt sleeve.

"I've eaten your sausages, Mr. Krooner," Zol said, without blinking. "Are you going to let us in on your secret ingredient?"

Krooner kicked at a solitary pebble on the floor. The edges of his mouth curled upward, exposing his eye teeth. "There's something about fine ranch mink and the luxury market. Rich dudes just can't get enough of it. Inside and out." He chuckled and looked to see if his captives got the joke. He narrowed his eyes, seemed to ponder a moment, then sneered at Zol, "Hey, now I know who you are. You're the bastard that ratted on me. Called I and W. And ruined everything."

Colleen wasn't smiling, but her face exuded motherliness. "Look, Lanny. Killing Morty must have been an accident. Why don't you clear out your safe and get the hell out of here."

"I'm gonna do that, little lady, but before I go I'm gonna euthanize you. That's what we call it in the business. Euthanize. It means you're gonna fall asleep. Just like the mink. Carbon dioxide. Completely odourless, as they say. You won't smell nothing, and it won't hurt a bit. Trouble is, you're never gonna friggin' wake up." He backed out of the door, and Zol heard him turn the key in the lock.

Zol watched through the window as Krooner's figure retreated. He counted to five before he whispered, "Jesus, Colleen. What are we going to do?"

"Act fast. He's a nutcase. Been eating his own sausages, by the look of him."

Zol surveyed the spotless kitchen. The counters were clear, all Krooner's machinery put away in cupboards. "This place is immaculate. But there must be plenty of knives somewhere."

"You're the expert with a knife. Free our wrists and our ankles, then cut the rest of the tape just at the back, and under the seat, so he won't notice. When he puts down his gun, we can jump him."

"But what if he sees we've fiddled with the tape? He'll shoot us on the spot."

"You've got a better idea?"

Zol hopped, chair and all, to a chest with three drawers under the counter beside the sink. The top two drawers opened easily but contained nothing the least bit sharp. Not even a fork or a corkscrew. He leaned down to snag the handle of the bottom drawer and nearly toppled to the floor.

"Quick," Colleen whispered, "get over here. He's coming back."

The chair legs thumped and clattered as he hobbled back to the table.

Krooner threw open the door, his face like thunder. "What's all that racket?" he asked, brandishing a heavy-looking wrench as if it were a billy club. His scowl dissolved into miffed surprise at finding his captives in the same spot as he'd left them. He checked their bindings and grunted in satisfaction. He went out again and returned almost immediately wheeling two large gas cylinders on a dolly. Stencilled lettering on the side said, *Medical Gas — Carbon Dioxide.*

Zol's heart pounded in his ears as he watched Krooner stuff two tea towels under the back exit then confirm that it was locked. He checked the windows above the counter, then ripped the phone cord from the wall. Zol looked at Colleen for a flicker of encouragement. All he saw was stone. The confidence, the motherly concern had vanished from her face.

The cylinders hissed to life when Krooner opened their valves with two spins of his monkey wrench. He said nothing as he pocketed the wrench and backed out the door, pulling it shut behind him. Keys jangled, the deadbolt clunked, his shoes crunched on the gravel path.

Zol pointed to the floor. "It's okay. CO_2 is heavier than air." The gas would settle first along the floor and, with luck, take some time to reach their noses.

"Easy for you to say," Colleen told him, and pointed at the shorter distance between her nose and the floor.

He hopped to the counter and the set of drawers. If he were to have any chance at finding a knife, he had to open the bottom one. But he couldn't reach the handle, even with his arms outstretched, his shoulders straining in their sockets. Again he leaned too far. The chair wobbled and started to topple. He jerked backward to regain his balance, then shook his head at the close call. He would never get himself upright if he crashed to the floor. And his nose would be right in the thick of the carbon dioxide.

Maybe he could hook his shoe under the drawer handle. He eased away from the drawers and lifted his two bound feet off the floor. With his legs extended, his feet hovering opposite the bottom drawer, he worried the handle with the toes of his shoes. But his Florsheims wouldn't fit under the slender handle, and with his ankles bound together he couldn't slip the shoes off and try a bare toe. He kicked at the handle in frustration. Sweat streamed from his face. His thighs trembled at the strain. His feet crashed to the floor and his arms to his lap.

Colleen's chair clattered as she hopped toward him. She lifted her foot, fit her toe under the handle, and pulled. Nothing. On her third attempt the drawer flew open, the weight of it toppling her. She crashed to the floor, her chair knocking the drawer shut on the way down.

"Shit," muttered Zol. "You okay? Did you hit your head?"

On her side, she blinked, then groaned a few words that sounded like *I'm okay*.

He slid her sideways so her fingers approached the drawer handle. "Here," he said, "pull it open."

She reached for the handle. Though her hands and wrists were bound, her fingertips were agile enough. She tugged. The drawer opened. She lay too low to see into it, but from his chair Zol spotted a paring knife underneath a metal spatula.

"Oh, thank God. I see a knife."

Colleen's cheek scraped against the floor while her hands fumbled in the drawer. He directed her to move her fingers to the right, a bit further right, then farther back. She closed on the spatula.

"No, that's not it. That's a spatula. The knife is underneath it. Feel for the handle. It's wooden. Skinny. There, you're touching it. Careful. No, you're pushing it away." Damn. Why couldn't she just pick the stupid thing up? "Start again. Just small movements. I'll talk you through it. Okay, just a little to the right. No, that's left. To the right, toward me. No, the other way. Come on, Colleen, the other way. An inch further toward me. Hey, what are you doing?"

She wasn't listening. Her fingers twitched aimlessly over the implements in the drawer.

"Come on, Colleen."

He'd been so preoccupied with directing her hands that he hadn't been watching her face. When he looked at her, nausea filled his belly.

Her eyelids looked like they were made of lead. Her breaths puffed in and out like a steam locomotive at full speed. Pathological hyperpnea. Damn. The effect of the carbon dioxide.

"Come on," he shouted, kicking her chair. "Colleen. You've got to stay awake. One more try. The knife is right there, next to your fingers. Scoop it up."

She raised her chin and opened her eyes, gritted her teeth, and pinched the small handle between three fingers. She started to lift it but it slipped. She found it again but again it slipped. Finally, she squeezed it between her fingertips and managed to lift it from the drawer. But before Zol could catch it, the knife clattered to the floor. Colleen's eyelids flickered then closed, and her head slumped to the linoleum.

Zol's mind boiled. Should he tip her chair upright so her face was out of the worst of the carbon dioxide? No. She was unconscious, and safer on her side where she wouldn't choke on her tongue. If he could free himself, he could carry her into the fresh air. But how was he going to reach the knife if he couldn't reach the floor?

His eyes found the kitchen counter. Maybe he could grab the edge, tip himself forward, and ease onto his knees. Damn, he should have thought of that before.

The back of the chair whacked him in the neck as he went down. His vision clouded, but he managed to grab the knife. He angled the familiar-feeling tool toward his left wrist. A strange way to handle a paring knife, but his fingers seemed to know what to do.

The blade only skipped across the duct tape. He tried again. Same thing. He scanned the kitchen. Nothing sharper in sight. He had to make this work.

He adjusted his grip so he could use the part of the blade closest to the handle where often a little sharpness remained on a dull knife — a chef's trick he'd never imagined might save his life. He pressed the blade against the duct tape and felt a short rent. More sawing action lengthened it. About halfway through, his fingers cramped into uselessness.

A glance at Colleen showed she was still breathing. His gut clenched at the sight of her so helpless.

He gripped the knife and struggled with the last bands of tape at his wrists. His head throbbed. He felt giddy, as if he'd just guzzled three glasses of merlot. He yanked his hands apart, hardly noticing that the tape wrenched the hair from his wrists.

On his knees, his feet tucked under the chair, he couldn't reach his ankles, couldn't cut them free. He lumbered to the counter, grabbed it, and heaved into a sitting position. The effort left him breathless, but his nose was again well above the floor, away from the worst of the carbon dioxide.

He had to get Colleen into the fresh air before she asphyxiated. The front door was no good to him. The deadbolt needed a key even from the inside. And he had to stand up to open the sliding bolt on the rear door. He had to cut himself free from the chair.

It seemed to take ages to force the short, dull blade through the sticky layers of duct tape binding his ankles, his thighs, his chest. With the passing minutes, his fingers felt heavier and clumsier. His temples pounded with a killer of a headache.

When he was finally free, he rubbed his knees, pushed himself to his feet, and limped on stiff legs to the rear exit. He reached for the bolt, slammed it back, and threw open the door. He gulped a few breaths of crisp December air and looked toward the farmhouse. No sign of Krooner. The Mercedes was gone.

Zol ran to Colleen and rushed her outside — chair and all.

He set her on the frigid concrete stoop and knelt beside her, then worked at her bindings with the nearly useless blade. He ripped her free and rolled her on her side. Her hands, white and cold as marble, dropped to the ground. He lifted her chin to open her airway and dipped his ear to her face. He felt the purr of her breathing. She didn't need mouth-to-mouth, just plenty of fresh air. But Jesus — that purple-blue of cyanosis on her lips. He prayed the lack of oxygen wouldn't mean brain damage.

Shivering inside his cotton shirt, he arranged her ponytail like a scarf against her neck. He wished he had his coat to shield her from the icy gusts blowing from the Escarpment. Pressing his body close to hers, he maintained the forward pressure on her chin, breathed in her jasmine, and kissed her forehead.

CHAPTER 33

"Are you sure this is necessary?" Dr. Trinnock asked Natasha after Anne hustled her into his office. "All the information you need should be in those cabinets in the library." He peered at his watch. "Dr. Szabo must be up in Campbellville right now, checking out — well, let's say, a different line of inquiry."

Natasha stood her ground, hands clasped behind her back, hoping the slight smile on her face presented a picture of innocence. She was not going to let on she knew about the mink meat in the sausages. "I do think this is important, sir. As I said, with four of our victims —"

"Yes, yes, I understand. You've uncovered yet another association. But viral meningitis is a mild disease. Doesn't affect the brain, only the superficial membranes. And what you're talking about was — what? — two years ago?"

She nodded.

He wrinkled his brow and closed his eyes, then pulled a crumpled hankie from his pocket and snorted into it. "Sounds like water under the bridge." He wiped his eyes and looked up as if surprised to see Natasha still standing beside him. He sighed his displeasure. "I suppose you already have the form filled out?"

"Right here, sir. All you need to do —"

"I know what to do," he said. He grabbed a pen and scribbled his name on the bottom of the paper. He waved a warning with the ballpoint. "Don't overstep your bounds. We're only entitled to the test results of people residing in our region. Don't get us into trouble by asking for anything more than that. The Ministry is touchy about confidentiality."

As soon as she was out of Dr. Trinnock's office, Natasha rushed to the fax machine, sent her fax, then phoned the public health laboratory in Toronto. The receptionist connected her with the technologist in charge of the virology division, who said the fax would be somewhere in her pile of mail, and she'd get to it later this week.

"But Dr. Trinnock is counting on having the information this afternoon," Natasha said. "All he's asking is that you check your records from two years ago. July to December. See if you have virus-culture results on the three patients named on the form."

"This afternoon? You should have submitted the request last week if you needed the information today."

"I'm very sorry to trouble you like this. We — I mean, Dr. Trinnock only realized the potential significance of these results today." Natasha had no idea how much she should tell the woman, how far she could push. "We're investigating something pretty dramatic here and we would be *so* appreciative of the information."

"From what I've seen on TV, you people in Hamilton have had plenty of drama already."

"I'm afraid so."

"Well," said the technologist, her tone softening, "if it's only three names, and the time frame is really as narrow as you say, maybe I can have the results to you in an hour or so."

"Oh, thank you so much. Dr. Trinnock will be incredibly grateful that you went the extra mile."

Thirty minutes later, on Natasha's third trip to the fax machine next to Anne's desk, the device began to beep and whir. Her heart raced at the sight of the public health laboratory's letterhead scrolling from the machine. Her hands trembled as she grabbed the sheet, her eyes almost afraid to scan it.

The three names, Hugh McEwen, Delia Smart, and Joanna Vanderven, as familiar as long-time friends, jumped off the page.

McEwen, Hugh: *No specimen submitted.*
Smart, Delia: *November 29, Spinal Fluid, Coxsackie B5*

She knew she needed to read the next line slowly, so her brain could digest it. She sat, then read the third line.

Vanderven, Joanna: *December 3, Throat Swab, Coxsackie B5*

Her fingers rode the galloping in her chest as they rubbed at her pendant. From the carpet near her foot glowered the wrinkled face of Father Time. She blinked and glowered back, and saw it was only a coffee stain on the industrial broadloom.

She pictured Joanna Vanderven, her mascara smudged, her head pounding, her body sweating with fever as she refused the needle of a lumbar puncture but gave in to a throat swab. The swab hadn't proved meningitis, but it did prove infection with a virus that could cause meningitis. The same virus, at the same time, as five other victims of CJD.

Natasha closed her office door and took her phone off the hook. She called up Google on her computer and typed in *Coxsackie* and *CJD*. In a millisecond, up came a long list of Web documents. The first reported a case of CJD in a man who lived in a place called Coxsackie, New York. A detailed map showed the town to be south of Albany and east of both Climax and Surprise. She rolled her eyes then opened more than a dozen other links to find that they mentioned Coxsackie and CJD somewhere in the same document, but many pages apart, with no implied connection between the virus and CJD.

She knew Google wasn't the best tool to retrieve articles from sophisticated scientific journals. The gold standard was PubMed, the search engine of the U.S. National Library of Medicine. She called it up, typed in *Coxsackie* and CJD, hit enter. "No items found" flashed at the top of a blank frame.

Had she found something new or just concocted a meaningless association between CJD and a common virus? She tapped her nails on her desk and stared at the screen. What if she had discovered that a third factor was necessary to initiate tulip CJD? If it took three factors working simultaneously to cause the illness, maybe there would be no huge epidemic. And if Max never had meningitis . . .

She had to share this with Dr. Zol. He'd be so relieved. Her hand gripped the knob of her office door, but she felt sheepish, almost ashamed to face her boss, to look into those penetrating eyes of his. He wouldn't let on he was angry she'd been late this morning, but he wouldn't be able to hide his disappointment. And that would be ten times worse.

Anne looked up from the stack of reports on her desk as Natasha approached. "He's still not back yet," she said, and glanced at the clock on the wall. "Maybe they stopped for a bite on the way home. He likes that little place in Lowville."

The two women turned at the sound of heavy footsteps in the stairwell. The door burst open and crashed against the wall. Natasha braced for the snarl of yet another citizen ready to rant about contaminated gelatin imperilling his family.

Hamish Wakefield let the door slam behind him and leaned against the wall, his chest heaving beneath his bulky coat. He ripped his scarf from his throat and stared at Natasha through wild blue eyes. "Where's Zol?" he gasped. "Got to — talk to him."

Natasha pointed to a chair beside Anne's desk. "Dr. Wakefield, you'd better sit down."

Anne extended her arms. "Here, let me take your coat."

"Just gotta talk to Zol." Hamish extracted an inhaler from a pocket and sucked back two puffs.

"Dr. Zol isn't here right now," Anne said as she helped Hamish out of his coat and placed it on the rack. "But we expect him soon."

"I'll get you a glass of water," Natasha said. "And when you're ready, we can go to my office and wait for him there."

Hamish dropped onto the chair, his shoulders heaving with every breath.

When Natasha returned from the water cooler, he was breathing more easily and clutching his briefcase as if it contained the Holy Grail. He looked around, as if embarrassed to be sitting on display. "Okay," he said, pushing himself to his feet, "where's your office?"

She pointed. "Just down there," she said and led the way. They entered her office, and she gestured to the chair in front of her desk. "Have a seat, and I'll try Dr. Szabo on his cell."

After one ring, a recorded voice said that the customer was currently unavailable. Natasha shook her head as she hung up. "He must be out of range."

"Where the heck is he?"

"Still at the Krooner farm, I suppose. Or maybe he stopped for lunch. Is there something I can do?"

He opened his mouth as if to reply, then drew his case to his chest and looked at the open door.

She closed the door and raised her eyebrows.

He nodded as if to say, *Yes, that's better* and sipped from the glass. He licked his lips then unbuckled the two straps of his briefcase. He stopped short of opening the flap and frowned, his face uncertain. "Are you completely up to speed on all this?"

"You mean, do I know about the mink meat in the pies and sausages?"

"And the possibility of transmissible mink encephalopathy?"

"Yes. Dr. Zol told me you've been waiting for news from the prion lab in Guelph. Don't tell me you've heard."

"Just a few minutes ago," Hamish said, lifting out a single printed page.

Her hands flew to her mouth. "Oh my God."

"Here," he said, handing her the sheet of paper, marked with the unmistakeable headers and footers of a fax. The letterhead, studded with an array of federal and provincial logos, said *University of Guelph: Canadian Research Institute for Food Safety.*

She read through the message three times.

Hamish extended his hand to retrieve the precious page. "Doesn't leave much room for doubt, does it?"

"And they can even tell they're *mink* prions."

"Prion food science has become sophisticated in a big hurry."

She pointed to the fax. "Why didn't the chocolates get sent to that same lab?"

"They did," he said, waving the sheet, "and these guys didn't find a single prion in any of them."

"But the Canadian Food Inspection Agency and the Ministry are still chasing them. And the gelatin."

"These boys in Guelph are just food scientists," said Hamish. He tsked and rolled his eyes. "Not far enough up the political food chain."

"Because they don't directly investigate outbreaks of human disease?"

He nodded and made a face.

"So," she said, "no prions doesn't mean no prions until the testing's been sanctioned by Winnipeg and Atlanta?"

"You got it."

"And," she added, "proving a negative is a lot more difficult than discovering a positive."

"Exactly."

"But now," she said, feeling confidence returning, "we've *got* the positive."

"And as soon as Zol gets back, we'll run with it."

A shiver gripped her shoulders. She pulled her cardigan tight. "Dr. Zol and Colleen should have been back ages ago. We'd better call the police."

"What?"

"Technically, Lanny Krooner is a murderer. And by now he knows we're on to him." She jumped at the piercing trill of the phone on her desk. She punched the button for the speakerphone.

"Natasha?" said Anne. "Dr. Zol is on the line."

"Is he okay?"

"He's at the hospital. In Emergency. Wants to talk to you."

There was a pause. Then: "That you, Natasha?" Zol's voice was strained, exhausted.

"Yes. And Dr. Wakefield."

Hamish leaned toward the phone. "Zol, what's going on?"

"I'm here with Colleen. Krooner tried to kill us. Gassed us with carbon dioxide, just like his mink. Colleen got the worst of it."

"Oh my God," Natasha said. "How is she?"

"Started coming around a bit in the ambulance."

Hamish raised a finger. "Good thing he didn't use carbon *mono*xide. You'd both be dead by now. What happened to Krooner?"

"He took Colleen's car. He's probably across the border by now."

Hamish asked, "What year is her Mercedes?"

"Don't know," Zol replied. "They all look the same."

"Does it have GPS?" Hamish asked

"Yeah," Zol said.

"Then it must have Driver's Cocoon."

"What?"

"All the best cars have it."

"For heaven's sake, Hamish, what are you talking about?"

"It's a satellite communication system. You push a button in the car and get connected with an operator, no matter what's wrong."

"But shit, we don't have the car."

"You phone a toll-free number and give them your ID and a password. If Colleen has the platinum edition, they'll pinpoint the location of her vehicle, shut down the engine, and lock the thief inside until the police arrive."

"Seriously?"

"I'm having it put into my next Saab."

"Where am I going to get the ID number and the password? Colleen's still pretty out of it."

"Check her purse. Look for a wallet card."

The speaker emitted an ear-splitting crash as Zol dropped the phone. Natasha and Hamish heard agitated voices; Zol must have phoned from a very public place. An ice age could have come and gone in the time it took him to come back on the line. "Still there, you guys?" he asked.

"We're here, Dr. Zol," Natasha assured him.

"Her purse must be in the car. But I found her wallet in her coat." In the background, a child screamed and a deeper voice cursed. "This must be the card. "Driver's Cocoon. Platinum edition."

Hamish beamed and sat back in his chair. "Perfect. Are the police still there?"

"Yeah. And no end to their questions."

"Show them the card. Get *them* to make the call. They won't need the password."

Natasha blurted into the speaker, "One more thing, Dr. Zol."

"Yeah?"

She threw Hamish a knowing look. "Dr. Wakefield has something else to tell you."

Hamish sent a puzzled look her way. *What?* he mouthed. His face brightened a little as she pointed to the fax from Guelph. "Right now?" he whispered.

She nodded.

"You sure?"

She nodded again and gestured toward the speaker.

"I — I heard from Guelph, Zol," Hamish said. "This morning. They found the prions. In everything I sent them. Krooner's sausages, his pies. Even his head cheese."

Zol said nothing. Natasha pictured him head down, eyes closed, fingering a loonie. Should she tell him about the Coxsackie B? Buoyed by the exhilaration in the room, she blurted it out. "I've found what seems to be an obligatory third factor."

Both men shouted, "Third factor?"

"At least six of the cases had aseptic meningitis. Two years ago. All caused by Coxsackie B5."

Hamish stared at the wall; he looked as if his mind was light-years away.

Another distant wail echoed from the phone's tinny speaker; gruff voices muttered, their impatience obvious.

"I — I can't take this in," Zol stammered.

Bit by bit, Hamish seemed to shake himself out of his trance. "Well, Zol," he said, wagging his professorial finger, "aseptic meningitis with Coxsackie B5 isn't all that common, and if six of the seven CJD victims were infected with it . . ." He ran a hand across his flat-top. "There has to be some significance there." He paused and narrowed his eyes, then smacked the desk with his hand. "The inflammatory effects of the meningitis must have broken down the blood-brain barrier and allowed the Extendo-Tox and the prions to enter the brain."

"Wait a minute," Zol said. "You're saying it took *three* factors to cause this tulip CJD?"

"From what Natasha just said, it looks that way."

"Max never had meningitis. I know that for sure. And he certainly doesn't have it now. That means he's going to be okay? He won't get CJD? Oh, Natasha." Zol's voice faltered. "I . . . I could kiss you."

She opened her mouth, but her tongue didn't form any words. She caught Hamish's mischievous smile and turned away, covering her lips with her hand.

"Listen, I've gotta go," Zol said. "I'm at a pay phone." He lowered his voice. "And the biker guy behind me is getting impatient."

The speaker clicked off. Natasha felt the air in the office hang strangely quiet.

Hamish pushed at his cuticles. His smile had faded, replaced by a spooky look of anguish. "I wish I could share Zol's enthusiasm about Max and the absence of a third factor."

"What do you mean?"

"How do we know Max doesn't have a mild case of aseptic meningitis right now? He could be incubating as we speak. Many cases have no symptoms whatsoever."

"Oh, Dr. Wakefield. Don't tell me. I was so sure that Max . . ."

"He must be loaded with Krooner's prions, and he got quite a dose of Extendo-Tox." Hamish stuffed the fax into his briefcase. "Never mind. We can do Max's serology. If there aren't any Coxsackie B5 antibodies in his blood, then we'll know he never got infected."

"How long will it take?"

"If it's sent to Atlanta — a month. But maybe less if we talk to the right people."

"And that will be the end of it?"

His face hung like the clouds that hadn't let up the entire month of November. "If it's negative."

CHAPTER 34

Natasha hated loose ends. She always had. Every question deserved a proper answer based on logic and sound data. As a child, it drove her to distraction whenever her mother answered *Because I said so* and refused to provide details to support one arbitrary edict or another. When freckle-faced girls in the schoolyard used to taunt her with *That's for us to know and you to find out,* Natasha was driven wild with frustration — well, as wild as a model student ever got.

She stared at the headline on the front page of the Hamilton *Spectator.* Mad Mink Murders: Politicians Push for Public Inquiry. The loose ends of the case tormented her. She knew she could do nothing to speed up the labs in Toronto and Atlanta, which were processing Max's Coxsackie blood test. But she could get to the bottom of how Tonya Latkovic — a strict vegetarian — had become infected with Lanny Krooner's mink-meat prions.

It had been Colleen who'd interviewed Mr. and Mrs. Latkovic. She'd gained their confidence and discovered that Tonya's anti-migraine injections contained not sumatriptan but Extendo-Tox. Ordinarily, it would be up to Colleen to ferret out — that phrase would never be the same for any of them again — how Tonya had come to ingest the prions. But Colleen had gone from the emergency department to intensive care. She wasn't on life support, but no one was saying how long it would be before she was strong enough to leave hospital. Dr. Zol was with her now.

Natasha cupped her morning peppermint tea in her hands and let out a long sigh before taking a sip. It was clear that Dr. Zol and Colleen had become more than colleagues during the course of the CJD investigation. Dr. Zol was so distraught that he'd messed up buttoning his coat as he strode past the lunchroom on the way to Caledonian Medical Centre a few minutes ago. Natasha gazed at her university degrees, expensively framed and carefully hung on her office wall. It wouldn't take book learning to tie up Tonya's loose end and recapture Dr. Zol's attentions — if only in a professional sense. Intuition and good old-fashioned epidemiological footwork were needed. Just like the E. coli–contaminated canapés at that Croatian wedding.

She retrieved the telephone directory from the bottom drawer of her desk, found the number of Tonya's high school on Hamilton mountain, and spoke with the secretary in the principal's office. The woman sounded wary at first, but once Natasha established that she really was calling on official business, the woman gave her the information she needed.

The workday at the health unit dragged on, but three thirty finally arrived. Natasha hurried to her car and drove to the parking lot behind the high school. She did as the secretary had directed and checked in at the office before making her way through the maze of corridors that separated the classrooms at the front of the school from the gymnasium at the rear. Twice, she came to the ends of hallways that led only to fire escapes. The halls were deserted, but she knew she was finally on the right track when she smelled the unmistakeable odour of sweaty rubber then heard the thump and squeak of running shoes hitting a hard surface. The first door she peeked through led to a gym flanked on one side by bleachers; the court raged with testosterone and resounded with boys shooting hoops in some sort of drill. She stepped back and closed the door. From across the hall, she heard higher-pitched shouting, a whistle, and more squeaky runners. She cracked open another door and found two dozen girls playing basketball in a smaller gym without bleachers.

She pulled off her winter boots by their fashionable but noisy heels, took a step into the gym, and pressed her back against the wall. She stood absolutely still, clutching her boots and remembering how intimidated she'd been by every gym teacher she'd had. She spotted a coach, a brown-haired woman wearing a white golf shirt and navy blue sweatpants, who punctuated her commanding arm gestures and stern facial expressions with toots of the whistle clenched between her teeth. Thankfully, she didn't look Natasha's way even for a millisecond. Just as Natasha began to wonder how she would get the cloying smell of sweaty bodies out of her skirt, the coach whistled four times in rapid succession, and the game came to a halt.

The coach told the girls to take a water break, then turned to Natasha and frowned as if to say *No boots or skirts welcome in here.* After a moment, the woman's face softened. She smiled and approached with an outstretched hand. "You're from the health department, eh? The office told me to expect you."

"You . . . you look busy, miss. I should come back another time."

"Now's a good time. They said you only wanted to ask a few questions." She turned toward the players guzzling from water bottles and kibitzing on the other side of the gym. "Girls, this is —" The coach turned to Natasha. "I didn't catch your name." Natasha told her, and the coach cupped a hand beside her mouth and called, "Ms. Sharma is here from the health department. She's got a few questions to ask."

A blonde — a teen-pageant beauty even in her ill-fitting polyester uniform — blushed and hid her face. The girls beside her giggled and made catcalls until the coach silenced them with a snappy admonition that this had nothing to do with anyone's private health concerns.

"Come," the coach said to Natasha, "I'll introduce you to the girls who knew Tonya. Maybe they can give you the information you're looking for." Her face darkened. She yanked a Kleenex from her pocket and wiped the sweat from her forehead. "We're all still feeling pretty raw." She called four girls by name and led them and Natasha to a corner of the gym. After she'd made the introductions, she blasted three toots on her whistle and shouted instructions to the remaining girls. She turned to the small group huddled around Natasha and said, "I'll keep the others occupied while you remember happier times with Ms. Latkovic."

At the sound of Tonya's name, the girls morphed from confident ballplayers to sad youngsters who had lost someone dear. Natasha started with the customary condolences and said she knew it would be difficult for the girls to talk about Ms. Latkovic after her illness and then her accident. "Have you been reading in the newspapers about this prion business?" she asked.

Three girls nodded. The fourth, a brunette with her hair tied back in a ponytail, covered her eyes.

Ignoring the silent tears, Natasha said, "What I really need to know is she how she got infected with the organisms — those prions — that affected her brain."

The girls shrugged, studied their sneakers, then gazed longingly toward the other side of the gym.

"Prions usually come from animal products," Natasha explained. "But I understand that Ms. Latkovic was a strict vegetarian."

After a long, silent moment, a girl with a large letter C sewn to her uniform rolled her eyes.

"Perhaps not so strict?" Natasha ventured.

Silence.

"Girls," Natasha pleaded, "I know you don't want to say anything bad about Ms. Latkovic, but if she got infected from a source we don't know about, more lives could be in danger." A hint of interest lit the faces around her. "Yes, any of you — every one of you — could be in danger if we don't find *all* the sources of those prions."

The ponytailed brunette clamped a hand over her mouth then turned to the captain and pleaded with her eyes.

"For heaven's sake, Breanne," said the captain, glaring, "stop being so histrionic."

"Yeah," said a blonde girl with a neat white scar through her upper lip. "Neither you nor Tonya had *that* many."

"That many what?" Natasha asked.

There was a long moment of silence, then the captain shrugged, rolled her eyes, and said, "We may as well tell her about the dogs."

"Technically, they weren't dogs," said a studious-looking girl, the shortest of the lot.

The captain flicked her hand dismissively. "Sarah, you're always splitting hairs."

"But maybe it's important," Sarah replied.

Natasha felt suddenly very hot in her winter coat. Dogs? This sounded worse than the mink. "Please, what can you tell me?"

The captain scratched at an itch near her elbow. "It's about our breakfasts."

The brunette remained silent while the other three told the story of their school's Saturday breakfast tradition. Every year, during the four weeks leading up to the basketball championships, the coach and the players indulged in an unshakable Saturday ritual that had been going on for as long as anyone could remember: a breakfast of bagels and sausages at Four Corners Fine Foods. The tradition, it seemed, had always got their school into the finals.

"Ms. Latkovic was a really good sport about the sausages," Sarah said, "because she didn't want to break the spell of the gourmet hot dogs and have us miss the finals on account of her."

"Yeah," admitted the captain, "but she always ordered a Viennese because the spices helped disguise the taste of the meat."

CHAPTER 35

Christmas Eve found Zol steering a cart through the aisles of Four Corners Fine Foods. The proprietor had wasted no time in restoring the place to its festive glory. Crimson bows and golden baubles festooned the walls. The customers — fickle but eager — had returned in flocks on the heels of the Ministry's pronouncement that chocolates and gelatin were officially safe, but Escarpment Pride products were to be avoided at all costs.

In a televised announcement lasting a scant thirty seconds, the province's chief medical officer of health had looked terribly lonely. The only person at the podium, abandoned by his consultants, his colleagues, his minister, Elliott York had the hangdog look of a man awaiting deportation to Moose's Testicle. He conveyed only the barest of facts while waving a press release that promised further details.

Wyatt Burr, of course, was long gone. AWOL, bolo ties and all. He'd fled the spotlight the moment Guelph confirmed they'd found the prions not in Wyatt's gourmet sweets, but in Lanny Krooner's tainted meats.

Extendo-Tox, facing an armada of lawsuits, had locked its doors. The wonder drug was a pariah, its licence suspended by the

Canadian Therapeutic Products Directorate; the drug was at the mercy of the American FDA. Julian Banbury had found high concentrations of Extendo-Tox in the olfactory bulbs, tucked beneath the brains of all seven victims of tulip CJD. After a little coaxing from Hamish, he posted the details on ProMed when he notified Extendo-Tox's CEO. Through the magic of the Internet, the entire globe buzzed with Banbury's Triad as the cause of tulip CJD: *ingestion* of mink prions, *injection* with Extendo-Tox, and *infection* with Coxsackie virus B5.

Health Canada directed everyone who had ever received Extendo-Tox to undergo testing for antibodies to Coxsackie B5. Those who tested positive and might have eaten Escarpment Pride products would be watched for the first hints of CJD. But as Hamish said in that bloodless way of his, early diagnosis wouldn't stop the relentless, untreatable mindlessness that would beset anyone marked by the triple whammy of ingestion, injection, and infection.

Zol broke into a sweat at the sight of the deli meats. He couldn't take his eyes off them. He pictured Lanny Krooner in jail, the charges against him so disgusting he'd been placed in protective custody. That was too good for him. The bastard had made it as far as Windsor. Two more kilometres and he would have slipped through the tunnel under the river and made it to Detroit. At Hamish's insistence, the police had phoned the operator at Driver's Cocoon. Contact was made just as Krooner was steering Colleen's Mercedes into the Casino Windsor parking lot. He'd probably planned on stealing a less conspicuous car, one with U.S. plates. While Krooner was trolling for a parking spot, the engine cut out, the door locks clicked, and a woman's voice came from a speaker in the ceiling: *You are advised to relax in your seat. Don't try to start the engine or open the doors and windows. Assistance is on the way.* According to Dave Hatala, Zol's lawyer, the police report said Krooner was still hollering when they found him three minutes later. The instant the officers told the operator to unlock the doors, Krooner leapt from the vehicle and punched a female constable in the abdomen. Her partner neutralized him, cuffed him, and tossed him into the back of the cruiser. The police told Dave Zol's antique Parker had been among the possessions seized at the time of Krooner's arrest. Dave was confident Zol's treasured link with the great Dr. Osler would be safely returned in due course.

Zol bypassed the meats, picked up two loaves of focaccia and a frosted yule log, then headed to the chocolate aisle for treats to stuff into Max's stocking. In half an hour, Zol and Max would be setting off for a condo overlooking the ski slopes of Blue Mountain. They'd spend their Christmas break three hours' drive north and a world away from Hamilton. And what a wonderful break it would be. This morning's fax from Atlanta had burned its image forever into Zol's retinas: *Maxwell Szabo, age seven, Coxsackie B virus IgM and IgG nonreactive.* Thank you, God. It would take the best part of a year for the Extendo-Tox to wear off, but the prions would be out of Max's system by the spring. Coxsackie infections were seasonal, and hardly ever occurred in the winter. Max was never going to suffer the devastating triple whammy that caused tulip CJD. Zol wiped his eyes and picked up a box of Lorreaux Chocolate Fruit Explosions. He stared at the little bird. Was there more to the CJD story than the honeycreeper was letting on? He cursed himself for his superstitions and tossed the chocolates into his shopping cart.

Hamish and Ken were spending Christmas in Florida at a clothing-optional resort for gay men. Zol couldn't imagine Hamish doffing his swimsuit in public, but maybe Ken could help him loosen up. Before he left, Hamish had gone through Joanna Vanderven's expensive bag. He found ginseng, bee pollen, and echinacea, as well as two heavy-duty narcotics, two types of sleeping pills, a diuretic, and a nearly full bottle of erythromycin dated the day before her death. Her autopsy had shown no signs of serious infection; maybe she'd had just a cold or smoker's bronchitis. Hamish had found two more medications at the bottom of the bag, both for heartburn: cisapride, sold by prescription, and cimetidine, packaged for purchase over the counter. The cimetidine had been the final nail in her coffin. There'd been warnings in the journals and in the press: the combination of cimetidine, cisapride, and erythromycin could produce a deadly cardiac cocktail. Joanna's cocktail would have been made all the more potent by the diuretic. The original pathologist had been correct in his autopsy report: Joanna *had* suffered a cardiac arrhythmia. The electrical system controlling her heartbeat had short-circuited. Her heart had stopped as suddenly as if someone had pulled a plug. Joanna Vanderven had not been murdered.

A mechanical Santa, ankle-deep in the cottony snow of the Four Corners window, waved at the shoppers from a chocolate-laden sleigh. Zol pictured another wintry scene: Max whizzing down Blue Mountain, both hands waving ski poles high in the air. Max had really taken to Colleen. She'd insisted on being discharged after five days in hospital; Zol had insisted she come to his place every night for dinner until she regained her strength. It had been a delight to see her with Max these past couple of weeks. The music in her accent made her a natural at bedtime stories. One night, she settled Max with a baby-elephant snuggle and explained that while hippos could be dangerous, their hugging unpredictable, elephants never forgot how much they loved you. Zol was certain the wistful look in her eyes said she'd always wanted to be a mother.

Zol inhaled deeply and imagined the scent of blossoms wafting from the flawless groove above Colleen's collarbone, from the cleft between her breasts. He flipped open his cellphone and scrolled to her number. Maybe he could convince her to join them at Blue Mountain for the week. And bring her jasmine. He'd supply the bergamot.

ACKNOWLEDGEMENTS

I may have inherited some writing genes, but turning me into an author took the unstinting encouragement of my parents, Archie and Barbara, and my siblings, Sheena and Tim. My talented writing buddies, John Hewson and Mark Walma, helped mould this work into something approaching a novel, ready for the insights of my trusted readers, Ross Blundell, Birgit Elston, Martha Fulford, Larry Kramer, Bob Nosal, and Anne Westaway. I'm very grateful to Jack David, Crissy Boylan, Simon Ware, and all the others at ECW Press who placed their faith in me as a novelist, and to Edna Barker for buffing my manuscript with her professional eyes and hands. But most of all, I wish to thank my darling Lorna, without whose love, patience, and shared joy in reading I would never have completed this book.

Ross Pennie
Ancaster, Ontario
April 2009

Here's a sneak peek at Ross Pennie's
next Dr. Zol Szabo medical mystery

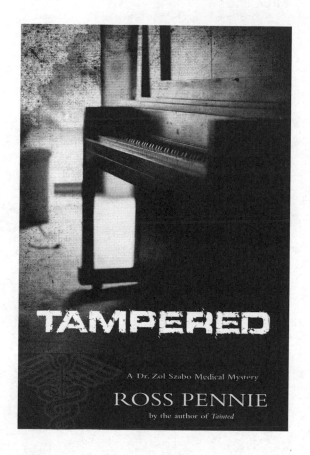

TAMPERED

A Dr. Zol Szabo Medical Mystery

ROSS PENNIE

by the author of *Tainted*

CHAPTER 1

Zol Szabo peered across the sea of silvery heads bobbing in the buffet line at Camelot Lodge. Usually, he looked forward to these monthly Sunday brunches with Art Greenwood, his ex-wife's granddad. Art, the only member of Francine's family who hadn't smoked himself into an early grave, sparkled with wisdom and wit in defiance of his age and physical restrictions. Best of all, Art and his tablemates never let political correctness get in the way of a candid opinion or a good story.

But today, Zol saw only clinical diagnoses smouldering through the retirement residence: the wobbly knees of rheumatoid arthritis, the stooped backs of osteoporosis, the trembling hands of Parkinson's, the vacant eyes of macular degeneration.

Zol forced another smile at Art, who was taking his place at the piano in the sitting room on the other side of the archway. Zol hoped Art was well enough to play. He'd looked pale and drawn when he'd greeted Zol a few minutes ago and confessed he'd been hit by another bout of fever and the runs earlier in the week. That made it his third bout in the past couple of months. And he wasn't the only one. Dozens of others had been hit with the same bug. Art denied any headache, thank goodness. When headache compounded the fever and diarrhea, the result was lethal. In the past month alone, two of the converted mansion's thirty-eight residents had died within hours of a blinding headache compounding their explosive stools.

Art warmed up with a few bars of "Bicycle Built For Two." His chording was tentative, not as sharp as usual. He switched to an improvised version of Beethoven's "Moonlight Sonata." Art played everything by ear. He couldn't read a note, but if he heard something once, he could play it forever. Despite the advancing muscle disease that had forced him into an electric scooter, he still glimmered with the genius that had made him an engineering whiz-kid in the telephone industry fifty years ago.

The understated elegance of the dining room's caramel walls and burgundy accents reminded Zol of a café in one of Hamilton's nicer hotels, except the bucolic vista through Camelot's windows was considerably more handsome than any view of the city's down-at-the-heels central core. Here on an elegant cul-de-sac a few blocks from downtown, stately homes abutted the woodlands at the foot of the Niagara Escarpment. Known locally as the Mountain, the imposing ribbon of limestone and old-growth forest snaked through the city like a giant's doorstep, its flora and fauna protected by the United Nations as a World Biosphere Reserve. Zol thought of his own renovated house a couple of kilometres above as the seagulls flew, perched on a generous treed lot on the Escarpment's edge. He was thankful once again for the two million in lottery winnings that had sent him to medical school and bought him such a gorgeous piece of real estate with its jetliner view. He could cope with Hamilton's overgenerous share of shysters and gangsters if, at the end of the day, he could tuck Max safely in bed, then sip a Glenfarclas while watching Lake Ontario shimmer in the ever-changing light.

Camelot's dining tables boasted smooth white linens, shiny cutlery, and imitation crystal that sparkled as brightly as the stuff his mother reserved for special occasions. Today's spread of poached salmon, eggs, bacon, French toast, salads, and gooey desserts looked a treat. As a former professional chef himself, Zol respected the care and effort that went into every dish. But as a public-health doctor, the table seemed to him less a chef's delight than a minefield.

Something nasty and undetectable — a microbe or a toxin — was poisoning the food. But intermittently. Not every dish and not every meal. As the Associate Medical Officer of Health for Hamilton-Lakeshore, second-in-command at the region's health unit, Zol's job was to quash epidemics, not wallow in them during Sunday brunch. Twice he'd sent his inspectors into Camelot. They'd examined every centimetre of the place with a magnifying glass. They'd collected scores of samples from the kitchen and dozens of specimens from afflicted residents. But they'd come up empty. The kitchen met all the health codes, and the laboratory detected no disease-causing pathogens.

Zol's friend and medical-school classmate, Dr. Hamish Wakefield, a savant in the field of infectious diseases, had raised the possibility of epidemic Norovirus. But even Hamish, an assistant professor at the city's Caledonian University Medical Centre, was stumped; he conceded there was no indication that anything as simple as the cruise-ship virus was the culprit here.

Zol helped the wait staff — invariably hesitant, awkward, and struggling with their English — park the walkers in a double row against the far wall of the dining room. He escorted the frailest of the gauzy-white residents to their seats, then joined the slow-moving buffet queue. He knew he'd soon be hunting down unsalted butter for one person and cholesterol-free scrambled eggs for another. He shrugged off the risk to his intestines and half-filled his plate with breakfast fare he hoped would be sterile: a rubbery fried egg, three crispy rashers of bacon, and a piece of charred toast. Bypassing the devilled eggs, sliced tomatoes, and potato salad, he took his place at Art's table where Phyllis and Betty were already seated.

Despite being past eighty-five, slow to move, and somewhat hard of hearing, Betty McKenzie and Phyllis Wedderspoon stayed fully abreast of the news. These days they'd be bursting with opinions on the latest Parliament Hill shenanigans and lamenting the deceptions that had triggered the stock-market crash now threatening their pensions.

Betty beamed at Zol, then peered over his shoulder. "Where's that handsome little man of yours, Zol?"

"Max sends his regrets," Zol said. "He's at a birthday party. One very brave mother is taking a dozen nine-year-old boys bowling."

"You tell him we missed him," Betty said. "And that his box of Godivas is here waiting for him. You will bring him next time, won't you Zol?"

"I'll have to check his social calendar. It's far busier than mine." It wasn't Max's calendar that would keep him out of Camelot until Zol got the place decontaminated.

He glanced at the buffet table. There was no one left in line. Earl Crabtree, a retired history professor, usually completed the table's foursome. Although Camelot's mealtime seating was officially open, Zol had noticed that most of the residents gravitated to their regular spots, like the four euchre-mad women, all former math teachers, who sat together and barely said a word to anyone else. Today, two of them were missing. And no one else had dared join them. Their intimidating impatience with forgetfulness, no matter how mild, was well known.

"Is Earl going to join us?" Zol asked.

"Not today," Betty said. "Dear Earl is staying in his room, close to the facilities." She gave Zol a knowing look and patted her abdomen.

Zol put down his fork. What must Betty and Phyllis think of him? Half their table was down with gastro, yet Zol and his staff were no closer to resolving the epidemic than they'd been two months ago. "Does he have a fever?" Zol asked.

"Just a gurgly tummy," Betty said. "And no headache. I made sure about that."

Phyllis lifted her chin and inspected Zol's plate through the bottom of her bifocals. "Well, Dr. Szabo, I must say it's a relief to see you're not a vegetarian, or even worse, a vegan. But what's wrong? Little appetite? You took barely enough to feed a chickadee. I trust it's not *your* belly this time."

"Let the good doctor eat in peace and not fuss about his tummy," said Betty, her voice a slight tremolo.

Phyllis lanced the yolk of her eggs Benedict. "I'm just saying that young people today are seduced by fads and schemes that distract them away from the tried and true. As I always say, *timeo Danaos et dona ferentes.*"

"For heaven's sake," said Betty, "we're not in your Latin class now. And there's no stranger with gifts we have to be afraid of here."

Phyllis was right on both counts: Zol was indeed an omnivore, and a Trojan horse was threatening Camelot's kitchen. He spooned strawberry jam onto his toast from a single-use packet and hoped the sugary hit would settle the disquiet he felt in his stomach.

From somewhere to his right came a sudden loud clang, the sound of metal bashing crockery. *Bang! bang! bang! bang!* Zol braced for shattered dinnerware skittering across the floor.

The more the clanging intensified, the louder Art pounded his rendition of "Camptown Races" from the sitting room.

Betty and Phyllis cupped their palms over their hearing aids and glared at the source of the unholy noise.

Eventually, the clanging stopped. Betty's face softened. "That's Bud," she said quietly. "Poor fellow. I do feel sorry for him."

"Poor fellow, nothing," Phyllis countered. "Bud doesn't belong here. Not anymore."

"He had a stroke, bless him," Betty explained. "And now he can't talk. Just bangs his spoon on his plate. It's embarrassing for his wife at mealtime. You know, with everybody watching."

Betty pressed her arthritic left hand on Zol's forearm. Despite her thinning hair and dorsal hump, she glowed with the grace and elegance she must have wielded forty years ago as the Prime Minister's executive assistant. Zol always found himself comforted by the quiet confidence of her presence. He'd never known either of his grandmothers, and as Art's girlfriend, Betty had become Zol's de facto grandma and Max's great-grandma. As a long-time widow, she understood Zol's years of single-parent loneliness. She'd coached him through it with more skill and empathy than anyone else. She'd really taken to Colleen, the private investigator he'd been dating since Christmas.

"Art plays our favourites so beautifully," Betty said, closing her eyes and drinking in the final chorus of "Danny Boy." The plump blue veins on the back of her hand, so clearly visible in their rich detail, reminded Zol of Gray's drawings in his anatomy textbook. Her skin felt warm and soft. "Without him, we'd never hear our kind of music anymore. They don't play our tunes on the radio."

"But Gloria should get that damn piano tuned," Phyllis said. "I've written to her about it over and over. It doesn't do the slightest good. The high notes are still flat."

In Camelot Lodge's well-defined hierarchy, Phyllis strutted in position number one. As the self-appointed grand peahen of the pecking order, she possessed a sharp mind and a strident voice. But the real source of her authority was her '72 Lincoln Continental. No one else had a car.

"None of us has a gramophone anymore," said Betty. She held Camelot's position number two, a status she didn't flaunt but that was hers nonetheless. "When my nieces and nephews moved me in here, they threw out all my seventy-eights and thirty-three-and-a-thirds."

Phyllis dipped her chin, her eyes piercing Zol over the top of her spectacles. "I believe you young people have taken to calling them *vinyl*."

Betty leaned toward Zol, still patting his arm. "Earl isn't the only one with a delicate tummy. I suppose Art told you. He hasn't been feeling himself the past few of days."

Zol stared at his plate and winced inside. He'd pleaded with Art to come and stay with Max and him until this gastro business got resolved. There was plenty of room in Zol's house for Betty as well. Zol had suggested confidentially to Art that the two of them could share a room or each have one of their own. Art had declined for both of them. It wasn't a question of the bedroom arrangements or the difficulty with the stairs. They would never abandon their friends.

Phyllis made a face. "No point in hiding it, Art has been down with *faeces liquifacti* for the past few days. I call it Gloria's Revenge. Montezuma had nothing on her." She stiffened and coughed into her serviette, as though forcing herself to stifle further criticism of the Lodge's manager, Gloria Oliveira. "But if we let the good doctor concern himself about Camelot's tummies, he'll have us in quarantine. Again. Every time we turn around, the place gets locked up like Fort Knox. No one in or out except the staff, who tiptoe around us as though we had leprosy."

"Now Phyllis, it doesn't help to exaggerate," Betty said.

Phyllis lifted a forkful of egg toward her mouth, studied it, then dropped it to her plate. "The Portuguese may be famous for their lace and celestial navigation, but they're hopeless in the kitchen."

"Zol has been doing everything he can to put a stop to our…our gurgly tummies." Betty dabbed her lips with her serviette and smudged her ruby lipstick into the wrinkles around her mouth. "Tummy troubles or not," she said, her tone of voice indicating she was changing the subject, "Art Greenwood is one of the best things to happen to this place. Just look around. Most everyone is smiling. Even the Mountain Wingers." She pointed to two tables at the far end of the dining room. "They've got their heads up."

Four of Camelot's Mountain Wingers were seated in wheelchairs, terry-cloth bibs tied around their necks. They lived in the eight-bed infirmary on the second floor and were allowed out of the locked ward only on special occasions such as Sunday brunch. They ate puréed meals out of plastic bowls and were never given knives or forks. Around them hovered uniformed staff with the gentle movements, rich black hair, and almond eyes of Filipinas. Watching the aides spoon beige mush into the toothless mouths, Zol shuddered. He'd promised himself he would jump off the Skyway Bridge and into a watery grave in Hamilton Harbour the instant he was diagnosed with Alzheimer's, or anything like it.

"I'll grant you that," Phyllis admitted. "Arthur's playing is almost like magic."

"Of course it is," Betty said. "It lifts the heads of those dear souls like sunflowers tipped toward the noontime rays. They wave their arms, tap their feet, and sometimes sing along."

"Hardly," Phyllis corrected. "It's really just muttering."

"When they hear that music," said Betty, "their faces get so bright you'd almost swear they could partake in intelligent conversation. Until . . ." A look of sadness misted her eyes — or was it fear? "Until it's time for Art to stop playing and Gloria locks the keyboard."

Two men in dark business suits caught Zol's eye from the far side of the common room. Betty and Phyllis had their backs to them, thank goodness. The men were pushing a gurney, their passenger draped head to toe in a white sheet. To the right of the men, the wall of floor-to-ceiling windows lit the room and flanked the side door to the parking lot. A black Craig & Lafferty van was waiting on the tarmac by the exit, its rear doors yawning.

Once they'd negotiated the awkwardly narrow side exit and wheeled their client to the van, one of the men tapped the gurney with his foot. The wheels didn't fold as they were supposed to. He tried again. Still, the undercarriage didn't give. The other man tried with a swifter kick but the wheels didn't budge. The two men kicked together — at the wheels, the frame, the mechanism beneath. The stretcher rocked back and forth. The corpse's legs slid off and pitched precariously toward the ground. Suddenly, the undercarriage collapsed, and one of the men caught the body just in time. They hoisted the gurney and flung their reluctant cargo into the van, then jumped inside. The driver slammed his door, and the vehicle careened down the street.

Zol dabbed his mouth with his serviette, then wiped the sweat from his forehead. He stared at the bits of cold egg and charred bacon on his plate, his stomach in complete revolt. Betty and Phyllis started at the sudden chime from Zol's belt. He grabbed his BlackBerry, ready to silence it. Whoever was calling could leave a message. He hated cellphones in restaurants. Nothing in public health was so important it couldn't wait fifteen minutes.

But the phone's display said Peter Trinnock was calling. That was strange. Zol's boss never worked weekends. He golfed a lot, skied a little, and often got heavily into the sauce. If he wasn't on the slopes today, enjoying March's last few weeks of spring skiing, he'd be into his third martini by now.

Zol excused himself and strode toward the common sitting room.

"Damn it, Szabo," Trinnock said, "where are you?" Zol pictured his boss's piggy-eyed gaze, the veins on his cheeks flaring like a tangled nest of spiders.

"Brunch with my ex's granddad. Camelot Lodge."

"Then you know."

"Know what, sir?"

"About the Prime Minister's aunt. Nellie something." Zol heard the shuffle of papers next to Trinnock's phone, then the yapping of a small dog. Trinnock cursed through a partly muffled mouthpiece, "Muzzle the damn dog, Marion. I'm on the phone." He paused and took a loud gulp of something that sounded more like beer than martini. "Nellie Brownlow, that's the name," Trinnock continued, his voice again loud and clear. "Died this morning. At that Camelot place. The Prime Minister's Office just called. The Prime Minister is very upset. The woman was his favourite aunt. It seems she got caught up in your epidemic. Stricken with diarrhea several times since Christmas."

Bile burned the back of Zol's throat. The Prime Minister's Office never interfered with health unit matters. "I'll . . . I'll look into it right away."

"You've dropped the ball on this one, Szabo. The guy from the PMO is saying people are dropping like flies at that Camelot place and that our Hamilton-Lakeshore Health Unit is asleep at the bloody switch."

"We've been doing everything possible to —"

"There are other Party favourites living at that place. The Brownlow woman wasn't the only one. They may be retired, but they're VIPs all the same."

Zol glanced at his table. He hardly needed reminding about Camelot's connections to the country's ruling federal party. Betty,

Earl, and a couple of sisters named Maude and Myrtle were living examples. Art stayed away from anything political, and Phyllis reckoned that all politicians were tarred with the same unsavoury brush. She loved it when the press discovered any of them *in flagrante delicto* and their careers got ruined.

"Any more of them gets wheeled out in a bag, an RCMP goon squad will be breathing down our necks." Trinnock downed another noisy gulp. "That's *your* neck, Szabo, now that the PM knows your name."

The Prime Minister?

The RCMP?

Zol imagined beer-bellied thugs in Kevlar vests waving fifty-thousand-volt Tasers.

He swallowed hard.

The force's boy-scouts-in-scarlet image had been shattered when shocking videos of RCMP brutality were broadcast to the world via the Internet. A brave guy with a video cellphone had recorded the nation's finest zapping a confused, unarmed traveller with a Taser at Vancouver airport. The guy died, right there on the screen. The scenario and the attempted cover-up had seriously jaundiced Zol's view of policing. Zol was sure many others felt the same way. The national anthem boasted that the True North was strong and free, but nowadays it felt like its citizens weren't safe if the RCMP took a sudden, arbitrary disliking to them.

"Does someone in the PMO suspect foul play?" Zol asked.

"You know these political types. Don't trust anyone. Which means you'll have to do better. Considerably better. And with due speed." Trinnock's English accent intensified when he got angry. "Shall I call in some assistance? Dare I say, our friends from Toronto?"

Ice filled Zol's veins. He pictured Wyatt Burr, the "consultant" who'd swaggered in from Toronto on his high horse and royally screwed up Zol's last big case. "I'd rather deal with our local experts. If you gave me the go-ahead to hire a couple more brains, I could —"

"Get the bloody thing fixed, whatever it takes. And keep us out of the papers."